Rip Van Winkle

Books by Sanford Friedman

Sanford Friedman

Rip Van Winkle

Atheneum

NEW YORK

1980

Library of Congress Cataloging in Publication Data

Friedman, Sanford, 1928–
    Rip Van Winkle.

        I. Title.
PZ4.F8989Ri 1980   813'.54   80–66016
ISBN 0–689–11099–5

To Jamie

Epimenides gave his oracles not about the future but about things in the past which remained obscure.

Aristotle

I

I

"Boy! Am I looking forward to this weekend," said Benjamin Spector as the Catskill Mountain Express pulled out of Weehawken and headed up the Jersey side of the Hudson. "Aren't you?"

Deep in thought, Andrew Spector turned from the window, next to which he was sitting (his brother Ben always made a point, when traveling by train, of sacrificing the window seat to his companion, whether young or old, male or female, just as he made a point, when taking a walk, of positioning himself protectively on the curbside of his companion), and mumbled something in assent.

"Be nice to have Letty with us." Ben, bothered now by his brother's lack of response, added pointedly, "Won't it?"

"Um." Having nothing more to say about either the weekend or their sister Letty, Andrew turned back to the window and resumed gazing at the newly christened George Washington Bridge. In the late afternoon light the long suspended span resembled a musical instrument, a fallen harp, waiting to be righted, raised, and plucked by some celestial hand. However ghostly, almost imperceptible the vertical ties appeared in the summer haze, Andrew saw them quite distinctly as a staff on which to note the opening measures of the hymn, scored for muted trumpet, whose solemn tones were issuing now—*molto grave*, serene—from the mountains to the north, not the nearby Catskills but far beyond from the Adirondacks, yet perfectly audible to Andrew, audible, he had no doubt, to anyone, whether

3

living or dead, willing to listen.

"Crooks! the whole damn bunch." Ben cuffed the front page of the *Times* to which he had reluctantly turned his attention. The epithet was meant to indict not only Roosevelt, Hague, Farley, and Hearst, but everyone presently assembled in Chicago for the 1932 Democratic National Convention—everyone, that is, except Al Smith for whom Ben had a soft spot. "You can't tell me—" Aware that he was virtually talking to himself again, Ben broke off and eyed in silence his brother who was busy at the moment jotting down some musical notes on the back of an envelope.

To Benjamin Spector, who knew nothing whatever about music—except, by God! what he liked—his younger brother's "hobby" or "avocation," as he preferred to speak of it to anyone outside the family, was pure Greek. It made him feel the way he had as a boy whenever his parents resorted to Yiddish to keep the kids from understanding what was being said at table—he felt in some way left out, excluded by music from a major portion of his brother's life. Maybe Pop—God rest his soul—had been right, after all, to dismiss a career in music as windmill tilting, a waste of time. Maybe he hadn't been quite so blind, pigheaded, and unenlightened as he seemed when he opposed Andy's going to Rochester. The fact that the boy had been awarded a partial scholarship made no difference to Pop. He wasn't thinking of the dough. Nor was he thinking of himself and the business, as Mamma—God rest her soul—sometimes implied; Pop had managed very nicely without Andrew's help during the war. No, the only thing the old man had in mind was Andy's future—the indisputable fact, according to Pop, that no American, other than Victor Herbert, had ever earned his livelihood composing classical music. In that, at least, the old man had been proved right. Over the last ten years Andy hadn't seen enough from his music to buy a bag of peanuts. Wasn't that what Pop had meant by windmill tilting? Funny that no one in the family, not even Letty, had ever tracked down the origin of that term. All they could suppose was that the old man had mistranslated some Hungarian adage, but he, of course, was much too proud ever to admit his mistake, always retorted haughtily, "What, my cultured *kinder*, ignorant of your classics? Go, ask the composer, surely he must know." But Andy didn't, didn't know a lot of things. . . .

Benjamin glanced sideways at his brother, who was mooning once more out the window, his strong profile in sharp contrast to the delicately molded brow, soft cheek, and large, dark, almost-womanly, watery eye. Somehow Andrew's self-absorption confirmed for Ben the sense he had of his own superiority, as well as of his brother's blissful ignorance. . . . No, Andrew would never know—no one would—what it had cost Ben to go to bat for him. If Andy had anyone in this world to thank for his education, for persuading Pop—forcing him, practically—to let Andy go to Rochester, it was Ben. *He* was the one who had made the sacrifice, borne the brunt not only of the extra workload at the office but of the old man's rancor. And not just at dinnertime like the servants or on Fridays like his sisters, but morning, noon, and night he had had to put up with the old man's rancor, his unending rancor. Because even afterwards, after Andy had failed to make a go of it, and Pop finally relented and forgave the loafer and took him back into the business (for all of which Andy also had only Ben to thank), the old man still held Ben responsible for Andy's marriage, his "unholy" marriage. "If you hadn't been so smart and taken his side, he would never have gone to that *farshtunken* place, never have met that piece of *traif*." . . . No, Pop had never forgiven Ben—the thought still pained him now—not even on his deathbed. That had been Ben's legacy, his birthright as first-born: blame, everlasting blame.

Nor had Andrew ever thanked Ben—not only for his education, but everything: the clothes on his back, roof over his head, for Ben's covering up for him, carrying him, keeping him on the payroll all these years, while the lazy loafer sat around on his can all day making those hieroglyphics. Sometimes Ben felt exactly like the Saint Christopher on that medal his customer Mickey O'Brien had given him years ago, which Ben had promptly pinned up (just like a born Catholic) over the windshield in the flivver for reasons which he himself didn't understand and couldn't begin to explain to Milly, who complained it made her "skin crawl"—he felt fated to carry on his back for

5

life the burden of his little brother. . . . Well, thank God, Pop hadn't lived to hear any of the music, especially —whachamacallit?—that ecclesiastical piece. Ever since Mickey O'Brien had told him that the title referred to bringing Mary news that she was to be the mother of Christ, Ben's memory had drawn a blank. And what would Pop have thought if he had had to go downtown to Henry Street last year to see that screwball dancer twitch her way through . . . whachamacallit? He would have bust a gut.

Still, there were occasional compensations, such as seeing Andy's name in print. Despite the fact that the reviews were generally unfavorable and, more often than not, corroborated Ben's own negative opinion of the music, he took great pride in showing off the clippings. And no matter how much he and Milly joked beforehand about putting in the earplugs, Ben really got a kick out of dressing up and going to Town Hall—except, of course, for that handful of hecklers who could always be counted on to boo at the end. But best of all was the time they drove up to Boston and stayed overnight for the premiere of . . . whachamacallit? and were introduced to Koussevitsky. Even Milly was impressed by that. It didn't make her change her mind about the music or, for that matter, about her brother-in-law, but it certainly gave her something to gab about. So did that comment of her cousin Adelle, the pianist, to the effect that, among professionals, Andy and some other guy were considered the first truly original voices in American music. After that, Milly kept her mouth shut, at least among her more knowledgeable friends for whom the mere fact that she was related to Andrew brought her automatic prestige. So maybe it was something more than windmill tilting, maybe even Pop—had the good Lord been merciful—would have found it in his heart to forgive and forget, after Koussevitsky. . . .

"What's it this time?" Ben, breaking the silence lightly, jutted his chin toward the envelope in Andrew's hand. "A ballad for the Hudson?"

"Just doodling."

"Something the matter, Babe?"

"No . . . why?"

"That envelope, you've been at it all day, ever since you came into the shop this morning. Business stinks, I'll admit, but still—something's on your mind, I can tell."

"Not really." As if to convince his brother, Andrew quit "doodling" and slipped the envelope into his jacket, which was hanging from a wall hook overhead.

"Everything okay between you and Peggy?"

"Um-hm."

"Better be—I'll break her pretty neck." Ben flashed a smile in an attempt to mitigate the violence of his words. "So, who's it from?"

"Who's what from?"

"The letter."

"Oh . . . Sarah." Andrew could tell from his brother's blank expression that the name meant nothing to Ben. "Kellogg." Still Ben showed no sign of recognition. "My dancer friend."

"The one we saw at Henry Street?"

"Um-hm."

"*Vildeh chaieh*." As was often the case when Ben wished to express himself colorfully, he resorted to Yiddish, in this instance characterizing the controversial modern dancer as a "wild animal." Then, coming to what was really on his mind, he raised the subject casually. "Thought it might be from that skirt."

"What skirt?"

"The one who called this morning, and Flo put through on my line by mistake." Ben's curiosity had been aroused by the young woman's anxious breathing, her hushed and intimate tone. "Anything serious?"

"Just a music student."

"That's not what I asked." After waiting in vain for a more forthright response, Ben put the question directly. "You two keeping company?"

Andrew laughed off the suggestion. "What gives you that idea?"

"The way she said your name."

"Company? Heavens, no."

"Better that way—keep it light."

Again the brothers lapsed into silence.

"Damn it!" The woman in the seat behind Andrew smacked her newspaper resoundingly. "It doesn't make sense, this article. Wish there were a lawyer on this train—preferably rich, young, and handsome."

"And traveling with a friend of the same ilk." Her female companion joined in the joke. "What article, Goldie?"

"About the Curtis trial. I don't get it, Lil, any of it— legally, I mean. What's the State trying to prove?"

"Fraud."

"Yeah, sure, that's what it *should* be. But what they're claiming is that Curtis was actually in contact with the kidnappers."

"What about that confession he signed?"

"Exactly!" exclaimed the first woman. "That's just my point. Either the guy made the whole thing up, like he says, and should be put in a nuthouse; or else it's true, every last word of it, in which case the son of a bitch should stand trial for everything in the book: conspiracy, fraud, extortion—"

"Mental cruelty," added the companion, her tone changing appreciably, becoming sober, almost grave. "That, most of all—for what he did to the Lindberghs—*all* of us, to all of us. Of course it was a lie! Christ! can you imagine that guy's noodle, how warped it must be to invent a yarn like that, Goldie, a yarn that kept a nation—the whole world! hanging by its teeth for weeks? What could make a man do a thing like that?"

"Money," the first woman stated simply. "What else? He said so himself, right here in the paper, Lil—wait a minute—here it is: 'According to Curtis the kidnappers were ready at one time to knock the Lindbergh baby down to the highest bidder just like'—and I quote—'just like any piece of merchandise.' How do you like that? Right here on the front page of the *Times*—'All the News That's Fit to Print.'" The woman sighed. "It's the depression, Lil, like everything else, the damned depression. I said so from the start. If it weren't for the depression, that baby would still be alive."

At this moment Ben whirled his head and glared at the women. "Come on, ladies, please!"

The women were taken by surprise, confused. "What? What is it, mister?"

"Keep it down! can't you, please?" Ben softened his tone, turned on the charm: "My brother's trying to work."

"Work!" By now the first woman, having regained her

composure, was able to voice her anger. "So who's stopping him!"

Her companion, on the other hand, was staring at Ben (as he himself was quick to observe) with obvious fascination. "Wait a minute, Goldie."

"No!" The friend refused to be mollified. "Who the hell does he think he is? This is still a free country, public transportation."

Ben waited while the woman who was ogling at him whispered something to her girlfriend, something, he imagined from her titillated expression, like: Easy, honey, he's a knockout! After a moment she said aloud, "Excuse me, mister, I was just remarking—has anyone ever told you how much you look like Roosevelt—Elliott, I mean?"

"Oh, sure, lots of people." Ben took the opportunity to turn around and face the women. Though neither was especially attractive, both were buxom, lively, in their late twenties. "Not Elliott, though," he corrected her, "James, the oldest, the one with the finest features. Sure, we hear it all the time."

"We? Who's 'we'?"

"My brother and I."

"You mean to say there's another one like you at home?"

"Home? Right here."

"Don't tell me you've forgotten, Lil? The man whose work we were disturbing."

"Oh, come on," Ben objected, "let's forget that now—a little misunderstanding. Hey, Andy, turn around and give the girls a thrill." Ben, whose hand was concealed from the women's sight by the back of the seat, nudged his brother and said in an undertone, "Come on, we'll have some fun." Then, stepping into the aisle, he continued aloud, "Sorry, ladies, didn't catch the names."

When the introductions were over, Ben suggested reversing the seat to get better acquainted. The women were delighted, but no sooner had the back been shifted than Andrew retrieved his jacket and excused himself.

"Hey, Babe," Ben said with both suspicion and concern, "where you going?"

"Somewhere where even the Roosevelts, presumably, gotta go."

9

"With your jacket on? In this heat?"

"You don't suppose," Andrew bantered, "they do it in the raw."

On his way up the aisle Andrew heard his brother explain that he, Andrew, wasn't really antisocial, just a little troubled by something of a personal nature which had occurred in recent months and from which the "poor kid" hadn't yet recovered. At the same time, Ben informed the women that he hadn't been pulling their leg earlier, when he said his brother was trying to work. "Here, take a gander at these." Without looking back, Andrew could visualize Ben getting out his wallet now to show off the clippings about the concert last year at Symphony Hall.

Once inside the toilet, Andrew locked the door. The air in the compartment was muggy, rank, in no way refreshed by the sultry draft, dense with grit and cinders, coming through the partly opened window. Andrew removed his jacket and hung it up. Out of the pocket he took the envelope, postmarked Bennington, Vermont, on which he had been "doodling" in the coach. Not bothering to unbuckle his belt or open his fly, he settled down to read for the third time the letter he had received that morning from Sarah Kellogg.

June 28, 1932

My dear Andrew:

I can't tell you how disgruntled I am. At first I thought, Well, old girl, if the answer's no, it's no—you'll just have to find someone else for the job. But then, after racking my grain for days . . .

Prepared though Andrew was for the typo, it made him chuckle again, more than at first, because now, when he considered the writer's Demeter-like temperament and Olympian energy, the mistake seemed almost intentional, a deliberate pun.

and picking Erskine's and getting nowhere, I realized, of course—we both did—that there simply isn't anyone else—at least not for me! There may be for Wigman or St. Denis, but not for Kellogg, not for Recovery. (By the way, what do you think of the title? Too insipid? Would Resurgence be better? Resurrection? As usual,

Erskine has coined his own title: <u>Tarantulas</u>.) So, there you are, that's why I came to you, Andrew, because you alone are right for the commission, can take (to borrow a phrase of your own) "soundings of the heights."

More than that, I came to you because in a very real sense we've <u>already</u> collaborated on <u>Recovery</u>. Don't you understand that, Andrew? Do you suppose the piece came out of the blue? Nonsense! Like everything else, it came out of everything else—particularly <u>Encounters</u>, our collaboration on <u>Encounters</u>—the Company's best work to date. And before that, it came out of everything you ever taught me—never mind that I was supposed to be the teacher—everything we taught each other, learned together in Rochester. Isn't that what both of us recognized almost at once on meeting—that we were kindred spirits?

I've spent the day mulling over your letter, trying to look at the situation from your viewpoint. Don't think I don't realize what a dirty trick it was to invite you to the studio like that, without a word of preparation, except to refer to my "little surprise." I can't imagine what you expected—certainly not a performance. I wish you could have seen your face when you came in and found the entire Company assembled—how we squealed about it afterwards. Never mind. We made history that afternoon, Andrew, if not a revolution. As far as I know, no choreographer has ever commissioned a composer <u>after</u> the fact, after the dance was finished, a <u>fait accompli</u>. That in itself must have come as a shock to you, even an affront.

. . . No, not at all. A surprise, yes, even an astonishment, but in no way an affront. Sarah was too much the healthy egoist to understand that. Because *she* would have been affronted by the reversal of prerogatives, she assumed that he had been. But she was wrong. Pride, protocol, hurt feelings—such things had really played no part in his decision to refuse the commission. . . .

You must have thought me mad, putting the cart before the horse that way. But why? Isn't that exactly what <u>I</u> did with <u>Presences</u>—took your finished score and created Encounters? All I'm really asking now is for you to return the favor.

You keep protesting you're a "slowpoke." I know that, Andrew, know what a perfectionist you are, how much you polish, pull apart, destroy, rework, how many years you spent on Presences, Intimations—all your pieces. And yes, of course, I know your longest piece to date lasts "little more than eleven minutes"— and here am I asking for thirty or thirty-five. (Not really, though. The simplest pulsations, drumbeats will suffice for the various "combats.") But that in itself is one of the reasons I thought it would be good for you —I'm speaking now as your friend, not as a choreographer, from your viewpoint, not mine. You've never done a piece to order—

To order, that was the problem in a nutshell: composing to order. It was all well and good for Sarah, having translated her vision into reality, into dance, to say, All right now, whip me up some background music—the simplest pulsations will suffice. Pulsations indeed! She knew damn well that that was not the way he worked—not the way *she* worked either—whatever she imagined about their collaboration on *Presences*. What came first, the indispensable element, was the *vision*. Where it came from, when, and how—whether in sleep or on the trolley car, after years of contemplation or in a flash, a flash of what was miscalled inspiration—remained a mystery, the sublime mystery, like life itself: a gift. Until it came, there could be no composition, no forced labor. Indeed not. Visions weren't made to order. Nor were they interchangeable, but altogether idiosyncratic, subject to the visionary. He could no more put on Sarah's vision, her concept of— what did she call it? (Andrew turned the pages of the letter, skipping ahead to find the phrase)—"body as biography" than she could put on his "soundings of the heights." Once you had the vision, the contour of the form, the rest—intervals, motifs—was nothing more than toil. How had he failed to make that clear in his letter? Or was Sarah simply unwilling to accept it? . . .

At times, I get the impression that you're afraid, Andrew—please don't get me wrong, I'm not finding fault, it's perfectly natural, human, to be afraid. But at others, you act as if accepting the commission would not only disrupt your life but demean you in some way, violate your integrity—that's the part I don't get. Can you imagine Fra Angelico taking that attitude? Or Michelangelo, responding to the Pope that way? (No immodesty intended.) For them it would have been tantamount to saying: I am not a painter. And actually, when you come right down to it, I wonder if that isn't what you _are_ saying, Andrew, haven't always said?

The surmise made Andrew's heart thump, filled him with inexplicable anxiety. He felt accused—but of what, he had no idea. Had his mind wandered, missed the point? Was he shielding himself against Sarah's words, the way the frosted glass blurred the passing scenery? _What_ had he always said? Of _what_ did he stand accused? . . . At this moment someone in the corridor tried to enter the toilet. Instinctively Andrew checked the door to make certain it was locked.

What else does the quest for perfection, taking three years to compose seven minutes of music, amount to, if not delaying tactics, a kind of metaphysical shilly-shallying, a refusal to accept yourself, your destiny, to say once for all, I am I, I am a composer? By rejecting my offer, don't you disavow the very thing I avowed in making it: your authenticity as a composer? In that you remind me too much of your brother with his preposterous "avocation." What on earth does that word mean? Either you do something or don't, are something or aren't. There's no such thing as avocation. Except, perhaps, for you, Andrew, with your double life: office downtown, piano at home, business world and music world, customers and longhairs. For you, I suppose, the concept _is_ a real one, has some real validity—so much so, I sometimes wonder whether you don't regard your whole life—life itself—as an avocation? You simply won't declare yourself.

Aware that he was having difficulty breathing, Andrew straightened his back, lowered, then loosened, his belt. . . . Though Sarah had meant it in a broader sense, he wondered

13

whether he could say those words even now, here in the solitude of this toilet, without a soul to witness them— just say out loud, for no one's benefit but his own. . . . Andrew hesitated. Could he even *think* them? . . . Apparently not. "Go ahead!" he enjoined himself. Still he hesitated, conscious of the racket of the wheels. At last, he murmured haltingly, almost voicelessly, without the least conviction, as if at the point of a gun, "I am a composer."

Andrew's chest swelled as he drew and released audibly a lungful of air. . . . Sarah was right. But why? What was the impediment? What prevented him from what she called declaring himself—from saying practically anything of late, talking at all? Was it just plain fear? Possibly, judging by his thumping heart. Or was it simply a lack of confidence, confidence in himself as a composer, compared with the masters—Handel and Bach? If so, could he state the counterpart: I am a businessman? No, that least of all. On that point Sarah was wrong—what he led was not a double life but a fractionated one. What, in that case, *could* he say? I am a husband? . . . I am a father? . . . I am a son? . . . Andrew grimaced, troubled by his inability to make any of these statements. Why should it be so easy for Sarah to call him composer, Peggy to call him husband, Mat father, Mamma son, but so hard for him? Why not take their word for it, accept himself because *they* did? Why was he unable—unwilling would be more exact; no sense fooling himself: It was a real refusal—unwilling to affirm himself? Where did it come from, that capability, the negative capability, to nullify oneself? . . . Andrew had an uncomfortable empty feeling in his chest, as if he didn't have the right to exist, hadn't earned the right. *Earned:* Was that it? Was it, like so much else, merely a matter of money? the fact that he hadn't succeeded as a composer, been a financial success? But then, who had? Was there anyone nowadays in any line of work who wasn't a failure? The whole country, America itself, was on the verge of bankruptcy. Did anyone feel different? Probably not. Practically everyone—not just the unemployed, but everyone, even those with jobs and a little money in their pockets like the people on this train, who could still afford to get away for the long Fourth weekend, yet looked no different from riders on the subway: their faces glum, eyes blank, bodies limp with anomie —everyone felt beaten, useless, worthless, disqualified from being. If money alone gave you the right to exist, if it wasn't yours intrinsically, then something was dreadfully wrong. So wrong, in fact, that everyone had begun to sense it—the depression had sounded the alarm, caused the rude awakening—sense that they were misspending, misusing, misliving, their lives. . . . Raising his head, Andrew brought his eyes to the open window and, gazing past the passing treetops into the colorless sky, remarked, as if to acknowledge himself to God, "Human . . . I am human." Perhaps that was the most anyone could ever say. . . .

Don't misunderstand. I'm not suggesting you choose between business and composing. Lots of businessmen have been composers. In any case you've already made the choice, at least as far as I'm concerned. All I'm asking is that you yourself acknowledge it—take a leave of absence . . .

. . . How glibly she proposed that, as if the leave were from an institution instead of from the family business, brother—his hot-tempered, overly protective, possessive brother who put family ties above all else, deemed them all but sacred. Surely Ben would take it personally—he had never learned that it was possible to take things in any other way—consider himself double-crossed, betrayed. At mere mention of the subject Ben would fly into a rage, call him Judas, curse him, kick him out, swear on their father's memory never to see or speak to him again. . . . Or would he? Maybe not. Maybe he would welcome Andrew's absence. Hadn't he said as much a thousand times? complained that he was killing himself because of Andrew, doing three jobs instead of one: his own, Andrew's, and someone else's, needed to rectify Andrew's mistakes; wasn't he always saying that Pearl, his eight-year-old, had more business sense in her little finger than her uncle, that Andrew couldn't sell a rosary to a nun, that he was nothing but a freeloader, a daydreamer, a longhaired lazy bum? . . . Was Ben merely bluffing, letting off steam? Did he need to do that, ridicule Andrew, in order to sustain himself, his image of himself as the long-suffering, self-sacrificing, hard-working, indispensable mainstay of the family? Or was it he, Andrew, who was deceiving himself, imagining that Ben would stand in his way, object to a leave of absence? Was he using Ben's inviolable sense of kinship to hide behind, dodge his own destiny, as Sarah suggested—using business to hedge music, music to hedge business, doing neither wholeheartedly, hedging both? Did he go on working with Ben solely to avoid being on his own, falling flat on his face not only as a breadwinner but also as a composer? Ben liked to refer to the glassed-in room—formerly a doctor's consultation office—in which Andrew worked at home as the "ivory tower." But wasn't it just the other way around: his workroom the battlefield; the office downtown the ivory tower? Hadn't he turned the office into a kind of cloister to protect himself from the world? . . . No, the analogy was inapt. In a cloister, at least, it was impossible to evade God. Wasn't that what Sarah really meant? what his rejection of her offer, reluctance to declare himself, commit himself, what all such shilly-shallying, side-stepping of life ultimately signified: the evasion of God? Even when, a moment ago, he had acknowledged his humanity to God, wasn't he fooling himself? Wouldn't it have been more accurate to say, I am no longer human? . . . no longer human because I've been evading You, evading myself? Wasn't he already on a leave of absence, a permanent leave from *life?* Wasn't that essentially what had been disturbing him of late: that he no longer seemed to be present in and to the world?

There were so many signs of it, new ones every day: his increasing absentmindedness (throwing the coffee measure instead of the grounds into the garbage this morning; finding, last night, the whole melodic line destroyed by that D-sharp where he had meant to write E-flat); forgetfulness (imagine calling Mickey O'Brien Wally after all these years, and not remembering the name of that chophouse on Thirty-sixth Street, the doctor in the Lindbergh case, the name of his own grandnephew—it was one thing to forget the cocker spaniel's, quite another to forget the little boy's—and even Monteverdi, the name of a *composer;* it had reached the point where he dreaded encountering anyone, whether a casual acquaintance or lifelong friend, for fear of being unable to address the person by name or, even worse, register just who it was he was deep in conversation with); misreading (for a while, perhaps, you could attribute misreading accidentals to eyestrain, a need for glasses, but not after you were tested and found to have 20–20 vision; and doing the same with words: not just scrambling or inserting letters, reading *tired* for *tried*, *bother* for *brother*, but hallucinating whole words, the way he had yesterday in that article about the Bonus Expeditionary Force).

Still, those were more or less ordinary signs of absentness, the sort Mamma would have classified as examples of "not thinking." But what really worried him was the sense he had so often lately of being absent *altogether*, not only mentally but bodily—absent from space and time. He could scarcely take a step nowadays without stumbling, tripping over something: the sidewalk, the curb, his own two feet; stepping into every puddle, pile of dog shit; bumping into hydrants, baby carriages, people on the street—all of which Mamma would have summed up with another phrase: "not looking where you're going." But that was years ago, when he was still a boy. Now it wasn't enough to call it not looking, not thinking, and let it go at that; it was something else, something more, closer to not *sensing*. Yes, that was it. He had begun to lose all sense of the ground beneath his feet, of whatever was supporting him—pavement, floor, a chair, this toilet seat. At times he felt as if he had no gravity, no substance whatsoever, as if his body were no longer corporeal, in contact with anything tangible, but cast adrift, floating aimlessly, shapelessly like fog. At others he felt inert, heavy as lead. At still others, he felt the opposite, an emptiness inside himself, not at his core, but in between the outer and the inner man, as if whatever bound the two together had come undone, leaving a gap, a layer of internal space, not easily traversable, separating him in both directions, distancing him not only from himself but from the world.

No wonder Dr. Oxenburg was puzzled, couldn't explain why anyone with blood pressure as normal as Andrew's should lose his balance repeatedly, feel unsteady, fear he was going to fall. Oxenburg may have been right to ascribe the condition to "emotional strain," but was altogether wrong about Andrew's need to "get away." He *was* away —that in itself was the illness, not the cure. He had done something to his senses, numbed them in some way, dulled or deadened them to the point where he had, quite literally, fallen out of touch with things—his own muscles, the air he breathed, objects he handled, other people, even Peggy —just think what they had been going through this entire year. Nor, for that matter, could he bear to *be* touched anymore, touched by almost anyone except, perhaps, his son, Mat. He had, indeed, fallen out of touch—not only out of touch, but out of time.

Why, just this afternoon, in making out the rent check, he had dated it '31 instead of '32—six months after the start of the year he was still in '31. Even so, if that were the extent of it, if all he had lost track of was six months, a year, the situation might not seem so serious. But every so often recently he found himself missing, dispossessed of great measures of time, whole decades gone by without a trace. Hadn't he had the experience just a little while ago when the train pulled out of Weehawken, and he was sitting next to Ben and staring at George Washington Bridge? Suddenly he saw himself as a boy, hand in hand with Benny, crossing Brooklyn Bridge—he, Andrew, for the first time, and terribly excited to be on an outing with his big brother, yet terribly frustrated, too, because he was much too short to see the steamboats he had expected to see from the pedestrian boardwalk in the middle of the bridge. That outing had occurred over thirty years ago, yet there they were, he and Ben, still together, sitting side by side aboard this train, staring now at the new George Washington Bridge as if no time at all had elapsed between the two events. At that moment in the coach he had had the disconcerting experience of being simultaneously a boy and a man. However much he knew himself to be thirty-seven (he could see the size of his hand, the size of Ben's), six feet tall, married, the father of two children—one, *one* —the composer of half a dozen pieces, he also knew himself to be five going on six, under three feet tall, and altogether limited in intellect, experience, strength, emotion, skills. What had made the moment shocking, though, was not the simultaneity between the child and the man but the awful gap in their chronology. One minute you were five, the next thirty-seven; one minute you were meeting a girl named Peggy Morand, the next marking your tenth anniversary. Though we lived our lives minute by minute, day by day, endured the daily struggle, the years did not accrue, amass in us the way they did in trees; we retained no evidence of ourselves, formed no annual rings, found no way of transmuting the years themselves into our very bodies, beings—quite the opposite: We seemed to hollow with age. Wasn't that what people meant when they spoke of time as "flying" and wondered "where it went"? Like so much else, it went in evading God—

Once again someone in the corridor tried the handle. Distracted from his thoughts, Andrew turned back to the letter.

. . . leave of absence—a paid leave—for six or seven months, and do what you were meant to do, born to do. That's what I mean by declaring yourself. I mean doing in your own way with Ben what Peggy did with me when she quit the Company. I'm not saying she was right or wrong—no one but Peggy can ever judge that —but at least I understand and respect her decision. You know what she said, after Mat was born and she asked me over—ostensibly to meet my godson, but actually to inform me of her decision? "I'm not stop-ping because I think I should or even of necessity—be-cause we can't afford a nurse; we could get along some-how—it isn't intellectual, my decision, it's physical. Something in my body's changed, in my guts. I don't quite know how to put it, but I can feel it, Sarah, as surely as I feel the pull of gravity. Before, I was a dancer—that was my pull of gravity—now it's Mat and Andrew." What Peggy was saying, though she never used the word, is: I am a mother, that is what I have become—to go on dancing now would be to belie my life.

Which brings me to a painful subject, Andrew. Christopher. I know what his death has meant to you, done to you—to both of you, but differently—in Peggy's case there are fewer outward signs. (Maybe a mother remains a mother even after her child dies.) When you came to the studio I hadn't seen you since February, I think. (Is that possible? Was I in absentia that long, preparing my little surprise? So there, you see, I'm a slowpoke too.) I don't quite know what I expected—some change, not radical but perceptible, some general improvement in spirits. But no, not at all. You were still in a state—perhaps shock is too strong a word, but certainly of dejection, if not despair, almost ten months after the fact. I realize, of course, that the Lindbergh case hasn't helped matters. Last month, when they found the baby, we had rehearsed quite late and didn't know a thing about it till we reached the subway and saw the crowd around the newsstand and heard the boy hawking the Extra: BABY DEAD. Erskine . . .

Now a series of staccato raps broke Andrew's concentration. "Hey!" came a man's voice from the corridor, "what's going on in there?"

From the man's impatient tone Andrew realized that it must be the same passenger who had tried the door earlier, if not both times. Apparently the fellow was determined now to rout him out. Hurriedly Andrew tucked the letter under his arm and stood up. But instead of reaching for his jacket, he undid his fly, dropped his trousers and undershorts, and sat right down again, needing now to use the toilet in earnest.

"Come on! You aren't fooling me. I can hear you in there. Don't play dead."

. . . Baby-dead baby-dead baby-dead, the train wheels echoed from the tracks. "Hold your horses," grumbled Andrew.

"Listen, mister, I've been holding them—"

"Is this the only toilet—"

"Are you the only passenger!"

"Well, go and find another one."

"The conductor! that's who I'll find."

. . . Baby-dead baby-dead baby-dead. . . . The wheels' refrain brought Andrew's eyes back to the letter.

Erskine couldn't understand why I took the news so badly, personally—not that everyone wasn't stunned, but somehow I knew the news would kick the whole thing up again for you, reopen the Christopher wound. When I got home I tried to call, but your line was busy for hours. Finally, I gave up and consoled myself with the thought of Recovery. At least he'll have that, I told myself, some outlet for his feelings, distraction from the personal. So, you see, that was another reason I hoped you would do the score.

Finally, a word about the piece itself. You know how long I've been obsessed with the idea of body as biography—personal, not to say, medical history revealed through movement—and what better proof of the pudding than Elizabeth Barrett Browning? Doubtless people will say—louder than ever—Oh, but it isn't dance (boy! haven't I given them plenty of ammunition this time—a veritable arsenal—choosing for the heroine a sofa-ridden cripple), and call it ugly, if not downright grotesque—especially when the whole Company starts clambering over the shawl like spiders. (Hence Erskine's Tarantulas.) I'm speaking, of course, not of the costume shawl but of the scenic one, the full-scale drop that will divide upstage from down in the performance. Oh, Lord! Please say a prayer for us, Andrew, that the shawl works. I don't mean technically—we'll make it work technically—and I know it works metaphorically (you understand, I'm sure, that the shawl is meant to suggest not only Elizabeth's captivity through invalidism, which is why Barrett keeps bundling her up in it, but also death, the past, the unconscious, the very fabric of her life that she herself has knitted—hence the moment when she becomes so desperately entangled in it or finds herself walled off from Browning by it or lands her long-since drowned brother . . .

Struck by a thought, Andrew stopped reading. Considering what Sarah said about *Recovery* providing an outlet for his feelings, he wondered now whether Elizabeth Barrett had actually had a brother who drowned or whether Sarah had invented the character partly for Andrew's sake —because she knew that Christopher had died in the ocean, not by drowning, to be sure, but—

A sob broke from Andrew's throat, and he covered his eyes to check the tears. In his imagination he saw again Sarah as Elizabeth circling the couch on which she usually reclined, an invalid, but on which the dancer who took the role of her brother sat now instead, cross-legged, as if in a canoe; saw the brother tumble sideways off the couch; saw Sarah, whirling twice full circle, cast her shawl like a life preserver out to him, over him, netting him; her brother thrashing, thrusting his arm through the shawl, straining for help, as she hauled him in and seized the outstretched hand only to be pulled down herself into the heaving net from which the brother presently escaped and drifted off, leaving Sarah landed, herself the twitching catch. . . . How brilliantly Sarah brought back that image of the brother's outstretched arm again and again throughout the dance. . . .

Andrew shifted his attention from the letter to the envelope on which was penciled a staff, designated by a bass clef, and numerous notes. He wondered now whether that little elegiac phrase he'd been fussing with all day wouldn't make a suitable theme for the drowned brother, hadn't, perhaps, been written for that very purpose; wondered, furthermore, whether he wasn't already at work, hard at work, no matter how unconsciously, on the score for *Recovery*.

Once again there was a rapping on the door. Too annoyed to care whether or not the man had summoned the conductor, Andrew snapped, "For God's sake, give me a chance to wipe myself!"

"What?"

"Oh, it's you, Benny."

"Yeah. What's up, Babe? Everything all right?"

"Sure, fine."

"You've been gone half an hour."

"Have I?"

"Yeah. Even the girls were beginning to worry."

"Those franks and beans—"

"Didn't I tell you to take the sole?"

"I know, should've listened to you, Ben." His jacket on, the letter hurriedly restored to his pocket, Andrew emerged from the toilet smiling.

"Look at you!" Ben exclaimed, "you're *shvitzing*."

"It's the jacket." Andrew wiped the perspiration from his brow. "Should've listened to you on that score too."

"*Shlemiel*, you mean to say you kept it on the whole time you were in there?"

"Not exactly." To evade the question, Andrew rubbed his eyes vigorously. When he looked again, Ben was studying him with concern.

"Tell me something, Babe—it's none of my business, I know, but—when—when did you see Oxenburg last?"

"May—end of May. Why, do I look that bad?"

"No, don't be silly. Terrific! you look terrific. It's just —well, sometimes, even at our age"—Ben brought his hand to his heart—"guys get little flutters, murmurs—nothing serious, but still, the old ticker. . . . You're sure—you'd tell me, wouldn't you—"

"I'm fine, Benny."

"On the level?"

"On the level."

"Better be—there'd be no shop without you, loafer."

Unprepared for this ill-timed reversal of Ben's usual position, Andrew challenged the statement but tactfully. "Thanks for saying so, even if it isn't true."

"In a pig's eye it isn't."

"Oh, come on, Benny, you know as well as I you don't need me—"

"Like hell I don't."

"Why, you could run that shop with one hand tied behind your back."

"Like hell I could."

"You know you could."

"Not without my partner—never!"

The finality of Ben's tone discouraged Andrew from continuing the argument. At the same time he had a nagging feeling that something was missing, lost, and he checked his pocket for Sarah's letter.

"What now?" Ben inquired as Andrew re-entered the toilet. "Those beans again?" Moving to the doorway, Ben watched his brother stoop and pick up from the floor the envelope on which Andrew had been "doodling" in the coach. "Oh, *that*." Ben did nothing to conceal his disapproval. "Listen, Babe, do me a favor," he entreated his brother with outstretched hands, "forget the doodles, just this once, for-forget—" Ben faltered.

Andrew watched his brother's fingers recoil like tentacles from some encroaching danger, watched the wavering arms themselves subside, sink slowly out of sight, the counterpoise to yet another arm, the drowning brother's, rising to the surface, reaching toward the sky, taking soundings of the heights— Baby-dead baby-dead baby-dead came the clatter of the wheels, to drown out which Andrew started humming to himself, but audibly, *lamentabile*, the first few notes jotted on the envelope in his hand.

"Is that a deal?" concluded Ben, who had been talking the while. "No doodling, no windmill tilting, no politics. Let's just relax and take it easy with the kids and have ourselves a real old-fashioned, bang-up Fourth."

Andrew, smiling halfheartedly, stuffed the envelope into his pocket. "Deal."

"Who's your best pal in the world?"

"You are, Benny." Andrew gave the perfunctory reply.

"That's the ticket!" Pleased, Ben made a fist, cocked the middle knuckle like the hammer of a pistol, and punched his brother playfully but hard on the upper arm.

"Hey!" Andrew protested in a rising tone, the immemorial tone used since boyhood to protest his brother's punches. "That hurts," he added, rubbing the spot, much as he always had in boyhood, partly to soothe the hurt, partly to enlist their mother's sympathy.

"Just a little love tap."

"That's what you always say"—Andrew smiled skeptically—"to justify an eggie."

"Eggie." Ben smiled back, charmed by their boyhood term for the swelling that resulted from a punch. "Come on." Turning, he started back up the aisle, a spring in his step. "Those skirts'll think we got lost."

2

———

"There!" Lawrence whispered. "She's turned off the light. The baby's asleep. She's leaving the nursery, closing the door. Is the ladder ready?"

"Yes," said Mat with indifference.

"The chloroform?"

"No fair," Pearl objected. "They didn't use no chloroform."

"Any," Mat corrected his cousin.

"Shut up, Sis," Lawrence said. "You, too, Mat."

"But they didn't use no—"

"Shut up, I said. You're supposed to be asleep."

"How can I, when I know about the chloroform?"

"Shut up, I said, or I'll *put* you to sleep."

"Like Blackie, you mean . . . forever?"

"Right you are for Eversharp. Now go to sleep."

"Larry, was Blackie chlorosphyxiated?"

"Chloroformed," Mat corrected his cousin.

"Was he, Larry?"

"Just keep talking, and you'll find out."

"Oh, my Blackie." Pearl began to sniffle. "My dear dear doggie."

"All right, smarty pants. Let's give her a taste of it right now, Mat. Hand me the cotton."

"No! No!"

"Then shut up and go to sleep," commanded Lawrence. Pearl did as she was told: closed her lips with all ten fingers and feigned sleep. "Now, where's the ransom note?"

After a brief silence, interrupted only by Pearl's simulated snoring, Lawrence repeated the question, this time addressing his cousin Mat by name.

"Oh," Mat reminded himself, "here."

"Read it."

"Have fifty thousand dollars ready—"

"Nnno, not like that—in German!"

"*Dummkopf*," Pearl remarked, pretending to talk in her sleep.

"I don't know German," said Mat.

"Let me!" Pearl bolted up.

"No!" Lawrence shoved her back down. "I'll read it."

"No, me! me!"

"All right. But make it snappy. We haven't got all night."

"Hev a trillion dolluz redy—ull smull biltz, no mocked vones—have zem by zis veekend or *elz*. Ve varn you, ze baby—"

"Oh, come on, Pearly," Mat protested mildly, "that's not German."

"How would *you* know," Pearl rejoined, "if you said you don't know German?"

"I don't, but—"

"Well, I *do*, so just *Ruhe!*"

"But anybody can read it that way."

"Oh, they can, can they?"

"Sure. That's just the Katzenjammer Kids."

"Oh, it is, is it? That shows how much you know. *Sprechen Sie Deutsch? Nein? Warum nicht? Du bist ein Esel! Verstehen Sie mich? Nein? Essen Sie—*"

"Okay, Sis! Stop showing off."

"I'm not showing off."

"Just read the note."

"Okay. But I wasn't showing off! Now, here's what it says," Pearl announced, adding pointedly, "in German! *Geben Sie mir dreiundzwanzig Million Dollar mach schnell or du gets das Kartoffel down die Gurgel mit die Brillozaner up dein Unterhosen und die Enema gesticht und geschrect in de Hinie und—*"

"Okay, okay!" her brother stopped her. "Has it got three holes?"

"Has what got?"

"The ransom note."

"Holes?"

"Yeah, the secret sign."

"Secret sign?"

"So no one can forge it."

"Three holes."

"Quit stalling!"

"I don't know," Pearl confessed singsong.

"What is that supposed to mean? Either it has or hasn't."

"Well, where do they go?"

"Where do they go!" Lawrence mimicked her suggestively. "Did you hear that, Mat? She wants to know where they go. Should we show her?"

"I don't care," said Mat.

"Well, *I* do," Pearl declared. "Show me!"

"Okay. You asked for it, Sis. Watch this, Mat. The first"—Lawrence raised his hand slowly overhead and pointed the forefinger—"goes"—after doing several loop the loops, the finger ended up in Pearl's mouth—"there!" he concluded, causing her to giggle with delight.

No sooner had Lawrence finished probing her palate and Pearl finished teething on his finger and the finger been withdrawn than Pearl said eagerly, "Now the second."

"Goes . . ." This time, as Lawrence raised his hand and aimed the finger, he pulled up his sister's nightie; whereupon Pearl squirmed and squealed and raised her own hands in self-defense, even as she spread her legs co-operatively, awaiting with mounting excitement the meandering finger, which finally came to rest, to Pearl's sudden disappointment, in the cup of her bellybutton. *"There,"* Lawrence repeated in a deep voice, depressing the flesh as if it were a doorbell—which, indeed, it must have suggested, because in the next breath he said, "Knock-knock."

So unexpected and hilarious was this turn of events, Pearl could scarcely articulate the obligatory response. "Who's there?"

"Minnie."

"Minnie who?"

"Miniature golf course!"

Convulsed by the punch line, Pearl kicked her legs in the air and screamed with laughter. When, eventually, she quieted down, she said, "All right now, your turn, Matty."

"For what?"

"Number three."

"No, thanks."

"Why not?"

"I don't feel like it."

"No fair!" Pearl clapped her knees together impatiently.

"Haven't you ever seen one, Mat?" Lawrence put it man to man.

"Of course."

"Then come on." Pearl hiked up the front of her nightie to further expose the target.

"No."

"Afraid to touch it?" Lawrence pressed his cousin.

"Why should I be?"

"Bet you are."

"I am not."

"Then touch it."

"I don't want to."

"She won't tell Aunt Peggy."

"Cross my heart and hope to die," Pearl assured him.

"I don't care."

"If I die!"

"No, if you tell Mom."

"Didn't you and Twister ever—"

"Oooo!" Pearl gasped and brought her hand to her mouth as if she, rather than her brother, had violated the family taboo on mentioning their dead cousin. "All right, then," she finally said, as much to break the awkward silence as to change the subject, "if he won't do it, let's do it to him!"

"Good idea!" Lawrence said. "We'll stick the holes in him. Off with his p.j.'s, Pearly. I'll hold him down."

Almost before Mat had a chance to move, Lawrence piled on top of him and clapped his hand over his mouth, stifling Mat's protests, while Pearl started clawing at his pajama bottoms. Thwarted, however, by Mat's kicking legs and one free arm, Pearl had another idea. "I know!"

"What?"

"Let's chlorosphyxiate him!"

"Hot ziggety!"

"And then we'll leave the ransom note and drag him to the woods—"

"And bash his head in with a blunt instrument!"

"Goody-goody!"

"Quick! you get the cotton, Sis, I'll hold the Little Professor down."

Pearl snatched a handkerchief out of her bathrobe pocket —"Uch! it's gooky"—and handed it to her brother, who promptly slapped it over Mat's nose and mouth.

Afraid that he would indeed suffocate, Mat began to struggle energetically and protest against his cousins, but to no avail—the handkerchief muffled his cries, the combined weight of Lawrence and Pearl was more than enough to restrain him.

"Is he out yet?"

"Nope."

Though spoken in jest, the words frightened Mat. He suddenly felt that his cousins were no longer playing, that they really meant to do him in, that Larry would go on gagging him until he needed artificial respiration, and there would be no one around to administer it—Mom would be too upset, and there were no lifeguards in the mountains, and even if there were, it would make no difference—lifeguards never succeeded in saving your life— he'd be dead long before the ambulance. . . . Exerting more strength than he realized he possessed, Mat freed his legs with a terrific yank that sent Pearl sprawling backwards toward the window against which she bumped her skull and broke into tears while he proceeded in one continuous movement to swing his legs overhead, catch Lawrence's neck in a scissors hold, wrench him sidewise off his chest, and cast his cousin down, cursing and punching, onto the floor, just as all three, conscious simultaneously of someone outside rapping sharply on the window, fell silent.

"—not fooling! Open this door! Do you hear me? Open it, I said! If you know what's good for you, Larry, you'll open it this minute!"

Scrambling to his feet and brushing the hair out of his eyes, Lawrence obeyed his mother.

"Oh, my God!" Mildred Spector brought her hands to her turban in horror as if the children she beheld, when she switched on the overhead light and peered into the back of the sedan, were not merely disheveled but dead. "Look at you! Look at this car! Just wait till your uncle sees it! Not a drop of air. For God's sake, open the windows! All the way, all the way! No wonder you're *shvitzing*—it's suffocating in here. What were you doing, anyway, with the windows closed? Hmmm? . . . That's a question! Larry," she snapped, "I'm talking to *you*. What were you doing in here?"

"Playing."

"With the doors locked? A likely story. Who ever heard of locking doors? closing windows, and on a night like this? What kind of playing is that? Suppose something had happened: the motor started—God forbid"—she covered her eyes to protect herself from beholding the appalling calamity—"and all of you were asphyxiated?" Pearl tried in vain to stifle a giggle, which promptly infected her brother. "What's so funny?"

"I don't know."

"Then why are you laughing? You don't even know the meaning— Wait a minute, you. Let me—come over here, come to Mommy. Have you been crying? Look at me! Yes you have. Lawrence! What have you been doing to this child? Picking on her again? Answer me! Have you been picking on your little sister?"

"No."

"Don't lie to me!"

"I'm not!"

"Just wait till your father gets here—you'll see: There'll be no picnic, no fireworks—"

"I'm *not* lying!"

"We'll see about that. Matty"—Mildred turned to her nephew—"tell me—you're the only one I can trust—is your cousin— What's the matter, darling? Why are you all hunched up like that? What is it, sweetheart? Have those two been tormenting you? Tell me, and I'll break their necks! What have you done to him?" she demanded of her own children in a hushed, strained voice, but turned back to Mat before they had a chance to answer. "Tell me, darling, tell Aunt Mil."

For a moment, as Mathew stared at or through his aunt —she couldn't tell which—he seemed, though sad, quite serene, almost in a reverie, his thoughts on something far away. But all at once his face contracted to half its size, turned old with pain; he snorted, burst into tears, buried his face in his hands, and shook with grief.

"Oh, God!" Half in, half out of the car, Mildred tried as best she could to comfort him. "What—what is it?"

"Twister," he sobbed.

Shocked, Mildred sought some explanation from her children, both of whom promptly protested their innocence in dumb show. Before she had a chance to express her disbelief, she felt a hand on her arm, drawing her gently but firmly out of the car. Seeing her sister-in-law, Mildred shrugged and turned up her palms to indicate her perplexity. In response Peggy Spector motioned to Mildred to take Lawrence and Pearl away. Then, stooping low because of her uncommon height, Peggy mounted the running board, switched off the light, closed the door (just as Mildred opened the opposite one to evacuate her puzzled children), and sat down beside her son.

"Mew-mew." Wrapping an arm around his shoulder, Peggy pillowed his head on her breast and fingered his hair. "It's me, Mew-mew. . . . You know, sweetheart, sometimes things like that—like Twister's death—stay bottled up inside for months—years sometimes—till they finally come out. But when they do, it's good—nothing to be ashamed of—good to cry, my honey . . . have to sometimes. So don't hold back. Let it out. There's no one now but us; Pearl and Larry went away. We'll just sit here quietly like this, as if we were being chauffeured—there's time before the train comes—just the two of us, and have ourselves a good old-fashioned—" Unable to go on, Peggy began to cry, not painfully, privately, but openly, unashamedly, participating in their common grief as if it were some everyday activity like reading aloud or playing a duet on the piano—significant only because shared. "You know, sweetheart, when Uncle Oily died—"

"I wish you wouldn't call him that."

"Why? It was his name."

"His name was Oliver."

Amused by Mathew's pedantry, Peggy chuckled through her tears. "Still, that's what he was called, like calling you Mew-Mew, Chris Twister."

"But oily is a word."

"So is twister—that's what makes it funny."

"Not a very nice word either."

"Nicer than piggy," Peggy remarked.

"Didn't you hate being called that?"

"No, why should I?" She gave her nose a resounding blow, and Mathew followed her example. "That was my name."

"Well, I think it's dumb—Oily."

"That's because you didn't know him, don't associate a person with the name."

"You mean he really was oily?"

"No, imbecile! Am I really piggy?" She waited while Mat considered the question. "Well, am I?"

"That's what makes it dumb."

"Maybe someday, Mew, when you have a child of your own and you speak of Twister—"

"I'll never have a child of my own."

"Oh?"

"And never speak of Twister."

Troubled by this statement, Peggy tried to scrutinize his face in the shadows. "Why not?" Mathew pursed his lips, keeping his thoughts to himself. "Why do you say that?" In place of a reply came the distant cries of other children playing on the platform of the railroad station and, closer by, the sound of crickets in the grass. "Tell me, please, why won't you speak of Twister?"

"Because he died," Mat said rather brusquely, annoyed at having to explain the self-explanatory.

"You make it sound— He didn't die on purpose, darling, just to hurt our feelings, however much it does. You don't see me not speaking of Oily just because *he* died, and he's been dead—" Peggy stopped to count the years, but got confused because, instead of starting with her own age at the time of Oliver's death, she based her reckoning on the fact that Oliver, had he lived, would have been exactly Andrew's age. "Wouldn't do any good anyway, not to speak—I'd still remember, more than remember—the part of me that grew up with him has yet to learn he's dead . . . never will. . . . Don't be silly, darling, you *have* to speak of Twister."

"Dad never speaks of Uncle Martin."

"Martin!" Peggy scoffed. "What has he to do with it?

32

Martin was an infant. They never even knew him. And don't call him 'uncle.' "

"Why not?"

"Because he's not your uncle."

"He *is*."

"No one three days old can be an uncle. Don't be such a goose! I don't know what Ben was thinking of, showing you that grave."

"He just wanted me to know that they once had a brother, too, who died."

"It's not the same. In the first place he died before they were born. And secondly, there are still two other brothers, plus five sisters—God help us! That's what makes it different. You see, darling, when Uncle Oily died, Mère and Père were too old to have another baby. But we're not, we're lucky, we can."

"Like Twister?"

"No, different."

"Then what's the point?"

"Oh, stop being such a Spector!" she blurted out before she could check her anger. "Of course there's no point— how could there be? until we know—we don't even know who we're talking about. You'll know when you see him."

"When will that be?"

Peggy heaved an audible sigh. "Soon . . . I hope . . . soon." Then, holding her wristwatch up to the light, she said, "The train is late." In the next second, however, the whistle sounded down the track.

"No! There it is." Mat was already half out the door. "Come on! He'll have the binoculars."

The crowd, which had intermingled sociably while waiting for the train, was milling now, regrouping itself, lining up in family units along the platform and gravel path beside the tracks. As the headlight beam came closer and the signal bell began to clang and the engine, though still in the distance, started slowing down, Lawrence reminded himself of something. Taking a nickel out of his pajama pocket, he dashed off the platform (at which his mother screamed so loud, every head at the station turned) and placed the coin squarely on the near rail. The entire exploit took but a second. Before Mildred could go after him, he was back at her side, too excited and pleased with himself to pay much attention to her familiar frantic warnings about the third rail.

"I've told Aunt Mil a hundred times," Mat said to his mother under his breath, "there *is* no third rail on this line. Doesn't she believe me?"

"Apparently not," Peggy responded in kind.

"Why not?"

"Because she's nervous."

"About what?"

To Peggy's relief, the arriving train drowned out their exchange.

"What?" Mat persisted.

Now that there was no longer any possibility of being overheard, Peggy raised her voice and, enunciating exaggeratedly, exclaimed, "Things in general!"

Unsatisfactory though the answer was, Mat had to laugh at his mother's clowning. Then, seeing the engineer leaning out of the passing locomotive, he waved hello, and the man waved back in such a friendly easygoing fashion, Mat felt as important as the station master for a moment; while Mildred clutched both her children to her sides for fear that one would dash away again and be crushed to death under the wheels.

"There they are!" Mat, having spotted his uncle, led the rest of the family, excepting Lawrence who couldn't tear himself away from the coin, toward the rear of the train.

The greetings varied greatly. Those exchanged by the men and children were genuinely affectionate, spontaneous; those by the husbands and wives, more self-conscious: Ben's a trifle showy, Mildred's tense, Peggy's chummy, Andrew's constrained; as for the in-laws, both sets did their best—considering the amount of suspicion, resentment, and ill will harbored among themselves—to greet each other cordially: Mildred suffered Andy to kiss her cheek, Peggy gave Ben a halfhearted hug.

It wasn't long before Ben missed Lawrence. "Say, where's the big fellow?"

Mildred pointed down the platform, toward a crouching figure, and everyone headed in the boy's direction. As they did, the train began to move again, whereupon Goldie and Lil poked their heads out of a nearby window and said in unison, "Bye-bye, boys!"

"Who's that?" Mildred asked suspiciously.

"Just a couple of tarts"—Ben dismissed the subject, even as he doffed his Panama and smiled broadly at the women—"who tried to pick us up."

"I'll bet."

"*Andy* really," he added, glancing over his shoulder at Peggy, "it was Andy they were after."

"Do you blame them?" Peggy rejoined.

His bluff called, Ben backed down. "I'm only kidding, sweetheart. You know me."

"I sure do," Peggy replied in an undertone to Andy who, in turn, nudged her with his elbow, partly to shut her up, partly to express his approval.

"Dad," Mat said matter-of-factly, "did you forget them?"

"What?"

"The binoculars."

Andrew came to a standstill and smacked himself on the forehead. "Oh, no!" he groaned. "I had them out—right there on the hall table—"

"That's all right," Mat said sincerely, without a trace of incrimination. "It's just"—shielding his eyes against the station lights, he looked up at the stars—"we won't be able to tell the color— Ooh, look! What a night! Look at them!"

The clarity of the stars made Andrew blink as if at the sun. "I'm sorry, Mew. It was the letter," he said, more to himself than to Mat, trying, as they moved on, to reconstruct the sequence of events that had led to his forgetfulness.

"What letter?" said Peggy. "Sarah?"

Andrew nodded. "I'll show you later." Conscious suddenly that Mat was no longer at his side, Andrew glanced over his shoulder. The boy, though still gazing at the stars, was right behind him, trailing in his footsteps, something Mat did so frequently that Andrew had dubbed the boy his "shadow." "Come on, shadow."

By the time Andrew and his family reached Ben and his, the train had left the station, and Lawrence and Pearl were busily examining the retrieved coin.

"Can you imagine, Andy," Ben complained, "a boy too busy to greet his own father? Imagine one of us at their age doing a thing like that. Why, Pop would've—" So dire was the consequence, it made Ben laugh nervously. "You kill yourself all week for them and they can't even say hello."

"I said hello." Larry defended himself timidly.

"Not to your uncle," Mildred put in.

"Oh, hi, Uncle Andy."

"Hi, Buster." Andrew kissed his nephew on the cheek. "What have you got there?"

"A perfectly good nickel," Ben answered for the boy, "destroyed. For what? They don't begin to know the value of money—think it grows on trees. Go out and try to earn one next time, before you stick it under a train. Besides, it's against the law—defacing U.S. currency. You think Mr. Mellon has nothing better to do than mint you nickels? You don't see your cousin—"

"Hey, Mat," Andrew called, "come look at this."

"He's just as bad as they are," Ben remarked on his brother to Peggy.

"Worse," she added playfully.

"Say, that reminds me"—Ben turned to Mildred—"where are Letty and Wooly?"

"At the boardinghouse," Mildred explained. "They've had their supper already."

While Mildred recounted the arrival on the 12:59 of Ben's youngest sister, Violet Baer, her husband, and two sons, all of whom were actually Ben's guests (although he had invited them for the weekend, "all expenses paid," Ben's summer rental wasn't large enough to accommodate ten, including the nurse and cook, and he had had to put the Baers up nearby); Andrew and the children continued studying what was left of the nickel: a paper-thin two-inch ovoid. The Indian's feathers, enlarged almost to the size of canoe paddles, streamed away in one direction as if they had been sundered from the rugged nose and jaw, which spread out in the other like a receding glacier. Below the head, the date, though blurred, was still legible: 1913; the word *Liberty* was not.

"It's like that mirror at Coney Island," Pearl observed. "Isn't it funny, Uncle Andy?"

". . . I suppose." Andrew didn't really think so. The coin, worthless now as currency, seemed to depict the fate of the American Indian, if not of America itself, defunct in less than twenty years.

"Over!" Pearl demanded. "Turn it over again."

The tale told by the bison was much the same: Compared with the immense power amassed in the charging head and hump, the hind legs lagged feebly, as if disabled like the Governor's by poliomyelitis. Andrew glanced at his watch. The convention was well under way by now, and he wondered whether Roosevelt had won the nomination. "Any news from Chicago yet?"

"Let's leave politics out of it for once," Ben declared, "it's a holiday. Come on, kids, I'm starving."

On the way back to the cars Ben, who was in the lead, followed at short intervals by his family and then by Andrew's, asked of no one in particular, "What's on the docket for tomorrow?"

"Letty and Wooly are coming to us for lunch," Peggy replied.

"Why to *us?*" Andrew objected in a whisper.

"Because they're going to your sister-in-law's every single night."

"So what? *She* has help."

"I had to be polite."

"Why? They're not *our* guests."

"She's still your sister."

"I'll see her at the picnic."

"Shh!"

At the same time Ben, slackening his pace, said in an aside to Mildred, "Are we invited, too?"

"No."

"Why not? We're not good enough?"

"She has no help."

"So let her hire someone! God knows I pay the dilettante—"

"Shh!"

"So when are we going to see you?" Ben said aloud as his brother came within earshot. Though he sounded perfectly jovial, Ben looked forlorn, his shoulders hunched, palms upturned like a mendicant's.

"Sunday," Peggy said, "at the picnic."

"Not before?"

"Of course," Andrew assured his brother, "tomorrow."

"Of course we will," Mildred joined in. "It's not as if the houses were a hundred miles apart."

"Damn it!" Now that Ben was at the wheel he found the front seat adjusted, as usual, to the length of Mildred's legs, so that there wasn't nearly room enough for his. "How many times do I have to tell you?"

"Want to drive?" Peggy asked Andrew, before getting into their own car.

"Just to show who wears the pants?" he remarked softly. "No, thanks. Come on, shadow," Andrew said to Mat, who in response opened the back door. "No"—Andrew moved over to make room for his son—"up front with us."

"I'm all right."

"Mad at me for forgetting—"

Peggy touched Andrew's thigh to silence him. After what had happened earlier, she understood that Mat, always the rationalist, had reasons of his own for sitting by himself. From what she could see in the rearview mirror of his pensive expression and the placement of his hands, clasped loosely in his lap, Peggy guessed he was working out some problem relating to Twister.

"Everybody in?" So loud was Ben's question, he seemed to be addressing both households simultaneously.

"Doors locked?" Mildred asked her children.

"*Auf Wiedersehen*, Cousin Matty." Pearl flapped her hand in the open window.

"What?" Mat murmured abstractedly.

"That means good-bye—in *German*."

"*Auf Wiedersehen*."

"Bye, Mat," Lawrence joined in.

"Bye—"

"Quick!" Pearl interrupted. "What does g-r-a-v-e-y a-r-d spell?"

"G-r-a—"

"Quick! quick! no thinking!"

"Gravey—"

"Ha! ha! you fell for it—"

"Graveyard! graveyard!"

"Watch out, everybody!" Ben exclaimed as he pulled away in a cloud of dust, "here goes the Spector express."

"Here, the local," Andrew retorted, whereupon Peggy,

shifting into first, followed Ben's car very slowly, as if to illustrate Andrew's remark, as well as to obey the township's road sign just ahead:

S L O W   D O W N

You Are Entering The Land Of Rip Van Winkle

3

"No, Dad," Mathew said, "you must be looking at Vega —the brightest star—in Lyra." Mat was much too comfortable—stretched out supine on the lawn behind the house, his head pillowed in his palms—too full of dinner, and too engrossed in his own stargazing to get up and guide his father's.

"Lyra . . ."

"The lyre—not l-i-a-r—you know, the kind of little harp they had in ancient times."

"Yes, sweetie pie," Andrew indulged his son. "Lyra, the lyre." The consonance of the words pleased him. So, too, did the idea of the instrument set among the stars. Although he couldn't for the life of him see the image in the sky—had never, even as a boy, been able to make out any constellation excepting Ursa Major—he liked imagining the instrument up there, and wondered now how many sound-years it would take the tetrachords, struck by some seraphic wing, to reach the earth. . . . " 'Take him and cut him out in little stars.' "

"Who?"

Andrew wasn't certain; the line had come to mind involuntarily. "Lear, I think." He had a vague impression that the words were spoken by or about the King toward the very end of the play when Lear comes onstage distraught, carrying the body of the dead Cordelia. "No, that can't be right. It's Shakespeare."

"Little stars—that's a good one. They must not have had the telescope yet. You know how big Arcturus is—the one I'm looking at? Twenty-five times bigger than the sun. Can you imagine, Dad?"

"No, truthfully, I can't."

"The trouble is, you're facing the wrong way. It's behind you. If you go back to the Big Dipper and follow the line of the handle, it's the first bright one you come to—sort of orange—at least that's what the book says. I can't see it. . . . Think I'm color-blind?"

"All men are, according to your mother."

"That's why I wanted the binoculars."

"Don't rub it in."

"I'm not, Dad, really. That's not what I meant."

"I know, just teasing—guilty conscience."

"You'll have to turn your chair around, I think. Or else tilt your head back all the way, but that makes me dizzy."

Andrew did neither. Distracted by a light going off in the kitchen, he was watching Peggy make her way, now that the dishes were done, through the downstairs rooms, toward the opposite end of the house. In the stairwell she paused to pick up an envelope off the boot chest and then proceeded to the parlor. There, she went over to the Rip Van Winkle—a heavily upholstered, clumpish yet comfortable reclining-rocker of local manufacture whose trademark Mat had recently discovered embossed on the cast-iron frame—and settled down to read Sarah Kellogg's letter.

Andrew knew beforehand more or less what Peggy would say, but needed to hear her say it, needed her advice, support, encouragement, if ever he were to reverse himself and accept the commission. At the same time he knew perfectly well that words were futile—whatever she said would fall on deaf ears. But why? why would her words have no weight for him, no validity, no effect? Because *she* had none?

He could see her now radiant and concentrated as the lamplight illuminating her long full face, strong features, large slightly tilted head, yellow sun-bleached hair still pinned up against the heat of the kitchen. At this distance he had no difficulty recognizing Peggy's qualities: the rare balance she maintained between common and uncommon sense, divine and worldly wisdom. It came, he surmised, partly from her French ancestry, partly from being a woman, but mostly from being a dancer—so much about her did—from all those years of working with her body. What a boon to living it must be to come to grips right off the bat with your body, the very instrument of living. How could a dancer help but gain a sense of reality, become a realist like Peggy? It resulted from her training, just as her sense of the divine resulted from its practice: from movement itself. No doubt she knew precisely, intimately what nature had given her to work with, what its possibilities as well as limitations were, and honored both; knew, moreover, the relation of her body to the earth, the ground on which she stood—not only stood but depended for support and leverage to make her leaps away from it, the ground from which she took her leave in joy and to which she knew herself bound always to return, not begrudgingly but in joy as well. Yes, clearly she had found her place, located her position in the world, and once you've found your place, he supposed, everything else—yourself, the world, the selfhood of others—must fall into place.

How, then, was it possible for such a woman to have no effect on him? Only if he himself robbed her of it. The reason he could recognize her qualities now was that he found himself removed from her, observing her at a distance and in repose like her—the two of them arrested, as it were, in space and time. But in a little while, when she came outside to speak about the letter, up close, those qualities would become indistinct, confused with his own, as blurred and indistinct as if he were astigmatic; whereas she would remain clear-sighted. She would come across the lawn, bridge the gap dividing them, yet still be able to maintain her distance, still perceive him as she would were it daylight and she to glance up from the letter and see him sitting in this wicker chair a hundred feet away. She would see the man she lived with, had shared ten years of her life with, and loved for what they shared; would see an exceptionally caring husband and father; a conscientious diligent businessman (his brother's viewpoint notwithstanding); a composer of such-and-such scores serenely beautiful and dense; friend—most intimate, "best" friend of such-and-such people who, like Peggy, loved and admired him, turned to him for counsel, relied on his compassion for insights into themselves. It would be to *that* man, then, that she would come across the lawn to speak. Not that she was blind to other aspects of his personality—she couldn't help but be aware of the chronically despondent, sometimes suicidal melancholiac, the self-disbeliever, self-tormentor—but found no basis in reality to verify those attributes, mistake them for her husband.

For Andrew, on the other hand, who hadn't found his place, gotten hold of himself like Peggy, that man, her husband, was all but nonexistent. He scarcely knew a thing about the fellow except by reputation, hearsay—even his scores, when Andrew happened to look them over or hear them played from time to time, seemed, despite their familiarity, the work of someone else. He had lived too long by other lights or darknesses, too intimately with other images or negatives of himself, to give much credence to the man she would address. No, the minute she approached, the distance which now separated them, which made possible their integrity, their separateness, would disappear, and he would lose all sight of her, all sight of himself.

"You aren't even looking, Dad."

Andrew removed his hand from his brow. "Sorry, Mew." To demonstrate his attention now, he took Mat's previous advice: turned the chair around, tilted back his head, and looked up at the sky. The countless specks and spots and sparkles of incandescent light, diamonding the dark, astonished Andrew, made him feel all at once wide awake, acute as the stars themselves. Strangely, the light seemed to be coming not from individual stars, stellar bodies situated in and set off against the sky, but from some central source on the other side of it, shining through the deep rich blackness, as if through a loosely woven canopy spread overhead to protect the eyes of mortals from the glare of another brighter world beyond. Andrew inhaled deeply. "The Big Dipper, you said?"

"Yes, follow the handle—it's the first bright—"

"I see it now."

"Well? Does it look orange to you?"

"No, not really."

"Me neither."

"Don't you say another word about those binoculars," Andrew bantered.

"I wasn't going to!" Mat defended himself strenuously. "Know how far away Arcturus is?"

"No."

"Thirty-six light-years." Mat waited for his father to ask the next logical question, but Andrew remained silent, motionless, gazing at the star. "Know how many miles that is?"

"No."

It took Mat a moment to arrive at the sum in his head. "Two hundred sixteen million million miles."

"A mere nothing."

"Are you kidding, Dad?"

"Yes . . . and no."

"Why no?"

"Because—" Andrew started to explain but thought better of it. "I don't know. It's too complicated, too many ways of looking at it, more than we can understand."

"*I* understand."

"So I see."

"Except one thing."

"What's that?"

"Well, there are some stars—we can't see them now, 'cause we don't have—"

"Binoculars?"

"No! a telescope. Stop kidding around. Some stars," he began again, "are thousands of light-years away—millions! You can see them with a telescope, even though"—Mat's voice rose as he went on, grew thinner, uncertain, hushed—"they don't exist anymore . . . they're dead"—he lowered his voice as though in deference—"burned out, but we can still see them—their light, I mean—a million light-years later."

"The song is over," Andrew remarked to himself, "but the melody lingers on."

"What melody?"

"In music. It's like music, Mew. You know, in music there are separate tones, one after the next, in a series." Andrew stopped to illustrate the point by humming five or six tones—the first that came to mind—which, to his sur-

44

prise, turned out to be the very phrase he'd been toying with all day, the one he'd begun to regard as the Drowned Brother's theme from *Recovery*. "Well, that's on one level. But then there's another—at the same time—another level: melody. 'At the same time' because even though those tones come in succession, one after the other, we hear them altogether . . . now—the way we see Arcturus, even though the light was generated thirty-six light-years ago, we see it *now*, right *there*"—he pointed at the star—"this minute. Follow me?"

"Not exactly."

"Well, let's go back to melody a second. When we hear a melody, what we're hearing isn't a succession of tones— the way they're printed in a score—individual tones sounded once and then no more . . . like—like so many birds—a flock of birds flying by, never to be seen again. No, not at all . . . they gather. Those tones, though sounded a moment ago, in the past, *persist*—can still be heard—right now, in the present . . . even as they forecast tones still to come, in the future. It happens all at once—present, past, and future—like *that*"—he motioned toward the heavens—"up there." As he gazed again at the stars, the thought of Twister crossed his mind. "Dead," he murmured, "yet still visible, a million light-years later."

"Not without a telescope."

"The trouble with looking at it that way, Mew, scientifically, is that too much gets left out in the process—the process itself gets left out, the whole dynamics of the thing —yet that's what constitutes the melody: the ever-changing process. Leave out the process, and you lose the melody . . . the movement of the stars." Once again he looked up at the sky. "How serene, immutable it seems. And yet, they're furnaces, those stars, ablaze with energy, great blasts of creation . . . destruction . . . the whole universe in conflagration, exploding every second; and we, poor souls, pin all our hopes on permanence, would rather die than change. . . . And so we *do*, unable to accept the fact that without process there would be no life at all—no stars . . . music . . . nothing."

"I've lost you, Dad."

"No, you haven't, sweetie pie; I'm right here."

"So am I," Peggy added, coming up behind them, the

letter, Andrew was quick to observe, tucked under her belt.

"Dad can't see it either, Mom, the orange."

"That's because he's color-blind." Peggy and Andrew recited the saw in unison, and all three laughed. "What a pity for you boys," she teased, looking up to locate Arcturus, "orange as a Sunkist."

"Really, Mom?"

"Bet your knickers! Come on now: way past bedtime."

Mat, as if prompted by the power of suggestion, yawned deeply, prolongedly, after which he picked himself up without protest, kissed his parents good night, and started toward the house but stopped. "Are you going for a walk?"

"Uh-uh." Peggy turned an empty chair around and sat down facing Andrew. "Staying right here," she assured her son. "We'll be up in a minute."

"Watch out for the wickets," Andrew cautioned as Mat proceeded across the lawn, which doubled as a croquet court.

"Don't worry: I know where they are, every single one, even in the dark—unless you moved them."

The boy's suspicion made Andrew laugh out loud. "No. But that gives me an idea."

"Better not," Mat admonished his father from the distance.

"Night-night," Andrew said.

" 'Night, love."

" 'Night," Mat called back before entering the house.

"Why *don't* we go for a walk?" Andrew suggested.

"I don't want to leave him," Peggy explained softly, sadly. "A little upset . . . afraid, I think."

"Of what?"

"Before you came, at the station, they were playing—he and Larry and Pearl—some kind of kidnapping game: Mew broke down, cried his heart out."

"Afraid of being *kidnapped?*"

"No; of being left alone."

"This house, you mean?"

"No . . . not exactly. Something about the silence here . . . at night . . . the solitude"—Peggy scanned the dark horizon—"the mountains . . . summer—mainly that, I think, the summer: the first since Twis— In the city, at least, there's school, the two of us home, but here. . . . He can't get used to it somehow."

"Being without Twis?"

"Yes. Twice this week he had nightmares."

"About Twis?"

"Indirectly, I suppose—some sort of sea monster, trying to swallow him alive. Breaks my heart." There was a catch in Peggy's voice.

"Don't," Andrew said with sympathy. Leaning forward, he reached out as if to take her hand but didn't follow through. Instead, it was Peggy who completed the gesture: took Andrew's hand. Her fingers were moist with perspiration.

"He thinks he's so composed—prides himself on it—doesn't understand. . . . He's frightened, Andy."

"Who isn't? . . . Of nightmares—it's only natural."

"I don't mean the nightmares, I mean in general."

Andrew felt Peggy's grip intensify, tighten with need, telling him something by touch that couldn't be put into words or was better left unspoken, something about their son, themselves in relation to fear, about fear itself, perhaps —he wasn't sure. Presently she began to stroke the back of his hand, her thumb smoothing the skin in the same direction over and over again. In response Andrew squeezed the fleshy mound at the base of her thumb, not instinctively but deliberately to assure her of their solidarity, even as he disengaged and then withdrew his hand.

Sighing, Peggy tipped her head up toward the stairs. "You know," she said after a moment's silence, "in a way I'm glad you forgot the binoculars."

"*Et tu, Brute!*"

"They're too far away, the stars, too removed to satisfy —a child's needs, at any rate. He's too involved with things like that: the scientific, abstract—"

"Funny, that's just what I got finished telling him—"

"You!" Peggy laughed in his face good-naturedly. "How do you suppose he came by it in the first place?"

"From me?" Andrew said with irony. "The scientific?"

"I'm talking about the amount of time he spends inside his head."

"Comes from me?"

"Well," she reconsidered, "that may not be fair, it may be something deeper: the nature of the beast—men, I mean —something inherently male. I don't know. But what he needs, and badly, is to be touched."

"By what?"

"Hands! Literally, I mean, physically touched . . . all the time . . . all of us do. It's terribly important," she summed up solemnly.

"Because I took my hand away just now?"

The question surprised Peggy, who was deep in thought, confused her momentarily. "What? Oh, no"—she brushed aside the interruption. "Sarah's right, I think."

"Don't change the subject."

"I'm not. . . . A bit too much the high priestess"—she went on with her thoughts—"the vestal virgin—of art—all that stuff about Wigman, Fra Angelico, Michelangelo—art! art! art! Sometimes I think Sarah gets herself into a trance state—autohypnosis—you can't believe half the things she says. That part about me and motherhood, for instance. Well, I may have said something of the sort, about gravity— I don't remember now—but not a whole cosmology the way she would have it. How she loves to work things up. . . . Still, she's wonderful—impossible, spoiled, self-centered, willful, but absolutely wonderful, and *right*, what's more," Peggy added pointedly, "about you."

"That I'm a metaphysical shilly-shallier?"

"No, for heaven's sake! You *would* pick up on that. Don't be silly. That's just Sarah—all that—that philosophizing. I mean," she stated simply, "that you should do the score."

"I knew you'd say that."

"Well naturally. Don't sound so disappointed. It's not as if I were betraying you—taking her side against yours. I said so from the start, didn't I? Last weekend, too, when you showed me your letter— Oh! thank God she wrote back. I could kiss her feet," Peggy declared in a hushed, almost reverential tone, before turning chatty again. "I must say, you didn't give me much idea of it—*Recovery*."

"Didn't I? I told you—"

"About the shawl, yes, and Elizabeth Barrett, but I had no idea—I should have, I suppose, knowing Sarah. God! it sounds exciting."

"It *is*."

"I got all tingly just reading about it. Could hardly sit still." The wicker creaked as Peggy stood up now and began to pace the lawn. "Made me want to dance again, rejoin the Company."

"Seriously?"

"No, just nostalgia. That woman has a way of exciting me like no one else." Peggy paused, waiting for Andrew to speak. "Not you?"

"Yes."

"Well?" She came back to the chair, letter in hand. "What are you going to do?" While waiting once more for him to speak, Peggy fidgeted with the envelope, revolving it continually, causing the paper to crinkle. "Sorry, I didn't hear you, Andy."

"I said, I don't know yet," he repeated irritably. "Why do you think I showed it to you?"

"Oh, my honey"—Peggy sat down again, facing Andrew —"you know what I would do if I were you? Just what Sarah says: talk to Ben, take a leave of absence, spend the summer here with us—"

"Here?"

"That's what I meant before, when you thought I was changing the subject, I was thinking of Mew—how good it would be for him to have you here . . . for all of us, for you! You know what Oxenburg said."

"I couldn't work here."

"Why not? How do you know till—"

"Because I'm such a confounded creature of habit."

"So what? We'll recreate the habits here. If the upright isn't good enough, we'll rent a better one—switch Mew around: put him in the guest room, the piano upstairs. You can't imagine what it's like, that back room, in the morning: the sunlight in the valley—just one bright patch"—she established its boundaries with her hands, held out, as if to make him a gift of the patch—"the mountains still in mist; then all at once it starts to spill, the light, like a wave, spilling over, down the slopes. . . ."

"What about my books, scores—"

"We'll drive down to the city, load up the car—one trip should do it: everything you need. And maybe, if it works, we'll stay on, through the fall, Thanksgiving—think of it!

what it must be like—"

"You're forgetting the Laymans, aren't you?"

"They might be willing—who knows?—need the money. If not, we'll find another house."

"And school?"

"Oh, don't be such a worrywart!" she snapped.

"To think about a school?"

"I mean, creating obstacles."

"Creating!"

"I'm sure the school's all right—be good for Mew: kids from different—"

"Thirty-five minutes!" Andrew burst out. "She's asking for thirty-five minutes!" That in itself, the magnitude of the commission, was more than enough from Andrew's view to justify his opposition, if not to end the discussion.

Peggy waited a moment before replying with perfect equanimity, "So?"

"You think it's a matter of drumbeats, too?"

"No."

"Mere pulsations!" Springing to his feet, Andrew began to stride back and forth in the dark, muttering to himself. "Pulsations! The woman must be mad. Vamping! that's what she wants. Well, if that's what she wants—"

"Stop working yourself up."

"—let her commission Norton—commission Erskine—"

"She wants *you*."

"I *will not pad*," he exclaimed defiantly.

"No need to pad—or shout," she added, remaining imperturbable. "She'll wait."

"Ten years?"

"If necessary."

"What's the matter with you? Don't you understand? it's ready *now*, *Recovery*, finished!"

"That's *her* worry. No one told her to jump the gun. Let her wait, work on something else, till you're ready."

"Just take the money, quit the business, move up here—"

"Exactly."

"I can't."

"You must!" she declared with passion, dropping her former composure. So strong was her feeling, it brought her to her feet and over the grass to where Andrew had come to a standstill. "Must," she repeated, facing him now, confronting him with quiet intensity. "Don't ask me why—just a hunch, woman's intuition—something tells me you must. It's one of those moments, choices, that everything turns on—our whole life, I think—on what you decide. Oh, my love, even if it frightens you, seems beyond your means, utterly infeasible, you must, because we're *here*"—she dipped her body suddenly, emphatically, as if in preparation for a leap—"on earth, I mean . . . just once, not forever"—her gaze shifted to the sky—"like the stars."

"Don't fool yourself: the stars don't have forever."

"All the more reason to do it, then—take the risk. You must. If not—" She stopped herself.

Her silence filled Andrew with foreboding. "What?" he whispered, adopting her tone.

"I'm afraid . . . we'll get stuck."

"Aren't we already?" The question was rhetorical, voiced without a trace of sentimentality or self-pity.

"That's why"—Peggy ignored the question, implying agreement—"you must do it . . . say yes for once. Come," she concluded matter-of-factly as she turned toward the house and started to remove her hairpins, "let's sleep on it."

"Sleep," he scoffed.

"Don't act as if you never do." Peggy picked up her chair to return it for the night to its customary place on the back porch. Andrew started to do the same but was distracted by the sudden appearance of Mat, silhouetted in their bedroom window.

"I thought you said 'a minute,' " the boy called out.

"Right now," Andrew called back. "We're on our— goddammit!" he exclaimed, lurching forward headlong, as the chair flew out of his hands and he stumbled several paces before slipping and coming to rest on all fours.

Seeing him, Peggy burst into laughter and laughed so hard she had to set her own chair down and hold on to its back for support.

"What's so funny?" Mathew wanted to know.

"Your father, he"—she could scarcely get the words out for laughing—"he—"

"Tripped on a wicket," Andrew confessed to the further delight of Mathew and Peggy.

4

By the time Peggy tucked Mat in and came to bed her-self, Andrew was asleep, albeit restlessly. His feet were moving steadily, sometimes straining against the footboard (stretched out, Andrew was several inches taller than the length of the Laymans' bed), sometimes arching the instep like someone testing a new pair of shoes; at others digging down industriously, deep into the cleft between the mattress and bedstead, as if in an effort to back out, tunnel his way to freedom. Lying on his stomach, he had the pillow in a strangle hold, his head turned away from Peggy's side of the bed, teeth clenched and grinding audibly, pelvis pump-ing rhythmically. The bedclothes were already half cast off, revealing the small of his naked back and one pajamaed leg.

Quiet and considerate as Peggy tried to be, slipping into bed, Andrew stirred, grunted faintly, moved away. For a while she remained perfectly still, though wide awake, lying on her back, listening to his night sounds—the sounds of some subterraneous animal in distress—and gazing at the window screen, pussy willow–colored in the moonlight. Even the moths and June bugs had given up their struggle for the night, clung motionless to the outside of the screen. Only Andrew, stranded midway between sleep and waking, strove against both, working every muscle. After a moment Peggy reached over and placed her hand gently on his shoulder.

Andrew woke with a start, a stifled cry, his heart thumping, half-tumid penis deflating. "What!" he demanded indignantly, neither turning nor raising his head. The moment he spoke, he regretted the fact, wished he hadn't acknowledged consciousness, encouraged any exchange.

In reply Peggy moved her hand to his neck, taking firm hold of the nape and squeezing tenderly.

Perhaps she only meant to quiet him, soothe his nerves, nothing more. He waited with misgivings to see whether or not the hand would be withdrawn. Soon it was. Relieved, he released his breath, relaxed his jaw, subsided into the pillow.

Presently, however, she brought the hand to his head, placed two fingers on his temple, rotating the tips round and round, slowly, surely, with the finesse of a masseuse.

Yes, clearly her intention was to relax him—only that: the laying on of healing hands. Yet, to do so, she had had to change position, turn onto her side, moving closer.

Andrew twitched, feeling her nipple graze his skin, her breath on his arm, the heat of her body. So, she was naked! Despite his having made a special point of putting on his pajama bottoms in front of her, she had come to bed naked —the healing hands not half so selfless as they seemed. No, indeed. Those selfsame hands would soon be picking at the scab again, prying it off; the confrontation, clash, in progress since December, would resume, if not be brought to a head— Ha! Andrew laughed to himself, that was a good one: "brought to a head." How foolish he had been to assume that she would let him off tonight, simply because of the long weekend. Not a chance. She was more determined now than ever, he realized, remembering her remark about the need for being touched, to have it out. Ha! another good one: "have it out." If only he could fall asleep again or fake it, before—

Peggy moved her hand, not hopping this time from one spot to the next but in contact constantly, sliding her fingers ever so lightly the length of his neck, down the shoulder, into the armpit and out again, over the ribs one by one. At the same time she curved her body, brought it closer: one breast pressed against his side, her knee abutting his thigh, calf crossing his calf, big toe stroking the sole of his foot; whereupon she brought her left hand into play, exploring with her forefinger the passageways of his ear, even as she slipped the right, which by now had reached the obstacle of his pajamas, under the waistband, over the buttock, and began to knead the flesh.

Andrew was by no means insensitive to this stimulation—the caresses of her toe sent tremors of excitement through his body, the hand fondling his buttock evoked other tremors in his groin. Yet not for long. Straightway, consciousness intruded, intercepted the sensations. Instead of leading to further, more pleasurable feelings, they stimulated thoughts, reflections on what he was feeling or failing to feel, till the feelings themselves were lost in thought.

In recent months it had become increasingly difficult for Andrew to engage in and enjoy foreplay for its own sake. No longer a preliminary, a prologue, foreplay had become for both Peggy and Andrew the action itself, the very agon of their drama. After Christopher's death they had, by mutual though tacit consent, lapsed into a period of continence. In the beginning neither questioned it—their celibacy seemed perfectly appropriate, natural under the circumstances. But gradually, as the shock wore off and her grief abated, Peggy recovered, felt stirrings of desire. At first these stirrings had little to do with wanting another baby, at least not consciously—that came later. Nor were they the response of someone, frightened by a sudden recognition of mortality, clinging for dear life to a fellow mortal. No, they were purely instinctual, these stirrings, like the quickening of sap in the sugar maple before the snow is off the ground, the yielding of dormancy to liveliness, of winter to spring.

But Andrew had a rhythm of his own. Not ready yet to relinquish grief, he resisted her advances. She was patient, understanding, didn't press the matter. In time he came around, participated in her desire, but with a difference: His ardor, heretofore avid, seemed halfhearted now, willed; his arousal, formerly instantaneous, took some time and effort. Aware though Andrew was of the change, he was still too preoccupied with Christopher's death to attribute to the matter much significance. Nor did Peggy. Having had time to sort out her feelings, she found herself concerned less with pleasure than with procreation. Not only was she ready but determined now to conceive another child. To that end she dispensed one night with her diaphragm. Andrew, quick to sense its absence, shrank from her. What had, till then, remained an unspoken, unexplored, even, for Andrew, a nonexistent question—whether or not to have another baby—became an open issue, a point of contention. Andrew was reluctant, unwilling to be rushed. Peggy felt they had no choice, must conceive. Andrew procrastinated, pleaded for time. Again she waited, tried to be patient. Then something unexpected happened. On one occasion he had difficulty ejaculating, on another his penis prematurely lost its firmness.

At about this time the Lindbergh baby was kidnapped. Like most Americans, but more so, Andrew became obsessed with the crime. Because of Christopher he sympathized sorely with the Lindberghs, suffered every setback, worried about the little boy, brooded over the kidnappers, woke in the night crying out against the "underworld." Despite the marked differences between Christopher and Charles, Jr.—differences in age, religion, class; as well as the fact that one was dead, the other ostensibly alive—Andrew often interchanged them in his mind, blurring the particulars, till it seemed at times he had the notion that Christopher, too, had been kidnapped, was being held for ransom, and might yet reappear unharmed. When, at last, the Lindbergh baby was found dead, the news left Andrew stunned. Silent, sullen, withdrawn, he spent the whole weekend incommunicado, almost as if, as Peggy put it, he himself had been spirited away, kidnapped by those two dead children.

Throughout this period his impotence increased, became all but chronic, compounding his depression—so much so, that Andrew couldn't tell which came first, the depression or the impotence, which was causing which. He tried to cover up, compensate for his debility with kisses and caresses. Peggy wasn't fooled. She wanted to talk the problem out. He refused, couldn't bear it. They spoke, instead, through their bodies: he with his flaccid penis, she with her persevering hands, both with the sweat of their fruitless labor. Andrew fretted about himself, felt afraid, humiliated, filled with guilt and self-deprecation. She was ambivalent, torn between the necessity of her body and the necessity of his. Day after day they strove to overcome the problem (sometimes by pretending to ignore it), struggled doggedly, defeated themselves, left off, strove again. Night after night ended in failure. Nothing helped. The struggle went on, became a trial, a test of wills, esteem, of love itself—the measure of their marriage. Andrew started having palpitations, vertigo, weakness in the knees. He grew apprehensive. Peggy prevailed on him to see their doctor. He went but couldn't bring himself to speak of the problem, dwelled instead on his other ailments. The doctor, after examining him thoroughly and finding nothing wrong, attributed the various complaints to "nerves," the strain brought on by Christopher's death. Andrew was at once relieved and more deeply troubled. Suddenly the impotence loomed much larger, seemed symptomatic of something in general: an overall collapse of spirit, nerve, determination, a flagging not only of the flesh but of the will *to be*, lay claim to anything, including life itself. The doctor recommended rest, a change of scene. At Peggy's insistence, Andrew complied, rented the Laymans' house for the summer.

Now, Andrew turned his head, rolled onto his side to face her, not instinctively but deliberately, dutifully, determined to be responsive. Peggy moved closer, drew him closer with the hand that held his buttock, till their pelvises and chests were flush, lips touching, tongues in contact. He scarcely noticed, feelingly, the movement of her hands and tongue and toes, the warmth and softness of her body, so attentive was he to his own body, to what effect, if any, her actions would have on his penis. Before long there was a slight swelling of the shaft. Andrew strove to reinforce it by probing Peggy's palate with his tongue. She, in turn, unbuttoned his pajama fly, fumbled with the bow. He assisted her. Like a soloist struck by stage fright at the parting of the curtains, his penis recoiled. As she slipped her hand inside and started fondling him he thought for a moment of the unveiling of his father's grave. . . . Would they have to undergo the same ritual again next month for Twister? It would be a year on— Better talk to Ben—better yet to Letty, she would know exactly— "Will the baby burn?" Was that what he had said, the Lindbergh baby's kidnapper, the first time in the graveyard? "Will *I* burn"— wasn't that it?—"if the baby's dead?" Baby's-dead baby's-dead— "It would make my mother cry." That's what he had said. "What does g-r-a-v-e-y a-r-d spell?" Gravey . . . gravey . . .

At some point, unrecognized by Andrew, Peggy had taken his left hand in hers (caressing him the while with her right) and moved it to her breast. He was conscious now of her cupping his palm over her breast, applying the gentlest pressure with her hand, inducing his fingers to grasp the flesh, even as she fastened her lips on his nipple. Following her lead, he squeezed and stroked her breast, fondled her nipple with his middle finger, much as she was fondling his with her tongue. In no time both their nipples stood erect. His penis, too, though not yet erect, had begun to swell. She was quick to acknowledge the fact, contracting and relaxing her grip rhythmically on the rising shaft. He tried hard not to be self-conscious, continued fondling her breast with his left hand, while with the right he reached up (she was bending over him now, her knees astride his hips) and began to caress her belly. Peggy moaned softly. Gradually he moved his right hand to her vulva, the middle finger to her clitoris. She moaned again, but whether to express her satisfaction with the motion of his finger or with the progressive stiffness of his penis or merely to encourage him, he couldn't tell. She, meantime, having left his nipple, drew her tongue over his chest, licking in every direction, as she made her way down the center furrow of his torso, pausing briefly to rim and probe the navel, nibble at the pubic mound, buss the testicles, before taking his penis into her mouth. It was almost stiff. He was well aware of that, aware too of what would doubtless follow once it was erect. Wanting to forestall that moment, allay his anxiety, he reached behind her now, encircling her rump, and tried to swing her body around, bring her trunk into juxtaposition with his mouth, so that he could substitute his tongue for the finger on her clitoris. She resisted. He knew why: She wanted to hold herself in readiness. He tried again to move her. She wouldn't yield. Nor would he. To outwit her, he rotated his own body, taking care the while not to pull his penis from her mouth, till his feet were on the pillow, head beneath her groin, and drew her down forcefully on top of him. She interposed a hand between his lips and hers. He pushed it away.

"Please," she objected, but the word was almost unintelligible, muffled by his penis which stood, at last, erect.

He ignored her plea, inserted his tongue between her lips, already moist—g-r-a-v-e-y— She squirmed to free herself. He held her fast, locked in his embrace, licking her proficiently.

"Please."

This time he had no difficulty understanding; the word was perfectly distinct. Having removed his penis from her mouth, she held it now firmly in her fist, gripping it like a tiller, trying to turn him about on the bed. Again he paid no attention, continued licking, determined to acquit himself as best he could of his responsibility, alleviate his guilt, absolve himself, before the fact, of his culpability.

Thwarted for the moment, she encircled his penis with her thumb and forefinger, joining them securely, creating a band to bind his erection. He, meanwhile, went on licking, prodding, pressuring, till she began to moan again, much louder, longer than before, tensed her muscles, twitched, went slack, breathing heavily. He breathed, too, a sigh of relief for the temporary remission.

The relief lasted but an instant. No sooner did he relax his grip than she raised her haunches, rolled off him, and, using his penis (still erect and banded by her fingers) as a pivot, turned around face to face, whereupon she straddled his hips and, lowering her own, eased the penis into herself.

Andrew, behaving and at the same time observing his behavior—himself the subject and research team—went through, or, more precisely, submitted to, the motions of coitus, anticipating every instant his imminent collapse. If only he could stop worrying—what had she called him? sounded so ugly: worrywart—stop watching, witnessing himself, stop trying to sustain the stiffness by muscular control, by will instead of willingness; if only he could still his brain, stop thinking altogether, forget for once the messages, transmissions of self-consciousness, self-criticism, incurring certain failure; if only he could transpose heads, transplant his cortex in his cock, think with his glans, think the contact of the membranes, gliding in and out, the slippery sliding into rapture . . . rupture: the spilling of the gravey in the gravey yard, making Mamma die. . . . Andrew groaned, feeling himself peter out, feeling

58

through Peggy's body her sense of loss at his diminishment.

"Sorry," he murmured, but the apology didn't ring true, did nothing to ease his conscience. On the contrary, it made him feel more ill at ease, not only because it came as a confession, an open avowal of everything heretofore unspoken—his worthlessness, humiliation, failure, guilt—but also because the word had by now lost all significance, become a platitude, part of their nightly routine. *Sorry* was what he always said at this juncture, to which she invariably replied *Don't be.*

Tonight, however, Peggy didn't say a word. Instead, she disengaged herself in silence and moved to her side of the bed.

Uneasy though her silence made him, Andrew didn't break it, preferred it to the discussion that would necessarily ensue. All he wanted now was to fall asleep, forget the whole fiasco, lose consciousness completely. Without so much as saying good night, he turned over onto his stomach, hugged the pillow, and closed his eyes. Yet scarcely had he done so, when he felt the mattress shift, heard Peggy strike a match, saw, despite his lowered lids, the sulfur flare, signalling her wakefulness.

"Those girls," she began, but stopped, broke off for what seemed a full minute.

Was she waiting for him to admit he was awake, ask which girls she had in mind? Ought he to complain about her smoking in bed? No, better not, best keep still.

"The two who were on the train," she finally resumed, "the ones Ben made that joke about and then retracted, said he was only teasing. . . ." Again she paused.

Goldie and—that was whom she was talking about—Goldie and— Damn it! what was the other's name? He couldn't have forgotten already. Alice? No. Lois? Goldie and—and . . . Louise?

"Is one of them . . . ?" Once more she lapsed into silence, dropped the question, only to take it up again in the next breath: "Andy?"

Although he hadn't the vaguest idea what she was driving at, he knew perfectly well what she was waiting for: some sign that he was still awake, that she wasn't talking to herself. But why about those girls? Goldie and—and— What had they to do with anything? Lola? Liz? "Go to sleep!" He squirmed his shoulders as if to shake her off, reshaped his pillow roughly.

"Is one of them . . . the woman you've been seeing?"

Andrew was taken aback. Not only was the question startling but utterly unfounded, farfetched. "Wom— What woman?"

Peggy ignored his question, put another of her own: "Have you brought her up here for the weekend . . . to be nearby?"

He wasn't taken in by her assumed bitterness. Her voice was too high-pitched, too thin and frail to disguise her vulnerability. "Who?" He turned over to face her. She was sitting on the edge of the bed, her naked back to him. He rummaged for her bathrobe in the dark. It had fallen to the floor. He picked it up—"What are you talking about?"— and draped it over her shoulders.

She cast it off with a shrug. "Please!"

He replaced it. "You'll catch cold."

"I don't care," she replied petulantly, but let the bathrobe stay. "Don't lie about it, please. What's the use? We're only fooling ourselves. There's someone else. I know there is, have known for weeks. Even before Janet called, I—"

"Janet?"

"—I knew . . . my *body* did. How could it help but know?"

"What? What has Janet—"

"She saw you at the movies, couldn't wait to tell me— good friend that she is—called up bright and early—"

"Saw me . . . with whom?"

"How should I know? Some girl—'very plain,' she said, 'but young.' You were at the Stoddard—it was weeks ago, the first week I was here."

Mention of the movie house, rather than of the nondescript girl, elicited from Andrew a murmur of recognition. "Oh . . . Penny—"

"I don't want to know her name"—Peggy stubbed out her cigarette—"anything about her—whether she's gorgeous or plain—none of my business," she said sincerely, struggling to be reasonable. "Not that part anyway, only what happens here, its effect on us."

Now, at last, the pieces came together, made perfect sense

to Andrew. "You mean, you think my failure here"—he pressed his fingers into the mattress—"has to do with someone else, caring for someone else?" Peggy nodded. He didn't notice in the dark. "Is that it?"

"Well?" she answered almost voicelessly.

Her pathos penetrated his defenses, drew him out of himself toward her. She was still in her former position, sitting with her back to him, head now bowed; he was curled up on the opposite side of the bed. Rousing himself, he edged closer, till his chest touched her back, his cheek her hair. He made no attempt, however, to change her position; her turned back suited him, created a note of anonymity, of the confessional, which he welcomed. "Oh, my darling . . . silly goose . . . Those girls on the train, I never saw them before, will never see them again. The one that Janet saw me with, that's someone else, a student, student of Norton's. Only saw her twice . . . sort of—well—experiment, I guess you'd call it. I—I wanted to see—*had* to, it was driving me insane—whether I—whether or not—" Andrew lost his voice for a moment but quickly regained it by force of will: "—whether I would fail with her as well. Wasn't fair—she's only nineteen."

"And did you?" Peggy whispered.

"Did I what?"

"Fail?"

Andrew nodded his head against her back—"Pretty much"—whereupon Peggy's back began to swell, rise under him like a mounting wave.

"Then . . . it isn't *me?*"

"You?"

"Me alone that you're refusing?"

Andrew felt a surge of sorrow, sympathy, self-reproach. He tried in vain to check it. A coughlike sob broke from his throat. It was soon followed by others, a fit of sobbing. "No . . . not you." He pulled her close, clung to her back. "Not you, my love . . . would make it too easy."

Pivoting, she hugged him to her breast, held his shaking body. She, too, was shaking now with tears. "Oh, my Andy —thought—didn't understand—thought we—we stopped—" The word *loving*, which followed, turned into a little wail.

"No . . . no . . ."

For some time they continued crying, shaking, clinging

to each other. Just when one began to quiet down, the other started up again, but eventually the spell was broken. Peggy went away for a moment. He could hear her blowing her nose. Presently she came back with a handkerchief for him. He moved over to make room for her. She didn't sit down. Instead, she put on her bathrobe and began to pace the floor in silence, one hand on her hip at first, the other on her brow, as if to gauge her temperature, then bringing both together, palm to palm, in a prayerful attitude. "If it isn't me," she said at last, standing still to weigh her words, "and there isn't someone else, what—what is it?"

"What is what?"

"The thing you're opposing?"

Andrew closed his eyes to consider the question. After a moment he heaved a dispirited sigh. "Myself, I suppose." Peggy made no reply, merely scratched her scalp. "You don't agree?"

"I don't know."

"Neither do I—baffles me—why anyone would stand against himself . . . how it's even possible . . . no animal would ever dream—" Suddenly uncomfortable, Andrew brought his hand to his groin, shifted his position, drawing his knees up toward his chest to relieve the ache in his testicles. "Lately I've begun to think it's something else entirely—what I'm opposing; not me at all, but something, well, even more . . . more puzzling . . . irrational."

"What's that?"

"Sex. . . . Don't laugh."

"You!" she scoffed.

"Yes. I don't know why, what it is, this refusal, whether I'm afraid . . . repelled—I don't know what—but there's a part of me, very old—young, I should say, very very primitive—that seems dead—dead set against it."

Peggy sat down and, placing a hand on his thigh, shook her head and smiled. "That isn't true."

"I know," he conceded readily. "Loved it once . . . more than anything . . . mitigated everything—seems so long ago."

"Less than a year."

"A lifetime, it seems." Andrew sighed. "I can't go on like this, mourning him forever."

"No," she agreed categorically. "If that's what it is."

Getting up, Peggy resumed pacing, deep in thought again, her hand poked like a pitchfork into her hair, eyes trained on the floor. After traversing the span between the windows several times, she came to a standstill in front of the chiffonier, facing its mirror, elbows resting on the oak top.

Andrew could see that she was looking at neither herself nor him in the glass, but looking down, her skull domed by her cupped palms. "What's the matter?" he asked with concern.

"Shall I tell you what I think?" Turning to face him, she leaned back against the chiffonier, supporting her weight on her elbows. "I think it's everything"—her tone, like her attitude, conveyed both dominion and defeat, indignation and despair—"not just me . . . yourself . . . sex . . . Sarah; you're saying no to everything—life itself, I think." So abashed and saddened was she by the idea, Peggy expressed it in a whisper, as if afraid of being overheard, not by Mat in the next room but by the Avenging Angel.

"By not having another baby, you mean?" he inquired coldly.

"By holding on to Twister . . . refusing to forgive . . . life . . . for death, I mean. Oh, Andy!" Shifting her weight and leaning forward, she appeared about to take a step, go to him, to succor and console him, but something held her back. "I felt that way myself at first. But then it changed— I don't know why, what enabled me . . . *grace*, I guess," she decided with evident thanks. "Unless, of course, it's that difference again between women and men. I don't know. In any case, I began to see it differently, his death . . . helped me understand . . . nothing's cancelled out. Oh, don't you see?" Released at last from whatever had been restraining her, she came over to him, hands outstretched, as if they were holding the very revelation she had had and placed now in his lap. "His death makes possible another life, another birth . . . *because* he died, someone else can be born . . . *must* be. I don't mean to us —planned parenthood or anything like that; it has nothing to do with *us*," she declared apocalyptically. "I mean . . . that death itself demands new life, makes life itself obligatory!"

"Regeneration," he said after a long meditative silence, leaving unspoken the distinction, weighing on his mind, between regeneration and resurrection. "That may be so—I'm sure it is . . . for certain things: animals and crops . . . even women, maybe; but for men . . . for men? . . . I wonder."

Peggy looked down and sighed. "That's why your body won't co-operate—because you wonder."

"Or because I'm a man?" he countered stoically. "Or do I wonder because I'm a man? Which, I wonder?"

At this moment the stillness was broken by a series of screams. "I'll go," Andrew said at once as he hurriedly put on his pajma bottoms.

"Wait and see," Peggy said, "he may sleep through it."

Andrew paid no attention, quickly made his way across the hall, and switched on the light in Mathew's room. Having kicked off his sheet and blanket, the boy had retreated to the head of the bed and was half lying down, half sitting up, his head and shoulders propped uncomfortably against the headboard as though his neck were broken, his legs drawn up almost to his chest, hands covering his eyes to shield them from the light. Andrew went over to the bed and, sitting down, stroked Mathew's crown. "Nightmare, Mew?"

"Grinder," Mat recounted, still covering his eyes, "had me in it, crushed down to the bottom—worms! Legs ground up, coming out like worms."

Andrew examined Mathew's shinbones. "Look all right to me."

"Do they?" Tentatively Mat uncovered his eyes and blinked. His cheeks were tear-stained, his expression both angry and perturbed. "Were just getting ready to grind the rest of me."

"It's over now, the dream," Andrew reassured him, but Mat looked unconvinced. "Want to come inside with us?"

"Don't be silly," Peggy said from the doorway, "he's not a baby anymore. You're all right, aren't you, Mew?"

"I guess," Mat allowed grudgingly.

"Of course you are," she maintained. "Just tuck you in." As she spoke Peggy went about straightening the bed-clothes. When it came to pulling up the sheet and blanket, Andrew was in the way, and she asked him to move. He obliged but sat right down again as soon as she was through. "Come on now"—she raised the covers for Mat—"Aunt

Violin and Uncle Wooly and the boys will be here before you can say Jack Robinson."

Contrary to Mat's custom of instantly repeating *Jack Robinson*, the boy said nothing as he slid down under the covers, his usually bright countenance enveloped in gloom.

"Say good night to Dad now," Peggy prompted.

"No," said Andrew, "I'll stay, I think, till he falls asleep."

"Good!" Mat smiled and gave his father an appreciative nudge, while Peggy looked on critically.

"What's the point of that?" she said. "Neither of you will fall asleep that way."

"Oh, yes," they disagreed in unison.

"Come on, Andy," Peggy said, losing patience.

"You said yourself—" He started to throw back at her her earlier observation that Mathew needed to be touched, but stopped himself. Instead, he slipped his arm around the boy's pillowed head and clasped Mat's shoulder. "Just turn out the light. I'll be there in a little while."

Without a word, but with a cold cross look of disapproval, Peggy switched off the light and left the room.

In the dark Mathew reached up, took hold of his father's hand, and kissed it. " 'Night, Dad."

" 'Night, my love." Andrew squeezed Mathew's cheek. "Sweet dreams—this time, I hope."

"Hope so."

As Andrew settled back against the headboard he thought of his sister Letty, "Aunt Violin," and reminded himself to remember to ask her tomorrow about unveilings—whether or not the ceremony of unveiling Twister's tombstone was required by Jewish Law. If it was, he had better get a move on, call the cemetery, and make the necessary arrangements. If not required, he would just as soon forget it, going to the grave—g-r-a-v-e-y . . . gravey yard . . . baby in the gravey yard— As if to dispel Twister's ghost, substantiate Mat's corporeality, Andrew gently tightened his grip on Mathew's hand.

"Mmm," the boy, already half asleep, murmured in response.

5

Halfway down the stairs Violet Baer, who was following her husband and preceding her brother, thought it behooved her to say something about the Laymans' house, through which Andrew had just conducted her and Monroe. "It's very . . ." she started to remark but stopped, unable to find a suitable yet polite epithet. At the same time her glance fell on the seat of Monroe's sharkskin trousers, shiny as the marble counter in her savings bank. He had had that very pair, his only pair, of summer-weight slacks as long as she knew him—eleven years next month—and Lord knows how long before that. How typical of Monny to make suits for the boys, dresses for her, overcoats for all of them, but not a stitch for himself. ". . . neat," she found the word at last, adding in a teasing undertone to her husband, "unlike certain people's trousers."

Monroe, who was slightly deaf in one ear (contrary to what the children thought, the condition had nothing to do with his being fourteen years older than Violet), stopped to turn the other. "What, my angel?"

"But not gaudy," Andrew put in from the landing where he was waiting for his sister to reach the bottom step. "Isn't that what Mamma used to say? 'Neat but not gaudy.' "

"About clothes and people, yes . . . and Papa's beard," Violet remembered almost in a reverie, not over the saying but over her father's black goatee.

"Straight ahead, Wooly." Andrew guided his brother-in-law, using the family pet name, whose origin was in dispute (both Ben and Violet claimed credit for coining it) and whose meaning few of the Spectors agreed about. Some attributed it to the fact that Monroe was a tailor; others related it to what they considered his fuzzy thinking and utopian ideas; still others, the majority by far, took it to connote his gentle lamblike nature. Only Essie Sachs, who among the sisters had the sharpest tongue and most devious mind, connected it, via the tribal herdsman of Transcaucasia where both Monroe and Stalin had been born, with the Communist International, a cause with which Monroe was known to be in sympathy, if not in league. "The parlor's a mess."

Monroe followed Andrew's directions: proceeded down the hall and out onto the back porch where he took a seat to watch the croquet match in progress between Barry, Kenneth, Mat, and Peggy. Violet, however, paid no attention to her brother. His warning merely provoked her everlasting curiosity, impelled her straight into the parlor.

The room was indeed a mess. At right angles to the piano was a collapsible bridge table at which Andrew had worked without stop from early morning till noon when Peggy had fetched the Baers from their boardinghouse. On the table was the envelope on which Andrew had been "doodling" the day before, as well as numerous sheets of paper, some still blank, others already ruled with staff lines and covered with notations. In addition to these there was an Art Gum eraser whose vermicular leavings were visible everywhere, a straightedge, emptied coffee cup, box of dried prunes, pencils, and colored crayons. The ashtrays were full of prune pits and cigarette butts, the wastebasket crammed with lumps of crumpled paper, the floor strewn with three or four work sheets, blown from the rack by a breeze.

Despite the fact that Andrew reached the parlor only moments after his sister, by the time he did, Violet was already busy examining one of these work sheets, picked up from the floor. Caught red-handed, she flinched, compressed her lips with guilt. "A gust," she explained, whereat she set about to pick up the rest of the sheets, making a show of her helpfulness.

Andrew said nothing. Much as he resented anyone looking at his work at any stage before completion, he knew better than to waste his breath on Letty. She simply couldn't help herself. Had the sheets not been on the floor, she would have scattered them there to create an excuse for prying or else gone straight to the rack on the pretext of tidying up. A born snoop and dissimulator, Letty spent most of her life covering tracks that no one was on the trail of, spinning a web of lies so flimsy, the strands were forever snapping, forever in need of repair. As a result, she suffered chronically from a guilty conscience. Even her most innocent act—brewing a cup of tea or doing a piece of needlepoint, at which she had become a master under Monroe's tutelage—was performed on the sly. Yet Violet was not the only member of the family marked by this trait; all the sisters were (Letty had merely carried their example to extremes), had had to be, had had to learn to do things on the sly, if only to survive in their parents' household.

Their father, Solomon Spector, a stiff, exacting, old-fashioned man transplanted in the New World, had found himself a long-stemmed beauty, Sophie Marcus, whom he married after an uphill courtship, and then—running counter to everything he had witnessed in the old country, every boyhood memory of his drunken tyrannical father, hectored mother on her hands and knees, scrubbing floors, toiling like a bondwoman—Solomon promptly instituted what he took to be a democratic reform: placed his already-Junoesque bride on a lofty pedestal and, still not satisfied, stanchioned her off with velvet-covered cords. Sophie, who was by nature an exceptionally strong, active, capable woman, an accomplished cook and housekeeper, was never again to lift a finger except at the piano, never to risk soiling her idolized beauty, never to be questioned, disobeyed, or contravened, never treated with anything but the utmost deference and adoration; in short, Sophie was to be sovereign. To assure her sovereignty, Solomon worked fourteen hours a day, six days a week, until he was able to set up his beloved in a brownstone house, staffed with no less than three servants whose salaries he could scarcely afford, at least at first, without considerable sacrifice. Later on, when the children were born, the female ones were pressed into service so rapidly it almost seemed that Solomon's sole purpose in begetting them was to enlarge his wife's domestic staff. Under the circumstances the girls grew up both in awe and secretly disrespectful, if not derisive, of their father, resentful yet envious of their mother, doting on while dominating their brothers, manipulating each other. Stealth and deception became second nature to them. One by one the girls discovered, and then schooled each other in duplicity to satisfy their father's inhuman standards and demands, hypocrisy to sustain their mother's exalted station, and dreams and self-delusion to make bearable their own sore lot in life. Their only hope was to find husbands for themselves someday as uxorious as their father, over whom they in turn could be sovereign. Such hope was anything but vain, since all the girls, without exception, were uncommonly tall and beautiful, far more beautiful than their mother—a fact from which each of them derived secret pride and satisfaction. So stately was their beauty that over the years their neighbors referred to them, depending on the fashion, as the John Singer Sargent girls, Gibson girls, Ziegfeld girls, and, when one or another was alone in the company of her brothers, the Barrymores. As it turned out, what each of them found was a man a whole head shorter than herself, altogether tractable, and, by any standard, homely. And the irony was that by the time Violet was born, sixteen years after her oldest sister Louise, she almost seemed a grandchild to her parents, a daughter to her siblings, all of whom (including Solomon who positively doted on her) treated her accordingly: indulged her every whim, pampered, spoiled, and babied her, so in reality there was no need for Letty ever to have mastered, let alone improved on, her sisters' underhanded ways.

"Working"—Letty's tone as she squared the gathered sheets on her raised knee was at once admiring and mildly reproachful—"even on the weekend?"

"Not really." Andrew took the sheets from her hand, put them on the bridge table, and set an ashtray on top of them for safekeeping. The ashtray's heavy glass rim magnified a group of notes: a B-natural, followed by an F and then another F. Something about the grouping displeased Andrew. "Excuse me a second," he mumbled, and, taking the top sheet along, sat down at the piano, sounded the tones, paused to ponder them, sounded them again, paused again, tried some variants. When at last he was satisfied, Andrew inserted a sharp sign in front of the first F.

"Sorry." He spun around on the piano stool to face his

sister, but Letty was no longer standing where he had left her. In the interim she had strayed to the bridge table (Andrew was amused to observe that the ashtray had been moved) to have another look at the sheets. This time, however, Letty made no bones about it for the simple reason, which Andrew also noticed with amusement, that while doing so she had helped herself to a prune and was now at greater pains to conceal her pilfering than her prying. "That's a pretty dress." Smiling, his sister glanced down as though to remind herself which dress she had on, but otherwise gave no sign of acknowledgment. Andrew wondered whether her silence was due to the fact that the dress was a hand-me-down (one of those that Letty acquired periodically from Mildred), or one of the many made for her by Wooly himself and worn by Letty not because she really liked them but just to spare his feelings; or whether she was, quite simply, reluctant to expose the prune.

"What is it," she said at last, enunciating normally despite the prune which, judging by the sudden swelling of her cheek, she had tucked to the side of her mouth, "you're working on?"

"Just some intervals."

"I can see that; I'd recognize them anywhere."

"My intervals?" His sister's pretentiousness tickled Andrew, and he couldn't resist leading her on. "How?"

Now that Letty had an excuse to indulge her curiosity openly, she picked up the ashtray, removed a sheet, and perused it at length. "They're so—so distinctly yours, so—tut! what's the word?"

"For what?"

"What you do."

"*Potchkees* around?"

"No!" In her laughter Letty had to bring a hand to her mouth to keep from either swallowing or spitting out the prune. "I'm being serious, Andy dear—for when you use those half notes—tones," she corrected herself, wishing to sound professional, "all those half tones."

"Chromatic?"

"Yes, that's it: 'chromatic.' "

" 'All those half tones,' " Andrew repeated with irony, sadly conscious of the fact that he had spent the better part of his musical life struggling to evolve a tonal system based on even smaller intervals. "I wish I could whittle them down," he said with feeling, turning away from his sister to face the piano again, "whittle them—"

"Andy," she interrupted, "don't you ever wonder about Mamma?" Having gone around him to the corner of the upright, Letty came to rest now, half slouched against the wall, half draped over the piano's frame. (Long before the flapper vogue had popularized poor posture, Violet's had been consistently round-shouldered and belly-out, giving her what Sarah Kellogg called the "Cranach look," a look which Sarah deplored because, as she was fond of saying, "Spirit itself depends on posture! The minute your eyes get out of line with your shoulders and the pelvic arch— *subito:* despondency sets in." Even so, Sarah's theory notwithstanding, Violet's spirits were generally lively.) In the course of her circumambulation Letty had absent-mindedly resumed munching the prune, but the moment she realized that Andrew had his eye on her, she packed it back into her cheek.

"Wonder what?"

"You think Mamma really understood or just pretended, because you were her pet?"

The question ruffled Andrew, not only because it seemed so patently loaded but also because it was so utterly ambiguous; he hadn't an inkling what she was referring to. "Understood what?"

"Your music."

"Oh, that." The letdown made him laugh. "She never claimed to understand. Who's looking for understanding, anyway? She did the best she could, the only thing you *can* do if you care for someone: respond."

Letty looked both skeptical and comical as she paused to ruminate on the prune, which she had since tucked into the space between her upper lip and gum, distending her mouth grotesquely. "If you ask me, she only wanted to appear cultured, more cultured than Papa."

Andrew refrained from pointing out how much more applicable his sister's comment was to herself than to their mother. "Don't fool yourself; Pop wanted it that way."

"To seem uncultured?" Letty objected. "Even if he did— for Mamma's sake, to put her in a better light—always better than himself, poor *shnook*," she added bitterly, before turning her attention to the work sheet still in hand, "it goes against everything the woman ever knew, ever liked, your chromatics, against melody, rhythm—"

Though Andrew thought better of correcting her misuse of the word *chromatics*, he couldn't let the rest pass unremarked. "Lilt, you mean, railroad rhythm, the 'simplest pulsations, drumbeats—' "

" 'Drumbeats?' Don't misunderstand; I myself happen to adore it, what you're doing, Andy dear, really I do. It may sound tortured—'constipated,' some people say—"

" 'Constipated?' " he repeated wryly. "Hope not; the opposite, I hope."

"You know what I mean—the New Music in general—all that straining and dissonance, all that tension— Not to *my* ear, mind; for me it's—it's so contemporary, *difficult* . . . like—like the times themselves. Of course Mamma didn't understand," Letty concluded. "How could she? It's asking too much; she belonged to another era."

The odd thing, from Andrew's view, as he looked up now at his sister, who for her part was looking down at him dreamily, her body all but hidden, except the head and shoulders, in the corner behind the upright—the odd thing was how much Letty resembled their mother. The nose alone was different (Letty's was the only nose in the family not perfectly straight, perfectly level), it deviated the least bit to the left, and the bridge was marred by the smallest rise, too slight to be called a bump. But in most respects— the gypsy hair, high forehead, chestnut eyes, widespread cheekbones, oval chin—she was Mamma's double. To be sure, Letty was much less ample, substantial in her body and her bearing—a sort of fluid, slightly lightweight version of Mamma. What was lacking was the presence, not self-presence—she was always present to herself—but presence for others. Right now, for instance: You would never have found Mamma slouching in the corner like that, half out of sight; no, she would have assumed a more commanding position, out in the open, made herself quite comfortable over there on the Rip Van Winkle—comfortable, not slovenly—her back erect, arms at ease on the upholstered rests (an attitude his sisters would no doubt have characterized as imperious, though he himself had never seen Mamma in that light—merely as munificent—perhaps because he had been what Letty called her "pet"), altogether sure enough of herself to put herself in abeyance, absorb herself in him, make herself receptive to whatever keys he might happen now to strike.

The keys that Andrew chose, in fact, to strike were struck at a very slow tempo, except for some sudden spurtive runs, more suggestive in tone of a harp than of a piano. The sounds produced were far from dissonant—if anything, they were lyrical, ethereal—the mood in no way tortured but distinctly contemplative. It wasn't that Andrew had deliberately set about to refute his sister's opinion of the New Music, though what he played certainly had that effect, or to win her approval, but simply to run through whatever happened to be on the rack—in this case the work sheet he had fussed with a moment ago.

Letty smiled appreciatively, egocentrically, as if the music were meant to be a serenade. "Debussy?"

Andrew smiled back, half amused, half flattered by his sister's mistake which, however, he overlooked. "You asked what I was working on," he said instead, and proceeded to tell her about Sarah Kellogg's commission.

Letty's unexpected response to this bit of news was to turn her back abruptly. For a moment, as Andrew watched her fish from her skirt pocket a shamefully soiled handkerchief and bring it to her lips, he was completely mystified by her actions. Only when, a second later, she turned again to face him, her smiling mouth agape, fist clenched, trying unsuccessfully to conceal the handkerchief, as she hurried over to congratulate and embrace him—only then did it dawn on Andrew that she had turned away—whether prompted by a sense of modesty, propriety, or stealth, he couldn't say—to spit out the prune. "Oh, how wonderful, wonderful! *Kain ein horeh.* I can't tell you how happy— How on earth did she do it—find a patron in these times? Sarah! of all people. I mean, Adele Astaire she's not! You have to take your hat off to her. Who *is* the patron, anyway? Or is it patroness?"

"She didn't say."

"Imagine that." Letty did nothing to conceal her disappointment. "Well, I suppose you have to be discreet about such things, especially in times like these, with people starving. It could start a revolution, I suppose, to broadcast it.

Imagine what someone like Wooly would think, commissioning a piece of music when— I'll keep it to myself," she confided, "not mention it to Wooly." Pleased with her own humor, Letty had to chuckle over this little family joke. In her excitement about the commission she had forgotten herself and begun to fold her handkerchief very carefully indeed, making a dainty parcel of it, as if the soiled linen were a piece of chamois and the prune inside a priceless gem. "Still, you mustn't let them take advantage of you, Andy dear—your lack of business sense, I mean, always the surest sign of the true artist. You'll speak to Benny, of course, let him look out for your interests. What—" Anticipating with some uneasiness the question she was about to ask, Letty used the gift-wrapped prune pit, which she reposited in her pocket, as an excuse to avert her eyes. "What sort of offer did she make, Sarah?"

Andrew ignored the question not only because no specific sum had been mentioned (even if one had, he knew better than to discuss money with his sister), but also because something else was on his mind. "Speaking of Ben, how do you think he'll react?"

"Be pleased as punch! Not that he'll understand, but he'll be pleased, proud."

"I mean to leaving, my leaving—for six or seven months, say—"

"Leaving?"

"The business."

The idea made Letty guffaw. "Oh, dear," she commiserated, foreseeing, if not foretasting with definite relish, the row that would ensue. Then, as if relishing the idea alone were not enough, too intangible, she began, one by one, to suck her fingertips, sticky from the prune. "He'll plotz, for sure—you know Benny—he'll never let you go."

"He'll have no choice."

"Then he'll never take you back."

Andrew looked solemn. "Think not?"

"Never. Unless—" A smile spread over Letty's face, swelling her sallow cheeks, kindling her eyes with a flamenco fire. "You want me to talk to him, Andy dear—is that it? Sort of break the ice?"

"No!" Andrew stated categorically. "Don't you say a word. I'll have a little talk—" As soon, he was about to say, as I get up the nerve, but the prospect itself so unnerved him, he hadn't the confidence to voice it, heaved a sigh instead. Just why "nerve" should be required and why his should fail him now, in mere anticipation of the "little talk," Andrew was loath to think. Nor, as it happened, did he have to, because in the next second a row broke out (to Andrew it was like a preview, however trivial, of what was in store with Ben) among the croquet players.

"Barry! I'll bet you anything," Letty speculated on her way to the window to investigate the fracas. "Sure enough —what did I tell you—cheating again, always cheats, that child, at everything: school, cards—can't do anything without cheating. If I have to go to that school one more time. . . . I just don't know how he comes by it, honestly I don't. If only he weren't always *caught*," she complained disgruntledly as she started toward the door. "It's so embarrassing."

"Letty"—Andrew stopped her—"that reminds me—unveilings, are they required by law?"

"I don't know. Let me think. No, optional, I guess, but almost always practiced. Oh!" She realized all at once why her brother was asking. "Maybe now with Papa gone—God rest his soul—it isn't so important. You'd rather not?"

Andrew nodded. "No."

"For Peggy's sake?"

"My own."

"Have you talked to Benny?"

Andrew shook his head. "Come"—he motioned her toward the door—"before someone gets *deharget* out there."

"I'd like to see him try, lay just one finger on the little one," she threatened the absent Barry, and headed out-of-doors to deal with the dispute.

Andrew followed her as far as the porch on which Monroe was still sitting, shaded from the midday sun. Though he had a perfect seat for the croquet match, plus a panoramic view of the meadow beyond, the outlying solitary barn and corn patch, woods and distant mountains, Monny was too absorbed in the *New York Times* to pay much attention to anything else. Occasionally he would glance up and smile with benign detachment at the shouting boys, as if they were not his sons but grandsons, and then continue reading. At the same time Peggy was doing her best to console the inconsolable Kenny whose outraged cries—"But I *saw* him! He moved it!"—were consistently denied by his older brother. Clearly guilty, Barry was indignant and kept stalking off, as much to cover up his culpability as to elude his oncoming mother who, for someone called upon to administer discipline, was going about it in the most perfunctory, casual fashion—at a shuffle. Mathew, meanwhile, had retired to the sidelines where he stood resting his folded arms on the head of his upended mallet, waiting stoically for the game to resume.

"Cheating again, Mat?" Andrew inquired playfully; in response to which the boy rolled his eyes heavenward and exchanged a knowing smile with his father.

Aware now of Andrew's presence, Monroe politely closed the *Times* and put it down on the table. ROOSEVELT NOMINATED ON FOURTH BALLOT, declared the banner headline.

"Well"—Andrew gestured toward the newspaper as he took the chair next to his brother-in-law—"that's something, at least."

"You think?" Clearly, Monroe didn't.

"You don't?"

"Roosevelt? . . ." Monroe, who by prolonging the vowel sound added a third syllable to the Governor's name, protruded his lower lip and made a comic face. "Seems a nice enough fellow . . . usual qualifications: good looks, good family, *gelt*—plenty *gelt*—not much more. You honestly think he'll make the difference?"

"*Something* has to."

"Oh, on that we're agreed. But it won't be Roosevelt."

"Foster, you mean? You'll vote Communist?"

"Who can say?" Monroe chuckled. "Please. Don't get me wrong. I'm not trying to dissimulate—not with *you*, Andy . . . but the others"—he wobbled his hand as if it were a scale coming into balance, and made a burping sound like an infant—"maybe. What I mean is: Who knows where Foster will be comes Election Day? Behind bars, more than likely."

"I thought they let him out last week."

"They did. They also put him back again, the Red Squad," Monroe replied good-naturedly, without a trace of bitterness.

76

Suddenly Barry, furious at his mother, pounded his mallet into the ground. "Stop saying that!"

"Why? You don't even know what it means. *Shvindler*, I called him." Letty let the others in on her comment, whereupon Barry protested again, and Peggy called for a resumption of play. Kenny, however, continued to hold out, so Mathew stayed as he was, resting on his mallet, motionless as a piece of garden statuary, a cast-iron dwarf.

Monroe chuckled. "That boy, the older one, he's going to be my retribution," he remarked with mirth, delighting paradoxically in the prospect, "going to turn into a full-fledged capitalist. Wait and see. . . . The little one? Harder to predict. . . . An artist, maybe—spends his life drawing pictures."

"A double retribution."

"Not necessarily. It all depends on function—for whom the artist is making the pictures. Just now, he makes them for his mother . . . naturally: a little boy . . . why not? In time, however— Oh, I see—" Monroe broke off and laughed at himself. "I'm slow today. You were being ironical."

"Not completely. I was wondering what your Mr. Foster would make of me—my kind of music."

"Mincemeat!" The older man laughed again, heartily this time.

"That's what I feared. Not that I blame you," Andrew was quick to add.

"No, no, my *shvonger*, I was only kidding." He patted Andrew's hand. "Sitting here, it's hard to imagine why anyone, given half a chance, would become anything *but* an artist. I myself could be an artist, sitting here. So beautiful: the children . . . mountains . . . bees—I keep hearing bees. My bum ear?"

"No. There's a bed of day lilies at the side of the house."

"Oh, so *that's* the perfume . . . I was wondering. It's a paradise. . . . How easy to forget in paradise those who aren't with you—those poor devils in Anacostia Park, for instance, trying to get what's rightfully theirs. . . . They'll shoot them down before it's over, just like Dearborn, mark my words." Monroe heaved a weighty sigh. "So much in life depends on whereabouts—where you happen to be at a given moment. No, my *shvonger*"—he patted Andrew's hand again—"if you're lucky enough to be in the mountains, you *must* make music—for those who aren't; it's your obligation, practically."

"Thank you, Wooly," Andrew said with feeling, returning the hand pat. "I *will*," he vowed, not to his brother-in-law but to thin air, as if he were making a covenant with the most distant mountain peak at which he was now gazing. "Imagine, going all the way up there only to bring back the Ten Commandments."

"Oh, but *they* were in the wilderness, not the Catskills. A ragged band of nomads, much in need of discipline. Here —who knows? He might have delivered the Song of Songs. Tell me, Andy, your sister"—Monroe seemed to be changing the subject—"isn't she a beauty?"

Letty was strolling toward them now, smiling broadly, the dispute evidently settled. Peggy handed down the ruling: Kenny was to "take croquet" against his brother's ball —"knock it out of the park," if he could—after which the game would resume without further ado.

Andrew nodded in answer to his brother-in-law's question. Yes, she *was* a beauty, might even pass for the Queen of Sheba, what with all those black rebellious curls meant to be bangs, Bakelite bracelets, and hoop earrings—a sort of lax, coquettish Sheba—if indeed Solomon had sung his song in praise of a woman and not, perhaps, of God. . . . Yet Andrew had scarcely nodded when Letty destroyed the illusion by removing the soiled handkerchief from her pocket, unfolding it carefully, and slipping the prune pit back into her mouth. This bit of byplay made Andrew laugh so hard he had to cover his face as his sister came up onto the porch.

"Well, he *is*"—Letty misinterpreted the laughter—"he is a *shvindler*—no two ways about it. They're Cain and Abel, those two— Please God, it doesn't come to that! Better Jacob and Esau. I'll prepare the hairy skin myself."

"Rebekah, my darling," Monroe put in, "a little deaf, I may be, but not yet blind—"

"Blind! Bite your tongue."

"—nor, in this case, is the birthright something to fight over—a handful of pins and needles."

"Speaking of cases, Andy"—Letty had picked up the

Times and was turning the pages—"the Curtis case—did you see?"

"See what?" Andrew asked with interest.

"It goes to the jury today," his sister explained, whereat she began, without being asked, to read aloud (juggling the prune pit as best she could) choice bits from the newspaper account of how Inspector Walsh had gone to the Lindbergh home on the night of May 16 and extracted from Curtis the confession that all the accessories to the crime were "figments of his distorted imagination." Monroe suggested that it wasn't the fault of the man but of the system, that under socialism there could be no such thing as kidnapping, but Letty was too engrossed in what she was reading to stop. " 'Now, Inspector,' said the defense attorney, 'has this investigation which has lasted seventy-four days gotten anywhere?' 'No,' snapped the Inspector. 'No, it didn't get anywhere. For that matter the New Jersey State Police and the whole metropolitan police force and all the United States Government forces haven't gotten anywhere.' You can say that again," Letty prompted the Inspector. Before going on to another item about a Czech who had falsely confessed to murdering the Lindbergh baby simply as a ruse to be extradited to the United States, she asked her brother how he thought the jury would vote, but Andrew failed to respond.

His attention had strayed to the croquet players, gathered now at the far end of the court: Peggy under that battered straw hat, bending over, feet apart, about to take a pendulum stroke; Mat, scrutinizing the field of play in preparation for his next shot; Barry, the future capitalist, his socks in rings around his ankles, prowling back and forth, impatient to revenge himself on his younger brother; Kenny, totally distracted from the game by the flight of a sulphur butterfly. Peggy's height, as she straightened up to appraise the shot, was almost ludicrous in contrast with the children's. She was, of course, pinch-hitting for Twister, that was the problem. Were Twister still alive, with them now, not merely as a spectre but in— Spector! Andrew stiffened, as if the homonym had never before occurred to him, and glanced down the porch, half expecting to catch a glimpse of his younger son, standing there and watching the game, a spectre like—*spectator*, Andrew corrected himself. Not that Twister would have made the match more even—far from it! He would have only added to the chaos, made his cousin Barry seem an amateur when it came to cheating, screaming, playing dirty, being sneaky, vicious, out for blood. It would have ended in pandemonium. There would have been no match at all without Peggy, good sport that she was, throwing herself into it so earnestly, committedly. Nor would the match have seemed less ludicrous without her, with Twister in her place. There was something strangely whimsical, make-believe about croquet, not only about the paraphernalia: all those mallets, balls, wickets, stakes—equipment enough for an archeological dig; but also about the activity itself: all that energy and emotion expended on knocking a set of wooden balls through a maze of wire hoops. What, in this case, made it even more unreal was the mountains in the background. Just as Peggy dwarfed the children, so the mountains dwarfed them all, belittled the players to the point of ridiculousness. What's more, the repose of the mountains made the movement of the players seem merely busy, nothing more: busyness for busyness' sake. Like the Lindbergh case, they too were getting nowhere. But then, who was? Was there any human activity, seen against the mountains, that wouldn't look ridiculous, give the impression of getting nowhere: the struggle last night in bed, ten thousand vets picketing Anacostia Park, all the United States Government forces? Was there, for that matter, anywhere worth getting *to*, except to the mountains themselves? (At this moment Andrew was seized with such a longing, a wanderlust so powerful, he instinctively gripped the arms of his chair to keep from becoming actual the feeling he had of being lifted out of his seat and transported bodily into the mountains.) Of course, mountains themselves got nowhere; but then, they weren't meant to, had no need to keep busy, be practical, purposeful, produce results. No, what made mountains matter was simply matter itself; they mattered because they *were* matter, without results. Whereas man? . . . Had man been meant for more than that, to matter more than as matter? *Could* anything matter more, be more holy, than matter? Surely not. What then were men to do in the face of mountains? Either emulate or celebrate them; come to rest or create music in the mountains. What composer was it who was said to have traced a mountain line and then transposed it intact to the staff? Apocryphal or not, that was one hell of an idea—more meaningful even than Monny's—to make music not only in but *of* the mountains. "Excuse me," Andrew said, getting up abruptly, "I think I'll go on working now, just till lunch."

The instant her brother went indoors, Letty rose and moved over, taking the chair on the side of Monny's good ear. Despite her urgency, however, she refrained from speaking until Andrew started playing the piano, sounding repetitiously an agglomerate of chords that all but drowned out her words for Monroe.

"What, my angel?"

"It's an illusion we're living." Though she had made sure that Monroe heard her this time, he still looked puzzled, so Letty tried to be more explicit. "The children, Wooly, how do you think they feel, being here?"

"Overjoyed."

"I mean seeing their cousins here for the summer, while they go back on Monday."

"I don't think they think that way, children—think ahead."

"Don't you? You think they have no sense—sense of being—well, poor relations?"

"Poor? Here!" Monroe found the contradiction laughable. "Look! just look." He gestured with his chin toward the playing field on which Barry was crowing at this moment over his little brother who, having failed to roquet Barry's ball, was chasing after his own as it rolled out of bounds into the timothy.

Letty paused, not to watch her sons but to maneuver the prune pit to the other side of her mouth, as if she were tacking a small craft. "Wooly dear, how much did you take in this week—ten . . . twelve dollars?"

"More," he answered tersely. "Why, my love, you're short?"

"How much?" she persisted.

Embarrassed, Monroe lowered his eyes. "The trouble is, people aren't picking up; they bring in, but don't take out—can't afford the finished work."

"*Vos noch?* . . . Pressing, even, they can't afford. And

even if they could, they wouldn't bother, don't care how they look—lost their self-respect." Letty stopped to listen briefly to the dissonant chords coming from the parlor. "How long can we go on like this, Wooly?"

"Like what, my love?"

"You, killing yourself, turning out unclaimeds—a shopful of unclaimeds! Your sons, assisting you: It's one thing in the summer, keeps them off the streets. One thing for the big one—who knows?—maybe Barry wasn't meant for more; but the little one, the little one has a gift, a gift from God, like his uncle—"

"How can you sit here, my darling, here in this paradise, and worry your head—"

"Because it *is* a paradise, that's how, puts things in perspective. . . . We're just a couple of *shnorrers*, Wooly." She put it plainly, causing Monroe to grimace. "Don't look so hurt. That's all we really are: here on charity, because I happen to have a big brother who has a heart of gold."

At a loss for words, Monroe shook his head in silence for a moment, then swallowed hard. "I—it—it's so unlike you, Letty. I—I never knew you to be envious."

"Not envious! not for *me*, my darling," she rejoined with passion. "Listen, Wooly"—she brought her chair closer—"suppose . . . just suppose there were a place for you downtown—at Spector and Son, I mean."

"For me? A place? In such times?"

"Never mind the times. Suppose there were an opening, and Ben agreed to take you in?"

"Why would he? What have I to offer? *Gornisht*—no experience, training. I'm not a businessman."

After glancing over her shoulder toward the parlor, Letty leaned forward with a twinkle in her eye. "Neither is Andy."

"All the more reason—"

"He'll do it for me, that's why, because you're my husband, not an outsider. He knows he can trust you, knows how honest, loyal, hard-working—"

"Wait! wait! What are we talking? Suppositions."

"Not at all!" Half rising, Letty leaned over and whispered in Monroe's ear, "Andy's going to leave the business."

"What?"

"Shh"—she brought her forefinger to her lips—"a secret. Ben'll give you the job, I know he will, if you show some interest."

"Show interest in a secret—how?"

"Not yet, of course, when the time is right."

Monroe looked troubled as he stopped to consider the question. "Work for Ben?"

"What's the matter, Wooly, it's against your principles?"

After a prolonged silence, during which he stared hard at the corn patch in the distance, Monroe said soberly, "Frankly, I would rather not."

"Not even for your family?"

"Please," he entreated her, "don't put it that way."

"How else? That's what it comes down to— Oh, look!" she interrupted herself, straightening up. "There he is." Ben, having parked the car and come around the far side of the house, could be seen now, in a white polo shirt, white leather belt, and white suede shoes, striding into the open, toward the croquet players. "Wooly darling, do me a favor," Letty said in an undertone, before hurrying off to welcome her brother, "no politics."

Ben's arrival broke up the game, but, as Peggy pointed out, it was time for lunch anyway, and she sent the children into the house to wash up. Monroe, on his way across the lawn to greet his brother-in-law, heard Ben say, "If the mountain won't come to Mohammed—" But whether the remark was meant for him or Letty or Peggy, Monroe was uncertain, not only because of his defective hearing but also because of Ben's early-morning visit to the Baers' boardinghouse.

After the greetings, Peggy offered her guests lemonade. Letty alone said she wouldn't mind. As the four—Letty linking arms with Ben, Peggy and Monroe flanking them— headed back toward the house, Ben turned to his sister and said, for no apparent reason, "Don't tell me you've caught cold?"

"No, Benny. What makes you think—"

"What's that you're sucking on?"

"A Jordan almond," Letty replied without hesitation. "You thought it was a lozenge? Count on Ben," she said to Monroe with pride, "always so observant, attentive to his family."

"Say," Ben went on, as if to prove Letty's point, turning this time to his sister-in-law, "where's the loafer—not up yet?"

"Mat?" Peggy rejoined pointedly.

"No." Ben laughed through his nose. "Not the little loafer, the big one."

Letty, who took it upon herself to answer the question, came to a halt, bringing her brother, with whom she was still arm in arm, also to a halt. "Listen . . ." From the house came a sequence of complex atonal chords, being sounded over and over. Ben made a sour face, in response to which Letty closed her eyes and grinned indulgently—an exchange that wasn't lost on Peggy, who gave them both an icy stare, while Monroe stood by, pulling at his earlobe, not knowing why the group had stopped.

Peggy was the first to move on, stepping forward rather brusquely. "Are you staying for lunch, Ben?"

"Didn't know I was invited."

"Of course you're invited."

"Thanks, but no thanks"—he flashed a smile—"I can't."

Letty was disappointed and tried, as they came up onto the porch, to make her brother change his mind, but Ben stood pat. To demonstrate his good will, however, he changed his mind about the lemonade, which Peggy promptly went indoors to fetch. Letty waited till her sister-in-law was all but out of earshot before calling after her to ask if she could lend a hand.

"Thanks, but no thanks," came the cheerful reply.

Letty shrugged. "Can't do more than ask, can I?" Now that she had established her solicitude, she felt free to sit down, whereupon Letty engineered Monroe into the chair on the far side of the table, took the center one for herself, and left the near one empty for her brother.

Ben, for his part, preferred to perch on the porch rail, facing but not looking at his sister and brother-in-law, focusing instead on the parlor window from which the dissonant chords continued to come forth by fits and starts. "So, Wooly," he said compatibly, "*vos neies?*"

"Not much, Ben. No complaints."

"Complaints!" Letty cut in. "You'll never know what this means to us, this weekend, Benny. How can we ever thank you?"

"Don't thank *me*," Ben declared enigmatically, his haughty belligerent tone belying the modesty of his words.

Letty could see that something was bothering Ben and, guessing the provocation, tried to mollify him. "I'm sure there's more than enough."

"Enough what?"

"Lunch."

"What makes you so sure?" Ben countered slyly, his eye still on the window.

"She looked!" Monroe snitched on his wife, who couldn't help but giggle.

Ben, on the other hand, didn't crack a smile. "Does he even know *you're* here?"

"Oh." Letty was quick now to discern the source of Ben's irritation. "You know Andy; once he's in his ivory tower—"

"Certainly," Monroe said almost simultaneously in answer to Ben's question. "He gave us the grand tour; that's when my darling took herself a little look-see in the icebox."

"Well, that's something, I suppose." Ben hopped down from the rail and headed for the door. "I'll just step inside and introduce myself."

Before entering the parlor, Ben stood in the doorway a full minute, waiting for his brother, who was sitting with his back to the door, to intuit somehow, and then acknowledge, his presence. But Andrew went right on playing, pounding the life out of a repeated progression of chords. At last Ben stole across the room and, coming up behind Andrew, ruffled his hair. "Hi ya, Babe!"

Andrew jumped. "Oh—Benny! Didn't hear you."

"Me—it's a wonder you can hear yourself."

"How long have you been here?"

"Must be"—Ben took a deliberate look at his watch—"half an hour."

"Really? Gosh, I had no idea I'd been at it that long."

"Thought you were going to give yourself a rest this weekend?"

"I was, but—"

"Do you even know your guests are here?" Ben asked with an edge of reproach.

"Oh, sure, I showed them—"

"Funny way to entertain—leave them sitting alone."

"Alone?" Surprised, Andrew stood up and started toward the door. "Where's Peggy?"

"Getting lunch."

"You staying, Ben?"

"Was I invited?"

Andrew remained silent long enough to swallow his annoyance. "Of course you are. I'll go tell—"

"No, no, don't bother, Babe."

"No bother."

"No, no, Mil's expecting me—just stopped by to say hello. You know the old adage: If the mountain won't come to Mohammed . . ."

The adage brought to Andrew's mind his earlier thoughts about the mountain, brought back as well an image of the solid mass, rising so sedately out of its surroundings into itself, its summit, beckoning him to do the same: rise above the bedrock, come into his own—*I am a composer*—make music in the mountains. "Ben"—he cleared his throat—"there's something I—I—we should talk about."

"Sure, what is it, Babe? I knew it all along—yesterday on the train, didn't I say so?—knew something was bothering you. Nothing serious, I hope." Ben was wary of his brother's grave expression. "Go ahead," he added, sitting on the leg rest of the Rip Van Winkle, "shoot!"

Andrew, who was standing now within a yard of Ben, facing him, felt acutely uneasy. Preparing to speak, he licked his lips, shoved his hands deep into his trouser pockets, avoided his brother's expectant gaze. "I— It's—it's about—" The word *office* stuck in his throat. Unable to go on, he turned away, drew a breath, and let it out audibly. His heart had begun to race, and he felt a bit lightheaded, unsteady on his feet.

"What?" prompted Ben, puzzled and frowning. "About what? Your health?"

"No."

"Wouldn't fool me, would you?"

"No."

"What, then? What's so hard to say?"

Going to the piano, Andrew sat down on the stool in defeat—shoulders hunched, head hanging—and heaved another sigh. "Unveilings."

"Unveilings?" Ben was visibly relieved. "What about them? Oh—" He hesitated, his sense of relief suddenly dispelled, superseded by concern. "For Chris, you mean? Is that what's on your mind?"

Andrew nodded. "Do we have to have one?"

Ben shrugged. "Customary. But you don't *have* to, I don't guess, if it's going to kick up—" In thinking through the question, Ben happened to glance at the window and was surprised to see his sister. With her head in profile, an ear pressed to the screen, she was as much in the room with them as out on the porch with Wooly—the only person in the world capable of being in two places at once. "Look who's there!" Ben remarked playfully to Andrew. "*Schwester ziseh*—she'll know."

"Know what?" Letty played dumb. She had been waiting the while for Andrew to broach the subject of the commission.

"About unveilings," Andrew was quick to respond.

"I told you already," Letty said, "with Papa gone—God rest his soul—it's hard to say. Still, I think you should—it's—it's expected."

"I don't get it," Ben declared skeptically. Though he was addressing Letty, he was eyeing Andrew with mounting suspicion. "If you told him already, why is he asking—"

"Lunch!" Peggy sang out from the stairwell. "Lunch, everybody."

"Know something, Babe, on second thought maybe I *will* stay."

"Now, that's more like it," Letty said.

"Otherwise," Ben continued to his brother, "it'll be the picnic before we get together again."

"But that's tomorrow, isn't it?"

Ben stiffened. "Would you rather I didn't stay?"

"Lunch!" Peggy, outside on the porch now, appeared within the frame of the second screen. "Oh, Ben, I put your lemonade out here."

"Ben's going to stay," Andrew informed her.

"Oh, good," she said with just enough conviction to satisfy her brother-in-law as the children came storming down the stairs.

6

"I wish the sun would stop doing that," Ben complained as a cloud interfered with his basking.

"It's not the sun," said Mildred matter-of-factly, not to contradict her husband but merely to give him the benefit of her direct observation, since she was sitting up on the outspread blanket, her eyes wide open. "It's a cloud."

"Never fails," Ben remarked with irony to the others, none of whom, with the exception of Letty, was listening. "If I say black, she says white."

"Gray," Mildred reported further on the cloud, ". . . not too big . . . won't take long . . . patience. . . ." Actually, her request for patience was directed more to herself than to Ben. Of all the picnickers, she alone felt really restless now, not because of the temporary disappearance of the sun—she had never had any use for the sun, nor the sun for her; it simply didn't "agree" with Mildred who, at this very moment, was wearing a fringed straw hat, appliquéd with scallop shells (a souvenir of Havana), to protect herself from its harmful rays—but restless because she felt so completely out of place in this savage eyrie. She was a thoroughgoing city girl, born and bred in Manhattan, and damned glad of it! If there was one thing in the world she had no patience for, not even for an afternoon, it was roughing it. To begin with, she could never get comfortable on the ground, never sit still, no matter what she did. How could it be otherwise? Human beings weren't meant to be down on all fours like snakes and bugs; it flew in the face of evolution. Besides, there was something especially inhospitable about this godforsaken spot, however "scenic," something downright hostile. . . . Mildred placed a finger on the crown of her hat to keep it from falling off as she tilted back her head and looked up mistrustfully at the surrounding mountain peaks, some so close she guessed she could count the wrinkles on their stony faces. Yet it wasn't just those jutting crags and looming ledges, all of which seemed on the verge of closing or caving in on her, that gave Mildred the willies; it was the whole *genius loci* of the place, the awful silence, solitude—that damned brook notwithstanding! She had felt it last week when Peggy first proposed the spot for the picnic—how the woman ever found it to begin with was a miracle—and drove her up here to have a look around. Had the choice been left to Mildred, she would have picked that little beach (much as she detested sand) on the far side of the lake where, at least, there was a concessionaire, should the children want to buy a bottle of pop—exactly as they *had*, of course, a little while ago, and were having now to hike a hundred miles for it. She hadn't made an issue of the beach last week only because she realized that it was still too soon after Chris's drowning to have a picnic by the lake. So, they had settled for this spot. In truth it made no difference, none at all. She had felt uneasy right off the bat, even before they reached the parking lot; halfway up the mountainside she had begun to feel the gathering menace. It was nothing you could put your finger on—no one but a fool would have let go of the safety strap long enough to try— just a feeling, a distinct feeling that she wasn't wanted there. By whom or what, Mildred couldn't say—*forces*, call them, forces of some kind. Never mind that you couldn't see them, you could *feel* them, their presence all around you, forces of a destructive nature. No, there were no two ways about it: The Spectors simply weren't wanted there. And not only by nature, but also by their fellow men, the ones who patronized those snooty restricted hotels on the ridge, for *goyim* only. No wonder her sister-in-law had picked the spot—you couldn't blame her—she had wanted to be with her own kind. Fair enough. But they weren't

Mildred's kind, not by a long shot! Nor did she want them to be, want to social-climb—*climb* in any sense of the word! The sooner they got out of there the better. . . .

The thought of departing brought Mildred's eye to the picnic baskets over which Letty was at present crouching, her back to the group, so that Mildred couldn't see what she was doing. . . . *Gott in Himmel!* why had Hallie wrapped the plums in *that* of all newspapers? How had the woman ever laid hands on it in the first place—that particular edition of the local *Daily*—two months after the fact? Mildred could have killed herself on the spot, *would* have, thrown herself right off the mountain, had they been closer to the brink. Thank goodness Peggy didn't seem to mind, didn't even notice till Letty made that ridiculous fuss, trying to conceal the headline from the children. . . . What *was* she up to anyway? "What is it, Letty? Looking for something?"

"Ants."

"At the fruit?" Mildred exclaimed with unwarranted alarm.

"Can't tell yet," Letty drawled, "that's what I'm looking to see."

"Liar," Mildred muttered under her breath.

"We've loads of chicken left in ours," Peggy said, showing no sign of life other than the movement of her lips. Like Ben, she too was worshiping the sun, though still beclouded, waiting for its re-emergence.

"Oh, no, I'm *shtupped*, stuffed," Letty protested mildly, translating the word as an afterthought for the sake of her gentile sister-in-law. "Couldn't eat another thing."

"Even a cookie?" Peggy tried to tempt her.

"Not for me, thanks. Wooly!" Letty called out. (In order to read the newspaper in peace, Monroe had moved away from the others, down to the nearby creek where he was sitting now, propped comfortably against a sizable rock.) "Cookie?" After waiting in vain for an answer, during which time Ben put in a snatch of the song "Lookie, Lookie, Lookie, Here Comes Cookie," Letty said to no one in particular, "Didn't hear," whereupon she helped herself to several cookies and set off in Monroe's direction.

Mildred, who was forever on the lookout for evidence of her sister-in-law's deceit, kept an eye on Letty until the latter, less than halfway to the creek, stopped, much as Mildred had anticipated, to sample one of "Monroe's" cookies. "Ants indeed," she muttered to herself and, smiling smugly, turned to her other sister-in-law. "I don't know how you do it, Peg."

"Do what?"

"Lie still like that, like a mummy."

"Egyptian blood."

Mildred nudged Ben on the sly to make certain he hadn't missed this remark which seemed to her all but tantamount to a signed confession on Peggy's part of being in the Pharaoh's pay.

Ben, responding less to the nudge than to the continued absence of the sun, raised his head off the blanket, rolled over, and, resting on his elbows, looked around. "Say, Babe, aren't you facing the wrong way?"

It took Andrew a moment to decipher his brother's question. Contrary to what he thought at first, it wasn't meant as criticism of him but of Peggy for being in a better position than Andrew to take advantage of the sun. (Andrew was, in fact, facing north, at an angle to the sun, while Peggy was stretched out perpendicular to him, her head on his thigh, facing directly into it.) In truth, though, it was Andrew who had settled on the blanket first and Peggy who had adjusted her position to his. He had chosen to face north deliberately in order to obtain the best possible view of the scene, not only of the astonishing escarpment, a hundred yards or so to the right and running abreast of the creek, but also of its many flat-ledged promontories, receding in tiers toward the summit of the mountain, the highest in the neighborhood.

He could see it now, the opal-colored crest, almost indistinguishable from the opal-colored clouds engulfing it. Just how far away it was, he couldn't judge; it seemed at once remote and near, accessible and inaccessible. . . . Was it only yesterday that he and Wooly had been sitting on the porch, looking at these mountains? *Was* it these, these very peaks or some others they had seen? It was hard to say. Without knowing in which direction the Hudson lay —whether on the far side of the escarpment or over that crest ahead or beyond those slopes to the left—it was hard to keep your bearings here. . . . *If you're lucky enough to be in the mountains, you* must *make music.* Wasn't that what Wooly had said? Well, he was wrong. You couldn't. Maybe down there, looking at the mountains from the valley, seeing merely their mass and form, distanced almost into immateriality, the Platonic Idea of mountain, you might make music, but not up here—in them, on them, all but at their summit. Their presence was too powerful, too challenging to allow for any sort of diversion. (Andrew scanned the escarpment, his eye moving from the nethermost promontory—so rugged, solid, vivid as to seem the most substantial thing he had ever beheld, pure substantiality—to the more remote and balder cones of dull gray stone that resembled heaps of unmixed cement, until his eye came at last to rest again on the distant fin-shaped crest.) They took you out of yourself, the mountains, out of the familiar into an altogether alien realm, one in which there was no time for music, no time for anything ordinary, everyday—no time at all! That was why you couldn't make music in the mountains, because they were devoid of time. They seemed, instead, to hold out the promise of something else, outside time, some secret in their custody, some answer—even as they waited redoubtably for you to answer to *them.* That was another false impression, caused again by distancing, that he had had yesterday on the porch: to think that mountains were serene, a place where you might come at last to rest, find repose. No, indeed! If anything, the encounter was a confrontation, clash! The minute you set foot in them, the mountains challenged you to come not to rest but terms, different from any you had ever known before, terms entirely *theirs*—challenged you, moreover, in a way that was all but inescapable, unshirkable. . . . Even now, as Andrew gazed at the summit, he could feel its tug, its power of attraction. The summit seemed to beckon him, bid him leave behind his family, leave this lovely glen— How had Peggy ever found it, any place this secluded (imagine! having it all to themselves the day before the Fourth), genial, idyllic? More puzzling still, how had it ever found *itself*, established itself here in this wilderness of unremitting rock? In contrast to those barren crags and slopes surrounding it, this glen was like a little meadow misplaced on the moon, a veritable Eden with its covering of moss and grass and wild flowers (what were they called, those with the star-shaped petals?), clumps of fern, re-freshing creek (how clever of Wooly to have taken refuge behind that boulder down there), thrushes singing in the evergreens—*theirs* the only music. Yet, despite the beauty of this cloistered spot, the summit held an even greater lure for Andrew, continued to beckon—more than beckon, it seemed now to be summoning him.

"You're losing out on the sun that way," Ben, unwilling to accept his brother's silence, pursued the subject.

"*I* have no Egyptian blood," Andrew quipped.

"Damn tootin'!" Ben was more than thankful to agree.

"Personally"—Mildred looked askance at the heavens—"I think we've seen the last of the sun for today."

"Shh," Peggy objected, "it'll hear you."

"Let it!" Mildred flailed her hand at a stone fly. "Who are we fooling anyway? We know the forecast was for rain."

"Shh."

Restless and bored, Mildred struggled to her feet and turned around to eye the picnic baskets. She had half a mind now to pack them up—her own, at least—in prepara-tion for departure. At the same time, she was curious to check on both the ant situation and the number of cookies her sister-in-law had copped.

"Where are you going?" Ben stopped her.

For a moment Mildred looked confused, gazing off ab-stractedly into the nearby woods, as if she herself didn't know. "Just what do you suppose has become of those children?"

"Berrying," Peggy said.

Burying *what?* Andrew wondered, before he grasped the meaning.

"Not the *little* ones," Mildred rejoined impatiently, "I'm not worried about them, they're with Fräulein—she's used to it, the Alps—it's Lawrence and Barry that worry me. Shouldn't they be back by now? They've been gone— If those two brats"—she broke in on herself, beginning to boil —"disobeyed my instructions and went into the water—"

"What if they did?" Ben challenged her.

"It's less than an hour—"

"Say"—he cut her off pointedly—"where's my little sis-ter?"

Mildred shot an accusing finger in the direction of the creek. "*Noshing*, for a change."

Ben repaid his wife with a dirty look, before rolling over to face the creek. "Hey, Letty!" he called out, wiggling his fingers to entice her as though she were a two-year-old, "come and join the grownups."

"Coming," she called back, but delayed a moment to brush the crumbs off her dress and to appropriate the front page of Monroe's newspaper.

In the next second the sun reappeared, evoking from Peggy a groan of such deep satisfaction it sounded to Andrew as if she were being inseminated by its rays. To further this impression, he presently felt her hand on his cheek, applying gentle pressure, much as it had in bed last night . . . the night before . . . petitioning his seed.

"You saw?" Letty held up the newspaper in both hands, displaying it like a visual aid. "Guilty—they found Curtis guilty."

"Please!" Ben protested, "can't we forget the Lindbergh case for five minutes?"

"Certainly, Benny, but why?" Letty inquired innocently. "The children aren't here now."

In answer to her question Ben cocked his thumb and motioned surreptitiously toward Andrew. "Why is Wooly being so exclusive?" He changed the subject.

"Oh." Letty winked in collusion, whereupon she proceeded like a prestidigitator to fold the newspaper in half and then in half again, four times, till it was no larger than a calling card, secreted in her palm. "You know Wooly, when it comes to keeping abreast of the times." Aware suddenly that *times* might be misconstrued as a reference to the newspaper she had scarcely conjured away, Letty laughed self-consciously and also changed the subject. "Benny dear, how's about a little stroll? There's something I'm dying to show you."

"What's that?" Mildred put in with more suspicion than curiosity.

"A profile in the rock down there—looks just like Papa."

"No kidding." Ben was intrigued. "Where?"

"Toward the hotel. Come"—Letty held out a helping hand—"it's really the spitting image."

"Well"—Mildred was quick to step between them—"*I'm*

94

going to go and hunt for those brats." She paused a moment, her eye on Ben, waiting for him to decline his sister's invitation and offer to accompany her instead, but Ben remained impassive. "You mean to say"—she turned next to her sister-in-law—"you aren't even worried, Letty?"

"About that *vantz?* Never. He'll find his way."

"How? By smell! in woods they've never seen before—they're Boy Scouts suddenly? For all we know they may be lost this very minute."

"Don't get so excited," Ben remarked with disapproval, adding, as though purposely to rankle her, "Hey, Babe, want to come along?"

"Oh, no," Letty put in before Andrew had a chance to speak, "look how comfortable he is."

"Truer words . . ." Andrew agreed, disregarding Peggy who was nudging him to go.

"Lazy loafer," Ben remarked good-naturedly, while Letty slipped her arm through his and started leading him in the direction of the escarpment. "Never mind; make it easy on yourself. *À bientôt.*" Ben bade them farewell with a mincing gesture, illustrating thereby one of his pet theories: that all Frenchmen were effeminate.

"Be careful!" Mildred called after them. "You saw those signs about the rocks, falling rocks! And don't go too far! . . . You hear me, Ben? I told Fräulein to be back by three. . . . Ben! you hear?"

"They can hear you in Albany, sweetheart."

"Very clever." Mildred was scowling as she turned back to Peggy and Andrew, talking to herself as much as to them. "Ridiculous! everyone striking out like that in different directions—not my idea of a picnic at all. . . . Profile in the rock, my backside! That woman wouldn't care if Barry—" She clapped a hand over her mouth to silence herself.

Andrew guessed from Mildred's pained expression that the stifled word was *drowned.* Oh! he suddenly reminded himself, he had forgotten to mention to Peggy his stopping by the library this noon to find out whether Elizabeth Barrett had actually had a brother who drowned. "Milly"—sitting up, he moved over to make room on the blanket—"come sit with us."

"No thanks. I'm really worried about those kids. *That*

one"—she motioned her head toward Letty's receding figure—"can do what she likes—when *didn't* she? Some women simply don't deserve to have children. Sorry, Andy," she added quickly, as if only then remembering that Letty was his sister. "Ben would kill me. . . . The love affair between those two." Mildred rolled her eyes heavenward, but whether to indicate the magnitude of Ben's and Letty's incest or to beseech God's intercession was hard to tell.

"Why limit it to *those* two?" Peggy muttered, going her sister-in-law one better. "*All* of them."

The remark nettled Andrew, but rather than take Peggy up on it in front of Mildred, he let it pass. "Don't let Letty get your goat, Mil. She can't help it. Being the baby has its disadvantages—lifetime disadvantages."

For a moment, as Mildred tucked her skirt between her legs and squatted facing Andrew, she seemed to have changed her mind about staying, but the position was only provisional. "How are you feeling, Andy?" she said with evident concern, her manner uncommonly forthright.

"Fine."

"Ben was worried yesterday, couldn't get to sleep last night . . . said you'd been to Oxenburg."

So unusual was Mildred's attitude (Andrew was perfectly aware how much she ordinarily resented him, considered him the bane of Ben's existence) that he was prompted to press her hand but stopped himself, knowing the extent to which she shared his phobia about being touched. "It's nothing, Mil, not serious."

Mildred lowered her eyes, looked at the ground contritely. "Sorry . . . about before."

The allusion escaped Andrew. "Letty?"

"No, at lunch, the Lindbergh headline." Mildred brought both hands to her forehead, creating a kind of visor, not to shield her eyes from the sun, but to circumscribe her vision, turn it inward. "I keep seeing that pile of newspapers in the pantry, keep asking myself what made Hallie reach for *that* one, that one in particular—of all the papers stacked up out there—the pile must be two feet high—how did she ever come to lay hands—"

"Don't," Peggy said with kindness, wanting her sister-in-law to spare herself the *autocritique*.

"And what made Mrs. What's-her-name save it in the first place? For what? What earthly purpose could it serve except to satisfy some morbid—"

"Look, Mil"—now for the first time since lunch Peggy sat up—"you mustn't take it on yourself that way. I don't mean Hallie—that was an accident, pure and simple—but us, trying to protect us all the time. You can't, you know. No one can. What's more, there's no reason to. With all due respect to Ben, you can't pretend what's happened hasn't happened. The Lindbergh baby's dead. Twister's dead. That's all there is to it. Life goes on. There'll be other babies. Look at Anne Morrow, she's pregnant already."

"*You* look!" Andrew snapped.

Peggy was taken aback. "What?"

"Obviously," he declared, determined to set the record straight, "she was pregnant *before* the kidnapping."

Whatever Peggy thought (she looked at once reflective, sad, and bitter), she kept it to herself, resumed sun-bathing without another word.

To break the silence Mildred stood up and said, "That's right, her baby's due any— Ooo," she complained, rubbing her thighs, "my legs aren't used to that. Well . . . I better go and hunt up those brats." Despite her pronounced intention, she didn't move; evidently something else was on her mind. "I—I know it's none of my business, kids, but even so, Ben and I—we talk about it constantly—speculate, I should say—you said yourself we shouldn't pretend. Well"—she finally overcame her reserve—"what about *you two?* Don't you think it's time to think about—"

"We think about it all the time," Peggy declared unequivocally, not to put her sister-in-law down but merely to end the discussion.

"Of course you do—how could you help— Dumb of me."

"Not dumb at all," Andrew reassured her, "kind."

"Well"—Mildred went to fetch her pocketbook from the adjacent blanket—"if Ben gets back before I do, tell him . . ." She hesitated, then shrugged irritably. "Tell him I've gone for a swim."

Andrew watched in silence as Mildred set out somewhat stiffly, unsteadily, impeded by her inappropriate pumps, yet determined to maintain her poise—set out not directly toward the lake but obliquely, branching off toward

Monroe with whom she stopped to have a word or two before venturing on. Turning back, Andrew regarded Peggy, her sun-tanned face glistening with baby oil, sun-bleached hair several shades lighter now, or so it seemed, than at noon. Once again she was in a state of perfect union with the sun, the sort of union Andrew yearned for, too, though not with the sun and earth like Peggy, not even with Peggy herself—no, that least of all just now. . . . He looked away, toward the summit. It beckoned still. How unalike they were, the summit and the sun. In return for union the sun asked nothing but submission, effortless submission, instantly rewarded; whereas the summit insisted on assertion, rigorous assertion, in return for . . . what? Andrew frowned for lack of an answer. Why bother, then, make the effort? In hopes of finding out the answer? Or merely to escape the family picnic—the basted flesh . . . baby oil . . . endless talk of babies . . . backsides . . . burying—What? What was it those children were burying in the mountain? . . .

"Has she gone?" Peggy asked without opening her eyes.

"Um."

"Why didn't you go with Ben?"

"Why didn't *you?*" he retorted sharply.

"It would have been the perfect—"

"Did you really want three children?"

"You mean"—she drew a breath—"had I known that one would die?"

"Known!" he kept up the attack. "You think the Lindberghs knew?"

"But they had only one—"

"Exactly! So why bring up Anne Morrow?"

"Don't." She tried to quiet him by bringing his attention to Monroe.

"He can't hear anyway," Andrew muttered. From the prolonged silence that followed he assumed that Peggy had dropped the argument in favor of the sun, but presently she took it up again.

"It would have been the perfect opportunity . . . to talk to Ben."

"With Letty there!"

"Even so—"

"Why do you keep harping on Ben?"

"Why do *you* keep putting it off?"

"I'm not! Tomorrow—I've decided—I'll tell him on the train." Peggy looked unconvinced, and he himself felt in some way unconvinced. "You *know* I'm going to do the score—you've seen me at it since I came—I even stopped at the library this noon—Sarah didn't make it up; she did have a brother—"

"Who?"

"Elizabeth Barrett—who drowned." Andrew lapsed into silence. It struck him now that he should make Barrett's theme, as well as Browning's, variations on the Drowned Brother's theme, since both the father and the lover were embodied in the brother. Like the father, the brother carried with him all the dead weight of his geneaology, the personal impedimenta which overload us till we sink and drown; at the same time, being dead, the brother, like the living lover, personified the possibility of being disencumbered, released from such impedimenta into the lightness of Being itself.

"*Yours* is very much alive."

"My what?"

"Brother."

"Would you rather see him dead?" Andrew said sardonically, but Peggy ignored the question. "Why Ben again? What has Ben to do with it?"

"I don't know exactly," she admitted, growing pensive, "just a feeling . . . there's some connection."

"Between what and what?"

"Us . . . the impasse—"

"In bed you mean?"

"I didn't say bed—"

Getting up, Andrew started pacing the border of the blanket. "It's what you meant! what you said the other night—about the commission—that we'd get stuck if I didn't accept. Well now I *have*, and still we're stuck!"

"*You* said," she reminded him, "we were stuck already."

"We *are*. So don't blame Ben! Don't blame—"

"I'm not blaming—"

"*Me*," he shouted in exasperation, thumping his chest, "you're blaming me!"

"I'm not!"

"Then why bring up Anne Morrow?"

"Sorry, Andy."

"That's all you ever are—both of us—sorry; me at night, you in the day—sorry for this, that, something every second! Well?" He looked at her despondently. "Isn't that what it boils down to? Being sorry every second of our lives—a sorry—" His voice quavered, broke. "Sorry couple."

"No," she disagreed gently but firmly. "We're talking about ten years, not months. I'm not the least bit sorry for *anything*, Andy, not for living with you all these years—I expect to live with you the rest of my life . . . I love you—"

"Unlike *me*, you mean—"

"What?"

"—who, if I really loved you, would give you another baby!"

"I didn't—"

"You did! It's what you meant! Like Lindbergh! that's what you want. Well, if that's what you want, go get Lindy to fuck you! I'm sick of it! Goddamm it"—he suddenly whirled on her in a passion, his shoulders hunched, fingers splayed—"I don't want another baby!"

"That's perfectly evident," Peggy said at last with muted bitterness. "To everyone on earth now," she added, glancing toward Monroe.

Monroe had gotten up and was heading toward them, newspaper in hand. Despite his sluggish gait, it was clear to Andrew that his brother-in-law had overheard their argument and was coming now like God to expel them in their shame from Eden.

Once he reached the blanket, however, Monroe raised his fists not to smite them but merely to stretch his bony arms and facilitate a yawn. " 'Scuse me . . . dozed off. . . . And to think"—blinking, he looked around the glen with delight—"I thought I was in Eden *yesterday*."

"Funny," Andrew murmured, "your saying that—that's what I was thinking." Peggy gave him a sharp, disputatious glance. "About Eve," he explained pointedly, "the tree of knowledge."

"Poor Eve," Monroe commented. "It's taken the world five thousand years to see the light, but surely she was right; no question: We have no choice but to eat of the tree."

Andrew was reminded of the consequence. "Then surely we must die," he declared.

"Surely," Monroe agreed cheerfully. "For the moment, though, it's not a problem. Unless, that is"—he indicated a nearby balsam fir—"you find pine cones tempting." Having made his little joke, Monroe looked around again. "Where did Letty go?"

"With Ben."

Puzzled, Monroe paused an instant to consider the newspaper in his hand. "And the front page?"

"Went with her," Andrew was amused to report.

Monroe chuckled. "How like my Letty not to realize that a front page is also a back page on which the news is likewise printed. No matter. And the children—swimming?"

"The little ones," Peggy said, "are berrying—"

Once again Andrew was teased by the question, *Burying what?*

"Barry and Lawrence went to buy some pop."

"So all's well with the world," Monroe concluded.

"More or less." Peggy made no effort to conceal her skepticism.

"Oh, look!" Monroe pointed south, in the direction of the escarpment. "There they are!"

Turning simultaneously, Andrew and Peggy were surprised to see Ben and Letty coming back already, no longer arm in arm. Ben was in the lead now, taking bold purposeful strides toward the glen, while Letty, scampering to keep up with him, was gesticulating animatedly. That they were in some sort of discord was soon apparent to both Andrew and Peggy who exchanged a questioning look; while Monroe, after squinting a second, shaded his eyes as if he couldn't quite believe what he was seeing. "An argument?" he wondered aloud. To dispel the idea, he shook his head and waved to his wife, but Letty didn't respond.

As the two drew closer Andrew could tell from Ben's stiff posture and stony expression, as well as from Letty's rapid hand and lip movements, that what they were in the midst of was not an argument but an entreaty on Letty's part, to which Ben was paying little heed. When at last they came within earshot, Monroe raised the newspaper overhead and called out, "Letty angel, so what's with the front page?"

In her distress Letty dismissed the question with a flick of the wrist, only to reverse herself the next second. "Oh my goodness!" She laughed in embarrassment, whereupon, conjuring back the front page, she began unfolding it methodically. "What a *draikop*. Would you believe it, Benny, I walked right off—" Her voice died out, hands suspended in midair, as she watched Ben make a beeline for Andrew.

"Got a minute, Babe?"

"Sure." Andrew wasn't taken in by his brother's apparent casualness. "What's up?"

"You have no objections, have you, sweetheart"—Ben gave Peggy a broad, winning smile—"if I borrow the bruiser for a minute?"

"Not at all," she answered civilly, her eye on Letty who, in turn, had her eye on Ben and Andrew, even as she began excitedly to relate something to Monroe in a voice so subdued it couldn't be heard over the rattle of her Bakelite bracelets.

"Let's take a little walk, Babe," Ben suggested, to which Andrew acquiesced in silence.

Scarcely had the brothers started off, when Letty broke from Monroe and made a dash to catch up with them. "Benny, please—"

"What now?"

"I wish—oh, please—Andy, I—mistake—I—I assumed—"

"Never mind, now." Ben laid his hand on Letty's cheek in such a way that she herself would have been hard put to say whether he was giving her a love tap or repulsing her. "Just go back and enjoy yourselves. We'll thrash this out in no time."

Before Letty could say another word, Peggy slipped an arm around her waist and escorted her over to Monroe who looked both worried and confused. "What is it, angel?"

Letty was too upset for the moment to deal with the question. Only after she had hidden her face in her hands was she able to utter a few disconnected phrases. "*Vai iz mir!* . . . trying to be good . . . what happens— How was I supposed—never! it never occurred—"

"It's all right." Peggy tried to comfort her.

"No!" Uncovering her face, Letty began to shake her head from side to side. "It's not! not! He'll think— *Vai!*" she moaned, covering her face again. "What? what have I done?"

"Whatever it is"—Peggy glanced coolly over her shoulder at the brothers, their bright polo shirts visible through the trees—"they're big boys now."

The farther they went, the more conscious Andrew became of the silence between them, the sound of twigs cracking underfoot. At last he stopped and said uneasily, "Thrash out what, Benny?"

Ignoring the question, Ben kept on moving as if he alone were qualified to decide just where to stop, when to speak. It wasn't long, however, before they reached a clearing, created by a number of fallen trees, in which Ben came to a halt. "Sit down," he muttered. But no sooner had Andrew done as he was told, selecting a tree whose snapped trunk provided a fairly level seat, than Ben fell silent again, planted his hands on his hips in a combative attitude, and paced back and forth, prolonging the strain. "What's all this about quitting?"

So *that* was it; Letty had repeated—" 'Quitting?' Who said—did—did Letty say—"

"Never mind what Letty said, I'm asking you."

"I never said 'quitting.' "

"You must have said something. She isn't smart enough, our little *Schwester*, to make it up out of whole cloth, a rigmarole like that—I should train Wooly, show him the ropes, so that when you abandon ship . . ." Ben turned up his palms in genuine perplexity. "Something about a commission?"

"Well"—Andrew drew a breath—"that part's true, I *have* been offered a commission."

"For what? Who works on commission? Shopgirls."

"To compose a score."

"So compose. Who's stopping you? What has that to do with quitting?"

"I can't do both, business and the score."

"Why not? You've been doing both for years." Ben paused a moment to appreciate his own wit. "For ten years—"

"It's a long score, very long, for me, thirty minutes—"

"Thirty minutes. *Gantseh megilleh.* So take it! Take an hour. Be my guest: take twenty-four."

"It'll take me months—months and months; she's already—"

"She? Who's she?"

"Sarah Kellogg."

Ben grimaced. "I might have known. Who else could it be, the instigator, but that one, that *vildeh chaieh?* And *she's* going to pay your rent," he inquired dryly, "your food bills all those months?"

"She's giving me a grant."

"A what? That's a good one, 'grant.' Grant's Tomb!" he hooted. "Why, the woman hasn't got a pot to piss in."

"She's found a patron."

At this, Ben's smug but otherwise good-humored expression turned into an ugly sneer. "Oh, she has, has she! Well you just tell her to go fuck herself—you *have* a patron!" He drove the point home with a fierce stare. "Your whole life you've had a patron; you don't need *two.*"

Though Andrew remained silent, he was anything but calm. Ben's menacing show of might, learned to perfection from their father who had menaced them both with the selfsame show since they were boys, had its desired effect: caused Andrew's threatened heart to throb, transformed the heart of the man into that of the boy who, despite the man's better knowledge, took the show for omnipotence itself.

"No brother of mine's going to take charity from anyone—anyone, that is," Ben added with a mixture of irony and martyrdom, "but me."

Andrew braced himself, gripped the tree trunk. "It *isn't* charity."

Ben whirled on him. "What then?"

"Payment."

"For what?"

"Work."

"What work? When were you ever paid, except by me? Don't give me that payment crap! I know all about payment. I've been paying through the nose for years."

"Well"—Andrew tensed his stomach muscles, took a breath—"now you can *stop*," he said defiantly, albeit in a hushed and shaky voice. The fact that he had finally shown some pluck, made a stand against his brother, brought him no relief. On the contrary, it served only to intensify his apprehension, accelerate his heartbeat, because he knew full well the brutal force of his brother's temper, knew the one thing Ben could not abide was opposition: To oppose him was to goad him, drive him all but wild.

"Don't get fresh with me—"

"I wasn't—"

"Don't you raise your voice to me! I can still cut you down to size—big as you are, miserable punk! Just who the fuck do you think you're talking to—one of your miserable longhairs?" The ferocity with which the question was put precluded an answer. Construing Andrew's silence, then, as submission, Ben turned away and strode to the edge of the clearing. "Imagine it!" he next remarked, as if to an interested bystander, "the whole world's in the throes of a depression, and that one's going to make music—fiddle while Rome burns. Well"—he wheeled to face his brother again —"just forget it, buster! You've still got a family to support, obligations like the rest of us—longhair or no longhair— and don't you ever forget it! Savvy?"

Andrew had been silenced too effectively—silenced not only by his fear of Ben's fury and the throttling of his own, but also by his thumping heart and irregular breathing—to utter a word. Short of that, he felt he had but one recourse: to leave the clearing straightaway.

"Wait a minute. Where are you going? I haven't finished yet. Sit down."

Despite the fact that Andrew's legs felt weak enough to buckle at any moment, he willed himself to remain standing.

"Sit down, I said." Instead of lessening the tension, Ben's modulated tone, combined with the satanic look in his eyes, made his words doubly sinister.

Still unable to speak, Andrew suddenly discovered that he was also unable to breathe, unable to quiet his heart, unable to do anything but resist his brother's command.

"Sit down, before I knock you down!"

Aware of how imperative it was to speak—whether

merely to excuse himself or comment on the futility of further talk—Andrew opened his mouth, but no words came.

In response Ben's expression quickly changed to consternation. "Wh—what's the matter? Why do you stand there gape——" Now it was Ben's turn to be left speechless, mouth agape, as he himself stood staring, pondering some question whose unexpected answer brought a flash of recognition to his eyes. "Not the commission at all," he conjectured quietly. "It's your health . . . your heart, isn't it? It's Oxenburg; he's the one, the one who ordered you to quit."

Andrew shook his head. "No . . . only a change, 'change of scene' is what he said, recommended a little rest."

"So take it! For God's sake, why didn't you say so in the first place, not have Letty— Stay! stay the month, relax, do the score, come back in August. You'll feel refreshed, a new—"

Andrew shook his head again and said with deliberation, "It's not my health."

"Not?" Ben frowned. "What then? You've got to level with me, Babe. You haven't got a better pal—" He broke off and squeezed his lower lip till it yielded a different thought. " 'Change of scene' . . . Oh, now I get it." A crooked, painful smile came to Ben's lips. "What do you take me for, a dunderhead? Don't you think I know what it is, what it really is at bottom? You don't have to be a doctor, Babe. 'Change of scene.' Let's not kid ourselves; what he really meant was not to go back to the shore. Isn't that why we're here this summer?" Even as Ben sought some sign of confirmation from Andrew's guarded eyes, his own eyes grew sadly tender. "Chris, it's Chris—should have known it yesterday: 'unveiling'—that's what's got you so *farmisht*, don't know whether you're coming or going— Who could be expected to? Christ! what an *umglick*"— he swallowed hard to stem his feeling—"lose a little boy like that. . . . Christmas!" At a loss for further words, Ben lapsed into silence. "Still"—he rallied himself—"you mustn't let it get you down. Got to pull yourself together, pick yourself up by the bootstraps, you and Peggy, and go on. That's the only answer. Want my advice, the advice of Dr. Spector? Have another baby—that's what I prescribe, home remedy: *Shtup* her good, *shtup* her like she's never been *shtupped* before and have another baby." Ben chuckled unexpectedly. "Remember that cheer we used to give? '*Shtup* her again, harder! harder!'"

Andrew shook his head, turned away. "I don't want to *shtup* her."

"But—but that's what I—didn't I ask you on the train: Was there something wrong between you two, were you playing around—that—that music student—you said no."

"I'm not." Abstracted, Andrew broke a branch off a dead tree and started picking at the bark. "It's not the music student," he explained almost wearily, "not Peggy, Twister, Oxenburg—none of those things, the reason I have to leave."

"What then—what exactly—would you mind telling me?"

Andrew dug his thumbnail into the dessicated wood. "Me."

"You?"

"I have to do it for myself."

Ben pulled back in surprise. "Yourself?"

"Do *something*—"

"Leave the business?"

"—for myself."

"For you!"

"For once I—"

"Once? When *wasn't* it for you? Everything! all I've ever done—putting you on the payroll, pleading your marriage, music school—everything was done for you, you and your sisters. And this is my thanks? Walk out on me in the middle of a depression?"

"But that's exactly why, with business slow—"

"Business! Don't hand me that business crap! A lot you know, sitting on your ass all day. If you'd get off your ass and start doing something, hustling like— Goddamm it! stop doing that"—Ben snatched the branch from his brother's hand and, breaking it, tossed the pieces into the underbrush; "I'm talking to you. All you know, the minute the going gets tough—take it on the lam, like—like a rat from a sinking ship—twenty-three skiddoo!" Pausing, Ben smiled balefully. "Maybe that's what I should do, till you come to your senses, what Pop used to do when we were bad—put you in the cellar with the rats."

"No need," retorted Andrew, "I'm there already, you

put me there long ago."

Ben's cheeks flushed and his voice came from his throat in a dry hollow rasp: "What?"

Andrew dug his heels in, tried to maintain a tone of conviction. "I said, 'you put me—'"

"I"—Ben poked himself repeatedly, his eyes all but bulging from their sockets. "*I* put you? I?"

For a time neither man could speak, Ben because the words were stuck in his throat, Andrew partly because his brother seemed on the verge of apoplexy, partly because he himself seemed to be.

"*I* put you?" Ben was the first to recover his voice. "Through music school, that's where I put you! behind a desk like a big shot, five-room apartment on West End Avenue! 'Cellar,' he calls it! Penthouse practically! Don't hand me—tell me—if anyone, it was me! He put *me* there, the old man, for taking your side. Always, always! my whole life I fought your battles. 'He goes to work like everyone else,' Pop said. But no! sucker here"—Ben thumped himself on the chest—"wouldn't listen. 'Not on your life,' I said. 'He isn't *like* everyone else,' I said, 'he's got a gift, got to be given the opportunity—*I'll* do his share, give up my own chances for a decent—'"

"It was Mamma—"

"*What* was Mamma?"

"Who said those things."

"Like hell—"

"Paid my way—"

"Like hell it was!"

"Mamma's savings—"

"The hell you say! *Me*," Ben roared. "It was me! me and Pop! and don't—don't you ever forget it! . . . Give me that 'savings' crap! 'Savings,' my ass! Where do you think they came from, those 'savings,' the trees?" He flung his arms heavenward as if to designate every last tree in the wilderness. "Pop! from Pop—busted his balls for you, killed himself, so genius here could come up with thirty minutes worth of—of— Worth? *Bubkes*, that's what it's worth, your music. You'll never see a cent from it, not a fucking cent —never have!—went broke, in fact, so that sucker here had to bail you out, go to bat with you for Pop— Mamma"— he backtracked, though evidently without quite knowing why. "Don't give me that Mamma crap! She never—the woman never lifted a finger—not a fucking finger—for *anyone*—anyone except her precious—" The tears, which Ben had managed earlier to check, came now to his eyes, causing him to turn away. "God forgive me." He sobbed.

"Sorry, Benny."

"Never mind. Just don't hand me— Mamma! You think it was Mamma who made the old man take you back? Mamma who made him let you marry? In a pig's eye! Me! it was me! *I'm* your Mamma—papa"—he reversed himself in confusion. "A father to you, that's what I've been, my whole life—killed myself, carried you, took care of you—more than my own two kids—and now you think you can just walk out, leave me high and dry, while you go off to—to fiddle-fuck? Well, think again, buster! You're not—I'm not going to let you do it, destroy what the man—it took the man a lifetime—this name, this family—the finest in the industry—and I should stand around and watch you do it, tear down— Not on your life!" he bellowed. "Hear me? I'll see you in your grave first! bury you in—in a packing case with Spector and Son on the lid."

"Benny!" Letty cried out as she rushed into the clearing, followed at a short distance by Peggy and Monroe. "Stop! Boys! please! Andy—what is it—what's happening?"

At sight of his sister, Ben muffled his fury and began to pace back and forth like a caged wolf, traversing the same narrow strip of ground again and again as if a row of iron bars had suddenly materialized between him and Andrew. "Mamma—has the nerve to tell me Mamma—Mamma! Can you beat it?"

"Don't"—Letty reached out to pacify him—"don't excite yourself."

Ben shrugged her off. "Why shouldn't I? No one quits on me—no one!—and lives to tell—"

"Ben, please." Monroe now stepped forward. "A misunderstanding—"

"Misunderstanding *in toches!*"

"No, really, for once Wooly's right." Letty sided with Monroe. "Believe me, Benny—never, I would never have opened—"

"Yellow-bellied quitter!" Ben gave Andrew a deadly look.

"You're talking, Ben," Monroe remarked lightly, assuming the role of peacemaker, "about your one and only brother."

"Listen, Wooly,"—Ben turned on him—"do me a favor—"

"Gladly, Ben. But first, I must explain you something. It's about our Letty here; well, naturally she meant well—a troublemaker, she's not—but to be perfectly honest with you—"

"*Shveig!*" Letty tried to silence Monroe.

"No, my angel, for once—"

"Stay out of it, Wooly," Ben cautioned him in a tone so ominous Monroe had no choice but to comply.

Peggy, meanwhile, having made her way to Andrew's side, said under her breath, "Are you all right?"

"Go away," Andrew muttered.

"Wha—— Why? What did *I* do?"

In response Andrew merely glared at her accusingly as if her culpability were too obvious to merit an explanation.

Peggy drew a deep immoderate breath which seemed to help her swallow down the gall of Andrew's unjust blame, even as it gave her time to regain her composure. "Why don't we go back now?" she suggested matter-of-factly to the others.

"Good idea!" Letty jumped at the suggestion. "Andy—Benny—boys"—she oscillated between her brothers like the index of an ammeter—"come! please! no more now, make it up."

"Not on your life!" Ben stalked away. "No one quits on me—"

"Quits!" Letty pressed her temples. "Who said quits? He hasn't—"

"Like hell he hasn't! Ask him, go ahead and ask him! See if he denies it." Before she had a chance to speak, Ben himself put the question to Andrew at the top of his lungs. "Well, *mamzer*, do you?" Andrew stood mute. "Look at him! There's your answer—lousy *mamzer!*"

"Benny, please! don't talk, you don't know what you're saying."

"Don't I?"

"Tomorrow—you'll see—"

"*In drerd!* that's where I'll see him."

"No! stop now! please!" Letty implored. "Our brother—"

"No brother of mine!"

"What are you saying? Please! Benny, take it back, tell him—"

"Back! I wouldn't take him back if—if he came on his hands and knees. And you can tell him that from me!"

"Andy!" At this point Peggy, who had reached the opposite side of the clearing on her way toward the glen, stopped to take advantage of the momentary lull. "Are you coming?"

"No!" Ben snapped at her. "He's not!"

"I didn't ask *you*, Ben," Peggy replied softly but emphatically.

"Well, I'm *telling you*, sweetheart!"

Peggy looked him in the face. "No need to shout, Ben, I'm not your brother."

"Damned good thing—"

"Peggy!" Andrew tried to forestall her response.

"Benny!" Letty interposed herself between Ben and Peggy. "Please! for my sake—"

"Forget it, Letty!" Ben declared. "It's over—the honeymoon is over—"

"No!"

"He's out! finished!"

"No! no! *Gotteniu!* this mustn't—Andy"—Letty turned to him excitedly—"please! don't let—say—say something!"

"What is there to say?"

"Exactly!" Ben agreed with Andrew. "*Gornisht.*" To help himself think, Ben began to pace again and to jingle the coins in his trouser pocket. As he did, his expression altered visibly, growing milder, more relaxed, almost crafty. "Should have listened to you in the first place, Let. At least Wooly here would never knife me in the back—would you, Wool?" Monroe averted his eyes. "Didn't hear?" Ben wondered aloud.

"I heard, Ben," replied Monroe. "It's just . . . I don't exactly see what Andy—"

"Never mind what Andy! He's out! It's *you*, you I'm talking to. Well—" Stopping to pat Monroe on the shoulder, Ben looked around at the others and smiled ambiguously. "—How's about it, *shvonger?* Ready to roll up your sleeves and get to work?" Monroe maintained a pensive silence, while Letty, clearly torn between objecting and rejoicing, clapped a hand to her open mouth. Ben, for his part, seemed uncertain again whether or not his brother-in-law had heard him. "The job is yours, Wooly," he declared magnanimously. "You start on Tuesday."

Monroe hesitated. "Thank you, Ben, I'm beholden—"

"Don't thank *me*, thank my little sister."

"But the fact is—well, I already have a job, a trade—perfectly respectable—"

"Respectable! he calls it," Letty scoffed.

Ben stiffened. "What are you saying, Wooly?"

"My work—"

"You don't want the job?"

"It's not that—"

"You're turning me down?"

"Not you exact——"

"What then?"

Monroe shrugged and smiled sheepishly. "*Ich machen a leben.*"

"*A leben!*" Ben and Letty scoffed in unison this time, but Ben alone continued. "What's a matter, Wooly? Not good enough for you? Against your principles, an open shop, I exploit the worker? You'd rather stick it out in that stinking dungeon? Dress your wife in *shmattehs*—"

"They *aren't shmattehs*," Monroe objected with pride.

"What then? What makes her come to Milly once a month—"

"Benny!" Letty exclaimed.

"No!" he overrode his sister's protest. "Let him hear for once. He should know how you demean yourself. You think you made this garment?" Ben confronted Monroe with the quarter sleeve of Letty's summer print. "*A nechtiger tog!* Milly's! She comes to Milly once a month for castoffs; *my* little sister—for castoffs she comes, so she shouldn't look like a ragamuffin. Comes downtown once a month—'lunch,' she calls it—"

"Benny!" Letty tried to silence him.

"No! let him hear. For handouts! that's why she comes, charity—you understand? Not for herself—God forbid—for the kids—*farshtaist?*—to have enough to feed *your* kids, so that you, Mr. *K'nacker*, can keep your principles, your C.P. card!"

Monroe turned slowly to Letty. "It's true?" he asked in a subdued voice.

"You're goddamned right it's true!" Ben answered for her. "I'm a liar suddenly? Every month, the first of every month, as God gives the day— Christ! what an irony, that *I* should pay your C.P. dues."

"Letty?" Monroe put the question to her a second time. Unable to repudiate Ben's words, Letty, on the verge of tears, gazed in pity at Monroe, her own expression utterly pathetic. "About the dresses, I knew, not the rest. No matter." He took heart, tried to comfort Letty. "Don't look so *fardeiget*, angel, not your fault—the system. Sure, the system leaves you short, robs you of all dignity. Sure, you have to borrow, beg—what don't you have to do?— kidnap—what choice? But don't you fret, it won't be long. It's in its death throes right this minute, we're witnessing the death throes—"

"Go! tell it to the marines," Ben scoffed.

"No, *you*," Monroe retorted with forceful but quiet conviction, "you'll need them, Ben, marines—all you can get, the whole United States Government forces. Nothing will help, nothing. 'Ready to roll up my sleeves?' You bet! and thousands more, thousands like me everywhere, ready to *deharge* you your capitalism."

At this, Letty buried her face in her hands and broke into sobs. "Now! look what you've done," Ben accused Monroe. At the same time, tears came, too, to Andrew's eyes, and turning ponderously, he wandered off into the woods like someone in shock, the sole survivor of an automobile accident. "Just a minute, you!" Ben charged after him.

"Ben!" Peggy, raising her voice for the first time, cried out against her brother-in-law. "Lay off!"

"Stay out of it, *you*," he countered savagely.

"Ben!" came Mildred's voice, like an echo of Peggy's calling from the distance.

Andrew could see the three of them now—Mildred, Lawrence, and Barry—bearing down on him: Mildred holding up her pocketbook to protect her eyes from the underbrush as she hurried headlong through the woods; Lawrence tagging after her, almost keeping up with her, not out of a sense of duty but out of fear, his face white as cotton; while Barry, who by contrast seemed to be taking his time, brought up the rear.

"What is it?" Mildred questioned Andrew breathlessly. "Why's he shouting? What's—" Breaking off at sight of Andrew's tears, she bypassed him and hurried over to her husband. "Ben—"

"Why's Uncle Andy crying?"

"Be still!" Mildred silenced Lawrence. "Go back to the picnic now—the two of you—right away! Letty, take them— Wha-what's the matter here? Letty? Wooly? *Everyone* in tears? What is it? What exactly's going on?"

"It's quite simple, Mil," Peggy began to explain. "Sarah Kellogg—"

"Never mind simple!" Ben cut her off. "No one asked *you.*"

"Ben!" Mildred gaveled the air with her fists, restraining herself rigorously in hopes of restraining him. "It's your sister-in——"

"I don't give a fuck—"

"Ben!"

"—they both can go—"

"Stop it! *di kinder!*"

"—she *and* her *shtik drek* husband—"

"Stop!"

"—straight to hell—*all* of them!" So broad was Ben's sweeping gesture, not even the trees were exempt from his curse. "That one"—he singled out Monroe—"that one, too!"

Still pummeling the air, Mildred whispered frantically, "Stop! I said."

"No! I've had enough! up to here! I'm through, finished! killing myself—for what? So that *shtik drek* there—"

"Please!" Mildred stamped the ground.

"Let him rot in hell, I say—*all* of them, this whole *fekuckteh* family—"

Mildred, shaking from head to toe, made one last effort to silence him: "*Sha!*"

"—down the drain—flush them—where they belong! Flush my hands—"

"Peggy," Mildred appealed to her sister-in-law with sudden self-control, "*please*, take the children—"

"Come on, gang!" Peggy sang out. "You, too, Let . . .

Wooly . . . Andy—come on, now—everyone—let's go back."

At last Ben fell silent, his eye on Andrew, as Peggy and the boys set off in the direction of the glen, followed at a lugubrious pace by Letty and Monroe who looked for all the world (she, hunched to half her height, face buried in a handkerchief; Wooly, supporting her by the waist) the same as they had looked last summer at Twister's funeral. Ben, meanwhile, his eye still trained on Andrew, was obviously waiting to see which of them would make the next move. When, at last, his patience gave out, Ben said gruffly, "Are you coming?"

Andrew shook his head.

"Come on, Andy," Mildred coaxed him wearily.

"No—need to take a walk." Turning, Andrew headed now in the same direction—divergent from that of the rest of the family—he had chosen earlier. But no sooner had he taken a few steps than he heard Mildred cry out Ben's name, felt his brother's hand come down hard on his shoulder blade ("Come back here, you!"), restraining him, turning him ("—sneak off like that!"), tearing his polo shirt, at the same time that he saw Peggy break from the boys and start to run, zigzagging through the trees, in his direction.

"You're still part of this family!" Ben shouted almost incoherently, "like it or not—"

Before Ben could finish, Peggy and Mildred converged on him and, exerting their combined strength, pulled him away from Andrew.

"I'll *deharge* him!" Ben raved, as Mildred took charge of the situation (*"Bist meshugeh?"* she demanded sotto voce), positioning herself like a cop squarely in front of him; while Peggy went over to Andrew and, reaching out to him, her eyes expressing unutterable regret and concern, murmured tenderly, "Come back, now," unaware that the others, having done an about-face, were returning to the clearing—Barry and Lawrence in the vanguard, Letty and Monroe not far behind—like curiosity seekers to the scene of a calamity.

"—*deharge* him!"

With his teeth bared, chest heaving, Ben did indeed look capable of committing murder, but not for long. A moment later his whole bellicose manner collapsed—head drooped, facial muscles went completely slack, leaving him looking dazed and defeated as he shambled over to Andrew and said almost inaudibly, "Don't do it . . . run out on me . . . don't ever—please . . . I—I wouldn't be—" His voice broke and tears came to his eyes. "What do you want?" he asked in earnest, ready to grant any wish under the sun. "An *s*? Is that it? It's yours. I'll add an *s*," he promised, "but don't run out on me."

Puzzled though Andrew was by the word *aness*, he was all but moved to tears himself by his brother's tears and pitiable expression. "I'll come back."

"When?"

"In a little while."

"What's a little while?"

"After . . . I take a walk."

Ben paused a moment to digest the fact that they were talking at cross-purposes. "Make it easy on yourself"—he resorted to one of his favorite saws, adding out of habit, "lazy loafer." To make certain that the epithet was taken as intended, endearingly, he made a fist, cocked the middle knuckle, and punched his brother on the arm.

Expressionless, Andrew rubbed the "eggie." "Love tap?" he said, not with irony but simply to help himself understand.

"Damn tootin'!" Ben exclaimed. "Come on, now. Who's your best pal in the world?"

When Andrew failed to ventriloquize the anticipated answer, Mildred, her cheeks mascara-streaked by tears of sympathy for Ben, stepped forward quickly, placed a hand on Ben's arm—"Let him take his walk"—and led Ben away.

At the same time, Peggy turned to Andrew. "Want me to come along?" Andrew shook his head in silence. "Sure?" He nodded and started to walk away. "Andy!" she stopped him, but the distress in her heart prevented her momentarily from saying what was on her mind. "Love you," she declared at last scarcely above a whisper.

"Me, too," he murmured back, "*all* of us . . . that's the trouble."

Before parting, Andrew and Peggy exchanged a heartfelt look. Then, turning simultaneously, they went their separate ways.

7

On his way toward the summit Andrew wondered why. What was driving him? What had made him turn, as if his course were preordained, in that direction? Why had he set the summit as his goal, set a goal of any sort, rather than ramble about until he calmed down, collected his wits, was ready to rejoin the family? Would he ever be ready? Was he in flight, fleeing from the family, or in pursuit of something? He couldn't tell—both, most likely—didn't know. Nor did he know how far away the summit was, how long it would take to climb. Mildred had mentioned reassembling at three; wasn't it practically that already? . . . Stopping to check his watch, Andrew thwarted the impulse by shifting his eye, almost in defiance of the time, to the southwest. Some nimbus clouds had amassed above the mountain peaks, clotting and murking the sky. The weatherman had been right for once, it was indeed going to rain. Paradoxically, the threat of rain did nothing to deter Andrew, seemed instead to spur him on, up the gradually inclining slope (as yet the trail—if, in fact, it was a trail—was far from steep, requiring neither his full attention nor strenuous exertion), along what Andrew took to be the rim of the escarpment viewed earlier from the glen, leading him now roughly north, away from the parking lot and lake, the picnic ground and family.

"Family," he murmured aloud to impress on himself the fact that he was moving away from them, regardless of the time. Odd for someone who made such a fetish of regularity, reliability, routine, whose every move might have been determined by a metronome, not to care what time it was, whether he got back by three. Wouldn't they worry? Of course they would. Maybe not Peggy. She was reasonably relaxed about such things, not a Spector after all, a stickler for time like Ben—he'd call the troopers out. Letty, too, she'd have a conniption. . . . Imagine her doing that, trying to manipulate Ben that way, to say nothing of Wooly and himself. He could have cheered when Wooly said that about the marines, could have cried when Ben exposed the dress as Mildred's. That was what had hurt the man, despite his saying that he knew. How could Letty be like that, insensitive enough to take the dress from Mildred in the first place? or, if she *had* to have it, wear it in front of Wooly? Vanity . . . another Spector trait, so pronounced in all of them, boys and girls alike: Ethel, Ben, Irene; even Essie, gargantuan though she was, considered herself a raving beauty; only Weezie was a little different, more restrained, dignified like Mama; but Letty was the worst—worse than Mamma?—worst because in Letty's case she pretended not to be, concealed her vanity under a guise of indifference, slovenliness, whereas Mamma— What had Ben said about being a mamma to him? What had he, Andrew, said to evoke the *lapsus?* He couldn't remember now, not a single word—*aness* . . . a nurse? If he had to go to court tomorrow and testify— Testify to what? That his brother had threatened to murder him, bury him alive—no, not alive, no need to make it worse than it was—in a packing case with Spector & Son on the lid. Sticks and sons—stones . . . *aness* . . . had offered *aness* . . . amnesty? anes . . . thetic? . . . an— "An *s!*" Andrew declared, deciphering the cryptogram with a sense of satisfaction and real achievement.

So that was what Ben had meant: that he would add an *s* to Son, Spector & Sons, make Andrew his partner, if not legally, titularly, hire a letterer to redo the show window, stationery, trade name—had meant that he was ready now, after all these years, to make amends for Papa's slight. Could holding on to Andrew possibly mean that much to Ben? Apparently, if he was willing at last to concede, not only to himself but to the world, that there were two of them, that Solomon Spector had had two sons, both of whom worked in the family business; that Benjamin Spector had but one, a boy named Lawrence, not a second, older son called Andrew whose mother, as well as father, Ben took himself to be—the very mother Benny felt he had never had; just as Andrew felt he had never had a father. . . .

"Oh, Papa!" Andrew whispered feelingly as he raised his eyes, welling tears, toward the summit. "Why didn't you —couldn't you—you yourself have done it—found it in your heart to add an *s*? . . . And, Mamma—couldn't you have done the same . . . f-for Benny?" That was what had made Ben cry: the hurt of being demi-orphaned, the self-same hurt that was bringing tears to Andrew's eyes this minute. Wasn't it that, their orphanhood, that made them more than brothers; made each the other's surrogate parent —he, Ben's mother (Ben's *lapsus* notwithstanding), the mamma Ben could never quite forgive, forget, free himself from for orphaning him; made Ben his father, the papa he could never quite forgive, forget, free himself from; made each of them not only the other's brother, the other's sur-rogate parent, but also the in-law of the other, since each had been turned by his surviving parent into a sort of secondary spouse: he of Sophie, Ben of Solomon? . . . And Letty? Wasn't she doing the same, doing with Barry and Kenneth what Mamma had done with him and Ben? Thank heavens Wooly was too mature, too sensible and sane to collaborate with her—unless by default, by failing to oppose Letty, by being in the end as love-blind as Papa had been. . . . And he and Peggy? Had they done any better with Mat and Chris?

Andrew stopped short. Directly in front of him, ob-structing the path, was a boulder the size of a log cabin. Split in two horizontally—by what? lightning? flood? ice? —the upper portion loomed like a slanting roof over the lower part, leaving a three-foot gap in between, a sort of natural shelter into which Andrew peered now cautiously, half expecting to find— What? What exactly was it those children had been burying? All he could make out was a few deposits, whorled by wind or water, of dead pine needles, lichen, moss, cobwebs, and a clump of ferns, sprouting like whiskers from a corner of the shelter's mouth. The luxuriant fronds (involuntarily Andrew pro-truded his lips, flexed his nostrils, sniffed the loamy pine-scented air) made him think of reindeer, of all the herbivorous creatures that must once have roamed these woods, after the primal sea had receded, the algae turned into ferns, the ferns into lichen, the feed of reindeer, before the descent of man. Glancing over his shoulder—did reindeer have a natural enemy?—Andrew saw the luxe hotel, a snow-white dollhouse at this distance, on the neighboring plateau, as well as a patch of the lake below which looked now like a patch of ice against the darkening shore. Turning back, he tried to catch a glimpse of the summit but failed, couldn't see it for the trees. Had he lost his way already?

"Better get on," he prompted himself, skirting the boulder and picking up the trail again in the underbrush on the other side where, presently, he snagged his shirt, already ripped (*I'll* deharge *him*), on a brier, a blackberry bush. . . . So, there *were* berries after all, though not yet ripe. Had the children come this way? . . . The children. Of course he and Peggy had done no better, made the same or similar mistakes—at least *he* had. In his determination not to be like Papa, not to impose on Mat inhuman standards, rigid rules and regulations, demands for absolute obedience, absolute respect: the absolute authority that leads perforce to orphanhood; to be, instead, supportive, permissive, uncritical as possible, encouraging the boy's innate reflectiveness and curiosity, his every impulse, every whim, indulging, even coddling him—and when it came to coddling, not care, could any mother match a doting father?—in doing that, hadn't he overlooked one essential factor: Peggy? Hadn't he failed to take into account their differences: genetic differences, the difference, for example, between Mamma and Papa on the one hand, Mère and Père on the other; between Oliver and Ben; between being a daughter and being a son, being a sister and being a brother—differences which, when compounded by crossbreeding, multiplied out of hand? Had he stopped to consider those differences then, before he started raising Mat according to his own highly individual liberal lights, he might have foreseen that Peggy would react the way she did—exactly like her mother. Much as she disliked Mère's conventionality, had gone to extremes to be the opposite, thoroughly Bohemian, the minute Peggy found herself confronted by Andrew's laxity, she turned into a carbon copy of her mother: a missionary of propriety, conformity, good manners, whose ever-ready retort to what she called Andrew's "Deweyism" was "Spare the rod and spoil the child." So that if, indeed, he had achieved his aim with Mat, succeeded in avoiding Papa's mistakes, it had been achieved at Peggy's expense—by reversing her rulings behind her back, undermining her authority, ridiculing most, if not all, of her inherited views; while he and Mat drew ever closer, more intimate, inseparable, monopolizing each other's time and attention, loyalty and affection, till they virtually excluded her, and Mat became for him and Peggy their chief instrument of discord—

Confronted suddenly by a sharp incline, Andrew was forced to concentrate on the trail until he surmounted the modest hill. . . . No wonder, then, that by the time Christopher was born Peggy set about, however unintentionally, to redress the balance: make Twister *her* son, the way Andrew had made Mat his. And she succeeded, though naturally at Andrew's expense this time—his turn now to behave like Papa. Hadn't her success hinged, in fact, on Andrew's failure, the failure of his will not to be like Papa? Somehow with Twister he found himself behaving in ways that would have been insupportable with Mat. He became bad-tempered, carping, stern, even—God forgive him!—bullying: treating Twister pretty much the way Ben had treated him since childhood . . . and Papa had treated Ben . . . and Grandpa had no doubt treated Papa. Was that Peggy's fault? Never mind that he had always thought so, blamed her for his mistreatment of the boy—was it actually her fault? Had her proprietariness, her dominion over Twister, driven Andrew to get back at her, take out on Twister the resentment he felt toward Peggy? Was she to blame for his behavior? Or was there something about the boy himself that triggered it? . . . Even allowing for his size (ten and a quarter pounds at birth), his inordinate energy and physicality, Twister was by any standard, not just in contrast to Mat, a riotous unruly child whose only purpose on earth, it seemed, was to disturb the peace, create disorder. Was it that, the disorder, the everlasting mess and tumult—slamming doors, stampeding feet, hurtling objects, hounding of Mat, hoots and squeals and cries, especially in the evenings when Andrew was trying to compose; was it the disorder that had made Andrew act like Papa? Was that enough to blind him to the child's other qualities: his impishness and ardor, self-reliance, animal grace? Was there something about disorder itself that threatened Andrew, brought out in him the very trait he had disapproved of most in Papa: the spirit that denies? And, naturally, the more Andrew denied, the more intractable Twister became, drawing ever closer to his mother, ever more estranged from Andrew—all that self-reliance soon reversed, reduced to dependence on Peggy; all that energy and grace perverted into spite, aimed at Andrew, provoking and defying him, forcing him against his will to become ever more intransigent, ever more like Papa. "Oh, Twister!"

He had come now to what was clearly the end of the path. Directly in front of him, blocking further progress, stood a sheer wall of rock, tiered and cracked and crannied, a cliff against which was propped, some yards to the right, a fallen tree. Like the tree, Andrew used the cliff to brace himself, pressing first his palms, then his brow against the stone, partly to prevent his keeling over, partly to withstand the shock of his remorse. "I did it, too," he confessed brokenly, "did to you—oh! my little boy—orphaned you— forgive me. . . ." Facing the wall, arms over his head, hands flat against the pudding stone, Andrew resembled a condemned man, awaiting execution. "Forgive me . . . forgive me . . ." He was sobbing now, rolling his head, still pressed against the stone, from side to side as if in penance for his sins, as if the sins themselves were incised in the stone and he were trying to efface them, trying to efface himself. . . . Oh, Lord, what an irony! If he and Peggy had had to be proprietary, take the children one for one, it should by rights have been the other way around: Twister *his* son, Mew-mew *hers*. The gods had tricked or punished them by making Mat first-born. Had Twister come first, there would have been no problem. Andrew would have easily condoned—more than condoned, celebrated, the very qualities which, as it turned out, he censured in the boy; would have seen in those qualities vestiges of himself, the boy he himself would have been had Papa been less censorious.

"Myself!" The recognition struck him with the impact of a falling rock, the ones climbers hereabouts were cautioned to watch out for. Retracting his head, though not his hands, he opened his eyes and stared at the pudding stone as if glimpsing in the bits of quartz and pebbles embedded in the darker mass an aspect not of the cliff's face but his own. . . . He had done it to *himself*—mistaken Twister for himself as a boy, mistaken himself for Papa and Ben, and, being taken over by a force beyond his comprehension or control, had repeated his boyhood history, re-enacted with his son the ritual sacrifice of himself. Was that why he couldn't come to terms with Twister's death, because it seemed somehow his own—himself the slayer and the slain? . . . In answer to the question Andrew groaned, clenched his fists, and pressed his skull against the stone. . . . Yes . . . yes. . . . He had killed the Twister in himself, and being unable to live with the guilt—guilt of partial suicide, partial infanticide—he had shifted the blame to Peggy, since Twister was *her* son and she alone was with him when he died. No matter how irrational, untrue, didn't that explain why he couldn't, wouldn't "*shtup*" her again? (*I don't want another baby*, came the shocking echo—or was it distant thunder?—from the glen), because in some way he blamed Peggy for the death of his son, the death of himself. . . . Looking up, Andrew scaled with his eyes the wasted face of the cliff as far as the sunless sky. "And all for an *s*," he concluded soulfully, "the refusal of an *s*."

When he felt calmer, Andrew glanced at his watch. Twenty to three. He would go back now—what about the summit? forget the summit!—before it started raining. Back to what? he challenged himself as he turned from the wall and faced, without really seeing, the surrounding panorama of the Catskills. Back to the conjugal bed? to Ben? to Spector & Son? Son*s*—mustn't forget the *s*. Or back to *Recovery*? Interesting how much *Recovery* had to do with kinship, how deeply Sarah explored the subject— An image of the drowned brother, his outstretched arm like a battering-ram, broke in on Andrew's thoughts. How brilliantly, thematically, Sarah developed the brother in the course of the dance, introducing him repeatedly, using him in such diverse and unexpected ways—sometimes as the advocate of Barrett, sometimes of Browning, sometimes living, sometimes dead, unsaved by his sister, sometimes knitting the shawl in her stead, sometimes unravelling the yarn—always present, primal, even in absence, his appearances and reappearances like so many epiphanies of Elizabeth's daemon. Her daemon. That was the brother's role in the dance, why Sarah brought him back at the end, not, as Andrew had initially supposed, for Elizabeth to lay him finally to rest, but just the opposite. In order to accomplish her recovery, free herself from Barrett, elope with Browning, Elizabeth had first to recover her drowned brother, salvage her daemon from the depths. . . . But in that case oughtn't the brother to be with them at the very end, an indispensable party to the elopement? Probably. . . . He would write Sarah to that effect tonight, try to clarify the point, maybe even suggest that she incorporate the beshawled figure of the brother into the final duet—he would soon see how much "collaboration" Sarah was prepared to countenance—turn the final duet into a trio, giving himself thereby a better chance to compose an extended coda—Compose! (The prospect gave him the shivers.) A thirty-minute score, in what amount of time? Six or seven months —wasn't that what Sarah had allotted?—when in fact it had taken him three years to finish *Presences*. Impossible! he couldn't do it, lacked the discipline— No, surely not the discipline—that he had in spades. What he lacked was fluency, freedom, the free flow of his energy, creative energy, given him by God, the gift of God, unhampered by self-consciousness, self-criticism, self-contempt—the whole caboodle of self-undoing that was his legacy from Papa. Papa again. Had Papa undone the part of him that composed? Was that why it took months and months sometimes to wrest the briefest passage from himself, because Papa had killed the gift? But he had done it to himself, killed it in himself, the gift, much as he had killed the Twister in himself. Twister! Was that what choked the flow: the fact that he had denied—worse than denied—cut off the child in himself, leaving the Papa-like part in command? Yet the Papa-like part had no imagination, contributed nothing—nothing, that is, but willpower, discipline, control—couldn't begin to compose, could only do the drudgery. No wonder composition took so long, came so hard, so joylessly: He had cut himself off from God. "Oh, God!" he cried out, covering his cranium with both hands as if the mountain were about to fall. "You, too! . . . orphaned *You* as well."

In his desolation Andrew looked around forlornly as though for some way out, some way back, not to the family or business or even to composing—on that score he was only fooling himself: six months indeed! it would take him sixty to complete *Recovery*—but for some way back to God. There simply was no choice. Once you realized that nothing about your life, as you were living it, worked, could even be called living, in the sense of participation, that you weren't in fact a willing participant in being, weren't being at all, merely going through the motions—to go back then, whether out of fear or habit, and resume those motions as before would be a sacrilege, the worst of all impieties: knowingly to trivialize your life. No! There was no dodging or delaying it, he must go on.

Andrew's eye fell now on what he had taken earlier for a broken or lightning-blasted tree, propped against the cliff at a point where a slight recess in the wall concealed its top from view. Though certainly a sapling, stripped of its branches, the tree was neither broken, blasted, nor there by accident, he realized now, but served as a makeshift handrail for a crude wooden ladder whose weatherworn rungs, almost indistinguishable in this light from the pudding stone, scaled the face of the cliff. Yet if there was a ladder, perhaps he hadn't lost his way after all, perhaps the path continued.

Instinctively, Andrew ignored the handrail, felt more secure—not that the ladder was the least bit rickety—climbing on all fours, one rung at a time. However clumsily and slow, he climbed with keen anticipation, curious to see what awaited him, whether by blind luck he had happened on the summit. His disappointment was marked, therefore, when finally his eye, coming level with the surface, encountered nothing, not a single tree or shrub, scarcely a tuft of grass. Far from the summit, what he had reached was a grim plateau on which nothing but some further rocks and boulders could be seen. Like a child out to explore an attic but finding it empty, Andrew paused in disappointment, two-thirds up the ladder. Still, having come this far, he might as well go all the way.

Stepping off the ladder and straightening up, he reached for the handrail to steady himself, so vertiginous was the chasm at his feet, so breathtaking the sudden view. What astonished Andrew most as he surveyed the prospect, his eye moving in an arc from the little lakes (to his surprise there were two of them, twin lakes, cratered like livid puddles among the nearby peaks that looked, from his vantage point, delicate as dorsal fins) to a precipitous gorge through which the valley, a boundless plain, receded for what seemed a hundred miles into the vaporous horizon; while to his left, beyond a rolling dale of evergreens and cluster of faraway foothills, three more peaks, cresting like waves, crisscrossed under a turbulent sky (surely it was raining there), dense, plum-colored clouds purpling the upper slopes—what astonished Andrew most was the altitude. After so relatively short a climb he was simply unprepared to find himself above the timberline (he had forgotten in the course of the afternoon how far they had come by car), if not above the line of every living creature, including birds, in a place absolutely still except for distant thunder and the agitation of the sky; unprepared for the scale of things: the dwarfishness of trees and crests, whole communities and townships, the reach and sweep of the plain; unprepared for the range of view—were he able to penetrate the haze on the horizon, he would no doubt descry the silver span, spanking new, of George Washington Bridge . . . Where *was* the Hudson anyway? Glancing over his shoulder, Andrew saw nothing but a heap of boulders, like so many giant wisdom teeth, silhouetted against the sky. He was too far from the other side to see the opposite view. To satisfy his curiosity, he started diagonally across the plateau, surprised that the surface wasn't nearly as flat as he had supposed but full of cracks, deep fissures, which seemed in some spots bottomless. Was that wall down below, which he had assumed solid, actually hollow? this plateau the roof of a cavern? the entire setting delusory? like those boulders over there, so substantial a moment ago, yet, seen now from a different angle, unmistakably a grotto, unmistakably forbidding.

126

Andrew hesitated, suddenly uneasy. Behind his back a lightning flash prompted him to turn and take another look at the distant storm. The peaks, resounding with dull thunder, were all but shrouded now, the line between the sky and mountaintops a violet blur; the lower slopes, where visible, steaming. He hadn't realized that he was sweating, slightly chilled, not by the wind, which was really rather mild, but because he was standing still, utterly exposed. In haste he resumed crossing the plateau.

On reaching the opposite side, Andrew was brought to his hands and knees by a sudden spell of acrophobia. Yet even on all fours he felt imperiled, backed his knees away from the brink until he was stretched out prone. Even then, hugging the ledge, he dreaded looking over, had first to summon up his nerve. When at last he did, what he beheld was a drop, a hundred feet or more straight down, sheer rock, then green, mat of trees, mountain bulging suddenly, becoming slope, slanting forth, falling yet another two or three thousand feet down to the floor of the valley: immense in scope, fanning out flat in all directions right up to the Hudson—the river itself an endless banner, stately, trim, trailing glints of silver the length of the valley, dividing it in two, the land on the far side continuing flat for miles and miles till finally in the remotest distance—was it Connecticut? Massachusetts? possibly Vermont?—other mountains rose again to shadow the horizon.

Inhaling deeply, Andrew closed his eyes, lay his cheek against the sandstone, feeling the ledge firm underneath him, steadfast and secure, supporting his outspread palms, flattened chest, pelvis, and thighs, inducing some tumidity, making tangible his body, taking from the rock its inherent energy and heat: his chill dispelled, bloodstream quickened, coursing now, his consciousness altogether focused on the intimacy between his body and the rock. In that intimacy he found himself defined, distinguished from the rock yet fused with it, relieved of both his sense of separateness and overriding self, assimilated in no time into the mountain, extending downward deep through prehistoric strata of which he now felt bodily a part. Opening his eyes, he saw again the vast expanse below. Of that, too, he felt a part—far-reaching as the plain, yet still specific, anchored in the rock—felt at once finite and unbounded.

Something white entered his field of vision: a day liner, tiny at this distance as a child's bathtub toy, plying its way downstream. An instant later a sudden change in the light attracted Andrew's attention to the sky. One sun-drenched cloud, shaped like a lobster claw, stood out luminous against the denser darker mass. As he watched the shifting claw go after another nearby cloud, its spreading pincers released a triple shaft of radiance. In wonder Andrew craned his neck, trying to catch a glimpse of the sun (how many light-years away was Arcturus? the same number as his age, wasn't it? thirty-six—or was he thirty-seven?); but even as he did, the pincers closed, turned opaque, occluding the shaft, the claw itself dimming rapidly, its luster fading, eclipsed by denser clouds, till finally all trace of it was lost under a layer of inky blue. Yet, despite its disappearance, Andrew continued to gaze at the spot where the claw had been, penetrating with his mind's eye the murky atmosphere, espying gradually the hidden sun, the moon and stars, especially Arcturus, vivid in the daylight as a navel orange, millions of millions of miles away.

"Oh, God," he whispered ardently, feeling now the need to pray, pray without really knowing whether or not he believed— How *could* you know until you prayed? Yet neither did he know exactly how to pray, hadn't prayed since . . . If I should die before I sleep, Pray God my soul to take—*keep*— If I should die . . . Raising his shoulders and drawing backwards, Andrew assumed a prayerful attitude—rump resting on his heels, eyes closed, bowed head bolstered by joined palms—the sandstone ledge his prayer mat. "Oh, God—cleansed! I feel so cleansed . . . swept clean . . . like—like that plain down there looks from here: perfectly level . . . limitless . . . uncluttered . . . like—what's the word? What chefs do to butter . . . purify? . . . clarify—that's it! *clarified*; the way I feel— clarified of everything: myself . . . the family . . . impurities—all the sediment that settles over the years. Oh! thank You, God. Thank You for this rock which holds me . . . held by the mountain . . . held by the earth—the river flowing to the sea—held by the moon . . . the stars . . . the galaxy—all *all* held by You. . . . Thank You, God, for holding me . . . for bringing me this far. . . . Not—I don't mean from the valley, I mean—I—from the age of . . . fern, the age . . . I—I was a faun . . . these peaks not peaks at all but level, a far-flung forest . . . before the glacier came: eons of ice . . . endured . . . outlasted . . . melting into mountains . . . rivers . . . maize . . . generating man . . . emigrating north again . . . to this very rock. . . . Yet—strange—I feel . . . just begun, as though I have as far to go as I've already come. . . . At the same time—s-s-slipping—part of me is slipping back—no, not slipping, gliding backwards . . . steadily . . . receding like a star . . . receding from the earth . . . into everlasting solitude: two hundred million million miles old—yet visible . . . still visible, though dead, burned out a trillion years ago— Oh God! is—is that why You—why I—what brought me here? Ha-have I died before I wake? Do you hold us all—the living and the dead—hold Twister too? . . . Oh, my God! protect him, please! my little boy, protect him . . . as I failed— Please *please*, dear God, hold him fast . . . despite my readiness—forget it, please, my readiness to orphan You—hold us both: my son . . . my soul . . . taken while I slept. . . . Wake me! God, oh, wake me! . . ."

"Andy!"

On hearing his name, not merely spoken but exclaimed, however indistinctly, Andrew felt a tremor course through his body. Half in fear, half in ardent expectation, he opened his eyes and tilted back his head, prepared to see the heavens part. Instead, the clouds had thickened, merged into one undifferentiated indigo mass. No trace of his addresser there. . . . After a moment he glanced out of the corner of his eye. . . . Still no one, nothing, neither to the right nor left, nor behind his back. Was he hearing things? Had he mistaken for his name a distant thunderclap, the call of a bird? . . . Not a bird in sight. . . . Scarcely breathing, Andrew waited, listened. . . .

"Dandy! I said."

"I heard you."

It was the *children*, Pearl and Mat, their voices coming from— Where? Perplexed, Andrew scrutinized the ledge, lowered his ear to the stone.

"Well?" Pearl pressed Mat.

"It's dumb, I said."

They were somewhere down below, on the next subjacent level, if not directly under him, *inside* the mountain itself . . . unless, of course, the rocks, by some acoustical fluke, were reflecting their voices from afar. In quick succession Andrew cast a glance over his shoulder at the grotto, then at the ledge again, hoping this time to discover a fissure through which—

"I don't want to be kidnapped!"

"Shut up, Kenny!" Pearl put in.

"But I don't want—"

"No one's asking you!"

"Pay no attention, Kenny," Mat reassured his cousin, "no one's going to kidnap—"

"Oh, yes we are!" insisted Pearl.

"Stop acting like an infant, Pearl."

"Infant! You're the one— Whose idea—I'd like to know—"

"Yours," Mat stated coolly.

"Liar! Who said—ooh! you're such a liar, Matty."

"You're the one who's lying, Pearl."

"I am not! You! it was you—your idea—who said we should come in here in the first place!"

"To explore the cave, I said, not to kidnap Kenny."

"Never mind, never mind—still your idea, so don't call me—make me out the liar. Kill-joy!"

"Chil-dren!"

It was Fräulein Landau calling, the sound of her voice more distant and diffused than theirs.

"Yoo-hoo! . . . chil-dren!"

"Come on," Mat said, "let's go."

"Wait!" Pearl whispered urgently.

"For what?"

"Just wait! . . . Maybe she'll think we're kidnapped."

"Why would she think that?"

"Maybe it's his—his hide-out."

"Whose hide-out?" Kenny adopted Pearl's hushed tone.

"Chil-dren! . . . *Wo sind sie?*"

"Ze kidnapper, my little vun"—Pearl put on her thickest German accent—"ze killer of ze Lindbergh baby!"

"Obviously, Pearl, what it is," Mat explained, "is a bear den."

"A what! Oh, Matty! You don't—you—you think?—there ain't no bears—"

130

"Aren't, Pearl. And besides, that's a double negative—"

"*Bears.* . . . You don't mean— Oh, Matty—in here? . . . with us . . . *now?*"

"Ooooooooo!"

Mat's imitation sounded more like a giant owl than a bear.

"Yi!" Pearl and Kenny shrieked in unison. "Fräulein! help! help!"

"*Was ist los?*"

"Help! Bears! *Bären! Bären!*"

As their voices died away, Andrew had to chuckle. It wasn't long, however, before the sound of his own voice died away, deadened by an onset of questions. Oughtn't he to go after them, with them, back to the glen? Hadn't he seen what he came for? Could the view from the summit be much better? View? Had he come merely for the view? If so, what about this feeling—why did it persist?—of having come but halfway, of having still another leg, equally long, to go? Yet where? To what? . . .

On his feet now, Andrew surveyed the sudden steep incline just beyond the grotto, the handful of stunted evergreens—some like hat trees, stripped of all their foliage, standing dead—atop the next plateau. . . . Did he really expect to sleep up here tonight? in the rain? not return to the house? Ridiculous . . . a daydream, designed to escape the conjugal bout, the next round in bed . . . next round with Ben— Not at all! He could feel himself being drawn this minute, physically drawn, in both directions at once: one foot forward, pointing toward the next plateau, the other angled back toward the glen. ("*Macht schnell! Wir sind spät.*") . . . Still within earshot, still time to catch them. No, let them go. It made no difference suddenly whether he ever saw them again, *any* of them: Peggy, Ben— Terrible thing to say! No, not really; said not out of indifference but dispassion, a diminution of the need to possess. The effect of being clarified? Perhaps. What good was clarification, though, if finally you didn't bring it back with you, down to earth, to share with others? Not ready yet, too soon. Even so, oughtn't he to make his presence known, give them some message for Peggy? that he was perfectly all right, would be along in time. . . .

Andrew raced across the plateau to the ladder. On the

trail below he could see the little group, retreating hurry-scurry: Mat in the lead (who was whose "shadow" now? for once he, Andrew, was shadowing his son), Kenny at his heels, followed in short order by Fräulein and Pearl, hand in hand and carrying, in Fräulein's free hand, a sand pail— The berries? . . . But if he made his presence known, there could be no excuses—what with the storm coming on (no question now: it was pouring over there between those peaks) and the hour (Andrew glanced again at his watch: five to three); he would have no choice, *have* to go back, the minute he called out. No, better not, best let them go.

In silence Andrew stood and watched first Mat (he tended to forget sometimes, with so much emphasis on gray matter, just how agile and athletic the boy could be), then Kenny (was he Twister's age?), Pearl (why would a child want to play kidnap, as if she were playing house?), and Fräulein (her fiancé killed on the Marne, these her foster children): "Take care of them!" Andrew charged her quietly, as the nurse's white beret disappeared under cover of the trees.

Turning resolutely, Andrew went his solitary way, past the simple grotto (what had made it seem the least bit sinister?) and up the steeply rising slope. At the top, he didn't pause to catch his breath or look back at the view but went straight on, through the half-dead clump of evergreens out into an open space, flat and barren as the one below except for a tomahawk-shaped boulder, sheltering a blueberry patch, which Andrew promptly skirted and continued on toward what he began to see was yet another slope, steeper than the last.

Only when he reached the foot of the next slope did Andrew stop, deterred not by the prospect of a further climb (if anything he felt exhilarated) but by a fork in the trail. Besides the ascending path, a second one, level with the ground, branched off to the left through a sudden growth of trees and underbrush. Despite his impulse to take the lower path, Andrew hesitated. . . . Clearly the ascending one would lead in time to the summit, whereas the lower one would bring him—to what? He hadn't a clue. Why take it, then? In hopes that it would double back, down to the glen? Was that his secret hope: to hoodwink himself, return to the family? Not at all. Then why not take the ascending one? Because something told him not to, and why not trust his intuition? . . .

"Annn-dy!"

"Not again," he said to himself with a knowing smile. The children must have seen him on the bluff, feigned departure, and then sneaked back to take him by surprise. Well, he would play along with them. . . . Putting his hands into his pockets, Andrew looked around nonchalantly. "Yes?" he replied in a perfectly normal tone. In the ensuing silence he tried in vain to catch sight of them through the trees. . . . Hiding, obviously. But where was Fräulein? Hiding, too? Unlikely, considering that they were late already. (Andrew glanced again at his watch: five to three. Odd, must have stopped.) Even so, he couldn't have been hearing things, any more than he'd been hearing them down below. "Yes?" he repeated, clearing his throat of uncertainty. "Someone call?" This time, as he waited—sure enough!—he heard a rustling in the bushes. It was coming from the left, a little way down the path. Aha! he would turn the tables, sneak up on *them* this time.

Although the path was strewn with twigs and cones and needles, Andrew did his best to steal along it quietly until he came to the source of the disturbance: a deep bed of ferns whose fronds were being deflected every which way as if by a rolling dog. Yet who or what was actually responsible for the agitation remained a mystery. The only evidence of the intruder's presence was the fitful movement of the fronds and an occasional crackling of twigs. That it might be one of the children, hiding in the ferns, seemed now out of the question. Out of the question, too, was the idea that the creature in the ferns had been the one who summoned him. . . . But if not, who?

Andrew stood stock-still. Apart from natural curiosity, what kept him glued to the spot was his fear of startling the creature and scaring it off or, even worse, provoking it to attack. And so he waited, motionless and watchful, as the fronds continued to dip and sway. It wasn't long, however, before the movement ceased and Andrew heard, or thought he did, a muted grunt, halfway between a *hmm* of satisfaction and a *humph* of irritation. A moment later there emerged from the ferns a head of lank black hair, a hood, hanging down over a smallish pair of shoulders, rather shapeless under the bulk of a loose-fitting leather tunic—presumably brown once but faded now and time-worn—which, considering the season, made the wearer look overdressed. The wearer was indeed a child, but of what age and sex, Andrew couldn't tell because the child was standing with its back turned, elbows crooked, looking down at something in its hands or on the ground.

"Box turtle?" Andrew, taking care not to startle the child, inquired gently, too gently, perhaps, since the question went unanswered. "Excuse— Was it you who called?"

When the child, who took its time, finally turned around, what Andrew saw was a rather stocky boy, seven or eight at most, staring at him squintingly, as if the sun were in his eyes. But since there wasn't a ray of light visible among the trees, it was hard to know what to make of the lad's expression, whether he was trying to size Andrew up or waiting defensively to be sized up. With his mouth half open, brows knit, eyes reduced to slits, he looked at once accusatory and guilty, quizzical and knowing, pugnacious and hurt. In his pudgy hands he held something, about a foot long that looked like a stick.

"What have you got there?" As the lad looked down and fingered the stick Andrew observed that his eyes remained mere slits, permanently fixed in a squint; on the other hand he was relieved to discover that the boy wasn't deaf. "Have you lost your glasses?"

After lengthy deliberation, during which he trained his narrowed eyes again on Andrew, the boy shook his head.

Since he was getting nowhere, Andrew decided to be on his way. "Well," he concluded awkwardly, "so long." But no sooner did he turn and take a step than—

"Annn-dy!"

The repetition of the call not only stopped him in his tracks but gave Andrew goose flesh. Though he hadn't a doubt where the sound had come from—farther down the path, in the general direction he was heading—he nonetheless turned back to question the lad with his eyes. In doing so, Andrew's expression practically mirrored the boy's, which hadn't changed a jot: Both were squinting now, both knitting their brows.

In response to Andrew's searching gaze the boy, still

mute, still holding the stick in both hands, began to come out of the ferns, a step at a time, lifting his legs like a clumsy ibis to clear the fronds. In addition to the tunic, the boy was wearing baggy leather trousers, tucked into knee-high leather boots. Once in the open he came over to Andrew and handed him the stick in silence. Rid of the thing, he then started down the path but shortly stopped, looked back, and beckoned with his head for Andrew to follow.

Without a moment's hesitation Andrew complied, even as he began to examine more closely what he had mistaken for a stick. Carved from bone or horn—horn, Andrew was inclined to think—the object was pointed at the tip, barbed in three places down one side, perfectly smooth down the other, with a good-sized hole drilled in the shaft just above the roughly triangular base. Judging by its rich dark patina and primitive appearance, Andrew concluded that it must be an ancient artifact—Indian, perhaps—a weapon of some sort or part of one, a spearhead used in hunting or fishing. What puzzled Andrew, among other things, was the absence from the barbs and shaft and hole of any deposit whatever: Clearly the boy had not exhumed the artifact but found it in its present pristine condition; old as it was, it looked brand-new.

From time to time, as they went on, the boy glanced back, but whether to check on Andrew or the artifact was hard to tell. Nor could Andrew tell much about their course. He had the impression they were going downhill, descending the mountain, but the question, so consequential earlier, seemed less pressing now. Whatever their course, Andrew was content to follow his guide and presently, as he rounded a boulder rounded by the boy a moment earlier, was surprised to discover that they were already emerging from the woods. Through the trees ahead nothing could be seen but open space, while to the left, less than fifty feet away, a towering crag (around which the boy soon disappeared) loomed against the stormy sky. Evidently they had come to the verge not only of the woods but also of the cliff top.

A rather steep descent circled the crag halfway, then leveled off and headed through a narrow cleft, hard between the crag and the face of the cliff. To negotiate this rugged pass, Andrew was obliged to tuck the artifact under his belt and, gripping the rock with both hands, descend the slope step by cautious step until he came to the cleft, through which he had to sidle, crouching, almost on his haunches.

Once out the other side, he straightened up only to find himself, together with his guide, perched on a perilous ledge several hundred feet above a gloomy gorge. Pulling back, Andrew pressed against the cliff. While trying to allay his fear, he heard a sudden downpour but could see no sign of rain. What he did observe, however, was that the boy was scowling at him. For his cowardice? Unlikely. It soon occurred to Andrew that his companion's disapproval was prompted by the failure of his squinting eyes to locate something they were looking for. The artifact, no doubt. "Don't fret, I still have it." Producing the spearhead, Andrew offered it to his guide, but the boy, though clearly relieved, made no move to reclaim it. All that concerned him, apparently, was its whereabouts and safekeeping. Satisfied on that score, he turned away and plodded on—rather recklessly, considering the drop—until he disappeared around a bend.

Delaying only long enough to replace the artifact under his belt, Andrew followed gingerly, keeping close to the face of the cliff. No sooner did he turn the bend, however, than he came to a standstill again, not out of fear this time but out of surprise. In contrast to the other side, here the drop was shallow—thirty or forty feet at most—and instead of a gorge, the ledge on this side overlooked a natural arena whose central space was altogether open, bare, and flat, rather like a playing field. What doubtless suggested the resemblance, and what, among other things, took Andrew so completely by surprise, was the presence on the field below of a sizable group of youngsters—mainly boys, it seemed—who were on an outing for the holiday and engaged in some kind of sport. Just what it was, whether football or soccer—there were no goals, no lines, no sign of a ball—was it possibly a track meet? What made it hard to tell was the suspension of play. Evidently time had been called, and the players—all of whom were overdressed, like Andrew's guide, in tunics, loose-fitting trousers, and soft leather boots—were doing nothing at the moment—not even talking among themselves—simply sitting on the ground or squatting on their haunches, waiting for play to resume. Their unnatural silence made Andrew conscious again of the distant downpour which, he realized now, continued unabated, if not louder than before. At the same time, he noticed another, much smaller group of boys, four in all, equipped with javelins and crouching, unobserved by the other players, behind a huge boulder on the far side of the playing field. The four seemed to be hiding, preparing to make a surprise attack. From his lookout Andrew cast an eye over the rest of the field. Behind another boulder on the right he spotted another pair of boys with javelins, and yet another, hiding in the trees below. As far as he could see, there were eight with javelins, leaving the rest, thirty or so, unarmed.

All of a sudden—actually, it was in no way "sudden," since the boys with the javelins moved so slowly and with so much stealth, it was almost like watching the rerun in slow-motion of a scrimmage on Movietone News—the four boys, javelins upraised, showed themselves on top of the giant boulder while, simultaneously, the other two pairs emerged from their respective hiding places. At sight of the armed boys the players on the field roused themselves, but listlessly. Though they looked startled and even alarmed, they didn't spring up but struggled to their feet ever so slowly and started to trot, exerting themselves strenuously but making little progress, moving, exactly like the armed boys had, in slow-motion, as if against a gale. Yet even where Andrew was standing, much higher up and more exposed than the youngsters, there was no wind to speak of, not the slightest breeze; if anything, the atmosphere was unusually dense and sluggish.

By and by, one of the boys on top of the boulder heaved his javelin—paradoxically, the arm movements were made in slow-motion, whereas the javelin itself whizzed through the air with considerable velocity—at a passing player. Much to Andrew's relief—from his vantage point it seemed that the weapon had been hurled with an intent to kill—the javelin missed the passing player. Surprisingly, the player made no move to appropriate the javelin, which had landed upright in the ground nearby, but trotted on, leaving the weapon free to be retrieved by the boy who had hurled it.

As the boy worked it loose, however, and pulled it up out of the ground, the javelin came apart in his hands—the shaft separating from the head, to which it was attached apparently by a leather thong—and the boy was obliged to get down on his hands and knees—

In sudden recognition Andrew removed the artifact from his belt. As he re-examined with repugnance the pointed tip and deadly barbs he had no doubt that the player would have been seriously wounded, had the javelin hit its mark. Not a javelin at all but a spear! What had made Andrew assume they were playing a game? Just because they were boys? Partly. And partly because of their movements: Moving in slow-motion made everything seem so uncanny, so unreal. Yet there was nothing unreal about this spearhead. Why had he been entrusted with it? . . . Reminded of his guide, Andrew tried to spot the lad on the playing field, but to no avail; not only were the boys too numerous and dressed too much alike but too much on the move to distinguish among them.

Now, as he continued to survey the field, on the lookout for a javelin without a head, another javelin went hurtling through the air. To Andrew's horror this one hit the mark. Yet even as Andrew groaned in sympathy and watched the victim slowly raise his hands, then slowly lower one, bringing it to the javelin (which was lodged in his side and which soon came apart: the shaft separating, as the player tugged at it, from the embedded head), at the same time that he staggered slowly backwards and, slowly doubling up, turned and sank slowly to the ground—even as Andrew watched all this, he wondered whether his sympathy wasn't unfounded, whether the whole spectacle wasn't an act. He half expected the victim to break the spell at any moment by leaping up and laughing out loud. Oddly enough, now that he thought about it, Andrew realized that the entire attack had taken place in silence—the victim's outcry, if indeed there was one, had been voiceless; realized, moreover, that except for the downpour and the hiss of the hurled javelins, there hadn't been a single sound since he arrived. Nor could a peep be heard this minute as the eight armed boys, sprinting eerily in slow-motion, converged on the wounded player—was he really wounded? there was no trace of blood—and, taking hold of his feet, started dragging him, together with the javelin's appendant shaft, toward the center of the field. Once there, they plunked the feet down on the ground—none of the unarmed players lifted a finger to help their comrade—and gathered in a circle, a sort of football huddle, around the victim, who was beginning to show some signs of life: slowly turning his head, flexing a leg. Seeing this, one of his captors stepped into the center of the circle, directly over the prostrate body, and, holding his javelin in both hands, raised it overhead in slow-motion and then slowly downwards, as if to run the victim through.

"Wait!" Andrew shouted out. Although no one on the field so much as glanced in his direction, the outcry achieved its desired aim: Everyone, armed and unarmed alike, froze in place.

Turning quickly to descend the slope, Andrew was startled to see his guide who had reappeared unnoticed. "What's going on down there?" he demanded. As usual the boy said nothing, merely peeped at Andrew quizzically, his mouth half open, eyes asquint, as if he not only failed to comprehend the question but were being blinded by the sun, of which there was still no sign. Rather than waste more time, Andrew tried to pass the guide, but the boy, taking advantage of his forward position and the narrowness of the ledge, wouldn't let him, remained in the lead.

To reach the field they had first to complete their circuit of the ledge which, on this side of the bend, doubled back, away from the field, for about thirty yards, before ending in a thicket, covering the adjacent slope. Along the way Andrew caught a glimpse, through the treetops on his right, of something milky, moving in the middle distance down below. Just what it was he couldn't figure out until he became conscious again of the rush of the downpour, filling his ears, and realized all at once that what he was gazing at was the foaming crest of a waterfall whose cascade he couldn't see. He had no way of gauging its drop but, judging by the intensity and range of the roar, guessed it must be at least as great as the drop on the other side—two hundred feet or more.

By the time they reached the playing field Andrew found all the boys sitting cross-legged in a circle, as though around a campfire. But instead of a fire, in the center were a pair of boots—the victim's?—and a neatly folded garment which, however simple and incongruous, were endowed with a kind of sanctity by the solemn, tenaciously silent congregation.

From outside the circle Andrew couldn't find a clue to the victim's identity. Close as he scrutinized the faces he could see, all the boys looked equally innocent, equally guilty, perhaps because all of them were squinting like his guide. But apart from their eyes and winter clothes, there was nothing unusual about the group—just a bunch of city kids on an outing for the weekend.

Before Andrew had a chance to question them about the victim, his guide, long since inside the circle, beckoned him to follow, and Andrew, determined to get to the bottom of what he had seen, entered resolutely. Yet scarcely had he reached the center, when he was brought up short. What stopped him was the pair of boots. From the distance he had assumed they were a boy's, but realized now that they were large enough to fit a man, a man his size; whereupon it crossed his mind that he himself might be the chosen victim! The possibility prompted him to flee. Pivoting impulsively, he was reminded not only of how outnumbered he was but also of the ready arsenal of javelins. Not wanting then to betray his fear, he checked himself, came full circle, and continued walking toward his guide.

The boy was standing now in profile, just to one side of a tawny-faced lad who was sitting directly in line with the boots. Judging by the guide's subordinate position, Andrew surmised that the tawny lad must be the leader of the group. And yet he seemed in no way different from the rest, neither older, bigger, nor differently dressed. His one distinguishing feature, as far as Andrew could perceive, was that he wasn't squinting: His eyes were firmly closed. Nevertheless, the minute Andrew came into his presence, the boy held out his hand in greeting. Since the palm was upturned, Andrew was at a loss to know what was expected of him, whether to shake or pat or clasp the offered hand. Deciding on the latter, he crouched to touch the stubby fingers, but even as he did, the boy withdrew his hand. Confused, Andrew looked to his guide for assistance. In response the boy pointed at the spearhead, which Andrew was still holding but had forgotten about. He delivered the spearhead to the leader who, though his eyes remained shut, received it without fumbling, raised it ceremoniously, and returned it to the guide. That done, the leader tilted back his head as if he were trying, despite his lowered lids, to look Andrew in the eye. Whatever his intention, the gesture failed to convey it. Once again Andrew was confused. This time, however, the leader himself came to his aid. Brushing aside his lank black hair, he cupped a hand to his ear. Evidently he was waiting for Andrew to speak.

To his surprise Andrew found himself tongue-tied. Though he had come down from the cliff solely to confront these boys, he was silenced now by their leader's expression. Seldom, if ever, had he seen on any face such unguarded innocence, unless sometimes on the faces of his sons asleep. But this lad wasn't sleeping. And yet, as with Mat and Chris, Andrew had the urge now to caress the unseeing youth—his slightly smiling, upturned face seemed, in fact, *waiting* to be caressed; at the same time, however, the boy evinced the self-sufficiency and reserve, the virtual inviolability of a sage, and Andrew kept his distance. What created the paradox was the hidden eyes. Behind the lowered lids the eye muscles were working earnestly like those of a blind person. Yet Andrew was all but certain that the boy could see, certain, moreover, that he had closed his eyes only to find within himself the answer to a question as yet unasked by Andrew. That it ought to be a question, rather than small talk, Andrew grasped from the grave, almost oracular, set of the youngster's brow.

When at last the question surfaced (welling from what depths, Andrew scarcely knew), he voiced it in a dry whisper, quickened by a pressing urgency and a sense of loss that verged on tears. "What became of the boy?"

In acknowledgment the leader bowed his head and signaled to the guide who, in turn, moved to the center of the circle and took up the boots and garment. Simultaneously, the boy to the right and left of the leader stood up, came forward and, crouching like Andrew, began to unlace his shoes.

Andrew offered no resistance. On the contrary, he co-operated fully by sitting on the ground and stretching out his legs. The fear that had gripped him earlier was gone, replaced now by a feeling of extraordinary quietude, a quietude which seemed to complement at once the stillness of the circle, the serenity of the leader, the slow motion of the hands at work on his shoes, and the hush of the scene itself, including the soothing sound of the falls. Not even when the attendants, having removed his shoes, began to unbutton his shirt and trousers, did Andrew feel in the least afraid. He could tell from their solemnity, as well as from their hands, which, however cold, performed their tasks with tenderness, that the youngsters meant him no harm. Whatever they were doing was doubtless being done in preparation to answering his question.

Once Andrew had been stripped to his socks, the guide handed the attendants the pair of boots (they were hand-made, heelless), while the boy himself unfolded the garment (a hooded tunic much like theirs) and eased it over Andrew's head. As soon as Andrew was ready, the attendants helped him to his feet; whereupon every member of the congregation also rose, made a quarter turn, and began to move, maintaining the circle, counterclockwise. After two and a half revolutions, the leader struck out in the direction of the cliff; and all the members, leaving behind their javelins, followed double file. So long was the lapse between the moment when the leader set out and Andrew was able to start that he automatically checked his watch, forgetting that it, too, had been expropriated, together with his wedding ring.

As the silent procession moved slowly forward Andrew supposed it was heading for the cliff top. For some reason, though, those in the lead weren't mounting the slope. What they were doing, or so at least it seemed from Andrew's view, was filing into the cliffside itself, vanishing two by two. Incredible as it was, his perception soon proved true. In a recess, which he had failed to notice earlier, was a grotto large enough to accommodate the entire group twice over. He could see them now, as his guide stopped before the vaulted opening, assembled in the shadows on the right. Lined up at attention, shoulder to shoulder in a compressed body, the boys looked like they were posing for a class picture. Opposite them, on the other side of the grotto, two small jets of water, a foot or so apart, spouted from the wall into the basinlike crater of a big sprawling rock below. The only other feature of the grotto, as far as he could see, was a rather shabby deerskin, laying on the ground between the water and the boys.

In no time the leader, his eyes still closed, emerged from the recesses of the grotto carrying a squat bowl-shaped oil lamp. When he reached the foreground, the lad transferred the lamp to the guide who entered the cave and, carefully skirting the deerskin, moved toward the sprawling rock. The two attendants turned to Andrew and invited him to follow. The guide, meanwhile, having climbed onto the rock, was holding the lamp high overhead to illuminate three lines of writing on the wall above the right-hand jet. Andrew could barely make out the inscription in the feeble light. Observing this, the guide assisted him by moving the lamp from one word to the next:

DRINK OF THESE WATERS
AND ALL YE KNOW
SHALL BE FORGOT

Before Andrew finished reading, one of the attendants produced a dipper made of horn and, half filling it, passed it to Andrew. Almost too cold to drink, the water not only shocked his teeth but tasted acrid; when swallowed, it formed an icy clot first in his gullet, then in his chest, and made his head tingle slightly.

As soon as the dipper was drained, the guide hopped down from the rock, circled behind Andrew's back, and climbed up on the other side where, repeating the whole procedure, he illuminated one by one the words above the left-hand jet:

DRINK OF THESE WATERS
AND ALL YE SEE
SHALL BE REMEMBERED

Again the attendant half filled the dipper; again Andrew took it from him. This time the water was unexpectedly tepid and sweet-tasting, and Andrew downed it readily.

The ceremony done, the attendants turned Andrew around with care to face the congregation; whereat the guide, still holding the oil lamp, assumed his former position and lighted Andrew's way to the deerskin. There, the attendants motioned him to lie down, taking care, however, that he did so with his feet pointing toward the entrance. Only after he had stretched out comfortably, and the attendants were bending over him to adjust his tunic, did Andrew notice that they were no longer squinting. Their eyes were wide open now. More than that, there was no distinction whatsoever between the pupil and the iris, and almost none between the iris and the cornea; the entire orb looked translucent, bluish-gray like a moonstone. To satisfy his curiosity Andrew turned to see whether the guide's eyes were also open, but was distracted by two boys who stepped from the ranks, carrying a pair of levers. With these they soon set to work prodding the mossy floor just beyond Andrew's head. After a good deal of trial and error they finally jimmied up a disc of stone, about the size of a manhole cover, which released a sudden puff of stale dank air from the subterrane.

Once the cover was out of the way, a wide-eyed boy with plump cheeks stooped to place a bowl-shaped oil lamp in Andrew's palm. Simultaneously two other lads stationed themselves at the foot of the pallet, facing Andrew; while yet a fourth—a youth whose eyes, peculiarly, were closed —kneeled at Andrew's side. So soporific was the lamplight, playing on the sleek knobby ceiling, that Andrew thought he was drifting off of his own volition until he felt the coldness of someone's fingertips, gently closing his lids. No matter—he couldn't keep them open anyway. Nor did he have a mind to open them again, not even when, presently, he felt the foot of the pallet being jostled, lifted up off the floor, felt the blood flowing to his head, felt his head and shoulders slipping backwards off the pallet into thin air.

II

Flat on my back I'm inching forward, heeling my way, headfirst, along a cramped, downward-sloping tunnel. What makes the going slow is the angle of the slope—too slight to speak of. A little steeper, and there'd be no problem: I could slide. That's how smooth the stone is, even slippery in spots, coated with slime. From snails? Was this once a sea spout? Possibly, judging by the color of the walls: emerald green. Or are they ocher? Hard to tell. The light's too dim, flame too low, almost failing—not enough oxygen. I feel it, too, breathlessness, from more than mere exertion. But still, best go on the way I have: at a snail's pace—is the slime from *me?*—using my elbows and heels. My only fear, besides asphyxiation—my skull, it feels so vulnerable, exposed. We were never meant to come at anything headfirst. No matter. Doesn't bother me, nothing does, so long as the lamp stays lit. What bothers me—there *is* one thing: the silence. Absolute, except for the sound of my own breathing: labored, dry. Hate that sound. Makes you know there's nothing else; *nothing* . . . but extinction. Our sole hope. If only our bodies concurred, could even conceive of extinction, it would be a cinch: I could stop, doze off— But no, the body burrows on. . . .

Uh! What's this? Sudden dip—more, a drop! Sheer. Nothing to support my head, hanging upside down now— over what? A shaft? How deep? Hollow as far down as I can reach. I'm going back. To what? Wait! The air, isn't there more air? Wishful thinking. No, don't you feel it? a little current coming from below. Yes! The flame—yes!—a little fuller. Dampness, too. Water at the bottom? Maybe. Drop something and see. Such as? A boot. Need them. For what? If it lands, you'll retrieve it; if not . . . Go on. . . . Can't! can't reach it, too cramped. Pry it off. . . . Can't, too tight. Forget the boot, take the risk. And drown? No choice. Go on. Brace yourself, elbows against the sides, slow the descent. Ready? As I'll ever be. Then go! . . . slowly . . . slow-ly. . . .

At the bottom now I'm bent in two, trunk and legs almost upright, still inside the tunnel, hands as well, still holding the lamp; head and shoulders out, all but flat in darkness. Ludicrous position. No concussion though. Landing cushioned. Not by water. Mud, I think—maybe clay—head embedded in mud, up to the ears. Must get out, extricate myself completely. . . . Use your legs, arch them. . . . That's it. Now push! . . . push— Stop! Only getting in deeper. Try to wriggle out. That's it. . . . Stop! Sinking, mud too soft. Bring your hands out. What about the lamp? Let it go. And lose the light? There's none as is. Come now, right arm first. That's it. . . . Can't! stuck! Don't panic. Stuck! Relax— Stuck, I'm stuck! 'Ahhh!'

Some—something has me by the head! holding fast— hands! a pair of hands, powerful, clamped to my skull, pressing hard, crushing me, tugging, tugging at my temples— They're going to tear my head off! 'Help! help!' help *the hands*, co-operate. The only way. Don't resist. Use your legs to shove. That's it, in concert with the hands. That's it, with every tug a shove. That's it: Shove! . . . shove! . . . shove! . . .

Crying now convulsively. . . . Don't! . . . don't! . . . don't know why, whether from relief at being out of there or from terror at being *here*, on my back, twitching in the mud. Covered with mud: hair, face, eyes— Open them. Afraid. Open them, even so. . . .

Light! . . . wavering . . . lamps . . . three: squat, bowl-shaped lamps—not unlike the one I just lost—cupped in outstretched palms. . . . Figures! standing . . . three . . . no, four (one without a lamp), grouped around me, beyond my head. Four men . . . faces shadowed . . . beardless . . . bodies bulky, naked, scarred—no not naked, wearing tunics—a lot like mine—tunicked to the thigh, bare below

. . . legs quite short but muscular, slightly bowed . . . no boots. . . . Best sit up, thank them— Oh! two more, but youths, facing me . . . boys . . . tunicked as well . . . bodies hairless—can't be more than ten years old—stepping toward me now, one on either side. For what? . . . To sniff me! on their hands and knees: one savoring my groin; the other, armpits, scalp. . . . Satisfied, apparently, they help me up. 'Thank you.'

The words reverberate. This chamber must be cavernous. Can't see the roof, too high, the light too feeble. I turn to thank the men. Having set down their lamps, they're bending over, gathering up their gear: a leather pouch with thongs, a knapsack, buckets, bowls, a sheaf with different-length sticks— Or are they bones? No telling . . . what *anything* is, under all those wrappings, especially that hulking, dome-shaped object, which comes up to the knees, and is almost as broad as the armspan, of the man responsible for portering it. Despite its unwieldy appearance, he manages to lift and hold the thing with relative ease.

As soon as they're ready, the men fall in line. 'Come,' says the one in the lead to the youths.

'Come,' the youths repeat to me and show me to my place: at the very middle of the line, between the youths, preceded and followed by two of the men. All the men are shorter than I, by a head at least, and yet they've grouped me with the youths. The disparity's confusing, makes me feel at once older than the adults, younger than the youths.

We're moving along rather rapidly, very rapidly, in fact, almost double time, bearing left, about to leave this chamber, it seems . . . yes, the lamps up front already lighting the start of a passageway, just high enough for the men to hold themselves erect. I'll surely have to stoop. . . . As we reach the opening the boy ahead turns to caution me about the clearance. I nod my thanks and smile. More than stoop, I have to crouch, doubled over, hands on knees for support. . . . Really oppressive in here, clammy . . . insufficient oxygen again . . . still muddy underfoot, have to shuffle . . . wall slick with sludge— 'Sorry.' Bumped into the boy ahead of me. . . . Seems to have stopped all of a sudden. Everyone has. For what?

'Kos,' explains the man, second from the lead, speaking in an undertone to the men behind me. They crane their necks, peer down the passageway. I do the same. In the distance another lamp, another figure, also at a standstill, is facing us.

'Go back!' the figure shouts, his voice resounding through the passageway.

The man in the lead ignores the warning—command, I should say—resumes moving. The rest of us follow.

'Zon! Listen,' the figure shouts again, 'go back!'

The man in the lead, the one called Zon, pays no attention, continues advancing.

At the end of the passageway, in the center of a sort of rotunda, stands the man called Kos, together with another man, their shadows huge against the dome. Both are wearing tunics, bare below the thighs, exactly like the others, except that these two look much younger—in their late teens, I would guess. As we enter the rotunda Kos steps forward to confront Zon, while the rest of us fall out of line and crowd around. 'So, you still mean to go through with it, the instruction?'

Zon, who, I now see, must be twice as old as Kos, says nothing, answers with a solemn nod.

'Not before you give us back the blood you stole!' Kos reaches for the leather pouch, hanging now from the older man's neck.

Zon is quick to safeguard the pouch with his elbow. 'It's you, you despoilers, who stole the holy blood.'

'To keep it from the women,' Kos explains.

'In that,' replies the older man bitterly, 'you have succeeded.' Saying no more, Zon turns and starts to move on.

The younger men block his path, interpose themselves between Zon and the start of another passageway, opposite the one we entered by. 'Don't you understand?' Kos shakes his head impatiently, as though he were the elder and Zon the youth. 'The labor'—he gestures toward the far end of the chamber, drawing my attention to yet another passageway—'the labor has begun.'

'We understand.' In contrast with the younger man's perturbation, Zon shows nothing but restraint, dignity. 'The labor is what brings us, what necessitates the instruction.'

'The instruction,' Kos retorts hotly, 'is a pack of lies!'

Stiffening, Zon takes hold of a sizable amulet, also hanging from his neck, as if to protect it from hearing what the younger man just said. 'You call Holy Mother lies?'

'Don't twist our words.'

'The gravest lie is yours,' Zon declares, 'the lie of you despoilers: to pull down Holy Mother, put yourself in Her place.'

'We'll soon see who's lying.' Kos stalks away, comes over to the youths and me. 'Kala, Olo'—he lays his hand on my sleeve, taking me, as well, into his confidence—'pay no heed—'

Zon, letting go the amulet, slaps his thigh resoundingly. 'Kos!'

'It's not the holy blood,' Kos, ignoring Zon, continues rapidly, addressing me, 'not the Host—'

'Kos!' Zon, furious now, draws a weapon from his tunic. The other men in our group take the cue forthwith, turn on Kos, their daggers poised, flaked stone blades flashing in the lamplight. Kos releases my sleeve. Zon, mollified though clearly bridling, turns to Kos's comrade. 'Now let us pass.'

'Why not wait,' suggests the comrade, his tone, unlike Kos's, conciliatory, reasonable, 'till we see the outcome?'

'Of what?' says Zon.

'The labor,' says the comrade. 'No point in giving the instruction—'

'No point,' Zon is quick to retort, 'but the point of appearance itself! The instruction *will* be given,' he asserts with utmost authority, 'given them'—Zon designates Kala, Olo, and me—'just as it was given you, given us, given all who ever were or will be with the Mother, regardless of the outcome. The outcome—understand this, Kos—is of no importance, affects nothing.'

'Everything!' Kos disputes the point impassionedly, trembling from head to toe. 'Everything will be affected!'

'Nothing!' Zon stands fast.

'Once the infant appears—'

'*If* the infant appears—'

'—we'll have the proof!' Kos contends.

'Of what?' demands a stentorian voice—a woman's, if I'm not mistaken—coming from the passageway at the far end of the rotunda. Only her face—her round, full, uncanny-looking, lamplit face—is visible in the shadows. Just how long she's been standing there is hard to say. 'Proof of what?'

Kos hesitates, his bearing appreciably different now in the presence of the woman, less self-assured, belligerent.

'Well, Kos?' Zon goads the younger man. ' "Of what?" Mas asks. Answer her.'

'*This*'—Kos takes hold of his genitals—'the horn—us!'

'You!' The woman, Mas, silences Kos with contempt. 'If the infant appears, it will appear in spite of you, you despoilers—appear, like every infant always has, through Holy Mother's favor.' Pausing, the woman brings something to her lips; like Zon, she, too, has an amulet, which she kisses now devoutly. 'And if it appears only to disappear again, or appears deformed or blind, that, too, will come about through Holy Mother, in retaliation for your sacrilege. Either way, *you* don't enter into it. Now stop your bawling,' Mas commands, 'and let us go about our business.'

Kos does as he is told. 'Come,' he mutters to his comrade. 'Let them keep the blood, give the instruction—they'll never have the chance again.'

'Zon!' Mas calls out excitedly. 'You have it, the holy blood?' Zon hurries across the rotunda and shows the woman the leather pouch, at sight of which Mas heaves an audible sigh. 'Holy Mother, be praised,' she says in a reverential tone, whereat all the men and boys repeat the phrase in unison. Mas turns away, obscuring the light from her lamp, which quickly fades as she withdraws down the passageway.

We collect our things and take the other passageway, opposite the one we entered by, out of the rotunda. Oddly, the episode prompts no discussion, not a single comment. How I wish it did—if only to throw some light on what just happened. That somewhere a baby is soon to be born, and that during the labor we, the boys and I, are to be given some kind of 'instruction,' that much I understand, but little else: not why the younger men, the 'despoilers,' oppose the instruction, nor why Kos took hold of his genitals that way—as 'proof' of what?—nor who the Holy Mother is. Is the amulet an image of the deity or the deity Herself? Is Mas, perhaps, the Holy Mother—she certainly commanded that kind of respect—or merely Her priestess? And what of the pouch of blood? . . .

The men maintain their silence. Perhaps they're listening for something. Perhaps it's more important here to listen than to speak. Perhaps their lives—mine, too—depend on it, on keeping their ears— Is that the sound of water? . . . Yes. And not just ordinary water either, more like a torrent, a flash flood, roaring toward us!

Zon raises his lamp. Alerted this time, I take care not to collide with Kala, the lad in front of me, as the file halts and Zon sets down his gear. Thereupon, the second man steps forward and, assuming an audacious lunging stance—evidently we're at the brink of some sort of precipice: a shaft, perhaps, or gorge—holds out his lamp as far as possible over what must be a waterway below. At the same time, the two men from the rear hurry to the front and drop their gear next to Zon's. Zon? . . . Seems to have disappeared, no sign— Oh! now I see: The carrier of the dome-shaped object has begun to lower himself—by means of a heavy rope, held by a knob of rock—into the gorge, while the other man —flat now on his belly, head and shoulders protruding beyond the brink—starts, with the help of Kala, to hand the lamps and gear over the side.

Once the transfer's been accomplished, the man himself descends, followed in short order by Kala. My turn next. I step to the brink and look down. 'Please!' I appeal to Olo to go first. The lad obliges. What made me draw back was the drop, a good thirty feet sheer to the water—hazardous rocks in a raging river, rapids fed by a falls upstream, the men huddled on a ledge two-thirds of the way down.

'Now you.' The man with the lamp bids me descend. 'Go!'

Holding fast, I start down—not rope at all but numerous thongs, plaited into a heavy line. Not too bad, once you get the hang of it. . . . At the bottom someone helps me onto the ledge as the final man, the one with the lamp, using one hand only, follows.

The file reassembles, and Zon, after turning sharply left and guiding us through a sudden grove of stalactites and stalagmites, gets down on all fours. . . . We're entering a tunnel—the sound of the falls suddenly hushed—crawling at an incline over sand . . . perfectly dry . . . arduous going. Though not, of course, for Olo who's at my heels, nudging me along. Perhaps he's as eager as I am to get out of here. No air at all, lamps at their dimmest yet . . . heart throbbing violently. Can't even crawl now, roof too low; have to caterpillar on our bellies. . . . Don't think I'm going to make it, lungs not used—light fade. . . .

Must have blacked out for a moment—boy behind me, jiggling my foot. I recover, pick myself up. Better now, end in sight, lamps ahead a little brighter.

The tunnel leads into a spacious chamber—our destination, judging by Zon and the second man who are busy unpacking their gear. Before I have a chance to look around, Zon comes forward, lamp in hand, and makes a rotating motion with his forefinger. Kala and Olo do an about-face. I follow their example.

'Rest,' says Zon.

We sit down facing the black hole of the tunnel mouth, our backs to the chamber. The lamplight fades, leaving us in shadow. The stone is cold. Kala and Olo don't seem to mind. They're sitting perfectly still, arms wrapped around their legs, chins resting on their knees, waiting no doubt for the instruction to begin. Vexing word, *instruction*, ambiguous at best, even a trifle sinister. Can't imagine what those men are up to. I turn to see.

'Sssst!' one of the men hisses disapprovingly, motions me to look away.

From the little I could make out, the man who hissed was raised above the rest on a ledge at the rear of the chamber. In the open space below the ledge Zon, kneeling sidewise, was burying something in a shallow pit. Whatever they're doing is being done with their usual silent dispatch. No, just then there was the faintest rattle, suggestive of beads being handled. And now, someone has begun to intone a soft, somewhat eerie strain, which rises higher gradually, grows louder, sadder, more impassioned, almost inconsolable—an ululation, yet skillfully controlled, quavered, held longer than I would have thought anything but wind could wail. At last the mourner's breath gives out, but not the sound of the grief, which still reverberates through the chamber, even as the soft lament begins anew.

'Uhh!' Someone just tapped me on the skull from behind, scared me half out of my wits. Imitating the boys, I stand up and turn around. Facing us is the man, altogether naked now, who acted as our beacon at the gorge. Again he holds a lamp, the oil very low.

'We are ready,' he informs us.

Olo looks puzzled. 'El,' he addresses the man, 'do we strip, too?'

'Do nothing,' El replies, 'except by example.' Without another word he turns and leads us toward the center of the chamber.

Zon, also naked, is sitting cross-legged on a piece of hide, his body swaying back and forth, tossing slightly, hands covering most of his face but the lips, parted to release the continuing lament. Beside him on the hide is an array of articles: a medium-sized clamshell, still hinged, several stone tools, the leather pouch of blood, and a number of bowls whose different-colored contents I can't identify. The man who, earlier, hissed at me from the ledge, is on our level now, his naked back to us. At the moment, he's bending over, busily mixing something by the light of the third lamp. On the ledge are a couple of sticks—perhaps they're bones— of various sizes, two buckets, and several lumps of something black . . . charcoal maybe. As for the fourth man, he's nowhere to be seen.

El has grouped us side by side—Olo to the right of me, Kala to the left—facing the overshadowed rear wall, some fifteen feet away. Having stepped behind us, El removes Kala's tunic. As soon as he's naked the youth places the garment neatly on the ground, whereupon El undresses me. Stripped to the boots—surprisingly, it's not as cold as I thought—I, too, sit down cross-legged on my folded tunic. Kala, quick as usual to be of help, prompts me to remove my boots, while El attends to Olo.

Once we're settled, Zon, wailing without cease, un-covers his face. His eyes are closed. Presently he reaches out in our direction, his disproportionately large hands moving slowly, fingering the air as though searching for something tangible. Not finding what they're looking for, his hands diverge, branch off in opposite directions, explor-ing by touch the surrounding space, but to no avail; empty, the hands pull back, cover again the haggard face. At the same time, El has joined in the search, but far more actively than Zon. Moving about with a good deal of show and cere-mony, he stalks the shadows, using his lamp to explore the chamber's most remote and obscure reaches. Occasionally he lifts the lamp overhead, illuminating some fantastically convoluted swirl of stone.

'Where? . . . where? . . . where? . . .'

This sudden outcry returns my attention to Zon who has ended his lament. Sitting now with his head bent back, eyes shut, arms outstretched, he soon begins to speak—recite, to be exact—in a strained and husky tone:

> *Where have You gone*
> *Holy Mother*
> *Where have You gone*
> *Mother Moon*
> *We have searched*
> *Your seeping cavities*
> *Stone-trunked forests*
> *Beds of clay*
> *Searched even this*
> *Your secret hiding place*
> *Sacred lair but find*
> *No sign of You*
> *The ardent face*
> *The sweet white fat*
> *We cannot be without*

At least that clarifies my earlier uncertainty about the Holy Mother. The deity for whom this whole long trek—pilgrimage, I suppose you could call it—has been a kind of quest is neither Mas nor the amulet but the moon.

' "Sweet white fat" '—Kala nudges me to join him and Olo in the refrain. ' "We cannot be without." '

Once again Zon buries his face, resumes lamenting. This time, however, the lament is echoed not only by the chamber but also by the boys and men. Though El continues to move about, presumably in search of Holy Mother, the other man, the one at the ledge, has interrupted what he was doing to examine his right hand in the lamplight. His fingers are stained with blood. The 'holy blood,' I wonder, from the leather pouch? No, the pouch is where it was, next to Zon, who now takes up the recitation.

> *Holy Mother*
> *Let us know You*

Have not left us
Disappeared for good
Bring to light
Your surfaces—

I've been distracted by the man with the bloodstained fingers, who suddenly mounts the ledge and, bending over, picks up the lamp with his clean hand. Straightening up—heavens! are those pictures?—he smears some of the blood onto the stone. Although, at present, his body's in the way —not only of the wall, but of the feeble light—I could swear that what I just now saw, as he raised the lamp, was pictures.

—egg-filled fish
Tracked upstream
By dappled seals
Bring to light
Your tender shoots
Creeping lichen
Pale gray moss—

Yes, as the man steps aside, backs from the wall with his lamp outheld to appraise the drying smear of blood, I see a number of recognizable images: an eye, an ear, an antlered head, upraised muzzle, downward-sloping shoulder—reindeer! a sportive group of reindeer. Most of them are painted yellow, excepting the first in the group, the one with the antlered head, whose body is red, a rather dirty-looking shade which almost matches the smear— Perhaps that isn't blood after all but some sort of pigment, perhaps the man is merely an artist, matching colors.

A doleful outcry from Zon elicits from the others, men and boys alike, renewed moaning.

Light us Holy Mother
Light our failing lamps
In Your absence
We lose presence
Lose the place
Wherein we dwell
Your body the abode
We cannot be without

157

' "Your body the abode," ' the boys and I repeat, ' "we cannot be without." '

In the interlude between the lamentation and the ensuing verse, El comes into the foreground, sets down his lamp, and kneels in front of the articles lined up next to Zon. From one of the bowls he selects a cube of something white, from another a small gray ball of matted stuff. With these he moves on his knees toward Zon and, reciting prayerfully, ' "Light us, Holy Mother," ' eases the cube into Zon's lamp. After waiting a moment, he ignites the matted stuff and drops it, too, into the lamp. Soon the lamp burns brighter.

> *Look She smiles*
> *Holy Mother*
> *Shows Her teeth*

Now Zon, who has also risen to his knees, slides aside a slab of stone. Underneath is a shallow pit from which he takes an oblong object, wrapped and laced in chamois. While Zon undoes the wrappings, El repeats the lamp-lighting ritual, refueling first his own lamp, then that of the artist, who has left the ledge and joined his comrades, bringing with him both his lamp and the bucket of blood—or—or pigment.

Unwrapped, the oblong object proves to be the amulet, worn earlier by Zon. Carved from ivory or bone, it amounts to little more than a straight stout rod, a foot or so long, with two pronounced knobs a third of the way down the shaft and a hole at the top to accommodate a thong. Even as Zon gazes at the amulet with reverence, he reaches behind himself blindly and, picking up a pointed piece of flint, uses it to incise the rod. I see now that there are many such incisions on the shaft, see also— It's bleeding! S-smeared, I mean, with blood—or whatever; pigment—which wasn't there till Zon incised the bone. That done, he takes the shaft in both hands and, righting it slowly, raises the rod to eye level. Goodness! it's a figure—the angle changes everything—a female figure: The upper third constitutes the head and neck; the hole, its eye; knobs, the breasts; shaft, the legless trunk. Zon slips the thong over his head.

Rejoice rejoice
Holy Mother
Reappears
Releasing holy blood

The minute Zon falls silent, the artist whisks away the bucket and, returning to the ledge, starts to prime the wall. Almost simultaneously, a muted bellowing commences, issuing from a dark recess to the right of the ledge. At first the sound consists of one note only—a sharp urgent monotone, sustained for several measures; but presently the note begins to rise, becoming strident, shrill: a frantic, high-pitched shrieking, followed all at once by a series of low-pitched, oestrual grunts— There's an animal somewhere in this chamber! Gives me goose flesh. Kala, on the other hand, doesn't look the least perturbed, simply engrossed, excited.

Listen grunting
Far-off hoofbeats
Of the Host
Holy Mother's
Horn-crowned brood

Wasn't something said earlier, in the rotunda, about the 'Host?' ' "It's not the holy blood," ' Kos said, ' "not the Host." ' '. . . Hoofbeats' . . . Could be horses, I suppose, a herd of horses—no, not 'horn-crowned'—bison, maybe, yet all the pictures— Reindeer! that's what it is, the Host, a herd of reindeer. So, that's what bellowed a moment ago—they've got a reindeer in that recess!

Take up your horns
To greet the Host
Slake Her mighty thirst

Confused by 'horns' and 'horn-crowned,' I turn for guidance to Kala and Olo, both of whom have gotten to their feet. I do the same. Even so, Kala nudges me, as though I had omitted something, motions with his head toward El. The man is holding his penis. So are the boys holding theirs. El is waiting for me to follow suit. As I do he suddenly grows curious, brings the lamp close to my groin.

159

He looks perplexed. Letting go his own penis, El takes hold of mine to examine it. Evidently something troubles him. The boys look, too; they, too, are troubled. All three frown, exchange puzzled glances. Oh, now I understand, it's the glans that troubles them, the fact that I've been circumcised; clearly they've never seen the like, don't know what to make of it. For a moment El hesitates, turns toward Zon, as if ready to interrupt the recitation, confer about my penis, but soon thinks better of it, takes hold of his own once more, and lights our way to an area on the right. There, El groups us in a semicircle, facing him and the rear of the chamber. Beyond El's shoulder I can see the black mouth of the recess from which, I'm all but certain, the grunting came.

> *Pour yourselves*
> *Upon the ground*
> *Pour yourselves*
> *In pools for Her*
> *Pools of thanks*
> *Upon the lichen*
> *Laved to please*
> *The Holy Host*

El has begun to urinate—so have Kala and Olo—aiming the jets at a hollow in the stone at our feet. The power of suggestion induces me to do the same. When we're finished, El says, 'Holy Host, be pleased,' and we repeat the phrase. Then all of us, guided by El, back away from the font, withdrawing to our former places, except that now El has us sit facing the font instead of the rear wall.

> *Behold the boundless forest*
> *Of horn-crowned heads*
> *On the move*
> *The dun-brown sea*
> *Of bobbing backs*
> *White-capped coats—*

I've been keeping an eye on the recess, waiting for the animal to charge out. Not yet—thank goodness! Nor has it bellowed again, not a sound. Puzzling. There! just then, a distant rattle . . . beads once more, but not, as earlier, merely handled; this time they're being shaken, rattled deliberately, rhythmically, creating a definite beat. The beat is taken up by Zon who produces it with one hand only, sounding the fingers against the palm. No, it can't be his fingers; the sound is much too clacking, sharp. He must be holding something, striking together— Oh, now I see: the clamshell.

> *They come They come*
> *On spindly legs*
> *Huge splayed feet*
> *Clicking with each step*

Both the rattle of the beads and the clacking of the shell continue, but at different tempos, with different tones. As the rattle quickens, loudens, clearly coming closer, the clacking grows softer, slows appreciably (how deftly Zon handles, *plays*, that shell), arousing feelings of expectancy, suspense, feelings reinforced by El who moves now with his lamp to the far side of the recess. Zon, meanwhile, working the shell fervently, sounds a sharp arresting roll, prolonged to increase the suspense, command attention. All eyes are fixed on the recess. Suddenly the rattling is punctuated by a sharp report (a clack of the clamshell), repeated once! . . . twice!. . . . Silence. Even the rattling has ceased.

'Eeee-ya!' someone exclaims.

Oh, my! The tip of a horn just jutted into sight, emerging from the dark very slowly, calmly—perhaps they have the creature tethered; tethered or not, the horn strikes terror to the heart—several tips, in fact, tines, an antler, lowered to charge. Can't see the muzzle— Wait! the head's begun to rise. . . . There is no muzzle, merely a long pointed beard . . . large pointed ears . . . eyes outlined in charcoal—*human* eyes; a man, thank heavens! masked, his hands now visible as well, but held like paws: wrists crooked, palms turned down, fingers pressed together. Even the beard is false, a piece of fur cut into a triangle. Only the horns are authentic . . . and maybe, yes, the pointed ears.

Now, as if to put us at our ease, dispel all doubt, the man acknowledges the disguise, begins to bellow, shriek, and grunt once more. Ironically, the exploit has the opposite effect on me, makes me break out in goose flesh again. Though I see the man beneath the mask, I somehow can't believe human lungs capable of producing such sounds—bestial, awesome, terrible, especially the grunts! That it *is* a man, I have no doubt, though unlike the rest of us he hasn't disrobed. What creates the rattle is several pairs of anklets, composed not of beads but of largish canines.

Crouching now to half his height, the man bends forward until his chest is all but parallel to the ground, rump upraised, antlered head erect, hands still held like paws. In that position he begins to move—dance, I should say—no, move is better, less misleading; he moves out onto the open ground. What made me correct myself is that the movements aren't natural—to man, I mean. He's moving like an animal, a quadruped, working his arms as if they were forelegs—one arm advancing with the equivalent advancing leg, the other gliding backward—the gait extremely slow, stately, each step accented by a click of the clamshell, rattle of the anklets. Perhaps that's what made it seem a dance at first. But it's not. Nor is it mime, a man mimicking a reindeer, merely that. No. What makes it so equivocal is not the man's mimetic gift, not his concentration and superb control—those horns alone must weigh a ton—but his self-conviction, the firm belief, he plainly holds, that he *is* an animal.

Just now he's raking the ground with his forehoof, presumably trying to unearth something. After several strokes he lowers himself onto his right knee and elevates his extended left leg, dipping his head simultaneously—he *is* a dancer, after all—as if to kiss—no, lick, lick the ground, while Zon resumes the recitation.

> *How beautiful*
> *The curling tongue*
> *That crops its meat*
> *Greedily*
> *How beautiful*
> *The marrowbones—*

The artist just moved his lamp to another section of the wall on which he starts to draw, using a lump of charcoal attached to a piece of bone, the life-size foreleg . . . flank—I begin to wonder, is the artist, like the dancer, simply depicting what's being said? Not only has the dancer enacted

Zon's every word about 'sniffing the air, picking up the scent' but done so with such consummate skill as to make the words superfluous. Just at the moment the dancer is trotting, moving his arms and legs in alternating diagonal pairs, taking long, deliberately awkward strides across the open ground toward the font in which we peed.

> *—our offering*
> *The precious drink*
> *She craves and laps*
> *Into Herself*

I'm really at a loss to say whether or not the dancer, after getting down on all fours and dipping his head into the font, actually lapped up the urine—his beard was in the way. Furthermore, while drinking or feigning to drink, he was cast into shadow by El, who suddenly moved away, and seems to be heading for us, the youths and me. Before reaching us, however, El pauses to pick up one of the leather bowls next to Zon, leaving his lamp in its place. Then, motioning us to rise, he scoops from the bowl a generous glob of something that resembles lard. Whatever it is, he offers the stuff to Kala who, in turn, holds out his hand to receive it. Using his own free hand to demonstrate what should be done with the stuff, El works his fingers against the palm. Once Kala has been taken care of, El allots Olo and me, as well as the rest of the men, our respective portions. (The stuff must be lard, considering how readily it softens, spreads. Rather sweet-smelling, too.) When everyone else has been served, El comes back to us and helps himself to the lard. After coating his palm thoroughly, he smears the grease onto his penis. His penis is tumid. So, too, are Kala's and Olo's. Zon's is erect. Mine alone is flaccid. I set about to stiffen it, massaging— Not fast enough, apparently, for El, who comes to my assistance.

> *Holy Mother's*
> *Reappearance*
> *Brings about*
> *The reappearance*
> *Of the Host*
> *Reappearance*
> *Of the horn—*

There, at last, I, too, like the rest am perfectly stiff. Now, for the first time since the instruction began, Zon gets up—his left hand gripping his penis, his right upraising the amulet—and turns around to face the wall on which the artist—Goodness! it's almost finished, the painting, huge! must be ten feet long—a huge female reindeer—maybe even pregnant —outlined boldly in black, the outline all but circumscribing the jumble of smaller deer, the red and yellow ones I mentioned earlier, plus fragments of a few stray bison, bulls, and horses I hadn't noticed till now. El, meantime, having replaced the empty lard bowl, picks up a group of chopper-like tools and distributes them to me and the youths. Not really a chopper, I suppose, but some sort of weapon, a handleless dagger or axhead, perhaps, made of flaked stone. Imitating El, I grasp the weapon with my right hand (how neatly it fits into the cup of the palm), my penis with my left, and start to stimulate myself, as the four of us swing around to face the mural. We're standing side by side now, several yards in back of Zon, who still holds up the blood-stained amulet.

> Receive us Holy Mother
> Receive us Holy Host
> Receive the whetted horn

After checking to make certain that we continue to excite ourselves, El leads us forward, single file, past the dancer who is back on his feet now, twitching and trembling in some kind of transport. When we reach the mural, the artist helps us up onto the ledge. El, however, remains on the ground to see to it we line up facing the wall (in my case opposite the giant reindeer's flank), and that we raise our right hands, axheads poised to strike—continuing the while to excite ourselves.

> Give us leave
> To sheathe ourselves
> Buried firm
> Inside Your flesh
> Trade the flowing marrow
> For Your sacred blood
>
> Drive deep the horn

Confused by the injunction, I look again to Kala for guidance. The boy is rubbing his penis vigorously, his head thrown back, eyelids closed, mouth agape. 'Ya! ya! ya! eee!' he moans, as his muscles slacken and he slouches against the mural, gouges the reindeer's haunch with his axhead, and spatters the lower wall with sperm.

'Ya! ya! ya! eeee!' Olo moans.

'Eeee! eeee! eeee!' echo the men.

I close my eyes, feel someone's hand—it must be El's—replace my own. When, at last, I too begin to moan, he shoves my right arm sharply, sending the axhead's point hard against the wall. Almost simultaneously someone else lets out an explosive snort. Startled, I turn to see what's happening.

The dancer, struggling to his feet, charges us but comes to a sudden halt, a yard or so short of the ledge. There, he drops to his fists, then to his knees, and, sinking with another snort, soon keels over, his body quivering pathetically as he lifts his antlered head to stare at us; whereupon El moves in and, wielding his weapon, dispatches the creature with one quick thrust to the neck.

> See! the Loved One
> After loving
> Knuckles under yields
> Her nape to the blade
> Held thus—

El demonstrates how to grip the axhead, after which the artist, using the charcoal holder as a pointer, directs our attention back to the mural.

> —cut first
> The lower joint
> Then strip the meat
> Crack the bone
> Extract the marrow—

The butchering lesson is long, exhaustive—all the dressing done with this flaked-stone implement, called, like the penis, a 'horn.' Apparently, they make no distinction between fornication and killing; both are called 'love,' both are effected by means of the 'horn,' both result in orgasm. Perhaps they also make no distinction between themselves and the reindeer, consider themselves identical, except that all the deer, male and female alike, are regarded as female by the hunters, and all the hunters male, so that the wound created by their horns is probably thought to be vaginal, and the blood they receive in exchange for their sperm (the 'flowing marrow') to be virginal, and what they're doing when they 'drive deep the horn' is not killing at all but in some way inseminating the reindeer, invigorating themselves. . . . Toward the end of the lesson Zon cautions us to slit the throat with care, 'conserve each drop of holy blood.' Till now I had assumed that the holy blood related only to the Mother—was human, I mean, menses—but now I realize that it's reindeer blood.

Once the lesson is over, the artist dips his fingertips into the bucket of pigment and streaks the wall, below the groove left by Olo's blade, with red—a kind of sunburst, meant, I guess, to represent the blood spurting from the reindeer's wound. That done, he sets to work on the next groove, made by me. At the same time, El bids us turn around, our backs to the mural, and kneel on the ledge. The genuflection brings us to his level. El is holding the leather pouch. Zon, for his part, has restored the amulet to his neck and is holding instead the bowl of cubes used earlier to re-fuel the lamps.

> *Hear us hear us*
> *Holy Mother*
> *Thank You loudly*
> *For this gift*
> *Of pure white fat*
> *Our vital food*

Moving swiftly, El takes the bowl from Zon and gives him in exchange the pouch.

> *Louder still*
> *For the gift*
> *Imperative*
> *This holy blood*

> *Consume the Host*

Now El, taking much the same care he took with the lamps, places a cube on each of our extended tongues. However pasty, the fat tastes bland, even a trifle sweet. Must be reindeer suet, this cube of fat they call the Host, the basic staple of their diet, as well as the fuel for their lamps, whose light, like Mother Moon's, is indispensable to them.

> *Gone gone gone*
> *The horn-crowned Host*
> *To feed the daughter*
> *Feed the son*
> *Foster us*
> *Her fat become*
> *Fat of our fat*
> *Her blood our flesh*

' "Her blood our flesh," ' the boys and men piously repeat, raising for me a puzzling question. How is it that once the reindeer has been eaten, its blood, rather than the meat and suet, becomes their 'flesh'?

Zon turns and crosses to the dancer. Squatting next to the prostrate body, he unlaces the leather pouch and takes from it a lump of something, something solid—not blood at all, unless it's been preserved in some way, rendered by cooking or dried in the sun—about the size and color of a cherry. At sight of the lump, the men and boys cover their eyes and utter in unison, 'Holy Mother, be praised.' Then, handling the lump with veneration, Zon draws back the triangular beard and inserts the 'gift imperative' into the dancer's mouth.

> *Bear witness men*
> *How the Host*
> *Through Her disappearance*
> *Works our reappearance*
> *As we work Hers*
> *By grace of Mother Moon*

The dancer opens his eyes, blinks, attempts to raise himself on wobbling arms but fails, falls back to the ground. Again he strains to lift his antlered head and shoulders, the horns' great weight buckling his arms, one of which slides out from under him, sends him sprawling. He tries once more. This time he manages not only to stay aloft but to raise his rump as well. For a moment he stands unsteadily on spraddled arms, knock-kneed legs. Then he starts to back-step with his hands, causing his rump to rise with each retreating step, legs to unbend, till his hands leave the ground and, straightening up bit by bit, he gets to his feet at last.

'Eeee-ya! eeee-ya!'

Upright now, the dancer starts to swing his arms, crooked at the elbows, and bob in place, moving only his knees at first, then gradually his heels (the anklets accenting the beat), the balls of his feet firm on the ground, as if held fast by the weight of the horns. In contrast with the feet, the swinging arms are free to rise, and do: hands moving upward steadily, upward to the chest, the beard, the neck, until they reach the ears and, taking hold of the antler beams, hoist the horns high overhead, unmasking the face.

'Ya! ya! eeee!'

The dancer is the fourth man, the one who portered the dome-shaped— Naturally. Don't know why I mention that, since I knew it all along, except that, even so, the transformation took me by surprise. I had come to believe so completely in the dancer as a reindeer that to see the slaughtered animal, revivified by its own blood, rise and start to dance and then take off its horns and turn into a man was really quite astonishing. Besides, the transformation makes me understand more fully, or, at least, divine, the men's identity with the reindeer—how the animal's 'disappearance' works their 'reappearance,' how its holy blood becomes their 'flesh'—I just now saw it *happen*.

El has relieved the dancer of his mask and tunic. Unburdened now and naked like the rest of us, the man begins to move more freely, hefting his thighs, hopping from foot to foot, doing a dance in triple time, a kind of jig but circular, even as he makes the larger circuit of the open ground, his shoulders dipping from side to side, head tossing, hands clapping the beat.

'Enough!'

I alone seem to have noticed the arrival of Kos, accompanied this time not by one but three comrades, no, four— another just emerged from the mouth of the tunnel—all in their late teens, all 'despoilers,' I assume. They've spaced themselves at intervals along the entrance wall, as though to demonstrate that they outnumber us—discounting, that is, me and the youths.

' "Enough!" we said, it's done.'

Kala and Olo are the first to comply, hop off the ledge, as Kos and his men advance toward us menacingly, maintaining their open rank. In quick succession Zon and El and then the artist snatch up their lamps. The despoilers have but two between them. Obviously, without lamps either group would be at the other's mercy. Now only the dancer continues whirling, utterly oblivious of the intruders.

Kos claps his hands to break the dancer's concentration. 'Enough!' The dancer pays no attention. It may be that he's unable to stop, carried away.

'Careful,' Zon cautions Kos, 'the man's with Holy Mother.'

Kos accepts the explanation, permits the dancer to go on whirling, presumably until he drops. 'And you, boys'—Kos points to me, still on the ledge—'have you released the "flowing marrow," given thanks for the "gift imperative," the holy blood?'

Zon stiffens, glances down at the leather pouch, clutched now in his hand, as if to ask its forgiveness.

I scramble off the ledge. 'We have.'

'And has it worked your reappearance?'

The man's sardonic tone belies his seeming interest, makes me hesitate, wary of some trap, but finally I answer. 'It has.'

Kos looks skeptical but says no more, advances with deliberate steps toward the ledge. The rest of the despoilers follow, taking care, when necessary, to side-step the dancer whose spiraling has slowed appreciably. At the ledge Kos halts. 'Hold on. What's this?' He lifts his lamp to light the mural. 'Look here, men, an image of the New Deer. Nicely done, Muken,' he compliments the artist. In response the artist spits.

'Not so fast,' says one of the despoilers. 'Better look again.'

'What's that, Spar?'

'Aren't those horns?' Spar's question is rhetorical.

Kos hops up onto the ledge and raises his lamp overhead.

'Why, so they are. Odd.' He scratches his scalp in mock confusion. 'Tell us, boys—Kala, Olo—have you ever seen a New Deer, the female, with horns?' Neither boy speaks. 'Well, have you?'

Kala looks from Kos to Zon, who maintains a stoical silence, and back again. Judging by the boy's reluctance to speak and by his ambivalent expression, it's clear that Kala knows he's being used. 'No.'

'Neither have we. Not possible, since females have no horns! So Spar is right. This must be an image of the Host.'

'Holy Host,' Zon corrects the younger man. 'Hallowed be Her name.'

Ignoring Zon, Kos begins to pace the ledge as though he had already taken over the instruction and were merely pausing to collect his thoughts. Zon, for his part, seems equally determined to ignore the despoilers. He and El and the artist are busy putting on their tunics, packing the gear. Even the dancer has quit whirling, squats now in the shadows, composing himself.

'Now, boys,' Kos resumes, 'tell us this, have you ever seen the Host?' Once again the question puts Kala on the spot. 'Either you have or haven't—don't be afraid to offend.'

'Haven't.'

'Neither have we. Oh, yes'—Kos reconsiders—'*once*, when we were small—much smaller than you—they came, a handful of strays, or so the elders claimed. We didn't see them for ourselves, only the excitement—fires, feasting through the night, tears and prayers and offerings: "Thank You, thank You, Holy Mother," ' he recollects with irony. 'And they, the elders, have been waiting ever since, waiting while the Land of Ice backs off, the sea horns in, nameless animals appear, nameless plants—and still the elders go on waiting, waiting for the Host—*Holy* Host,' he corrects himself. 'Right, Zon?'

Zon interrupts what he's doing just long enough to remark dryly, 'Spare us, Kos.'

'No, *them*'—Kos points with sudden fury at the boys— 'spare them . . . the *lie*. Listen, boys—you, too'—he motions me to come closer—'that was the end of it, the last time any of us, young or old, ever saw the Host. Never again. The rest is rumor: Some roving band, encountered in the summer, reports encountering another band which, in turn, has had it from a third that somewhere in the Land of Ice a fourth has spotted the Host. But not us! Never us! For us the Host has disappeared—'

'Lies! She'll reappear!' Zon and El protest.

'Never!' counter the despoilers. 'Not until we ourselves disappear.'

'The Host is—'

'Disappeared!' Kos raises his voice above the rest. 'We tell you, boys, She's disappeared, nothing but an image now, an image in the elder's heads, an image on stone . . . like this!' He slaps the wall, hitting the mural smack in the center.

'Hands off!' comes the outcry of the artist, who promptly draws his weapon, provoking the despoilers to draw theirs.

'Wait!' Zon restrains the artist. Kos removes his hand from the wall. The mural is unsmudged. The artist puts up his weapon. The despoilers do likewise, whereupon Zon orders us to dress.

'Hold!' Kos stops us. 'We haven't finished yet. When we asked you boys if the Host had worked your reappearance, you answered, "Yes." But how? Tell us that. How, if it's disappeared? How can the blood of an *image* work your reappearance?'

'This blood'—Zon uplifts the pouch, his hand trembling with emotion—'is no image!'

'That blood,' Kos rejoins with equal vehemence, 'is the blood of the New Deer!'

'Yes! yes! The New Deer! Not the Host.' The despoilers stress the distinction.

'So what?' El breaks in. 'What if it is?'

'There! Hear that? They admit it!'

'What difference does it make?' El persists. 'Host or New, the woman is in labor!'

'Exactly!' Kos seizes on the point. 'Listen, boys, there's something you must hear—'

'Wait!' Zon breaks in, hastens toward the ledge.

'No!' The despoilers block his path. 'Let us speak! Let them hear! Out with it! once for all.'

Zon raises his hand for silence. 'We agreed to wait.'

'For what?'

'The infant's reappearance.'

'No! Now!' The despoilers stand fast. 'Let them hear it now, the lie!'

'The lie is *yours*,' Zon retorts.

'Listen, boys'—Kos turns back to us—'what you must hear—'

'We already know,' Kala states matter-of-factly. Every head, including that of the dancer, who has rejoined his companions, turns now toward the youth.

'Know what?' Kos looks both skeptical and pleased.

'That you've withheld the gift imperative, the holy blood.'

'From whom?'

'The women.'

'For how long? Do you know that as well?'

The boy holds up both hands, fingers spread.

'Right, ten moons. What else?'

'Erta is in labor.'

'That's it!' Kos heaves a sigh and grins complacently while the rest of the despoilers nod and comment among themselves. 'Now then, tell us this: Have you any idea what that means?' Kala shrugs. 'Olo?' Kos waits in vain for the boy to answer, then motions to me. 'You?'

'Nothing!' Zon asserts. 'It means nothing.'

'*Nothing?*' scoffs Kos. 'Don't you understand, boys?' Still on the ledge, he squats to meet our eyes, his own intense with concentration, his voice hushed. 'It means that something other than a bag of blood'—he flaps his wrist dismissively at the pouch in Zon's hand—'works our reappearance.'

'Only Holy Mother!' Zon declares.

'Holy Mother!' the elders repeat in chorus.

'She alone'—Zon removes the amulet and holds it high to substantiate his argument—'brings about our reappearance.'

'Don't be intimidated, boys'—Kos is quick to reassure us— 'not by a scrap of horn. They are not the only ones who have Her image. We have it, too.'

'What?' The elders are taken aback.

'You heard us.' Kos springs to his feet. 'Show them, Flint.'

Coming forward, Flint, the man who was with Kos earlier in the rotunda, reaches under his cape and removes an amulet which appears to be a perfect replica of the ones worn by Zon and Mas. At sight of it, the elders stiffen, seem at once affronted and dismayed.

'Bring it here,' Kos calls out. Flint, crossing to the ledge, holds the replica in the lamplight. 'Come closer, boys.' Kos beckons us. Surprisingly, the elders seem more curious than we to examine the carving. 'Explain it, Flint.'

'Look, boys, these notches here'—Flint runs a finger down the left side of the shaft—'these are the New Deer's moons, starting, mind you, with the rut. This last, in blood, marks the calving. Count them.' He motions to me.

All the incisions are alike except the last, the one stained red, which is slightly shorter than the rest. 'Nine . . . unless the last—'

'Half,' Flint enlightens me. 'Now, look at this side. These are Erta's moons, starting with the vomiting. This last, in blood, was cut tonight. Count them.' Again he designates me.

The marks on this side are altogether uniform. 'Nine.'

The answer causes Kos to burst into a grin—more, an exultant smirk. The same is true of Flint, of all the younger men in fact, all are smiling now, obviously pleased with themselves, proud of themselves, enjoying their triumph over the elders who, at a signal from Zon, turn away in silence and go about their business. Their departure from the ledge only encourages Kos to grin more broadly, knowingly, while he waits for us to return his grin, share his triumph, assuming that we share his knowledge, which, of course, I don't . . . nor, judging by their blank expressions, do Kala and Olo. 'Don't you see, boys?' Kos can no longer contain himself. 'Don't you understand? It's the same! the same for both of us—Erta and the doe. Just because they bleed each moon, doesn't mean— It's not the blood—never was—not blood that brings about our reappearance. It's *this*.' He grips his genitals demonstratively. The protests of the elders are drowned out by the younger men's wild cheers and jubilation. 'Understand, boys?' Kos rushes on excitedly. 'Not this'—he snaps up from the ledge the artist's bucket into which he thrusts and then withdraws his hand, exhibiting the pigment-coated palm, blood red—'but *us*.' Once more he slaps the wall. This time, however, he defaces the mural, leaving on the reindeer's flank a perfect imprint of his hand, fingers spread.

'Us! us!' Pressing forward, the despoilers, fired by Kos's example, vie with each other for possession of the bucket, one more eager than the next to leave his imprint on the wall.

Suddenly someone behind us lets out a terrible shout. Before I have a chance to see what's happening, the despoilers disperse, fleeing in panic from the center of the ledge, leaping to the ground, pushing and tripping over each other, as Zon cries out against the artist who, having seized the headgear, the horns from the dance, charges the crowd with such propulsion only the wall can stop him. The impact of the crash produces sparks, snaps the dagger tines, sends the artist staggering backwards—stunned, it seems—while the rest of the men, sobered by the incident, look on in silence.

'No more!' Zon enjoins elders and despoilers alike. 'We know what comes of locking horns: disappearance, for *both* combatants, pitiful disappearance, so let's not lose our heads. You've had your say, you despoilers, shown your copy of the Mother.' Pensive for a moment, he strokes the amulet hanging from his neck. 'Though why, if you were going to do the forbidden'—his fierce shrewd eyes fix on Kos—'you chose to do it in the Mother's image baffles us. You should have used the image of the horn.' A wry smile curls Zon's lips. 'No matter. What matters—and let's not dwell on how it's worked!'—he anticipates himself forcefully. 'However it's worked, it's surely not by *us*, scantest of all creatures—what matters, we say, is *reappearance*, the reappearance now in progress. Come.' He turns to me and the youths. 'Collect your things. The women are waiting. We must make haste, bring Mas the gift imperative.'

'Leave the blood!' Spar demands.

'No,' Kos disagrees. 'It makes no difference *now*, now that the woman's in labor. Let them take it.'

El returns the pouch to Zon, who loops the thong around his neck, as the dancer sets about somberly to gather up the bits of broken horn and deal with the antler. The artist doesn't move, continues instead to stare in sorrow at the mural. The quality of his sadness suggests that he's grieving not for himself, his painting, but for the animal embodied therein, the giant reindeer, scarred by the horns, reduced to chattel by the despoilers' brands: three bold handprints impressed upon its flank. After a moment the artist shakes off his sorrow, tramps across the chamber to retrieve the bucket from the younger men, who give it up without a struggle. The despoilers, for their part, are huddled together now, conferring animatedly but in hushed tones among themselves. Our group is all but reassembled, dressed and ready to leave the chamber.

'Zon!' Kos stops the elder, now on his hands and knees, about to enter the tunnel. The despoilers break up their huddle, step aside to afford us an unobstructed view of Kos holding overhead the other amulet. 'Look!' Very slowly, deliberately, Kos turns the replica upside down and grips it by the head. Amazing! the effect. A mere flick of the wrist and the Holy Mother's body becomes a lusty phallus, Her breasts a pair of testicles. 'See?' He smiles guilefully. 'The horn you spoke of.' The transformation make the younger men guffaw. The elders avert their eyes and spit. Without a word Zon ducks his head and crawls out of sight, followed in short order by El. While waiting my turn, I look back at the despoilers. By now they're doubled up, slapping their thighs and sputtering with laughter. To further convulse them, Spar gets hold of the amulet, sticks it between his legs, and struts the length of the ledge.

The artist pokes me hard. 'Move!'

I scramble into the tunnel.

Strange, but going back seems much shorter than coming, easier too. Though I understand much better now the dispute between the elders and the despoilers, I only vaguely understand the crisis that brought it about—the disappearance of the reindeer. What exactly made them disappear? Doubtless it has something to do with the Land of Ice—how did Kos put it?—backing off, the ocean horning in. Some sort of cataclysm has occurred, causing the reindeer to be replaced by a different species, what they call the New Deer. It must be that, the coming of the New Deer, that made the younger men start to question the 'holy blood,' question blood itself as the seed of generation, made them question everything, even Holy Mother.

Back now in the rotunda, we come to a halt at the mouth of the passageway from which Mas emerged earlier. In the distance can be heard the woman in labor, screaming. El whistles twice, very shrilly, to summon someone. (Presumably, there's some sort of code that prohibits the men from venturing beyond this point.) By and by a child appears, a little girl about Olo's age and dressed like him in a tunic, except that hers reaches to her knees. Zon informs her that we've brought the 'gift imperative.'

Standing aside, the little girl lights the passageway with the lamp in her left hand, while with her right she invites us to enter. 'Please, those new to the hunt.'

Kala looks up questioningly at El, who nods, whereupon the boys move toward the entrance. Just as I'm about to follow, Zon steps forward and hands me the leather pouch. Before entering the passageway, the little girl does a curious thing: touches the stone, then brings her fingers to her lips, partly to lick, partly to kiss them. I see now that the stone around the mouth of the passageway is stained red, the same red as the mural. Only after the boys and I have repeated the ritual does the little girl proceed down the passageway. We follow in the usual order, leaving the elders behind.

For once the clearance is high enough for me not to have to worry about hitting my head. As we move along in silence, I hear again the distant screaming. The passageway looks endless, yet presently the little girl signals us to stop. She alone takes a few more steps, cautious ones, and, turning, lowers her lamp. She's standing on a bridge—span, I should say, since it's nothing more than tree trunks lashed together and laid across a sluggish river. After pointing out, for our protection, the hazards of the bridge, the girl herself crosses it with ease. So does Kala. Wish I could say the same. Never; these logs are much too slippery, springy, and irregular to cross on foot; I crawl, the pouch secure around my neck.

On the far side the little girl pulls back some sort of drape (so heavy she has to heft it on her shoulder), exposing a cavity beyond: tree trunks, stumps—stalagmites, that's what they are. Only that, the glinting dripstone; empty otherwise, not a soul in sight. I follow Kala into the cavern. Oh, my!

The little girl has brought us into the delivery area. The pregnant woman, Erta, is supine on a deerskin between two stalagmites, slender ones, to which she clings, groaning, pulling herself up from the ground; at the same time, two other women, flanking Erta like the stalagmites, hold her drawn knees high, while a third applies systematic pressure to her abdomen in an effort to force down the fetus whose head is already visible. A fifth woman, older than the rest—it must be Mas, since she alone is wearing an amulet—is kneeling on another deerskin, her broad shoulders thrust between Erta's upraised legs, large hands poised to receive the infant's skull. The woman wiggles her fingers, but whether inadvertently, showing impatience, or deliberately, to beckon the baby, coax it into the world, is hard to say. The latter, I think, because she's moving her lips as well, mumbling to the skull. The others watch her closely. 'Thia'—Mas motions to the woman kneading Erta's abdomen—'more force.' The midwife responds with vigor. Erta groans. Mas watches narrow-eyed as the infant's head emerges fully and begins to turn. At last she takes the head between her hands and, jiggling it ever so slightly, draws it slowly toward her.

Once the baby's been delivered, Mas remarks, 'In no way different.' From her surprised, somewhat puzzled, though definitely relieved, tone I can only conclude that she's talking to herself, commenting on the fact that the baby resembles other babies, despite the complication of the despoilers' withholding the holy blood. Now she closes her eyes, takes hold of the amulet, and brings the figure's head to her ear, listening. After a moment she nods and says with obvious satisfaction, 'Holy Mother shows Her will.' Then in an altogether different, declamatory tone she adds:

> *Out of Holy Mother*
> *From whose perfect fullness*
> *All things first appear*
> *Reappears the disappeared*
> *In everlasting praise*

'Holy Mother, be praised,' respond the women and children—there's a second little girl, as well.

Almost simultaneously another woman emerges from the shadows. She's holding something in her hand . . . a knife, flaked stone. The baby has begun to cry. Mas pinches the umbilical cord near the navel.

By this twisted line
Mother Moon
Lowers us
The long way down
Into reappearance

Release the line

The surgeon severs the cord and binds it with a strip of chamois. That done, Mas, clutching the agitated baby, backs away from Erta (on whose abdomen the midwife continues working) and proceeds to wash the baby, who, by the way, is male. Before long the midwife jumps up and, dropping something she holds by its tail into a bowl, hurries toward the exit—oh! the afterbirth—stopping only long enough to peer at the baby and inquire anxiously, 'Is it—'

Mas dismisses the woman with a wave of the hand, sending the midwife on her way out of the chamber, as the other two assistants help Erta to her feet and walk her out of sight. Then, while Mas drys the baby with wads of moss, the surgeon reappears, bearing in both hands a receptacle of some sort, covered by a mantle.

'Take away the light,' Mas instructs the little girls, who promptly remove the lamps from the area, leaving as the only source of light the azure embers of a nearby fire. No sooner has the first command been carried out than a second follows: 'Take away your eyes.'

Imitating our guide, I turn my back on Mas. During the interlude the baby's crying gradually subsides, turns into a gurgle. After summoning Erta, Mas resumes her recitation in a deep hushed voice.

Wonder-struck
By Your presence
We give thanks
Mother Moon
For Your coming
Down to us
Into dark
Permitting us
To look on You

178

Your everlasting light
In the flesh

Bear witness women
To the reappearance
Of the disappeared

Turning back— Heavens! There's something luminous: the infant, glowing in the dark. Only its open eyes, slightly parted lips, and nostrils are black, black hollows in an otherwise luminous body. Still cradled in Mas's lap, the infant scarcely stirs, seems altogether pacified, content to give off its cool uncanny moonglow. Seeing it, all of us kneel in a circle, shield our eyes—not against the glow, but out of reverence—and bow our heads. 'Holy Mother, be praised.'

Now Mas begins to swaddle the infant (some traces of phosphorescence are visible on the woman's hands), using first a layer of moss, then of chamois. When all the light, except the glowing face, has been eclipsed, she calls for the 'gift imperative.'

The surgeon takes the pouch from me and brings it over to Mas, but even as she does, the midwife returns in haste. 'Mas!' the woman exclaims, muting her voice as she hurries toward us, 'they threaten—'

Mas silences the woman brusquely. Then, dipping the tip of her finger into a cup of pigment fetched by the surgeon, Mas stains the last incision on the amulet.

From the source itself
Your sacred cleft
We draw this gift
In everlasting praise

Opening the pouch, Mas extracts from it a lump of blood. At sight of the lump, the rest of the women, unable to contain their gratitude, close their tearful eyes, cover their rapt faces. Mas passes the lump to Erta, who receives it in her trembling palm. She too, in tears, closes her thankful eyes and whispers, 'Holy Mother, be praised.' Then, taking the lump into her mouth, she savors the blood in a transport of joy.

'Now, woman.' Mas turns back to the midwife.

'They threaten to burst in.'

'Who?'

'The followers of Kos.'

'Bluff! They would not dare.'

'No,' the midwife disagrees. 'Only the elders keep them out, block the bridge.'

Mas puts the baby down beside her, face up on a bed of sand. 'They know it has appeared?'

The midwife nods. 'Heard it crying . . . saw us at the river, disposing of the former skin . . . came and shouted from the other bank—in the middle of the prayer, mind,' she protests, 'broke in with their questions, so many: "Is it shaped as we are? hoofless? hairless? our color?" *Is* it?' the midwife interrupts herself, unable any longer to restrain her own curiosity.

Mas, evincing sudden pride, undoes the swaddling clothes, but only momentarily, just long enough to afford the woman a glimpse of the glowing limbs.

The midwife shades her eyes, sinks to the ground, thanks Holy Mother. In the next breath, however, she looks up with concern. 'But then—'

'Then nothing!' Mas cuts her short.

'But they are out of patience, demand to see the child.'

'Demand? Go and remind them that demands come from above. We do the Mother's bidding here, not theirs. When She is ready, they will see the baby. Go.' The midwife, despite her obvious reluctance, picks up her lamp and starts toward the entrance. 'Wait.' Mas brings the amulet to her ear again, as earlier, listening in silence. 'Much better, yes'— a crafty smile bares her teeth—'tell them, yes, tell them that it's hideous, deformed, that they must never look on it— never! no matter what.' She restores the amulet to its customary place between her breasts. 'Go!' The midwife hurries away. The rest of the women nod their approval, exchange knowing glances. 'Let us continue.'

Now all the women, including the little girls, are given a lump of blood, to which each responds as Erta did: with evident relief, words of benediction, tears of joy. Once the others have been served, Mas herself takes a lump, but is soon distracted by a sudden uproar outside. Instantly on guard, Mas dispatches the little girl, our guide, to investigate the cause of the disturbance. Before the child reaches the entrance, however, the midwife reappears on the run.

'They won't accept not seeing it,' the woman reports breathlessly, 'have gotten past the elders, to this side of the bridge.'

Mas scrambles to her feet and snatches up the baby, who begins to cry. 'Shh! shh! Take it out—shh!—take it along the wet way'—she consigns the infant to the midwife who, in turn, lifts it overhead and deposits the disquieted creature in the hood at the back of her tunic—'as far as the sump, then climb to the hanging ledge. Stay there and feed it—someone fetch a lamp—stay until we come. Be swift!' As the midwife hurries away, Mas turns back toward the entrance and listens for a moment. If anything, the hubbub has increased. 'So much the better. Perhaps they won't have heard the crying.'

Scarcely have these words been spoken, when the drape is wrenched aside, revealing Kos and Spar. 'Where is it?'

Mas whips off her amulet to hold the men at bay. 'Keep out! You have no part in this. Forgive them, Holy Mother.'

Kos looks uncertain, hesitates, but Spar, producing the amulet's replica, steps forward defiantly and flaunts it at the women. 'As much as you.'

'Where—wha—' Mas stammers, shaken by the sight of the replica. 'What have you done to Zon?'

'No need,' says Spar. 'We have our own. Now show the babe.'

'*Your own?* Well'—Mas regains her equanimity—'in that case you had better listen to it, keep out!'

'No!' Kos, emboldened by his companion, joins Spar. 'Not until we see the babe.'

'Never! You didn't hear what the woman said?'

'We heard.'

'And still you wish to see it?'—Mas affects surprise—'see it for yourselves—the bony snout, badger claws, filthy foul-smelling fur? Faugh!' She spits several times in rapid succession. 'Go and search the river, then, where you saw it dumped!'

'Don't try to fool us. You only dumped the former skin.'

'Both!'

'The baby, too?'

'Good riddance!' Mas spits again. This time the rest of the women, collaborating in the ruse, do the same.

Tensing, Kos brings his arms to his waist, half clenches his fists. 'You had it drowned?'

'Instead of looking furious, you should thank us.'

'For destroying—'

'We did you a favor, believe us.'

'You had no right!'

'More right than you have here,' Mas retorts. 'Now go!'

Kos turns, but not to go. 'Kala, Olo, tell us, was it snouted, furry—'

'Enough! That woman'—Mas indicates Erta, who has gone back to the delivery area—'is waiting to be bathed.'

'All right,' Kos acquiesces. 'But don't fool yourselves, you women, imagine that you've won—the blood will be withheld again—'

'No!' the outraged women protest.

'Just as before—'

'No!'

'Withheld until—' He breaks off abruptly, whirls his head.

Simultaneously Mas gets down—I don't understand what's happened—down on her knees and starts intoning loudly:

> Once again
> Receive our thanks
> Mother Moon
> For Your coming—

'Keep still!' snaps Kos.

'Thank You, thank You, Holy Mother,' the rest of the women are quick to join in.

'Quiet!'

'Thank You—'

'So!' Kos raises his voice above theirs, 'You thought you'd trick us.' The women fall silent. (Oh, now I understand: It's the infant, crying in the distance, so far away the sound is barely audible—don't know how Kos heard it.) Wasting no time, he snatches the lamp from Spar—'Wait here!'—and turns on his heels in pursuit of the midwife. As he does, the women rise as one to stop him.

'No!' Mas, still on the ground, intercedes. 'Let them go, let them see.' Her tone is resigned, almost weary.

The women comply. Kos sprints off. The surgeon, looking after him, shakes her head. 'That was a mistake.'

'Not so,' says Mas in her own defense. 'Sooner or later they were bound to know.'

'We knew all along,' boasts Spar. 'Knew it wasn't drowned, heard the crying *after* the skin was dumped.'

Mas struggles to her feet. 'What if you did?' The question is rhetorical, dismissive.

'Well then, if it isn't drowned, perhaps it isn't snouted either, isn't furry—'

'And if it isn't?' she challenges sharply.

'It's us, not you, *us*'—he grabs his genitals—'who work the reappearance.'

'You!' Mas hoots in his face. 'Hear that, women? Them!' The women hoot in echo. 'We, who have borne the weight, labored half the night, shoving the infant out of our guts—we claim no credit, know full well that we are merely Holy Mother's implement, Her hand tool here below. But you, who have done nothing, nothing but make trouble from the start—plaguing and tormenting us by holding back the blood—you stand there, horn in hand, and say it's worked by *you?*' The women guffaw, jeer at Spar, as Mas moves closer, meets him face to face. 'Tell us, then, if, as you claim, it's you, your horn, how come they don't occur more often, the reappearances, every single night?' Whatever Spar's response to this, if indeed he has one, is drowned out by the women's boisterous laughter. 'Fools! Now, leave us to our work!' Still laughing, the women, led by Mas, hustle him out of the cavern.

Pleased with themselves, they come back to the delivery area to deal with Erta, who is now reclining on the deerskin. She looks anxious, lifts her head to speak. 'What now? What will happen . . . when they see?'

'There will be a fuss,' Mas replies matter-of-factly.

A cheer goes up outside. 'It's begun already,' remarks the surgeon. 'Spar has brought the news.'

'No matter,' says Mas, 'means nothing. Means they're young, idle, restless from the winter. It will stop, once the Host returns, hallowed be Her name. Let them fuss; we have work to do.'

Reminded of their chores, the women busy themselves. The two who assisted Erta earlier now help her off the soiled deerskin, whereat Mas, setting about to clean it, pours a bucket of sand onto the fur and then has us, the boys and me, jiggle the skin energetically. Once the sand has turned lumpy and discolored, we pour it back into the bucket, and Mas says to the little girl, our guide, 'Show them where to dump it. Not in the river,' she quickly adds, considering the continuing ruckus outside, 'use the wet way.'

Picking up the bucket, I follow the little girl—just the two of us, as it turns out, the others stay behind—past the surgeon who is kneeling now in front of the rekindled fire, brewing something which gives off a rather spicy minty smell. The child leads me down an alleyway, made hazardous but exquisite by scores of low-hanging stalactites. Toward the end of the alley the ground grows slippery, slopes downward suddenly. The little girl turns sharply left, then, almost at once, sharply right, and we come into a kind of natural aqueduct: a long, low, rounded roof, overarching a series of descending limestone troughs. When we reach the small dam that separates the trough in which we're standing from the next, the little girl says, 'Here.' I dump the sand over the side into the trough below, while she begins to recite a prayer.

Shouting! someone shouting in the distance . . . a woman's voice, then a man's, ringing through the tunnel but indistinctly, words distorted by the resonance. Splashing! the sound of splashing supersedes the waning echo. A light appears, far away, coming toward us jerkily. The little girl tugs my sleeve, takes hold of my wrist, hurries me out of the tunnel. The moment we touch dry ground she breaks into a trot, doesn't stop until we reach the cavern.

Once there, the child goes straight to Mas who's sitting now, together with the other women, beside Erta's bed, eating. The young mother's also sitting up and eating, too, with evident relish. On the ground is a steaming bowl of brew, a dish of suet cubes, similar to those given us during the instruction, as well as another dish of something that resembles sheets of cardboard. The boys alone are neither eating nor sitting, but busy hand-feeding the women. 'Kos is coming,' the little girl informs the group.

Mas glances up unperturbed, interrupts her vigorous chewing. 'And the baby?' The little girl shrugs. 'Eat,' Mas says to the little girl, and she herself resumes chewing.

'Like us!' The silence in the cavern is broken by the sound of Kos's voice. 'Like us!' he calls out exultantly, but whether for our benefit or that of his companions is hard to say, since he's still out of sight. 'Isn't snouted! isn't furry' —the man whisks by so fast we scarcely see his back as he disappears through the drape—'like us! just like us!' Outside, the news provokes another uproar.

Mas pays no attention, looks instead in the opposite direction. 'Where is Thia? Someone go and bring them back.'

The surgeon picks up the lamp and sets off. Almost before she's gone a yard, she hesitates, stopped by the sound of wailing. The rest of the women, except Erta, spring to their feet. For a moment everyone stands stock-still, listening. The wailing continues, intensifies if anything, coming from the dark, utter dark, not a sign of the midwife. Raising her lamp, the surgeon moves ahead, followed by the rest of us. The wailing seems everywhere at once now, coming batlike from the dark in all directions, but still no sign of the midwife. Wait. There she is, emerging from the alleyway, one hand covering her face, the other out, groping the air; no lamp in either.

The surgeon hurries to her (the midwife's hair looks sleek—must be wet—slicked against her scalp), examines the woman's tunic, also wet, front and back, then turns to us and shakes her head.

'Not there?' says Mas. Again the surgeon shakes her head. 'Where is it, woman?' Mas confronts the midwife sharply. 'The reappeared?' The woman uncovers her tear-stained face, claps her fingers to her lips to stem the wailing. 'Speak!'

'Heard them coming after us, splashing through the wet way, louder every step. . . . Couldn't keep our lead, overtook us, tried to snatch the baby, crying from the chase. We turn around to face them, put the baby out of reach. They push in, grabbing at us, grabbing for the hood, crowding us, crowding, crushing us against the wall, the baby bawling loud. We break free, slip! lose our footing, fall backwards, land in water, the baby under us—'

'Drowned?'

'No. They pull us out at once, the baby sputtering, drag it screaming from the hood. Lost our lamp in the scuffle. They tear off the chamois—their teeth, use their teeth to strip the baby bare, see it in the light. "Eeee-ya!" they exclaim, thrust the baby overhead. "Like us! us!" They jump for joy, hold the baby by the neck, shake it, shake it hard . . . the baby . . . baby—' The midwife breaks off, covers her eyes.

'Tell us!' Mas demands.

'Silent . . . silent now, no longer screaming, squirming . . . nothing, just dangling slack, streak of blood—'

'Disappeared?'

'Don't know. They turn too fast, the baby underarm, start back. We start, too, calling after them, "Cover it! Keep it warm!" They give no heed, hurry on.'

Without a word Mas takes the surgeon's lamp and leads the way back to the delivery area. Erta is still sitting where we left her. We approach her from the rear. As we do, something stops Mas in her tracks, makes her kneel at Erta's side. Can't see what it is yet. . . . Oh! the baby, cradled now in Erta's arms, its body naked but no longer glowing, just a few faint traces of phosphorescence still visible between its toes and in the folds of flesh. Though Erta sits fingering the child's cheek, she does so absently, staring into space.

Mas takes the baby from the mother, listens for its heartbeat. After a moment she looks at us, her expression grave, and lays the baby on the deerskin.

'Disappeared?' asks the surgeon.

Mas nods. The rest of the women, in keeping with their leader, show little emotion: heave a sigh, set their jaws, or scowl. 'They stole the reappeared,' says Mas, more to herself than to Erta, 'and brought it back . . . like *this*?'

'Just dropped it,' Erta reports listlessly, 'as you would a sack, into our lap.'

'Unfed . . . never fed.' Mas lays her hand in sympathy on Erta's breast. 'The flowing marrow—Thia will show you how to release it.' She glances broodingly toward the entrance. The ruckus outside has ceased. 'Where are they now?' Erta shrugs. 'Celebrating, likely.' Mas closes her eyes, takes hold of the amulet, her face austere as dripstone. 'Holy Mother, we beseech You, punish them!' In contrast with her husky vengeful tone, a tear appears on her lashes. Letting go the amulet, she swaddles the baby once more, leaving the nose and mouth exposed, as though still needed for breathing—'Thia, you stay here with Erta; we'll go back'—then inserts the bundle into the hood of her tunic. 'The sooner we restore the disappeared, the sooner can Holy Mother work Her will.'

The boys and I help the women gather up their things. Once again I'm entrusted with the leather pouch. As soon as everyone is ready, Mas pulls aside the drape and leads us out of the cavern single file, the surgeon and I bringing up the rear. Erta and the midwife remain behind.

At the bridge the file comes to a halt while Mas confers with the elders. Can't hear what they're saying. After a while Mas raises and lowers her lamp, and the file moves on, the men now in the lead. It isn't long before there's another delay, this one caused by the entryway—all that touching-of-the-stone, kissing-of-the-fingers. . . . Surprisingly, on repetition the ritual begins to make some sense. If, as I surmise, the chamber that we just now left, the delivery chamber, is taken for a womb, and the red-rimmed entry for a vagina, then passage through the entryway, the 'sacred cleft,' must signify our emergence from the mother— whether the human mother or Holy Mother, I can't be sure, maybe both. Maybe the cave itself, not just this particular portion, but the whole extensive network of caverns, wa- terways, and tunnels, through which we crawled, is taken for the Mother, the body of the Mother, nurtured by the men, the hunters of the Host, who secure the holy blood to impregnate the women, the 'pure white fat,' their 'vital food,' to feed them—literally feed them, as the boys were doing by hand—infuse them with the 'flowing marrow,' which in time flows back, from the mother's breast, to nurture *them*, the men, when they 'reappear.'

Having traversed the cavern from which we originally set out (how long ago was that? no telling), we seem to have reached an impasse: a towering wall of solid rock, rising in tiers—can't see the top—each tier set back a yard or so from the one below. Some of the men have already stationed themselves on the tiers and are busy passing the gear from ledge to ledge. Once the transfer has been ac- complished, the rest of us start to ascend, aided by lines like the one at the rapids, as well as by the men, who remain in place to assist us.

As I mount the fourth ledge I finally catch a glimpse of

the top, what looks like stars, a patch of sky— No, couldn't be—too light for stars, stalactites maybe. . . . El, who's stationed on the ledge, permits no dallying, waves me on without pause. To my surprise, Spar is manning the fifth ledge. I say 'surprise' because since we left the delivery chamber, there's been no further sign of the despoilers.

'Ready yourselves,' Spar says in an undertone, as he helps me up.

'For what?' I ask.

'Ready yourselves,' he merely repeats, and sends me on my way.

Oh, my! it *is* the sky, a handful of stars visible beyond a broad, bow-shaped arch—the entrance to the cave. No moon in sight, starlight hazy, the sky itself the color of shale, mottled slightly—surely on the brink of dawn. After the darkness down below, the light, however dim, seems hospitable, inviting—not just the light but space, the sudden abundance of space, air, the freshness of the air up here: loamy, sweet, cooler, too, transmitting birdcalls—makes you want to walk right out— 'Sorry.' Bumped into someone underfoot. Best stand still.

Incredible, the amount of activity in here, despite the lack of light. Most of the lamps have been extinguished—all, in fact, but one: in a gloomy recess to the left of the entrance where two youths are engaged in some sort of manual labor. Everyone else is equally busy—some on their hands and knees, attending to domestic chores; others hurrying to and fro, storing and removing things, much of it, presumably, equipment used in the rites—though, come to think of it, no spears were used, and several men, Kos among them, have passed me carrying spears. Nor is the activity restricted to indoors. A number of people are also outside, some at work behind a long level wall, others clustered around a hearth. It's still too dark to see what the group behind the wall is fussing with . . . a bundle of some sort.

At this moment one of the women leaves the wall and hurries toward the cave, touching the arch and kissing her fingers as she enters. Once inside, the woman stops and shields her eyes. Shortly, she advances, stops again, surveys the chamber, apparently in search of . . . me! It's the surgeon, come to collect the leather pouch, which she takes without a word.

As she turns to go, the surgeon is accosted by another woman who addresses her with urgency in a lowered voice. 'They say they will leave—'

'Who?'

'Kos and the others, after the ceremony—say we *all* must leave.'

'To follow the Host?'

'No. Leave for good, they say, never come back.'

'Never?'

'Tell Mas.'

The women part: the informant to spread the news in here, the surgeon to pass it on outdoors.

The sky looks slightly lighter now, fewer stars. The central figure in the group behind the wall, the woman—I can see her more distinctly—the woman handling the bundle—not a bundle at all, but Erta's baby—is Mas, it's Mas, manipulating the baby's limbs, repositioning its legs. The other women—

A light, distracted by a light. Someone has entered the recess where the youths, now on their hands and knees, were working— Zon, it's Zon, holding a lamp overhead. All three are looking down, examining . . . a pit, it must be, judging by the mounds of earth that weren't there before.

The surgeon, meantime, has begun to remove from the wall various vessels, which she places on a paddle-shaped tray held by another woman. Once the wall's been cleared of everything but Erta's baby, the women cross to the hearth to have a word with their co-workers, who thereupon light a pair of lamps and, turning to lead the way, guide everyone down the uneven slope toward the cave. Mas alone, silhouetted against the dawning sky, remains outside, motionless as the baby that she's watching over.

The minute the lamp bearers, who repeat the touching ritual, enter the cave, those already inside, attracted by the light, drop whatever they're doing and join the procession. I take my place at the end of the line, behind a group of men, among whom I recognize two of the despoilers. Neither says a word, no one does, total silence, except for the birds outdoors, as the line moves slowly toward the recess.

All the light in the recess is focused on a piece of hide, stained blood-red. Four stakes—or, rather, reindeer tines used as stakes—loosely hold the corners of the hide, allowing it to sag, hammocklike, into the pit below. Beside the pit is the surgeon's tray, laden with food, a lump of holy blood, and all sorts of ritual articles. I go around the congregation, grouped in a semicircle facing the pit, and stand behind the two despoilers I was following. For once my height proves advantageous, provides an unobstructed view.

Mas just entered, is moving ceremoniously toward the head of the pit. Once there, she hands the baby to the surgeon, whereat she herself disrobes and spreads her tunic on the ground. Naked except for the amulet, she squats at first, then sits down squarely, back to us, and, stretching her legs, straddles the pit. The moment she's settled, Mas retrieves the baby, which she places in the hammock, face up and headfirst between her thighs. Thereupon she checks the baby's limbs, making certain that its arms are folded over its chest, legs drawn up and crossed just so. Satisfied, Mas calls for the 'holy blood.' Surprisingly, it's not the surgeon who steps forward but the artist, who scoops a glob of pigment from a mixing bowl and streaks the infant's body red. As soon as he's finished, Mas speaks again, calls for the 'gift imperative.' Now comes the surgeon, who carefully inserts the lump of blood into the baby's mouth. Next, Mas calls for the 'vital food,' whereat the surgeon takes the edibles and stores them one by one in the little hollow between the baby's folded arms, after which she insinuates a suet cube into the baby's fist.

'Secure the line,' says Mas.

In response the surgeon quickly trusses the infant's ankles with a plaited cord, the other end of which she hands to Mas who tucks it into her vulva. That done, Mas lies back, head and shoulders flat on the ground, and, gripping her thighs, swings her legs overhead—a convolution that takes up the slack but doesn't disconnect the cord. Immediately thereafter two women, the ones who helped the midwife, come to Mas's aid, support her hefty thighs, just as they supported Erta's. Strange, how much the re-enactment resembles the delivery, except for the inversion of the baby's skull. Mas, her hands now free, takes up the amulet and, righting it, begins to lament, making a moaning sound rather like the one Zon made at the start of the instruction. When, at last, her breath gives out, she draws another and makes the sound again, while the women continue to support her thighs efficiently and the congregation looks on engrossed. Again she makes the sound . . . and yet again . . . repeatedly, until she's moved to stretch her arms full-length and, placing the amulet parallel to her body, address it face to face.

> *Whether there*
> *Or here below*
> *In earth or air*
> *Our dwelling place*
> *Is one with You*
> *Holy Mother*
> *One space Your sky*
> *And cavities*
> *One light Your dark*
> *And radiance*
> *One migration*
> *Forth and back*
> *Through You alone*
> *Your sacred cleft*
> *We come and go*

' "Through You alone," ' repeats the congregation. ' "Your sacred cleft, we come and go." '

> *Holy Mother*
> *We entreat You*
> *Open to us*
> *Open wide*
> *That we Your children*
> *Disappeared*
> *May reappear*
> *Mother to ourselves*

> *Pull up—*

Mas breaks off, lowers the amulet halfway to her chest. Unable as I am to see her face, I can't explain the interruption. Nor, apparently, can the congregation, among whom it causes a stir. Mas readjusts her position, the women better their grip on her thighs, Zon and the surgeon shift their weight uneasily, while others crane their necks, exchange inquiring glances, baffled gestures. Presently Mas raises the amulet once more and resumes speaking.

> *Holy Mother*
> *We entreat You*
> *Open to us*
> *Open—*

Again she breaks off, except that this time she does so with finality: drops her hands, lays the amulet flat on her chest, disconnects the cord. 'She will not,' Mas reports solemnly.

These words are greeted by gasps. The congregation pulls back, confused and shocked and questioning. 'What? What did they say?'

'Release us,' Mas orders the women supporting her thighs. Despite the crowd's distress, the women let go of Mas, help her up from the ground. She turns, not bothering to put her tunic back on, and stares at us in silence, eyes intense and penetrating. In contrast with her gaze, her body looks relaxed, her bearing almost girlish as she stands holding the upright amulet in both hands like a flower. 'Holy Mother says She will not open.' The small challenging eyes scrutinize our faces, sweep the congregation from left to right until they come to rest on someone in my vicinity. 'Says that you, those who praise themselves, boast they bring about the reappearance— "Let one of *them*," She says, "take your place." ' Mas continues eyeing whoever it is— one of the despoilers—defiantly.

'Us?' Zon steps forward. 'Us men restore the disappeared?' His empty gestures, upturned palms express bewilderment. 'How can we—can She expect—' Glancing down, he covers himself, his groin, with both hands, as though in shame. 'We have no way.'

'Perhaps *they* have.' Mas juts her chin in our direction.

'No. There is no way for us,' Zon states simply, his tone at once practical and humble, 'no way but you.'

'You heard what Holy Mother said. She will not open, not to us. Perhaps to them. If not, perhaps they'll find some other means . . . use force, their *horn*, perhaps'—Mas can't resist the irony—'horn their way in.' After staring hard at us, she turns back to the pit, picks up her tunic, and puts it on. 'We leave the disappeared to you.'

'Wait!' Zon hurries over to her. 'Once more, try once more.'

'What use? We have. No, *you*, you men must try.'

Zon looks disheartened, shakes his head. 'Impossible.'

'You have no choice,' Mas ends the discussion.

Slowly Zon turns back to us, his expression sober, eyes fixed on someone in particular, much as Mas's were a moment ago. 'Kos.'

'Don't call on *us*,' the younger man protests, 'ask us to squat like them. We will not!—will not be made the butt of their scheme.'

'Scheme!' Mas turns on the despoiler. 'You call Holy Mother's will a scheme?'

'Not Hers but yours, you women.'

'Consult Her, then'—Mas fingers her amulet—'the copy you contrived.'

'You know we cannot,' Kos replies with bitterness, 'no one but you—'

'Then do as you are told!'

'We will not!'

'And you?' Zon quickly intercedes, calling first on Flint, then Spar, to straddle the pit. Both refuse.

'If not,' Mas continues calmly, 'what do you propose? How restore the disappeared?'

Kos considers the question in silence, eyeing Mas the while. After a moment he says, 'That's easy,' struts to the head of the pit and kneels, facing Mas and Zon, his back to the rest of us.

Before any of us can see what's happening, Zon dashes toward Kos with an outcry, grabs him by the shoulders, and wrenches the young man back from the pit, raising a cloud of dust. As it settles, the cloud— The piece of hide, it's empty, the baby gone. Kos must have pushed— No, the stakes—that's it—pulled out the two front stakes, releasing the hide and dumping the baby down into the pit.

The moment the women see what's happened, those up front fall on Kos, beat him with their fists, kick at his recoiling body. Emitting a battle cry, the despoilers hurry to their comrade's defense, try to pull the women off. Just as the scuffle seems about to turn into a free-for-all, Mas, who alone among the women has held herself aloof, claps her hands resoundingly. 'No more! "No more!" we said. Leave off!' The combatants comply, begin to separate, however grudgingly.

Once everyone is back in place, Mas moves with measured steps toward the pit until she reaches Kos, over whom she assumes a commanding stance. The despoiler is sitting up now, looking slightly dazed, one hand stemming the blood from his lip, the other holding his ribs. ' "Easy," is it?' Mas takes up where she left off, but with forbearance. 'And how will we get back?'

Kos, clearly in pain, struggles to his feet, hugs his naked sides, his tunic ripped off in the scuffle. 'We won't, will leave for good.'

'We don't mean *here*'—Mas loses some of her restraint—'back here, but back *at all,* back into appearance?'

'As we always have.'

'Understand, Kos! Holy Mother will not open.'

'Her daughters will.'

'Not if *She's* unwilling.'

'Erta did,' Kos is quick to rejoin.

'With what result?' Kneeling beside the pit, Mas lifts out the baby, its face besmirched with blood and dirt.

'There will be others.'

'Others?' Mas shrugs off the suggestion. 'What others? What does that mean? There is only *us*, this infant'—she holds it up impassionedly—'the disappeared.'

'No. It's you who do not understand,' Kos asserts, but with surprising sympathy, patience. 'Others, new ones will appear.'

'So you say. But how?' Mas looks genuinely perplexed. 'Tell us that. Appear from where?'

'Us! from us. That is our discovery. *We* will make them reappear.'

'You!' she sneers. Putting down the baby, Mas gets up, confronts the youth not only with the full authority of her presence but also with the amulet, once more in hand. 'Consider what you're saying, Kos.' The warning is portentous. '*You* will make them reappear, these "others" that you speak of? You alone? Without Holy Mother?'

Kos looks her straight in the eye, meets the challenge bravely. 'Without Holy Mother. Without the holy blood,' he adds, as though to leave no doubt he understands completely the gravity of his claim.

'No!' the women protest.

'And what of us'—Mas snatches up the baby again—'the disappeared? "Easy," you say. Forget the holy blood, the vital food, celestial line—forget it all, everything: provisions, prayers. No need to attend the disappeared. Just let us go! drop us out of sight, you say. But where? Into what? *This?*' She peers down into the pit. 'This hole, pitch-black, with no way out, no way back. Just leave us there, trapped, to rot? That is what you're saying, Kos: Let us disappear for good. *For good.*' She stares in dismay at the baby, then shakes her head, shuts her eyes. 'For good,' she repeats, continuing to shake her head. 'Hard as we try, we cannot see it, cannot picture "for good." . . . Can you?'

Kos, too, shakes his head. 'No.'

'Yet if the disappeared has no way back, neither have we. If the disappeared disappears for good, so do we. We *are* the disappeared.'

Still hugging his sides, Kos looks daunted, grimaces, but whether from pain or the impact of Mas's words is hard to tell. Soon, however, he straightens up, raises his head, overcoming by dint of will his discomfort. 'We must risk it.'

'No!' the women cry out in dread. This time the outcry is taken up by Zon and the elders: 'No! never!'

'Yes!' counter the despoilers. 'We must!'

'Risk! you would have us risk—' Mas breaks off, nonplussed. In her struggle to articulate the unspeakable she weighs the infant in her arms. 'Risk an end to reappearance?'

Kos hesitates, seems at a loss for words. Straightway Flint steps forward, fills in for Kos. 'An end to reappearance,' he explains, 'doesn't mean an end to appearance.'

'Nothing less!'

'Not so,' Flint continues reasonably. 'Consider the New Deer.'

Mas stiffens. 'We know nothing of the New Deer.'

'The New Deer—'

'Nothing!' She cuts Flint short. 'All we know is reappearance: Holy Mother in her phases . . . the stars in their courses . . . reappearance of the crows, reappearance of the lichen, reappearance—'

'Of the Host?' Flint puts in ironically.

'Us!' Upraising her arms, Mas elevates the baby, become once more the embodiment of 'us,' high overhead for all to see. 'Put an end to reappearance and you put an end to us! to everything!' Still holding the baby overhead, she makes her way back to the pit. 'Everything but *this*,' she hisses, louring over the pit as though about to hurl the baby down, 'this final trap!' Oh dear! she *has*: dashed the baby into the pit. The congregation groans. 'Consider *that*'—Mas whirls in passion on the men—'consider yourselves down there *for good*.'

'No!' Kos asserts his leadership. 'We mean to leave this place—'

'This place—'

'Whether you agree or not, *we* are going through with it, are going to leave this place—'

'This place,' Mas cries out, 'is Holy Mother!'

'Even so'—Kos stands up to her—'we must leave.'

'For what? Where? Where will you go? There is no *other* place!' the women and elders shout out. The despoilers begin to dispute them, but at a signal from Kos they desist, turn to leave the recess.

'Hold!' Zon calls after them. 'You know there is no going unless *all* go.'

'Then all will go,' Kos states flatly.

'Wait a bit.' Zon acts the mediator. 'We'll put it to a choice—'

'However you choose,' Kos maintains, 'we mean to go. And you will follow,' he adds with confidence.

'Never!'

'If not, you'll starve.' Kos turns away, retrieves his tunic. 'Come, boys.' He motions to Kala and Olo. 'Come,' he says to the older boys who dug the pit. 'Come.' He beckons to me.

'Stop!' Mas quickly interposes herself between us and the despoilers. 'On no condition! They stay with us!'

Kos shakes his head. 'They go.'

'No, you! you go, go where you like—they stay here!'

' "With us," we said.'

'And we say no!'

For a moment the two stare each other in the face, neither blinking, neither backing down, both intransigent, while the congregation looks on transfixed. Suddenly Kos draws a knife from his cape. 'Take them!' He gives the order to his men who instantly grab hold of us. None of the boys resist, all, in fact, seem perfectly willing, even glad, to go—all, that is, but me. The despoilers, their knives at the ready, put us behind them protectively—Kos himself is my protector—and start backing out of the recess.

'Wait!' I try to stop them. 'She's right.'

Turning on me, Kos turns his knife as well, the point pricking my ribs. 'Quiet!'

Despite his knife—it's already broken the skin, I think—I'm convinced that Mas is right, that it's imperative to stay. 'We *won't* get back.'

Kos shoves me hard, sends me stumbling backwards.

'By what right?' Mas pursues us fearlessly. 'What right have you to take them?' she demands, seizing my wrist to halt the retreat.

'This!' Kos flaunts his penis.

'That!'

'The source of them, their maker!'

Mas spits on the man, flaunts the amulet in return. 'None but Holy Mother makes!'

'Us!' he answers back with vehemence, wiping the spittle from his groin. 'We tell you they were made by us!'

All at once Mas lets go of my wrist, closes her eyes, clutches the amulet, claps her hands to her ears. She will hear no more. . . . No, that's not it. She's begun to mumble, is mumbling to herself: slowly, softly, virtually without inflection. The congregation edges forward soundlessly. Oblivious of everyone, Mas continues mumbling, even as she starts to waver slightly, swaying to and fro, shuffling unsteadily, staggering a step or two as though about to fall, then lurching just as suddenly back again to balance. Yet, despite the fitful lurchings of the body, the voice remains unchanged—measured, hushed, monotonous—so much so it's hard to say whether what we're hearing is the voice of the woman speaking to the amulet or the amulet speaking through the woman.

Presently the eyes begin to open—only the whites are

197

visible—the features terribly contorted, jaw horribly agape. 'Hear Us.' Faint as it is, the command brings us to our knees—all of us kneeling now before the tranced and teetering woman. 'If they were made by you, not Us, they will disappear. You will disappear. Those "others," looked for to come after—*all* will disappear . . . for good. Yet if you disappear for good, with no chance to return, then disappearance will determine all, even appearance—appearance, too, will come to nothing more than disappearance. And you will know it, through your "making" you will know it. And the knowledge will confound you, drive you to fall back more and more upon appearance. Oh! how you will cling to it, your brief appearance, cling for all you're worth to those you boast of making. But unlike tools you fashion now, for use of all, you will look on them, on those you make, as yours alone. And being yours, you will designate your handiwork accordingly: so-and-so made by such-and-such. Not by Us. No more Us. No more you. No band of you, made strong by Us, strong in numbers, Mother-made to reappear, but merely makers, separate momentary makers, horn-made to disappear. As makers, you will make and make, make all you can appear, as many new appearances as possible, multiplying and amassing them, hoarding and controlling them in hopes that those you make will somehow make you reappear. Yet all you make will only make you disappear. . . .'

The voice has died away, leaving Mas utterly wrung out: eyelids shut, facial muscles slack, head drooping sidewise as though the neck were broken, arms hanging limp. The amulet slips from her hand, lands on the ground noiselessly. She herself soon follows, seized, as her body sprawls, by a fit of coughing, gagging. Otherwise there's not a sound, not the slightest murmur, slightest movement among the congregation. Even the lamplight is motionless, unflickering, as Mas continues retching. When, at last, the fit has passed, her body stiffens, becomes motionless, too.

For the longest time the silence and the stillness prevail. Finally Kos gets up, moves cautiously toward Mas. Stooping, he picks up the amulet. . . . No one seems to have noticed or, if they have, no one—neither the elders nor the women—tries to stop him. Kos puts the amulet around his neck, then motions us, his followers, to withdraw, giving me another shove to make certain I comply. Again no one tries to stop us, no one even stirs, as we steal out of the recess, leaving the prostrate Mas.

The entrance area is lighter now, not bright, but light enough to see—no need for lamps. Without a word from Kos, without any talk whatever, the men and boys go about collecting their gear. . . . Not a sound; even the birdcalls have ceased. Must be early morning. No more stars, but neither is there sunlight—not a trace of blue anywhere, just haze, dense and uniformly gray.

As soon as everyone is ready—garbed in baggy deerskin trousers, tucked into knee-high boots like mine, and armed with spears, fitted out with detachable triple-barbed heads, hanging from leather thongs—Kos moves toward the entrance. Once there, he stops, this side of the arch, and waits while the rest of us fall in line behind him—the boys and I in the middle, as usual. He then moves on, but not without first touching the arch and kissing his fingertips. One by one, those who follow do the same. Though no one looks back, you can sense the men's uneasiness, see it in their shoulders and in the way their fingers linger over the stone —the uneasiness of departure, departure from the Mother, leaving behind 'for good' the 'sacred cleft.' When it comes my turn, I too feel uneasy, sad. . . . The pigment is moist, comes off on my fingers, tastes metallic, induces tears. . . .

Outside, the men put up their hoods, and Kos moves on, past the wall and up the slope. The downgrade on the other side must be fairly steep, judging by how cautiously and jerkily Kos disappears from sight. . . . No, not so steep, after all. What makes for difficulties is not the slant but slush. We're on a slush-covered hillside, a hundred feet or so above a barren plain . . . dun-colored, as far as the eye can see. Only in the distance, the remotest distance to the right —can't tell what direction that is, since the sun is nowhere to be seen, the sky completely overcast, lackluster—far far away there's a shadow, so vague as to be almost indistinguishable from the horizon, a long, low-lying shadow, flecked with white—snow perhaps—that might be another range. But otherwise there's nothing—not a tree or rock or river, a clump of grass, touch of green . . . not a sound, except the crunching of our boots; nothing to relieve the flatness, drabness, nothing at all to break the awesome silence.

We're veering to the right now, toward a snow-filled gully that runs all the way down to the foot of the hill where the snow is heaped in a towering mound. . . . What on earth! Not snow at all but bones, a gullyful of bones— heaven knows how deep—skulls—some with antlers, some without—skulls and antlers by the thousands, shoulder blades and shinbones, vertebrae and thighbones, bones of every conceivable size and shape, all picked clean, immaculate; many in a state of perfect preservation, others broken, splintered, pulverized, but none decayed. The cavern dump. . . . Looking back, you would never know there *was* a cave concealed behind that rise, would never guess how this bone-yard came to be, would probably attribute it to nature, the result of some disaster, an avalanche or flood, accomplished at one stroke, not piecemeal: bone by bone, deer by deer, herd by herd—and surely not man-made. How many meals, consumed by how many men, over how many generations, must it take to make an avalanche of bones?

Kos has stopped now at the foot of the hill, not to wait for the rest of us but to survey the huge expanse. After a moment he removes Mas's amulet and, holding it by the head, points with the phallic shaft in the direction of that shadowy form on the horizon.

'Eeee-ya! eeee-ya!' the men approve, as we set out across the waste.

III

Opening his eyes, Andrew Spector saw on a luminous screen, viewed through the brass bars of the bedstead, the looming lopsided silhouette of a tree monster or troll with threefold arms—were they legs?—limbs in any case, long sticklike limbs, supporting its clumsy bulk precariously. "Must have dozed off," he remarked, more to reassure himself he wasn't dreaming than to address the other person whose presence he sensed without seeing in the unlighted room.

"Oh, Andy," said Letty, "you're up."

The sound of his mother's voice sent a thrill through Andrew's body, brought tears to his eyes, tears of relief, refuting his previous conviction that he had done with tears, would cry no more. "You've come!"

"Hours ago." Letty, getting up from the settee, approached the bed. "Not five minutes after you closed your eyes. Just my luck. Look!" Her voice grew exultant as she pointed at the television set on top of the bureau facing the bed. "Can you see? They've done it!—landed safely. *Got tsu danken.*"

"At last," he murmured with feeling.

"Just now." She angled her wristwatch to catch whatever light was in the room. "It can't be more than—"

"You should have waked me."

"I wanted—was going to, but then you looked so peaceful—*umbeshrien*—I didn't have the heart."

"Been waiting."

"Ben? No, he's out with Mil and Peggy—poor thing, needed a breath of air. I urged them to go, gray as it is—no sense everybody sitting indoors."

"*Waiting.*" Andrew rolled his pillowed head from side to side to correct the misunderstanding. "Been waiting," he repeated, "so long."

"All you really missed was the landing. Look! It's still there. The module. Want to sit up?" Again her brother rolled his head. "They haven't come out yet, the astronauts, won't, for hours apparently. Have a million things to do in there, technical things—'housekeeping,' they call it; quaint of them, isn't it?—hours before they take their walk. Can you imagine! Just like Ben and the girls: out for a walk. Only not on Riverside Drive. I wonder if they know yet, that it's landed? Must, by now. All that cheering. People were cheering in the street, heard the news on their portables. It's what woke you, I think. You should have seen them in Houston—delirious! The whole world! cheering, clapping, crying—couldn't help but cry. My hankie's soaked." As though to substantiate her claim, Letty revealed a wad of cloth in her palm. "All that suspense, excitement. A miracle! that's what it is, landing that contraption on the moon."

"Holy Mother, be praised." Andrew stretched out his hand, fingers crooked to grasp, and made an effortful wrenching motion, forward and back, as though straining to open an obstinate jar.

"Turn up the sound?" Letty tried to interpret the gesture.

Only when he realized that she had moved away did Andrew finally withdraw his hand. "Off . . . please."

Disappointed though she was, Letty complied with the request. After all, the astronauts would not emerge for hours yet. Besides, the network had just switched back to the studio for a dental commercial, correlating the cavities of the moon with those of man.

Andrew watched the orb's pitted surface disappear in a flash, watched the flash diminish at once to a pinpoint of light, stellar light, burning incandescently, before it too disappeared. "Dark . . . too dark."

"The shades," Letty explained on her way to the windows.

"Shades," he echoed thoughtfully, "mmm."

"For your nap," she further explained. The first shade shot up with such a sharp report it made Letty gasp, giggle nervously, and she took more pains with the second.

The afternoon sky was cardboard-gray, completely overcast, lackluster like the sky above that dun-colored plain. Vividly as Andrew could see the barren waste, stretching for miles and miles, he couldn't for the life of him remember its name. "Trek." He needed to urinate. "Long long trek."

The swearword *drek* brought Letty back to the bed to see what was the matter. Andrew was struggling—the struggle coupled with grunts—to sit up, using his elbows to haul, heels to push, himself backwards toward the headboard. She offered to help, but he refused, didn't want her to strain herself. Even so, she tried to be of help: fluffed and stacked the pillows. He couldn't bear the fussing. "Bottle." He indicated the empty juice jar on the night table. She handed it to him and turned away discreetly.

As the urine began to flow he felt the sheet, then his pajama bottoms, to assure himself that both were dry, whereupon he shut his eyes and sighed with pleasure. In addition to enjoying the physical relief, he was pleased with himself for hitting the mark, not having an "accident," pleased by the sound of the flow, as well as by the flow itself, fluid and free, without burning or stoppage, pleased to anticipate Mamma's pleasure at sight of the specimen, collected especially for her, her delectation, pleased to be pouring himself "in pools for her"—but mustn't lap; pleased moreover to be warming his hands—cold hands, warm. . . . Blood? "Mammalian," he said aloud, warming his hands on the baby's bottle, that palpable extension, locked between his thighs, of himself, his mother. "There!" He produced the quarter-full jar with pride.

"Good boy," said Letty.

"But mustn't lap." He raised a finger of caution. "The reindeer."

Letty started to say it wasn't going to rain, but stopped herself, not really certain what her brother meant. Instead, she pinched together the sides of her lower lip and smoothed her skirt self-consciously. He was a bit "off" again today. Still, that was only natural, to be expected from someone suffering from hardening of the arteries, especially after a nap. Plucking a facial tissue from the box, she clapped it over the top of the jar, as though to trap an insect inside, and headed for the door.

"Don't go."

The entreaty made her hesitate. "Has to be emptied."

"Not in the river."

She had to laugh, couldn't help herself; his earnestness only compounded the incongruity. "No, no," she gave him her assurance as she whisked the bottle out of the room.

" 'They come, They come,' " Andrew recited to himself. A Pyrex bowl on the coffee table in front of the settee caught his eye. The bowl contained something red, a lumpy batch of deep red— He couldn't make it out. Leaning forward (his hip felt broken anew), he craned his neck and squinted, but couldn't bring to a focus whatever it was. From the hallway came the belch and gurgle of a toilet being flushed, followed by the sound of water running from a faucet. *Circulation*, that's what it came down to, everything: water, waste, money, blood. His eye reverted to the bowl. "Blood," he declared. Of course! what else could it be but blood?—lumps of blood, taken from him while he slept. His curiosity satisfied, Andrew eased himself back down onto the pillows, proud that he himself had become the donor of the holy blood, the gift imperative. It somehow justified, more than justified, made meaningful this whole ordeal, smoothed the way toward disappearance.

"Andy, darling"—Letty replaced the emptied bottle—"you look so much better today, much, much—"

Andrew shook his head, didn't want to hear it. "Don't," he said, his tone both brusque and pleading.

"You do," she insisted. "Some color in your cheeks. Even Oxenburg—"

He covered his ears till his mother's lips stopped moving, stood agape. "For you, only you, I've waited."

The distinction touched and flattered Letty, even as it filled her with foreboding. "Well," she tried to make light of it—"you know what they say: Blood is thicker than water."

"Too thick," he quipped, and chuckled sardonically.

The gaffe made Letty want to bite her tongue. In shame she averted her eyes, only to catch sight of the anticoagulant on the night table. Seeing it, she wondered whether the medicine did any good, whether it really thinned the blood, dissolved the—the—what did they call the clots?—em-embolisms. "Your medicine, have you—"

"Sit." Andrew jutted his chin toward the rocking chair beside the bed.

"One sec," she requested girlishly, glad for an excuse to turn away, compose herself. Slouching toward the coffee table, she picked up the Pyrex bowl—"What a funny thing to do, cover your ears like that"—carried it back to the rocker, and sat down with the bowl in her lap. "Is it Oxenburg? You mustn't have misgivings, darling. No spring chicken, I admit, but still, he's one of the top men in New York. You don't become chief of staff for nothing, you know. Besides, what other doctor makes house calls these days? A thing of the past." As she spoke, Letty poked among the cherries in search of the fattest one available which, when found, she sucked whole into her mouth. At the same time, she became aware that Andrew was watching her, and she felt a bit self-conscious, guilty, not because he disapproved—if anything, he looked positively fascinated, pleased as punch, kept nodding as though to encourage her—but guilty because she was hogging the bowl. "Have one?" She pouched the uneaten cherry in her cheek. "They're delicious! a *meichel*, go ahead."

He raised his palm to repel the bowl. "For *you* . . . you to eat. Only the mother—"

"Don't be silly, there's lots. Look!" She proffered the bowl. "I didn't eat *that* many—a quart—quarter pound at most."

"Recompense. How else can we repay you?"

"Pay?" Puzzled, Letty bit into the cherry, enjoying the firm juicy meat. "For what? Pay," she wondered aloud, chewing the while. "The money, you mean? Peggy told you?" Assuming she had solved the puzzle, Letty chewed more rapidly. In her haste to clear her mouth she almost swallowed the pit but coughed it up and spat it into her palm.

Andrew stared at his own cupped palm, disappointed to find it empty. "Pleases me—"

"No! you mustn't speak of it, Andy dear, whatever you do, promise, please, you won't speak of it— Ben! not a word to Ben. He—he wouldn't—doesn't know I— What's to know anyway? Just a little nest egg, not enough to speak of—"

"Egg?"

"From Wooly's life insurance—a pittance, really—"

"Pit," he remarked with gravity as he peered once more into the cup of his empty palm.

"That's all. Put into a savings account—you know how frugal I am—for the boys. And that *mamzer*, Barry"—mere mention of her older son aroused Letty's anger—"has the gall to call me miser! Married to an heiress, and accuses me of playing favorites, just because I give the interest to the little one. On what should Kenny live, stones? Starve for his art while his brother sails the Caribbean? A yachtsman suddenly. Cain and Abel, that's what they are, those two, always have been. Not like you and Ben, real brothers. But even so, don't speak of it. Promise?"

"Must."

"To Ben, I mean."

"Ben? What has *he* to do with it? *You*"—he reached for his mother's hand which she yielded readily—"only you, to thank."

In reciprocation of his sentiment Letty bent down and kissed her brother's hand, hooked now in hers, the fingers cold. His fingers were, in fact, burrowing into her palm as though for refuge. She laid her other hand on top of his to warm it, but still the fingers went on squirming, struggling to dig deeper. She became conscious of the cherry pit. Was that what he was after? Was he trying to get hold of the pit? Apparently. She felt embarrassed, not by him but by the messy pit, and clenched her fist. Her resistance only made his fingers struggle harder, burrow deeper. At last, feeling foolish, she relaxed her grip, relinquished the pit.

Andrew brought it right up to his eye, revolved it slowly between thumb and forefinger like a jeweler examining a gem. Till now, he hadn't an inkling that the gift imperative concealed a pit . . . "with no way out, no way back"—the pit of the despoilers that led, for good, to disappearance. Perhaps this was the clot itself the doctors kept referring to, the clot that clogged the flow, substantiated disappearance. What did they call it—that word they kept using *ad nauseum?* . . . To help himself remember, Andrew stared hard at the lumps of blood—*his* blood, taken from him while he slept—mounded in the Pyrex bowl. Bowl! Something with *bowl* in it, wasn't that the word? Yes. Bowl . . . *bowlinism*, that was it. . . . As he looked again at the bowlinism, to which traces of blood still adhered, Andrew wondered what its purpose was, what he was meant to do with it. He didn't know, only sensed that he must hold on to it for safekeeping. "Nasty little bugger," he remarked to his mother with a combination of scientific detachment, humor, and genuine curiosity.

"The pit." Letty identified it deliberately to make certain that her brother understood what he was looking at.

"Lot more than a pittance."

She laughed. "Perhaps. But not that much, not enough to beef about, begrudge your brother—"

"Not to be shared with him. For *you*, yours alone."

"I have enough."

"Not yet, you don't."

"Enough to make ends meet."

Andrew brought the tips of his fingers together, creating at the juncture a lozenge-shaped setting for the bowlinism, at which he gazed intently as though at a mandala. "All that matters finally—make ends meet."

"You mustn't worry, Andy."

"Then eat, eat"—his hand spiraled toward the Pyrex bowl—"more, another, eat."

"I'll get the runs."

"Don't speak." The request was made in a hushed tone, the sort usually reserved for libraries or churches. "Just eat." He waited tensely, toyed with the bowlinism, turning it over and over in his fingers, till his mother helped herself to another lump of holy blood and took it into her mouth. As she began to chew, he sank among the pillows with a look of utter contentment, matched only by her own. "Pleases me. So right. Didn't understand till now. Couldn't figure out. . . . Worried . . . worried so how to thank you. Not for"—a vague little gesture, a halfturn of the wrist, was meant to signify the entire process of gestation, labor, delivery—"but for the thing itself: the gift—"

"Please."

"—imperative."

"You promised."

"Should have known not to worry. Not my job. Holy Mother's. Should have known She'd take care of it, have some way, some master plan . . . to conserve the gift. Don't frown."

Letty had never known what to make of Andrew's Christianity. It nettled her. She had no trouble understanding his religious bent, that was only natural; after all, he *was* a Spector, and the Spectors, though never orthodox, were nothing if not good Jews. Yet for a Jewish composer to title a piece *Annunciation*, well, that was going too far: a real affront, if not a sacrilege. Unnecessary to boot, since the piece itself was in no way liturgical. He could have called it anything—Elijah! Why not? At first she had blamed Peggy for the title, Peggy's *shikseh* influence. Yet Peggy wasn't Catholic, nor was she especially religious, not even a churchgoer—an atheist, if anything—so how could she be held to blame? No, it was altogether Andrew's doing, only Andrew, something in the man himself had compelled him to choose *Annunciation*, some inexplicable quirk, the same dark quirk that had prompted him to set that Jesuit's sonnets, the Blake cantata, to say nothing of *Maurya*—selecting for his libretto a work by that Irish Catholic playwright. And what about *Recovery*, the score that Sarah Kellogg had commissioned for her work about the Brownings? A perfectly harmless secular title, yet never in all the years since its premiere had she heard her brother refer to *Recovery* as anything but *Resurrection*— a private whim, probably in deference to his beloved Tolstoy. Well, whatever you called it, his Christianity bothered Letty, created a kind of no-man's-land between them, a whole area of her little brother's life and work about which she knew nothing. (Amazing how many things brothers and sisters didn't know about each other.) On the other hand, she realized that she was the only member of the family, excepting Peggy, with whom Andy felt free enough to speak at all of the Holy Virgin, and so she tried to put aside her own feelings, be tolerant of his. "Was I frowning?"

"Yes. Mustn't. Distorts your features. Too beautiful. What if they froze that way?" Andrew smiled knowingly.

Letty smiled back, not to counteract the frown or forestall the freezing but to signify her awareness that he was quoting their mother, using one of Mother's pet expressions. "Mamma."

"Yes." He nodded and, smiling broadly, fondled her hand. "Mamma. Pleases me—you've no idea—more than pleases, overjoys, overjoys to see you eating. Another, eat another, please."

"All right, if you insist." Letty willingly obliged. As she disposed of the pit she had been savoring and selected a third cherry, her brother held out his hand in request of something. The pit again, she guessed, and though it struck her as odd to participate in such a crazy game, she nonetheless placed the second pit beside the first in his open palm.

"Divine," he whispered in a reverie, while his fingers began unwittingly to work the pair of bowlinisms like worry beads. "That's what it is, divine! . . . divine wisdom . . . justice . . . for you to take back at the very end what you first gave: the gift."

" 'Take back?' I didn't!" Letty brought the rocker to an abrupt halt. "Didn't take back! Who said—did Peggy say— She refused! didn't tell you she refused the offer? Wasn't me. Pride, her pride—she always—hurt her pride. Only natural, I suppose. I understand, went through it all myself . . . with Wooly. You don't want someone taking over, someone like that, a registered nurse, in your hair every minute—just a helping hand, someone like your Mrs. Lexy, compatible, kind, comes in and does her work, someone you can trust to s-stay, let—let you go, get out for an hour or so without worrying. But otherwise you want to do it all yourself, the—the care, caring for—" Letty drew herself up in the chair, rocked backward to take herself out of Andrew's line of vision, restrain her brimming tears. "You want—it's your duty, isn't it? your job in life, concludes the pact, vows you took . . . to look— Oh!" she cried out, unable any longer to hold back the tears. "My Wooly! cherished, cherished. . . . Knew that, didn't you? No one ever, no one else."

"Don't," said Andrew softly. "Please. No going back."

"Oh, Andy, there's something—secret, deep dark— Isn't that what we used to say? I'll tell you a 'deep dark secret.' Never told anyone before, not even Kenny, not a soul." She blew her nose noisily, then brought the rocker forward again till her knees touched the mattress, and she rested her elbows on the bed in the attitude of a sphinx, albeit a rather informal, chatty sphinx. "Remember Max? Max Kisselgoff: handbags. Well, Max and I, for many years we—we—off and on, Max kept—Max and I kept company. Never —don't misunderstand—we never—not—strictly platonic. After all, Max was married . . . estranged—who wouldn't be from *that* one?—but married all the same, just wanted someone to go out with, have a good time with once in a while. So did—you couldn't blame him—I—I did, too. Hard to explain." She gnawed on the cherry pit to help herself produce the explanation. "Not boredom exactly. . . . Alone, alone so much: Wooly working, always working, working late—if not the shop, his—those 'meetings' of his; the boys grown up, moved away—a little after the war, this was, forty-seven, eight, when Max first took me out. Swanky places, nothing but the best—you know Max, such a sport, so big-hearted, couldn't do enough for you —Twenty-One, Saint Regis Roof. Once! I'll never forget it as long as I live—Milly was there, Coq Rouge—we usually went at lunchtime, you see, so as not—more—more discreet that way. Well, she was lunching with a friend . . . Fanny Himes—I still remember—saw us, I think, Milly that is, *know* she did—the look on her face!—but never said a word—to Ben, I mean. Smart woman, Milly, have to hand it to her: knows how to use her *kop*. Saw me in a Jay Thorpe dress—not one of hers, you understand, I had a wardrobe of my own that would have knocked her eye out—but kept it to herself, kept—for Ben's sake, I suppose, not mine . . . her sake, too, of course, made her look big, generous in Ben's eyes—not only kept it to herself, but kept on giving me her castoffs." She plucked at the bodice of her summer print, as though at something soiled, to indicate that she was wearing one of the dresses in question at that very moment. "And I kept taking them. For Wooly, Wooly's sake, so that he would never guess, if he saw me dressed to the teeth, that it wasn't one of Milly's. Not to deceive him, don't think that. Just the opposite really: protect him, his feelings. I wouldn't have hurt that man for the world, have him think that someone else—*that* would have been the real deception: for him to think that someone else —anyone! Max or Frederic March—could ever take his place." Letty slid the cherry pit out of her mouth into her fingers. By now she no longer needed prompting, simply dropped the pit of her own volition into Andrew's waiting palm.

He took the bowlinism greedily, heartened to see it sucked clean, not a trace of blood anywhere on this one. Three! she had already eaten three whole lumps. A couple more and his worries would be over, he could disappear in peace.

"That was the trouble," she resumed, but Andrew interrupted her, jabbed a finger at the Pyrex bowl, shifted since from Letty's lap to the night table. She understood, helped herself to another cherry before lounging back in the rocker. The chair dipped with her weight, angling her face, white as the hair that haloed it, upward toward the ceiling. "Somehow Max, he never understood—no one did —what I saw in Wooly. 'A young woman like that,' they would say, 'a beauty, married to a man old enough to be her father.' A *'nebbish,'* they called him, 'pauper,' 'dwarf' —all kinds of names, but always 'father, old enough to be her father.' . . . Didn't understand." Letty's voice quavered, broke. "Little boy, not my father, little boy . . . my little boy!"

"Always will be," Andrew assured his mother, trying to console her. "No such thing as father, misconception to begin with."

"Exactly." She heaved a sigh of gratitude, wiped away the tears. "*You* understand . . . always did."

"Meeting of the ends." Andrew clenched the bowlinisms tight as he could in his fist. "In the end . . . you yourself" —he spread his thighs as though to facilitate, then and there, delivery—"miracle!—become the mother."

"Not only at the end, all along, almost from the start. A woman can leave a husband, a lover, but not a little boy. That's what Max didn't understand—couldn't!—the nature of our love, Wooly's and mine. Never! . . . never understood that what we had—whatever it was—we had *because* of Wooly, because we were so confident, sure of each other, Wooly and I, sure of our love, *unshakable*, I could go out with Max. The only reason. Otherwise our—our friendship would have been impossible. What made it possible with Max was—was what I had—the *certainty* of what

I had with Wooly. Does that make sense?" Andrew gave no sign one way or the other. Though his eyes were fixed on her, and he seemed to be listening attentively, he kept playing with the cherry pits, rolling them in his palm. Perhaps she was taxing his memory, perhaps the example of Max was too shadowy for Andrew, too remote for him to follow. "The same was true afterwards—you know yourself, with Josh—after Max had died, and Wool—Wooly, too, was dying, it was always Wooly, Wooly himself who kept urging me to go out with Josh. 'A beauty like you,' he would say, 'too young to sit at home, nurse an *alter kranker*. Go! go, my sweet, go out and have a good time.' You heard him yourself, a hundred times—no secret."

"What *is* the secret?"

The question took Letty by surprise. "Wha-what secret?"

"Deep dark."

"Oh!" As her face lighted up, she raised and lowered her brows, bulged her twinkling eyes, and smiled broadly, relishing beforehand the confidence she was about to divulge. "Money."

"Money!"

"Don't laugh. I'm a rich woman," she boasted solemnly, slowing her words for emphasis, whereat she rocked backwards, as though on her heels, and added with pride, "rich as Milly."

"That's no secret."

"Not?" Startled, Letty plunged the rocker forward again, toward the bed on which she planted both hands for support. "You knew, honestly knew?"

"Common knowledge, worst kept secret in the world."

"No," she reassured herself, releasing her pent-up breath audibly like air from a toy balloon. "Teasing me, I can tell. *Didn't* know; no one does. That's why I wear these *shmattehs*, so no one will ever know. No one but you, my darling." Letty inched the rocker closer to the bed. "Before Max died—he knew he *was*, people always do, I think —he came by the apartment one afternoon, had his chauffeur with him. Strange, I thought, to bring the man upstairs, carrying a valise . . . till I saw what was in it. Not the chauffeur, he didn't see, was sent back down at once.

214

What Max stopped by to give me— Well, it doesn't matter, the exact amount, it—it was quite a sum, substantial, I assure you, a—a lot more than a pittance—you were right! And all of it"—she lowered her voice—"in *cash*, securities and cash. Nothing crooked, mind, just didn't want it all, everything to go to Rosa . . . said I was his *true* wife." Letty paused in reverie. "And in a way, you know, I *was*: the wife of Max . . . mother of Wooly. . . . And they expect you to choose. . . ."

"Mother," Andrew obliged.

"Of course. What else?" She shrugged. "*Had* to be."

"No choice at all."

"To *our* way of thinking, no. But for Max—"

"Falsehood."

"What is?"

"Husband."

"Oh? I don't know," she hedged coquettishly, "I—I think he would have liked—"

"Father."

"Ooo-hoo!" Bursting into laughter, Letty flapped her hands to shoo away the notion. "No-no! going too far."

"Falsehood too, fatherhood, primary one," he declared. "So what's the *truth?* Tell the truth."

"I just got *finished* telling you—" She hesitated. "A hundred thousand . . . almost—cash!"

Andrew shook his head dogmatically. "No." Then, hunching forward like a conspirator and stretching his arm as far as it would reach, he placed his hand squarely on his mother's lap, fingers closed, clenched in a fist. Presently, however, the fingers began to unfold, opened fully to reveal the bowlinisms nestled in the palm.

"Oh!" Letty, who welcomed the opportunity to drop the subject, play his little game once more, took from her mouth the pit she had been sucking on and added it to the collection. The moment she did, the fingers curled, closed like a trap.

"It's *there*, the truth," he whispered ardently.

"Where?" she whispered in return, drawn into the conspiracy.

"In the blood."

Irrational as he sounded, she couldn't pass it off as that, attribute to senility whatever he was attempting to say.

His fervent tone, almost beatific expression, were too compelling to ignore. Clearly, he was speaking from his heart, sharing with her a truth which he, poor soul, took to be divine, a revelation. At the same time, the word *blood* unsettled her, and she rocked backwards to put some distance between herself and the bed, break the conspiracy. "I'm—I'm afraid—"

"Don't be. Nothing to fear. Replenished soon . . . replenished by the son."

Even as she glanced over her shoulder at the still-gray sky for some sign of the sun, Letty realized the folly of doing so and turned back to complete her previous thought. "I've—I've lost you, Andy."

"Not yet, you haven't," he retorted playfully.

She drew an anxious breath. "I—I didn't mean—"

"Never will," he added in earnest. "*That's* the secret: never will . . . so long as we revere Her."

"Who?"

"Holy Mother."

At a loss for an appropriate response, Letty picked herself up and went to the television set. "I wonder. . . ." She knew full well that the astronauts hadn't had time as yet to complete their preparations, but switched on the set, even so.

Andrew, meanwhile, having lain back contentedly, resumed toying with the bowlinisms. Their clicking sound evoked again the snatch of verse that he had recited earlier to himself. " 'They come, They come . . .' " Unable to remember the rest of the words, he tried to coax them from memory by repeating the opening phrase, but to no avail. "What *is* that?" he asked in frustration.

"Just a commentator." Letty switched off the set. "Still in the studio."

" 'They come, They come . . .' "

"Who?" She listened. "You heard the door?"

" 'They come, They come . . .' "

From the front of the apartment came a murmur of voices, the click of a closet door. "It *is* them. What ears you have . . . composer." She fetched her pocketbook from the settee. "Back from their walk."

" ' . . . On spindly legs,' " Andrew recited happily, pleased with himself for having recalled the missing words,

" 'Huge splayed feet/Clicking with each step.' " To heighten the effect, he worked the bowlinisms rhythmically like castanets in accompaniment to the verse, which he repeated in full for the benefit of his mother who, he failed to notice, had left the room.

On her way to the front door Letty stepped into the bathroom for a moment to powder her nose, fuss with her hair. In retrospect she regretted telling Andrew about the money. Supposing he told Ben? Chances were he would, the way his mind was wandering. What an *umglick* that would be! She should have kept it to herself, not have been in such a hurry. . . . What had made her do it? Vanity? . . . Mindful, suddenly, of her aged image in the mirror, Letty was taken aback, appalled by what she saw: hair in a flurry white as snow, skin no longer smooth but lined, creeping lines like window frost, cracking ice, soil in winter —everything, in fact, about her face, once so dark, Mediterranean, now betokened winter—now, in the dead of summer—dead! *That* was it, wasn't it? what had made her tell, confess to Andy. Confess? Till now she hadn't thought of it in those terms, but that was what it seemed, a confession, a kind of last— As if *she*, not he, were on—were seeking absolution, final—deathbed! The word couldn't be suppressed, avoided any longer. No, somewhere in her heart of hearts she *knew*—there was simply no denying it —knew that she was dying, that she would—he! he would, *he*. She had told him because some part of her knew he would take her with him, her secret, to the grave . . . *wanted* to be taken! *Gotteniu.* (Letty held on to the sink for support.) Her little brother was dying—*all* of them: Weezie, Wooly, Essie, Irene— dead, all dead! Only she and Ben and Ethel left . . . without Papa. "Oh, Papa!" she moaned, "Papa! take me too!"

By the time Letty pulled herself together and emerged from the bathroom, she heard Peggy's voice coming from the bedroom. After a moment's hesitation she decided against going back in there, went instead toward the living room to say hello to Ben. But as she approached the end of the hall she heard Ben say, "Can't, I can't!" and Letty stopped instinctively to eavesdrop.

"How can I?"

"We," Mildred corrected him.

"We," he conceded. "How? Tell me, how can I go to Europe, with him like that?"

"For yourself! that's how. You have your heart—your—your own health to consider. For once in your life—for God's sake, Ben!—do it—something, something for yourself!"

"Worrying, that's what I'll do, the whole way over—not a minute's peace. The minute we get there, there'll be a cable, have to come back."

"So, we'll come back."

"God forbid!" Ben exclaimed.

"At least you'll have had the crossing, a little rest."

"Rest? Who's going to rest with him in there, lying like—like a dog."

"He *isn't* dying—you heard what Oxenburg—"

"I didn't *say* dying!"

"Listen, Ben! If I have to give you knockout drops, you're going to board that ship."

"Not on your life. Couldn't. My conscience—"

"Then do it for *me*," Mildred snapped.

"Anything, anything, my sweets, you know there isn't anything— If only *she*"—he lowered his voice—"would listen to reason, get someone in to look after him, properly trained."

"*Him?* . . . He's out of it, Ben." Mildred put it plainly. "*Her*, it would be for her, a nurse, the only reason: give her some time for herself."

"I don't care *who* it's for, so long as she gets someone."

"Shh!"

Mildred and Ben fell silent. Letty, nonetheless, waited a moment or two before entering to make her appearance seem perfectly accidental. "Back already?" She went straight to her brother, ensconced in the club chair at the far end of the room, and kissed him on his suntanned scalp as if she hadn't seen him in ages.

Ben welcomed the fawning. "*Ziseh*."

"How is it out?" inquired Letty.

"Miserable." Mildred flicked the ash from her cigarette as though with an intent to kill.

"You saw the landing?"

"Now, how on earth could we have *seen* it, Letty?" Mildred carped.

"How *but* on earth?" Ben, coming to his sister's defense, enjoyed his own retort.

"It was just incredible, thrilling—"

"Not for *my* money. What do you call—" Mildred interrupted herself to pluck a piece of tobacco from the tip of her tongue. "In theatre, what's that called? Anticlimax, that's what it was. Too much ballyhoo, buildup not to be a letdown."

"You didn't even see it," Ben reminded his wife.

"I saw enough. All that money! For what?"

"To put a man on the moon," marveled Letty. "Andy was annoyed, I think, I—I didn't wake him."

"He's up?" Ben looked up at his sister who, having rested her bosom on the back of the chair, was looking down at him dotingly. Letty nodded. "How"—he lowered his voice as if Andrew were within earshot—"how is he?"

"Pretty good, *kain ein horeh*. We had a nice little chat."

"Lucid?"

Letty seesawed her hand.

Ben struggled out of the chair, trudged in silence toward the foyer, his shoulders hunched, eyes fixed on the carpet as though in search of something lost. To help himself think, he jiggled the coins in his trouser pocket until he reached the foyer. Once there, he turned to face the women again. "Never know what to do," he confessed, "whether to play along with him or try to bring him back."

"Play along." "Back where?" Mildred and Letty spoke at once.

"Reality."

"Oh, he's not that far gone, not what you'd call 'out of it,' " Letty reassured her brother, even as she slyly contradicted her sister-in-law's earlier claim.

"Want to say hello?" Ben, with a slight toss of the head, invited his wife to accompany him to Andy's room.

Little as Mildred looked forward to being left alone with Letty, she liked even less the prospect of trooping inside to sit with her brother-in-law. Not only did it make her uncomfortable, but it struck her as pointless, hypocritical, to go through the motions of chatting with a man who, likely as not, hadn't the vaguest idea who she was. What good did such pretense do either of them? At least with Letty she could discuss Chappa—Chappa—whatever-it-was-called—the Kennedy accident last night. "Before we go, I'll say good-bye. Ben"—she stopped him as he started down the hallway—"don't forget: We're meeting the children at seven, the *bon voyage* dinner," she added pointedly.

"How could I forget?" he muttered. And how, he asked himself, proceeding down the hall, could a woman you lived with forty-nine years fail to pick up your signal? not understand that you didn't wish to be alone with your brother? Though Ben made a practice, if not a fetish, of stopping by to see Andy almost every afternoon, there were times of late when he wondered whether the visits were worth it, worth how much they upset him. Not that he cared about the cost to himself; that was nothing! He was prepared to suffer anything, any amount of stress, jeopardize his own health, if need be, so long as it did some good: boosted Andy's morale, kept the poor guy going. But lately—

"He's up," said Peggy.

"Oh!" Ben brought his hand to his chest. "You startled me."

"Sorry. I was just coming to tell you he's up. A little hazy," she remarked matter-of-factly on Andrew's mental state.

"So Letty said." Ben had by now regained his poise. "When are the kids coming?" He wanted to be out of there before his nephew Mat arrived.

"Soon, I think."

As he stepped aside to make way for Peggy, Ben was surprised to see his brother emerge from the bedroom. "Oh, there he is, the bruiser."

It made Peggy somewhat nervous to see Andy walking by himself, without his cane—she worried about his hip—but as with a child, you had to let him try. Quick, now, to observe Andrew's outstretched hands, she said, "Want something, honey?"

Andrew ignored the question, as well as the old man, past whom he shuffled without a word, intent on reaching the white-haired woman. Although there was no need whatever to be rough (the woman offered no resistance), he nevertheless yanked from her hand the Pyrex bowl. He wanted to impress on her that she was not to touch his belongings without permission. To further emphasize how proprietary he felt, he curled his hand around the bowl, hugged it football-like to his ribs, and carried it, still at a shuffle and without a word, past the old man and back into the bedroom.

If Peggy was the least bit ruffled by the incident, she showed no sign of it, took it in her stride. "Sit with him," she said to Ben on her way now to the front of the apartment.

Ben followed his brother into the bedroom, but then hung back and waited in silence, just inside the doorway, till Andrew reached the night table. "How's it going, Babe?"

"They're all alike." Andrew replaced the bowl fussily. "Can't keep their hands off anything."

"Mustn't be too hard on her." Ben ventured a step or two into the room. "Poor girl's been under so much— Meant well, I'm sure."

"Rifle your sheets," Andrew complained.

"Had to, probably—freshen the bed."

"You can put up a sign: Please Don't Touch, and still they touch."

"Just to straighten up a bit."

"That's always the excuse: straightening up. Doesn't bring back the missing sheet."

"She had to change it? Accident?" Ben moved to the left side of the bed, opposite his brother, to examine the bedding. "No. Both here. See?" Pulling back the summer blanket and top sheet, he showed Andrew that both sheets were in place. At the same time, however, Ben spotted something in the bed, a pellet of some sort, so unexpected and incongruous, embarrassing and comical, it brought to mind a turd. He promptly took another look. At second glance the object appeared to be a pebble. Whatever it was, now that he had discounted his first impression, Ben broke into laughter. "Looks like you laid an egg," he joked as he picked up and examined the pellet, which, on closer inspection, could have been anything from a dried pea to a pine nut.

Until this moment Andrew hadn't paid much attention to his visitor, hadn't given a thought to the man's identity. Now all at once he realized who the old man was. Only his father used that disparaging expression, used it moreover to needle him about his music. "So," Papa liked to say about some new composition, "I see you've laid another egg." Mention of the egg prompted Andrew to check now on the bowlinisms in his pajama pocket. But since he didn't wish to expose them to his father's view, he went about it on the sly, fingering them through the lightweight cotton.

"Itch?" Ben tried solicitously to make sense of his brother's fidgeting fingers. "Handkerchief?"

"Fork it over!" Andrew suddenly exclaimed.

Ben had no idea what his brother was referring to. "What?"

"Egg!"

"Oh." Ben chuckled uneasily and handed his brother the pellet.

Once Andrew had restored the bowlinism to his pocket, he rejected his father's offer of help and got back into bed on his own.

The ensuing silence made Ben restless, impelled him toward the television set. "Shall we see how it's going?"

"What's going?"

"Apollo."

"Nowhere" was Andrew's laconic reply. "Sun god," he added with contempt, "no match for the moon."

"So, you saw it then?"

"Enough. . . ."

"Whatever you say; you're the boss." Irritated though Ben was by Andy's contrariety (the tyranny of the sick), he had no choice now but to forgo turning on the television set and sit down. Of the two available seats in the room he much preferred the settee to the rocking chair, which was placed too close to the bed for comfort, cramped his legs. "Letty thought you'd missed it."

"What does Letty know."

"She thought you were—" The ashtray on the coffee table caught Ben's eye. It was glutted with cherry pits. So that explained the "egg," but the explanation only left him that much more puzzled by his brother's eccentricity. "Thought you were annoyed with her for letting you sleep."

"Sleep!" Andrew mocked the assumption. "She thinks I was asleep?"

"While we were out."

"Nonsense! *She's* the one who slept. *I* . . . I saw it all."

His oracular tone made Andrew's words seem more than an idle boast. "Enough at least to differentiate between the sun and moon."

"I'll say." The distinction tickled Ben. "Can you imagine landing on the sun?"

"Can't imagine *not*."

"Are you kidding! You'd disappear in a puff of smoke."

"So long as man imagines he's the father, he'll come down on the son."

"Oh." Ben forced a laugh. "*That* kind."

"There is no other. All get landed on . . . and disappear."

This was one of those instances of uncertainty—so soon, at that—to which Ben had been referring in the living room. He didn't know now which tack to take, whether to "play along" with Andrew or try to "bring him back." "Oh, I don't know," he said, for lack of something else, equally neutral, to say.

"Look at yours," Andrew prodded his father.

"My what?"

"Son."

"Mine!" It took Ben a moment to comprehend the startling suggestion, whereupon he laughed it off. "Mine has no complaints."

"Maybe not. None at least that matter . . . anymore—too late in the day."

"Never did! None at all! You must be talking about some other guy, not me. If anything, I spoiled him."

"Mustn't blame yourself. Not your fault."

"Who said 'fault'?"

"Didn't know any better."

"I certainly did!" Ben all but turned his back on Andrew as he crossed his legs decisively and looked out the window at the lackluster sky. "Knew just what I was doing. Wasn't going to repeat the same mistakes— Not that Pop made that many . . . old-fashioned, that's all, European school: strict —strictly European. Swore I'd do it differently, that's all, give the boy some of the advantages we missed. Not you," he quickly corrected himself, casting a glance over his shoulder at Andrew who, to Ben's annoyance, had resumed fiddling with his pajama pocket. "You at least had an education . . . thanks to me. That's all I ever wanted," he summed up, "to give the boy an education, plus—well, some—some of the amenities."

"Eumenides?"

"That's right." Ben turned again to face his brother. Feeling more expansive now, he spread his legs, rested his elbows on the back of the settee until he all but occupied the entire seat. "Some of the comforts, the little"—he searched with his fingers for the right word—"what would you call them?—allowances—I don't mean money, though God knows I always saw to it the boy had plenty in his pocket, a more than liberal allowance—liberties! that's what I mean, the little liberties we had to do without. That's what I gave him."

"But not me," Andrew admonished his father with irony but almost no vindictiveness.

"What you did, you and Peggy, with Herr Doktor, that's your business, no ones but yours. To each his own, I always say. You did it your way; we did it ours—Milly and I, God bless her! the best little wife a man ever had. Why, I wouldn't trade my boy— The best son in the world, couldn't ask for better."

"Easy enough to say now."

"Always! always said it! You never heard me say a word against—"

"Practically disowned him."

"Like hell I did!" Ben burst out, but quickly checked his anger, mindful of his heart. "What are you talking about?" Looking away, he rubbed his eye self-consciously as though to dislodge from it his brother's irritating accusation. "The marriage, is that what you mean? Christ! what a memory you've got. So long ago I'd clean forgotten. The boy was too young to know the score, had to marry the first skirt he *shtupped*—never mind she didn't have a pot to piss in, love conquers all. Still,"—Ben put aside his bitterness, turned magnanimous—"if that's what he wanted, *abi gezunt!* I don't interfere with my children. They have to do it for themselves, make their own mistakes, no one can do it for them. Sure"—he slapped his knee for emphasis—"we had some words, a little spat—happens in the best of families, but don't exaggerate, say 'disowned.' "

"Ownership . . . that's the crux."

"Of what?"

224

"Everything! . . . the whole business."

Andrew's austere gaze, plus his juxtaposing of the words *ownership* and *business*, neither of which would have attracted Ben's attention by itself, put Ben on his guard. To change the subject, he motioned to his brother's blanketed hand with which Andrew was now vigorously scratching his groin. "Something bothering you?"

"Horn."

"Come again?"

"Turned it upside down."

"What upside—"

"To create the covenant."

Ben held up his hand to stop the conversation. "Now don't—"

"Made yourself the maker—"

"Don't, please, I beg of you, don't start that again or—"

"Gave yourself a trade name."

"I—I'll have to leave the room." Ben, dramatizing the threat, made as if to get up.

"Not until you give it back," Andrew stopped his father.

"What back?"

"What you took."

"Nothing! nothing that wasn't mine—"

"Ownership!"

"Mine!"

"Title!"

"Mine! mine to begin with."

"Not by rights."

Ben fell silent. In a visible effort to regain his composure, exercise patience and restraint, he sat up tall, drew a deep swelling breath, expelled it audibly, and then settled back, as though deflated, against the tailored cushions. "Look, Babe, I don't know who—who it is put this bee in your bonnet, but it's got to stop. We've been over it a hundred times. Just not fair to keep coming back to it like this. I know you don't know—well, know exactly what you're saying, but even so—"

"*Covenant*, I'm saying."

"Contract, yeah—no need to get so highfalutin, biblical about it."

"The covenant," repeated Andrew forcefully, "must be dissolved."

"Was! was dissolved—don't know why you keep harping on it—legally dissolved, nine years ago, ten almost, ten this fall. Christ! would you believe it?" Ben paused to muse, "How time flies. Ten years ago . . . ten years the shop is gone." He shuddered. "Ten years, and suddenly you get this bee—ten years after the fact—suddenly I chiseled you. Me!" He shook his head in bewilderment. "Best pal in the world, and suddenly— You don't know what you're saying, Babe. And yet," came the disturbing afterthought, "you keep on saying it. Why?" Ben waited in vain for an answer. Though Andrew's eyes were fixed on him, his thoughts seemed elsewhere, removed like the fidgeting fingers under the bedclothes. "You don't believe it, do you? honestly believe— Couldn't. Who was it—think back—who insisted— wasn't it me?—you get your own accountant, lawyer, let them take their time, look over the books, papers? Why, do you suppose, for what reason? Precisely *this*"—he extended both hands as though to serve his brother, there and then, the reason on a platter—"to avoid this—this kind of pickle: post-mortems—er, accusations. That's why I insisted: to keep things businesslike, strictly business. *You're* the one who saw no reason for it, couldn't understand, trusted me, you said, would trust me to the ends of the earth. . . . Well, look around you, Babe, we're *there*, the ends of the earth: accusing me—" Ben swallowed hard, his eyes welled tears. "You—you got exactly—to the penny—exactly what was coming to you, not a penny less. Christ!" He brought his fist down on the cushion, as much to restrain his tears as to release his anger. "When I think of it, the irony. I didn't have to give you anything, the way Pop set it up, not a fucking cent! When Mamma died—" Ben broke off, distracted by the memory of their mother who, before she died, had made Ben promise that he would give her share of the business, held till then in trust, to Andy. Ben had hedged the promise by assuring her that he would "always look after Andy," and God knows! he had kept his word. "I don't say Pop was right, doing what he did, cutting you out completely, but still, let's be fair about it: You *did* walk out on him, run off to make music; and Pop, as you know— both of us know—was not one to forget . . . forgive. . . . Never mind!" He brushed aside the bothersome thought. "Right or wrong, when Mamma died, the shop was mine!

226

Not just 'title' either, but lock, stock, and barrel—property, premises, inventory, everything! all the assets, mine! 'Took,' " he muttered. "Burns me up: 'took' from you— nothing! Gave! gave you, always! everything! whatever you got, came from me, out of my own pocket, the bigness of my heart. And this is the thanks: accusations." Part of Ben was ready now to drop the subject, let it go at that, but some other, more commanding part drove him on. "Milly warned me this would happen, begged me not to do it. 'Give him a raise,' she said, 'if he needs incentives, double his salary, do what you like, but don't make him your part- ner—you'll only live to regret it.' 'Regret? Why? why would I regret? Never,' I said, 'what's fair is fair. Pop was wrong. It's coming to him, Mamma's share.' " All at once Ben was struck by a new idea, and he tried to draw closer without getting up, slid forward to the edge of the seat. "*That's* it, isn't it? what's eating you: the split, that it wasn't fifty-fifty. All these years and not a word, now suddenly I gypped you. What else could it be but that? Took more than my share, you think."

On his feet now, Ben began to wander aimlessly, plod- dingly, lost in thought, his steps guided by his thoughts, following his thoughts, rather than his eyes, wherever they happened to lead: first to the door, then to the television set, next to the wheelchair in the corner, then over to the window, and finally to the foot of the bed where he came to a standstill, both hands on the bedstead as though forcibly restrained by the brass bars. "For myself, you think? Did it for myself?" He shook his head in answer to his own ques- tion. "Larry . . . for Larry. We're going back some, Babe, don't forget, some thirty years—what am I saying, thirty?— forty, almost forty. Larry was a boy still, little boy, still had hopes—I–I–hope—" Again his eyes filled with tears. "Can you imagine having a great-granddaughter . . . and never setting eyes on her? Pearl's Sally—you know she had a daughter?—must be eighteen months by now. A child named Hope, and never— Beats me. Breaks Milly's heart." Again, as earlier, he stemmed the tears, this time by smack- ing the bedstead. "Where—where was I? Oh, yeah, hope! Forty years ago, well, I still had hopes, hopes that Larry— maybe even Pearl—who knows? some future son-in-law . . . Who could have guessed there were going to be *four*?

Four sons-in-law, one bum worse than the next! . . . Larry, though, Larry for sure. Someday Larry would come downtown, take an interest in the business: That was my hope. Not—not so easy for you to understand, I realize, don't expect you to. That's why you never understood how Pop felt—still don't—because you never wanted it for Mat, never wanted it for yourself, the business. But *I*— I—I'm not criticizing," he backtracked, wary now of both his own emotion and Andrew's perplexed expression. "You did all right, better than all right: lots of honors, prizes, grants. But—but I had something else in mind—for Larry, I mean, not you. Hoped—more than hoped—what kept me going, the only thing! I—I— Never dreamed the boy would turn his nose up." Unable any longer to control his emotion, Ben burst into tears, shook with sobs. "That's why I held on to it"—he clutched the bedstead for support—"extra twenty, for *him* . . . not to chisel—never; never chiseled! gave you the shirt—" Too upset to go on, he buried his face in his palms and made his way—however unsteadily, blindly, bumping into the coffee table—back to the settee. Once there, he lowered himself, doubled up as though from internal bleeding, onto the cushion, and, slumping into the corner, continued crying.

"Don't." Andrew tried to comfort his father. "Too radical for tears."

"Sorry."

"Tears won't dissolve it."

"Don't know what came over me."

"Only by giving back what you took—"

" 'Took' again."

"—can it be dissolved."

"Contract, you mean?"

"Covenant."

After a moment Ben fished a handkerchief from his trouser pocket, blew his nose resoundingly, and then sat up, staring at his brother. He realized now that Andy hadn't understood a word he'd said, not a blessed word, would never understand, would go to his grave— Ben rapped himself for even thinking such a thought. Andy would go on lying there; no matter what Ben said, he'd go on lying there the rest of his days, convinced— Unless! Maybe if Ben "played along," made a settlement of some sort, a cash settlement, actually *paid*— After all, he had wanted to pay for a nurse, had pleaded with Peggy for months. Another woman would have jumped at the opportunity, gotten down on her hands and knees to thank him, but not his sister-in-law—too damned stubborn, proud, proud enough to put her pride before her husband's health. Well, this way she would have no excuses, *have* to take the money. . . . Ben stood up and strolled over to the rocking chair. As he sat down, his eye fell on the bowl of cherries, and he automatically helped himself to one.

"Put that back," said Andrew sternly.

"What back?"

Little by little Andrew brought his hand out from under the bedclothes and pointed at the holy blood. "Not for you."

"Sorry." Ben replaced the cherry. "Didn't know they were reserved." Flummoxed though he was, he couldn't really take offense at his brother's childishness. Not his fault, poor fellow. Wasn't that the very nature of the illness, the disease itself, to become increasingly childish? "Listen, Babe, I've been thinking. Know something? I think you're right, *was* unfair, the way I did it, should have been even Stephen all the way. I see that now, would like to make amends. Know what I've decided? First thing in the morning I'm going to get hold of my accountant, have him reopen the books—Christ! what a job that'll be—figure out exactly what I owe: ten percent across the board. How's that sound? Give you back exactly what I owe."

"You *must*."

"Now wait a minute." Ben took umbrage. "Not so fast. No musts about it. It's what I want, choose to do; there's a difference. Can't stand this kind of bickering—divisive. That's why I'm going to call him in the morning, because I *want* to, not because I *must*, want to call him in the morning."

"Can't wait till then. *Now*."

"How? It's Sunday, Babe."

"Please," Andrew implored his father. "Let me disappear in peace."

"Don't talk like that: 'disappear.' " The word made Ben uneasy. "No one's going to 'disappear.' "

"*Everyone*," asserted Andrew, "unless it's given back."

"Jesus! I—I've no idea what—what amount, what's in-volved—"

"The covenant!"

"Okay, okay." Getting up, Ben pulled out his wallet, re-moved a blank check, sat down again, and began to write rapidly. "There you go," he said, when finished, handing his brother the check.

Andrew stared at the paper blankly. "What's this?"

"On account, till we see what's involved. I—I made it out to Peggy—"

"For what?"

" 'Deposit only,' don't worry."

"What's it *for?*"

"To dissolve the contrac—— er, covenant."

"This?" Andrew looked incredulous. "Piece of paper?"

"Can't give cash—Sunday."

"No good." Andrew tossed aside the paper.

"What! *My* check?" Ben retrieved it. "Good as gold. Not enough, on account, five grand?"

Andrew shook his head. "Horn tip."

"What?" Puzzled, Ben grimaced, rehearsed the word to himself. "Haunt . . . haunted?"

"Horn tip." Andrew took pains to make his father un-derstand.

"I— Sorry, Babe, s-still don't get it."

"Give back . . ."

"Yeah, that I get."

"Horn tip."

Ben made one last effort to grasp the word, if only be-cause it seemed of such crucial importance to his brother. "No"—he gave up after a moment—"just don't get it. What? What must be given back?"

"*This.*" Casting off the bedclothes, Andrew fumbled with his penis, threading it through the pajama fly till it was exposed.

"Now don't, don't"—Ben promptly replaced the bed-clothes—"don't do that."

Andrew cast them off again. "This"—he pointed with his free hand to the glans—"this is what you took: the *flesh.*"

"Please." Ben was both embarrassed and unnerved. He had seen enough plays in his time to know that when people went mad they often turned obscene. "Cover up, now, please."

Andrew ignored the plea. "No right! you had no right to cut it. Not yours to give, God's to claim—no matter what was promised in return: makership," he scoffed, "assurances of makership. By making Him the Maker, your Maker, He in turn vouched for you as mine, the maker of me. The proof is in the trademark." Andrew designated the scar on his glans. "That was your covenant, sealed by a scrap of flesh. So much, it must have seemed, for so little, a little scrap of flesh. Yet not just any scrap, cut from any part, but *this*, the sheath, cut from the man-child; that must be the token. Why? Did you stop to think what God for His part stood to gain?" He paused to let his father speak, but the old man backed away from the bed. "Authority!" Andrew stopped him. "The instrument of authority—that's what you gave, put into His hands, not just a scrap of flesh, but the instrument itself, the instrument unsheathed. *This*"— he shook his penis impassionedly, causing his father to blurt out, almost voicelessly, the name Peggy—"this is the rod by which He rules!—more than rules, is bodied forth; the rod you take for your rod and staff. *This*"—again he shook his penis, tugged it to the utmost; again his father uttered the woman's name—"this is the god himself, the god with whom you made your covenant." Andrew let go of his penis disgustedly, as though in repudiation of the living god. "No covenant at all! Confraternity! is what you made—for men only, women not allowed. *That's* why it had to be this scrap, no other, not for promises of makership—just the opposite: disappearance! deicide! did away with Holy Mother; turned Her upside down; put God the Father in Her place. No use! It's *Hers*, this flesh, Hers by rights, no matter what you claim. By cutting it off, you cut yourself off, too, from Her, Holy Mother . . . cut off Holy Mother," he repeated ruefully. His sorrow, however felt, lasted but a moment, whereupon Andrew, recovering his force, said in a redoubtable tone, "Now, give it back!"

"Peggy!" Ben called out.

"Give it back!"

"I'll just get Peggy."

"Give it back, I say!" Andrew shouted.

"Peggy!" shouted Ben.

In answer to the call came not only Peggy but also Mildred, Letty, Mathew and his wife, Lois, both of whom had been in the apartment but a few minutes. Of the five, only Peggy, Mathew, and Mildred entered the bedroom; the other two remained outside. In Letty's case staying in the hall had nothing to do with indifference. Ben's call had alarmed her just as much as the others, if not more, alarmed her at once about Andy's condition, Ben's heart, and the fate of her deep dark secret. The only reason she remained in the hall was that Mildred had pushed ahead of her, reached the bedroom first, and Letty, intimidated as always by her sister-in-law, had hesitated to follow. In that respect she felt ostracized from the bedroom, relegated to the hall by Milly, who always treated her like an inferior; but in another she felt that she was there by choice and thus more dignified, superior to Milly, who was utterly incapable of exercising comparable restraint.

As for Lois, she remained outside partly because that was the way she saw herself, had always seen herself in relation to the Spectors: as an outsider; partly because she, like Peggy, was gentile and therefore viewed the Spectors' appetite for family drama as something exotically Jewish; and partly because over the years she had gained a deep respect for her mother-in-law, whom she took for a model of sorts and wished in many ways, especially in temperament and spirit, to emulate; so that the moment a scene such as this occurred, Lois was only too ready to step aside and let Peggy act in her stead.

In the bedroom now Peggy by-passed Ben, went straight to the bed to check on Andrew. His eyes, to her relief, were open, alert—more than alert, intense; his breathing, though somewhat rapid and shallow, didn't seem unduly labored; his cheeks showed signs of color, and he even responded to her inquiries, albeit crabbily (another good sign), muttering a word that sounded like "faker." Catching sight of his genitals, cupped in his palm, she asked if he needed the bottle, to which Letty answered for him, calling from the hallway that he had used the bottle earlier. Since that didn't preclude his having to use it again, Peggy offered the bottle anyway, but Andrew pushed it aside; whereupon she set about to straighten the bedclothes. Mildred, meantime, having put her mind at ease about Ben's heart, turned her back on Andrew, whose dishabille embarrassed her, and tried to ascertain what had prompted Ben to call out. Though he promised in an undertone to tell her "later," Ben was unwilling to discuss the matter now, would say only that his brother was a little batty, but even then he used the word *tsedrait* so that neither Peggy nor Mat, who was standing within earshot at the foot of the bed, would understand. Despite Ben's precautions, Mat, who by now had assured himself that his father was all right, took up Milly's question. Ben remained evasive, unwilling to shed any light on the subject. Only when pressed by his nephew did he finally say, "I—I took a cherry; he got enraged."

"With me, too," Letty chimed in from the hall, "the cherries."

"Maker," muttered Andrew.

"What's this?" said Peggy. She had come upon the check among the bedclothes. "Ben?"

"Oh, that." He stalled.

"Made out to me?" Peggy was having her difficulties reading the check without glasses. "Five thousand! For what?"

The others were equally curious. Milly cast a questioning glance at Ben. Mat, wanting to have a look, reached for the check, but his mother, while making no show of her refusal, held on to it. At the same time Letty, always on the qui vive about money but especially so now with the deep dark secret on her mind, dropped her reserve and slipped into the bedroom.

Ben's first impulse was to take back the check, but for some reason, no less intuitive, he promptly changed his mind. The idea of leaving the check appealed to him even more, promised somehow to put things right, restore the status quo. Never had he felt more convinced of Andy's need for professional care. "Look, sweetheart," he said to Peggy, "you've been under a terrible strain—months and months; you can't go on like this, alone, without anyone—"

"There," said Peggy to Andrew as she pulled the overfold of the sheet up to his chest. "Hungry?" Andrew spited her with silence. "Mat, you stay with Dad. The rest of us will go back inside." Thereupon, Peggy, implementing her own decree, extended her arms and, wielding them like a staff, herded Milly, Ben, and Letty out of the bedroom.

Left alone, Mat scrutinized his father with a penetrating, impersonal gaze, the kind of gaze with which he received his patients at the office, trying to determine Andrew's state of mind. For several months now he had been weighing the pros and cons of placing his father in a nursing home. More and more he tended to favor the idea. So, too, did Dr. Oxenburg with whom Mat had twice this month discussed the matter privately. The more Andrew's condition worsened, became virtually untreatable, the more Peggy became the focus of Oxenburg's attention and concern, as though she, rather than her husband, were the patient. Strong as she was, remarkably strong, her strength was of the will, and both Mat and Oxenburg worried about her endurance. Accordingly, the doctor, urged on by Mat, had finally broached the subject this very morning. Peggy, of course, had scorned the idea, wouldn't consider a nursing home. Mat understood, fully appreciated his mother's attitude. After all, since she alone would have to live with it, the decision rested solely with her—her and the gods. At the same time, however, Mat couldn't help but feel especially qualified, by virtue of his training and experience as a psychoanalyst, to counsel her. He wanted to make sure his mother would do what was best not only for Andrew but for herself. With that in mind he welcomed this opportunity to be alone with his father. If, as Mat suspected, Andrew had practically lost his ability to recognize the members of the family, know exactly who or where he was; and if, as Oxenburg had put it, the situation could go on like this "for years," then Mat saw no alternative to a nursing home.

Observing now his father's pensive, somewhat disgruntled expression and inward-looking eyes, as well as the blanketed hand, engaged like the hand of a sleeper in fingering his groin, Mat wondered whether Andrew was even conscious of his presence. Uncertain, he drew closer, skirting the bed, and sat down in the rocking chair. "Too much excitement?"

"Wouldn't give it back."

"Who?" Mathew waited for the answer. "What back, Dad?"

Andrew, glad as always to foil that woman who kept tucking him in, cast the bedclothes off again, and was about to call attention to his glans, when suddenly he stopped and took a long hard look at his visitor. "Don't call me 'Dad.' "

The son in Mathew was amused, the analyst attentive. "What would you prefer?" So long as Andrew seemed to be considering the question, Mat was content to wait, but after a full minute he could only conclude that his father's mind had wandered. "Did you see the landing?" Again Mat waited, while Andrew stared at him in silence. "Funny, the kids took no interest—Rafe, at least. Wendy would have watched, I think—I'm sure—if Rafe had let her, hadn't induced her to go to the movies. 'A greater tribute to the reality principle,' he called them, movies, than the space program." Mat chuckled. "How he loves to use the terminology. Witty, in a way, but disaffected, too—the disaffected generation. Gosh, when I think how much it meant to me as a kid, astronomy. Remember, Dad?" To Mat's surprise, this time, as he waited, his father broke the silence.

"Babe." Andrew, responding at last to the original question, stated his preference.

"Yes, Dad."

Having put it plainly once, Andrew saw no reason to repeat himself, say again how much he disliked being called Dad. Instead, he dismissed the offensive appellation with a scowl. "So *you're* here, too."

Andrew's undisguised enmity all but convinced Mat that his father didn't recognize him. "Who do you think—" he began, but thought better of making him guess. "It's Mat, Dad."

"I know . . . just who you are."

Mat remained unconvinced. "Who?"

Andrew, staring intently, took his time, transfixed his brother with unblinking eyes. "First-born."

The unexpected answer caught Mat off guard, affected him diversely. For one thing, it made him reconsider his assumption that Andrew didn't recognize him; apparently he did, but then why the enmity? For another, it touched him like an undercurrent, faintly stirring dormant sentiments about his brother Christopher. "That's true, of course. But—but why put it that way? Unless you mean, not Chris?"

"Privileged one is what I mean, preferred one, receiver of the birthright."

"In what way privileged? Because I—I survived? Is that

what you mean by birthright?"

"Don't act so innocent. You know perfectly well."

"The word, yes, but not—no idea what you have in mind."

"Mind?" Andrew hugged himself as though against the elements. "Body," he corrected his brother. "The right to lord it over the second-born, slap him into servitude, slavery! . . . liquidate him, if need be."

Once more Mat was unprepared, surprised not only by the statement but by his father's virulence. Too much of Mathew's history had been affected, if not determined, by his brother's early death for him to take impersonally such an allegation; nor could his father's choice of the word *liquidate*, in reference to a son who had drowned, be purely accidental. For years Mat had struggled with the problem of his brother's death, and though it had been resolved eventually, he remained anything but insouciant about Chris. However much he tried now to concentrate exclusively on his father, tried to consider what *liquidate* revealed about his father's thoughts and feelings, Mat nonetheless had difficulty maintaining his neutrality, keeping himself, his own thoughts and feelings, out of the discussion. "Is that the way you see me, Dad? A despot, lording it over my brother?"

"Despoiler," Andrew put it to his brother plainly.

"You think I liquidated him?"

"Think? I know."

"Drowned." Mathew tried to state it gently. "He drowned."

An image of an aqueduct, which seemed more dreamed than actual—perhaps because it was subterranean and so poorly lighted—appeared before Andrew's inner eye. At the same time he had no doubt the place existed, that he had been there in reality. "A kind of waterway."

"Ocean."

"Baby-snatcher."

"The ocean?" Mat tried to follow his father's thought.

"Abducted him."

"Only swimming."

"Battered him."

"Calm that day, according to Mom."

"Hurled him down."

"Not rough at all."

"Fatal scuffle."

"Hemorrhage, Dad."

"Cracked his skull."

"Cerebral hemorrhage."

"You cracked his skull!" Andrew charged his brother.

"I—" Irrational though the accusation was, Mathew could see that his father believed it unequivocally. No wonder there was enmity. "You must feel awf— . . . hold yourself responsible in some way, Dad, to say a thing—put—put it onto me like that. You mustn't—blame yourself, I mean. No one was to blame; not you, not me, not Mom. . . . Fate."

"Exactly! Always! . . . always hated him."

"I didn't say—"

"Couldn't bear the sight—"

"Why do you—what basis—"

"Wait to do away with him—"

"How? Fights, you mean?" Provoked now, Mat was both curious to hear the charges and ready to refute them. "Tell me. How did I show it, my hatred?"

"*Physically*," Andrew growled. "Fists, boots, belts, buckles—"

"Even if I did," Mathew allowed for the sake of argument, "he gave as good as he got."

"Brass buckles." Demonstrating, Andrew made a fist, cocked the middle knuckle like the hammer of a pistol, and aimed it at his brother. " 'Eggies,' you called them, 'love taps,' the blows, bruises you delivered, black-and-blue, burst the vessels—started *then*, with *you*: bowlinisms."

While his father stopped to fiddle with his pajama pocket (his other hand, the fist, still at the ready, knuckle cocked, trained on Mat), Mathew tried to puzzle out "bowlinisms," linking the word with vessel, vein, blood, embolus . . . "Embolism?"

"Pits! produced by you . . . choking the gift, hardening the art. . . ."

Scarcely had Mat begun to deal with this second puzzle —had his father left unfinished the word *artery* or did he, in fact, mean *art?*—when it became clear to him that Andrew was referring to himself, speaking of himself as the victim. "Arteries?"

Andrew's mouth opened wide, revealing what remained of his decaying, gold-filled, almost gumless lower teeth. From his windpipe came a ghastly sound, half arid whisper, half the harsh dredging noise that precedes expectoration. "Heart!"

The word evoked Mathew's sympathy, did away with his defensiveness. He had the impulse now to touch his father's hand, smooth down the still-cocked knuckle, but as soon as he acted on the impulse, Andrew pulled his hand away. Despite the rebuff, Mat remained convinced that his father had been speaking of himself; in which case, it followed, he must also have been speaking of his brother, his *own* brother, not Chris. "Ben, you mean, it's Ben—"

"You!" countered Andrew. A confusion of words— *gainer, nelson, strangle hold, kidney punch*—came to mind as he struggled to remember the wrestling term used to describe the hold in which you first grabbed your opponent's wrist, then twisted and wrenched his arm behind his back. "Twister!" he vilified the bully in his brother.

At mention of his brother's nickname Mathew broke out in goose bumps. "Not Uncle Ben?"

"*Uncle*," Andrew pounced on the word, "yes! made him cry uncle, lick your boots."

A pang of remorse forced Mat to draw an anxious breath. He suddenly felt vulnerable, defenseless, unable to refute the charge—doubtless because it was true! He had indeed made his brother cry. But then, what older brother hadn't? No, it wasn't culpability that was causing him now to feel eight years old, but his father's vehemence—the immediacy for Andrew of the injury, the outrage which triggered his resentment, the truculence with which it was released, as though the alleged bullying had taken place but a moment ago, and Mat had been caught in the act. Yet even if he had, his father's response was entirely out of line, exaggerated, irrational. No matter . . . just because Mat was culpable, because he once had made his brother cry, he found himself susceptible now to his father's irrationality, susceptible to his own. No matter that his brother had been dead for almost forty years and that his father, too, was dying—dying! . . . Usually the awareness made Mat feel that much more capable and vigorous, virtually parental,

238

as though *he* were Andrew's father, but not today, not now; he suddenly felt eight again and altogether blameworthy, to blame not only for his brother's death but also somehow for his father's dying. . . . Bowing his head and leaning on his elbows, Mat brought his brow to rest on his intercupped hands. "Did I?"

"Know you did—anything! to prove your superior strength, protect your precious birthright."

"Sorry." Though Mat had grown tearful, the apology was not for that. About tears he felt no inhibition or embarrassment (what prompted him now to bury his face in his palms was not self-consciousness but sorrow's instinctual need for privacy); nor did he try to stop the tears. On the contrary, he had trained himself to be in touch with his emotions, experience intrepidly whatever he was feeling; and what he was feeling at present was penitence. "Sorry . . . if I did . . . *did*," he confessed openly. "Didn't know any better . . . boy, a boy . . . what child does? . . . pecking order. . . . Would have been all right—hadn't drowned"—the utterance was muffled, as though Mat himself were drowning—"if only he hadn't drowned! . . . Had to live with it so long, most of my life . . . mark of Cain . . . for killing him, killing a brother I *didn't* kill. Oh, Dad!" he pleaded in innocence, "I didn't kill him—please remember that."

"Didn't you?" Andrew challenged his brother.

"No," said Mat, as much to reassure himself as his father. Then, taking out a handkerchief, he wiped away the tears. "Look, Dad"—he met his father's steely gaze—"you—you won't understand this—what I'm— What makes it hard, your saying that, is not that *you* believe it—*have* to for some reason—but that *I* do—did," he corrected himself; "once . . . once believed it, too. That's the trouble. Took so long, years and years, therapy, for me to come to terms with it, make my peace with Twister." A knowing smile suddenly enlivened Mat's expression. "Let's face it, Dad, he wasn't half the innocent—not by a long shot—you seem to think, have turned him into in memory. No child is. Every child wants to kill his brother . . . from time to time . . . father, too. Doesn't mean we act on it. The same holds true of fathers," he added pointedly. "Every father wants to kill his son at times—didn't you?"

"Kill?"

"Umm."

"Son?" Andrew knitted his brows.

"Sure." Mat shrugged lightheartedly. "Why not?"

"Wanted only to adore you."

The bittersweet avowal had an instantaneous effect. Once more Mat was reduced to tears, welling this time from a depth much deeper than before, a depth that knew nothing of bitterness, responded only to the sweet, the sweetness of unqualified, unguarded love. "Me, too. Did . . . did adore . . . loved you so." Bending over, he lay his head childlike on the mattress, as though on his father's lap, and sobbed unabashedly. "Oh, my Dad! *you* were the one . . . guarded . . . after . . ." He pressed closer, needing to touch and be touched by his father, express physically the feelings of their emotional communion. Yet the moment his fingers reached his father's cheek, Andrew recoiled again, backed toward the headboard, breaking the communion. "What stopped you?"

"Twister."

"From loving *me?*"

"Forced to keep my distance . . . harden. . . ."

"I? I did, forced you, or his death?"

"You! . . . despoiler."

"Despoiler? Of what?"

"Learned from you."

"Learned what?"

"Taught us all."

"To what?"

"Kill!" Andrew used his knee, as though his pitiless accusing eyes were not enough, to drive his brother from the mattress, make him fall back to the rocker. "Yes!" he hissed, showing his decrepit teeth, "he wished to kill . . . learned from you—*had* to, had to learn: self-defense, but always lost—no match for you: superior strength—always beaten, beaten down. . . ." Rooting through his pajama pocket, Andrew fumbled for and finally came up with one of the bowlinisms, poised between his fingertips. "Beaten into *this.*"

Though Andrew's knee had succeeded not only in repulsing Mat but in tempering his subjectivity, he nonetheless rocked forward now, compelled by his father's passion, to see what Andrew was holding. The discoloration of whatever it was, made the thing look bruised, unclean, made Mat grimace. "What is that?"

"Egg . . . 'egg,' he called it—imbecile!"

"Who?"

"*Once*,"—Andrew ignored the question—"once was that: gift imperative, circulating freely, fluently, through all— one body, blood, bearing all. . . . No more. Hardened now." He revolved the bowlinism between his thumb and forefinger, studying it closely. "Eggie now . . . 'eggie,' you called it. Pill!" he disparaged his brother. "Bitter pill, medicine we're made to take, force down at the end . . . where once there was no end, only reappearance. . . ."

Having figured out what his father was holding, Mat was concerned now to keep Andrew from swallowing the pit in his confusion. "Not your medicine, Dad. Your medicine is here." He indicated the night table. "That's a cherry pit."

"Pit. That's right, pit into which you cast your brother, sold him into bondage—with no way out, no way back—so that you could be first-born . . . self-made, say 'I,' say 'mine'—me! me! mine! mine!—where once there was no singular, only *us*. Singular? Listen!" he cried out, "either each of us is first-born or no one is, all are quadrillionth! . . . Excepting you! would stop at nothing—kill!—to keep your title: first-and-only born . . . first to kill. Couldn't bring yourself to share it any longer, share with the women; had to hog it all—strip the flesh, crack the bone, suck the marrow—flesh and bone and marrow of your *brother*. Fratricide!" Andrew showed no mercy in pronouncing the judgment. "You took the gift imperative and turned it into *this*" —once more he exhibited the bowlinism—"a bone yard, mountain-slide of bones. Took the Host, Holy Host, and turned it into livestock, to feed yourself—never mind generating others—just feed yourself, on *him*, your brother, while he was given piss; you made him drink your piss!" Now all at once it dawned on Andrew what the bowlinism was for: to undo the work of the despoilers. "*Your* turn now!" he declared savagely, shoving the bowlinism at his brother. "Eat it!"

Hard as Mat tried to maintain his composure, exercise detachment, he felt intimidated, frightened, not by his father's ranting but by his demonic appearance. Never had he seen Andrew look so ugly, ferocious, his face contracted to half its size, mostly snout, mouth contorted cruelly, crookedly framing his bared teeth (the lowers degenerate and crude in contrast with the artificial uppers), from behind which bulged his coated tongue. "Take some water, Dad."

"Eat it!"

"What good would that do?"

"You heard me!"

"Won't bring him back."

"*Eat it*, I said."

Glancing at the medicine tray, Mat spotted what he was looking for: the container of tranquilizers. "Let's both take one," he suggested, reaching over the bowl of cherries for the Thermos jug. "I'll just pour—"

"Eat it"—Andrew, growing more aroused, swung his legs over the side of the bed and, struggling upright, thrust the bowlinism to within an inch of his brother's face—"or I'll kill you!"

Mat had only to see the malevolent look in his father's eye and hear his cold-blooded tone of conviction to know that Andrew meant what he said. It would be useless, if not inciting, either to oppose or try to reason with the man. He therefore took the cherry pit and, palming it while pretending to put it into his mouth, went through the motions of chewing.

After a long silence, during which Andrew eyed his brother first with suspicion, then gloating, he gave a new command: "Swallow it!"

Mathew did as he was told, and though he only simulated swallowing, the function seemed as difficult as if the cherry pit were actually passing down his gullet. What made it difficult was the pronounced discrepancy between his father's passion and appearance. On the one hand was the fiery autocrat issuing commands and taking cruel pleasure in watching them carried out; on the other was the pitiable, almost broken figure hunched now on the edge of the bed, his right hand still outstretched, still issuing the last command, the fingers of his left gripping the mattress to keep himself from keeling over, legs awry, fly undone, genitals exposed—a senile, moribund old man in a pair of striped pajamas transmitting angry oracles from God-knew-what

242

repository of the unconscious.

"So much for the pit," Andrew summed up, adding mockingly the afterthought "despoiler."

Even as Andrew was enjoying his moment of triumph—a moment that, ironically, also served to liberate Mathew from his father's authority—Mat suddenly became aware of a distant ruckus. He was able to distinguish some of the voices (his uncle's, followed by those of both his aunts speaking at once), but none of the words. Yet the minute he started listening in earnest, the outburst ended, stifled no doubt out of consideration for the "patient." "Want to get back into bed?" Mat stood up, ready to assist his father.

"Oh"—Letty insinuated herself into the room—"sitting up —how nice." As she approached the bed her nephew waved her away. "Oh"—she caught on immediately—"bottle again."

Once Mathew realized that his father hadn't the slightest intention of either getting up or going back to bed, but, quite simply and demonstrably, was staying put, his back to the room, Mat left the bedside and went over to speak to his aunt. "What's going on in there?"

"Tut!" She flapped her hand and made a face, a comical one meant to suggest that she alone was above the fray and rather bored with the carryings-on of the others. "You know your mother and Uncle Ben when they get started."

"Over what?"

"Birthright," muttered Andrew.

"No, my darling," Letty explained, "that check of Ben's. I trust you remembered your promise, didn't say a word—"

Mat made a sign for Letty to save her breath. "Agitated." He described Andrew's condition in an undertone.

"Who's agitated?" Andrew wanted to know.

"Ben," came Mat's quick reply, after which he turned back to his aunt. "Where's Lois?"

"In the kitchen with the children."

"Mine?"

"Yours?" Letty lost the thread of the conversation.

"Rafe and Wendy—they're here?"

"Quite a while—you didn't know?—helping with the supper. That Wendy of yours—*umbeshrien*—is she a beauty, the men had better—"

"Ben, you say?" inquired Andrew. "Still around?"

"You bet your life!" Ben answered for himself as he

sailed into the bedroom with the aforementioned check fluttering pennantlike in his hand and with Mildred steadfast in his wake. "Around and kicking."

Andrew looked perplexed. Still facing the window, his back to the room, he peered out at the overcast sky. "Didn't disappear?"

Ben was taken aback until Letty explained, without once removing her eyes from the check, that Andrew was a bit "off" again. Mathew, meantime, opened his palm to consider the cherry pit. Mildred for her part was impatient to get the good-byes over with. To begin with, the quarrel in the living room had upset her, especially the part about "conscience money"; and now the air in the bedroom all but turned her stomach. It was foul with flatulence and a caseous smell which for some reason she associated with death. Obviously Peggy had no idea of the number of room deodorizers on the market nowadays—even Chinamen used incense! "Andy?" she said as she approached the bed somewhat gingerly, wanting not to startle him, but Andrew showed no sign of recognition. "We're going now." Mildred stopped at the foot of the bed. She preferred to keep her distance. "Stay well."

"He better, the loafer." Ben joined her but ventured no closer than his wife had.

Letty alone showed no hesitation: sat right down in the rocking chair, face to face with Andrew, and took his hand. The hand was limp, unresponsive. She would have thought him dead were it not for signs of breathing. Even so, she thought he might be dozing, and bent over to see if his eyes were open. They were, however listless. "See you tomorrow, my darling."

Emboldened by Letty's example, Ben sat down beside his brother. "Wish I could say the same, Babe." His evident regret was tinged with resentment as though the decision to go abroad were not of his own making. "We're going away—not for long—couple weeks," he fibbed. "*Ziseh* here" —Ben glanced over his shoulder at Mildred who, in turn, shook her head and made a gesture as if to say, Don't knock yourself out, he doesn't understand a word—"she needs a rest."

"Never mind"—Letty stroked Andrew's hand—"*I'll* be

here; every day, as God gives the day, I'll be here. Don't worry, Benny."

Ben resented his sister's proprietary attitude, resented her usurpation of his rightful place. "Not worried"—he feigned indifference. He was not only worried but conscience-stricken to leave his little brother in the lurch like this.

"He'll be all right, Ben," Mat assured his uncle.

The sound of his nephew's voice reminded Ben of the check in his hand, and he began to toy with it, flexing it like a bow, even as he stared blankly into space. " 'Conscience money.' "

"What?" said Mat.

" 'Conscience money,' she called it, your mother."

"Why?" said Mat.

"Stubborn! always—"

"Ben!" Mildred was anxious to head off any fresh out-break of hostilities.

"Mat." Ben held the check overhead. "Do me a favor, will you please?" he requested humbly. "Take it."

"Sure, but why? What's it for?"

"Conscience . . . con—— cov-covenant—"

"Never mind what it's for!" snapped Mildred, disturbed by Ben's crumbling poise. "Just take it!" she commanded her nephew, and, snatching the check from Ben's hand, transmitted it to Mat's.

Mathew had no choice but to comply. Now, with the cherry pit in one hand and the check in the other, he felt like an unwilling participant in an enigmatic game of scav-enger hunt. The feeling lasted but a moment, interrupted suddenly by strains of piano music coming from the next room. "Wendy." Mat took pride in his daughter's playing. "Hear it, Dad? For you, I'm sure." Everyone stopped to listen, grateful for the soothing interlude. The poignant little piece suggested the composer's struggle to overcome some painful sense of loss and heartache. Its delicate rippling tones were reminiscent of Chopin, yet Mat could not be certain—it might be Liszt—so much had Wendy's repertoire grown in recent months. "Who's the composer, Dad?" he asked, not to test his father but to draw him into conversa-tion.

Well as Andrew knew the names of both the piece and

the composer, he couldn't come up with either. Not that it really mattered; such things as names and dates no longer made a bit of difference. The best he could do was to give an impression of the composer's appearance by tugging the hair at his nape.

The peculiar gesture caught Ben's eye. "Haircut?"

"Longhair?" Mat built on his uncle's guess as if they were playing charades.

"Liszt," Letty hit upon the answer.

"Good-bye, Andy." Mildred seized the opportunity to take her leave. "Come on, Ben. We'll never get packed at this rate."

"Bye, loafer." Ben made a fist, cocked the middle knuckle, and poked his brother tenderly twice on the upper arm. "Keep punching."

"Eggie," said Andrew.

"Soon," said Letty, "you'll have your supper."

"He doesn't mean—" Ben started to explain, but thought better of it. He hadn't heard the expression *eggie* in a dog's age. Something about it saddened him. So, too, did the soulful little melody coming from the next room. As he stood up he had a presentiment that he would never see his brother again, never in this life. One minute you were giving your brother an eggie, and the next you were burying him; and the seventy years in between were as nothing, a twinkling . . . already past.

"What's the matter, Ben?" Mildred was quick to notice his grieved expression.

"Nothing . . . music." He bent down, as much to hide his sorrow as to kiss his brother's crown. "God bless you."

Letty, taking her cue from Mildred and Ben, wished her "darling" a peaceful night and tiptoed after the others out of the room. Their departure coincided with the end of the music, and a murmur of voices ensued. The voices distracted Mat, who in the meantime had been prompted by his father's reiteration of "eggie" to examine the cherry pit once more. But now he pocketed the pit, together with the check, and, going to the corner, rolled the wheelchair toward the bed. "Dinner, Dad."

Andrew shook his head: He had no appetite at all.

"Well, come inside anyway."

Again Andrew shook his head, but otherwise remained

inert, perched, as he had been all the while, on the edge of the bed, his back to the door.

"Dad!" Raphael stuck his head into the room and called out in a stage whisper, "Wendy wants to know, should she play another piece?"

Mathew nodded, then raised a finger, requesting his son to wait; he wanted to have a word with him at the door. "How was the movie?"

"Like it is." Rafe's highest praise, by which he also meant to put down the Apollo landing, was followed by a qualifier. "A little dull."

Mat laughed, uncertain though he was whether the qualifier was intentional. "Sit with Grandpa, will you? I want to see what's happening."

Raphael was only too willing to stay with Andrew. No sooner did his father leave the room than the boy made a beeline for the wheelchair. The chair brought out the child in Rafe, induced behavior that in someone seventeen could, he realized, be called regressive. He didn't give a shit! loved to play with the contraption, imagine it a chariot, a motorboat, a sports car, anything but what it was: irrefutable evidence of Andrew's infirmity; loved to drive it forward, shift into reverse, execute a hairpin turn. Such maneuvering required skill, mechanical admittedly, yet no more mechanical than playing the piano. At least it took some imagination to turn a wheelchair into an Alfa Romeo, not just dumb technique. Face it! what could be more mechanical than all that drilling, all those scales? In that respect Wendy took after Mom and Dad, the technicians, while he took after Andrew and Peggy, the artists. Poor Wendy, no matter how proficient she became, how rich and famous, she would never amount to more than a performer, an interpreter of other people's passion, other people's inspiration, whereas he was destined to express his own, become, like Grandpa, a creator, a maker of great movies! Like Grandpa, he had been given the gift of the gods, and Grandpa knew it, had always known it; right from the start, in childhood, Grandpa had spotted the gift in him. That was their special bond, what made them more than grandfather and grandson, made them kindred spirits, fellow artists, almost peers— the gift had a way of wiping out all kinds of phony distinctions: time and generations—made Grandpa love him more than Wendy, more than all the other children in the family, even more, Rafe sometimes thought, than Dad himself. Poor Dad had been skipped by the gene that bore the gift. Most likely that was why Dad had left the room, because he didn't know what to say to Andrew anymore, didn't know how to talk to him, relate to him. No one did but Rafe. After all, he was the only person Andrew continued to recognize consistently, the only person who could still converse with Andrew, draw him out, cheer him up—all of which Raphael now set about to do. "Hi, Andrew."

Hard as Andrew stared, he couldn't quite make out his visitor against the light. "Who is it?"

Raphael brought the wheelchair closer. "Me."

"You!" A tremor, strong enough to make Andrew grip the mattress, spread through his body, and his eyes welled tears. For a moment he gazed at the boy adoringly. Then, letting go the mattress, he reached out with both hands, as though mistrustful of his failing sight, to touch Twister.

Raphael, attentive to the old man's need, promptly took the gnarled and bony hands in his, held them tenderly. "Yes, me."

"You've come back!"

"Don't, Andrew, please"—with his thumbs the boy caressed the bulging tendons of his grandfather's hands—"don't cry."

"Can't help it. Never dreamed you'd reappear."

"Why wouldn't I?"

"No longer possible . . . I thought." As the tears streamed down Andrew's cheeks he squeezed with all his strength the smooth and hairless hands in his, as if to verify their corporeality. "Here! . . . you're here! . . . and in the flesh."

Rafe patted his belly self-consciously, tried to make a joke of it. "A little overweight, I know—don't rub it in."

"Have I come to you? . . . or you to me?"

Raphael, wanting to play down his grandfather's restricted mobility, evaded the question. "What's the difference?"

"All the difference in the world."

"Me to you—I'm younger." The boy resorted to logic, whereupon he yanked a facial tissue from the box with a flourish (Rafe did nothing, if not demonstratively), helped his grandfather blow his nose, and then soaked up the tears.

"How did you do it, get here—in *that?*"

The idea of riding around the city in a wheelchair delighted Rafe, and he nodded enthusiastically. "Like . . . like—what's-his-name?—the sun god in his chariot."

"Apollo?"

"No! never—are you kidding, man—that's the moon, command module."

"Moon?" Andrew looked about discreetly as though the orb were present somewhere in the room.

"Those astronauts, they're up there for only one fucking reason—excuse the language—to distract us from this fucking war."

" 'Moon,' you say? Is that—" Andrew hesitated; when he spoke again, his voice was hushed: "Who sent you?"

"No one 'sent' me."

"Not . . . the Mother?"

"Mother!" The mere suggestion offended Rafe's pride. "No one tells *me* what to do, least of all Mom and Dad— God love 'em—too compulsive. Anally." He summarized his parents in a word. "I came here on my own—own steam" —impetuously the boy backed the wheelchair up to the wall behind him, as if to demonstrate his "steam"—"own man. Don't underestimate me, Andrew."

"Oh, no, I don't, believe me." Andrew had to chuckle. "But if you weren't sent, wh-why have you come?"

"Take care of you."

"Take? . . . take me? In *that?*"

"Right on!" Raphael drove the wheelchair back at once and hopped out like a chauffeur. "Ready for a ride, sir?"

"Not yet. First, there's . . . something we must talk about." So disturbing was the subject, however, that Andrew failed to make himself understood, murmured something unintelligible.

"Come again."

"Absolution."

Now that Raphael heard the word, he was doubly puzzled because he didn't know its meaning. "Solution?"

"Do-do you," Andrew stammered in a whisper, lowering his lids, unable to look Twister in the eye, "forgive me?"

"Forgive? . . . For what?"

"Everything, all I did," came the anguished reply, "made you disappear—I—I made you disappear."

Frowning, Raphael glanced down at his sneakers as if to reassure himself that he was really there. "How—how do you mean, 'disappear'? I don't get it."

"Didn't understand at first, when you came originally, just where you had come *from*. . . . Wasn't ready for you —what man is?—all too young, too old, set in our ways for kids. Far as I could see, you came like an onslaught—kicking, screaming, trailing chaos. That alone seemed to be your purpose: disturb the peace, disrupt the order, the very peace and order by which I lived. Had to put a stop to it, restrain you in some way. And so I set about to change you," he recounted sadly, "turn you into something you were not, never meant to be—model child."

"Me!" The notion sounded laughable to Rafe. "Model?"

"Yes . . . yes. . . . You wanted to wear your hair uncombed, wild—wouldn't let you, insisted on a part" (this statement prompted the boy to finger questioningly his long ungovernable locks) "nothing crooked either, had to be straight, straight as a rule . . . rules and regulations—hair slicked down, fingernails clipped, clean—cleanliness . . . 'next to godliness,' you were told, taught to wash your hands before leaving the john—'all employees must wash their hands,' piss only in the urinal, never in the bed—forbidden! 'But I like the way it feels!' you answered back, shouted, always shouted, could never say anything, whatever it might be—'Pass the pickles please' (except there would have been no 'please')—without shouting, grabbing the pickles before anyone had a chance to pass them—boardinghouse reach, your—your body itself had boardinghouse reach, always on the run, rampage, bumping into everything—bull in a china shop, breakage, shaking the piano strings, glassware on the shelves, shattering the peace — Couldn't, couldn't think"—Andrew brought his hands to his temples as though to deaden the assault—"couldn't bear the chaos—threat-threatened me, my work, couldn't do my work."

"Not because of *me*," the boy objected. Since so much of what Andrew had said rang true—who the fuck had blabbed about the bed-wetting?—Raphael was relieved now to realize that Andrew was speaking not just of him but of Dad as well, lumping the two of them together; the part about the hair gave it all away. Had Dad been a bed wetter, too? "Couldn't have been me, Andrew, never kept you from working."

"Of course not—*me*," he stated simply, "only me. That's just the point"—Andrew leaned forward to confide in his son—"mistook you, mistook you for myself. That part, at least, that once had been rampageous, too, raising cain, running riot, releasing all that energy—inborn energy, held in check, channeled into work, solely into work, to make myself a model child . . . *perfect* really . . . punished otherwise."

"Were you a bed wetter, too?"

"Sure. Still am." Andrew grinned at his own little joke, and the boy grinned back.

Besides fascinating Rafe, the subject aroused in him a good deal of nervous energy to which the boy now gave vent not, as some people do, by jiggling a leg or jangling a set of keys, but by rubbing his groin with vigor. "Is that how you know about me? Or did—Dad told you?"

Though Andrew observed what Twister was doing, he refrained from comment. "Saw you, saw for myself—all I ever did see—nothing good, commendable, only what was 'bad,' forbidden." He brought his hands to his eyes, shading them as though with blinkers, to shut out what the boy was doing. "Distracted me, the rioting, unruliness—couldn't concentrate, do my work. Had to take measures, lay down the law." The phrase had been a favorite of his father's, and as he heard himself speaking it Andrew was saddened to recognize in his own tone the tone of Solomon, speaking through him. "Like my father, father did with me . . . and his with him no doubt—made you walk, not run, made you tiptoe, talk in a whisper, keep your hands— Stop doing that!" he blurted out.

"Doing what?"

"That!" Andrew pointed accusingly at the boy's crotch.

"What's wrong with 'that'?" said Rafe in perfect innocence.

"Nothing—sorry—nothing at all. Always like that—couldn't help myself—finding fault, criticizing, criticizing everything, least little thing: the way you held your pencil, laced your boots—nothing ever right—criticized you out of existence. Forgive me! God forgive me! Didn't mean—don't stop—didn't mean to stop you."

Raphael shrugged. "No big deal, if it bugs you." He left off rubbing his groin, sat back down in the wheelchair. "Little nervous energy, that's all."

"Not nervous, *natural*, all that natural energy, exuberance, nipped in the bud, high spirits quashed! For what? So that I could do my work. But couldn't!" he was quick to confess. "Couldn't work, couldn't let up on myself, let up on you." Overcoming his guilt, Andrew paused to look at his son searchingly, as though seeing him, truly seeing his winsome face, for the first time in his life. "Trouble was, you see, I didn't recognize the gift."

"What gift?"

"Yours, the one you brought."

"Gosh, Andrew"—Raphael ran his hand through his hair again, tugging at it this time—"I don't know; if *you* didn't, I sure don't know who did."

"Did I?" A flicker of hope enlivened Andrew's eyes.

"Always, from the start, recognized the gift we share, the two of us."

"*All* of us," he corrected the boy as the flicker disappeared, giving way to a dazed mournful stare. "No. Didn't understand. In my ignorance, assumed that you were mine, of my own making, come from me. Not *to* me—that I didn't understand till later, much later—but *from* me, to do with as I pleased. And what I pleased was to make you over . . . my own image. . . . No." He closed his eyes and lowered his voice, solemnifying what he was about to say. "Didn't understand, never did, that you were sent by Her."

"Who?"

"Whom," he corrected the boy, "sent by whom."

"That's what I'm asking!"

"Mother."

"Want to bet!" The suggestion made Raphael squirm with impatience, causing the wheelchair to squirm as well. "Why do you keep saying that? I just got finished telling you—"

"Sent by Holy Mother." In his fervor Andrew ignored Twister's denial, went right on, his tone devout and hushed. "Her agent here on earth—sent by Her to animate . . .

252

create— You alone made possible creation."

Raphael eyed his grandfather skeptically. "*Yours,* you mean, composing?"

"You alone."

"Gee, I—I—flattering, Andrew."

"You were the force that informed the work, endowed it with a shape, with—with everything—intervals, smallest intervals, semitones—the tones themselves came from you, nowhere else."

"Like, you mean, like I was—well, kind of your inspiration?"

Andrew nodded eagerly. "All *I* had to do was listen"—as if to demonstrate, he jerked his head, cocked an ear—"and, having listened, jot down what I heard, juggle it around a bit—orchestrate! that's all, orchestrate all that natural energy, imagination." His upraised hands fell back feebly into his lap. "Simple enough, you'd think, but not for me—too self-important, arrogant; assumed that everything was up to me, my responsibility, solely mine—me! the maker, mistook myself for the maker, you, you for—for the despoiler."

"Spoiler? Come on, man!" The Indian giving angered Rafe. "I thought— Didn't you just say I made the whole thing possible?"

"Did! you did . . . till I stopped you . . . blocked you —I! I was the despoiler—fearful I would lose control. *Control,*" Andrew repeated bitterly, "that became the crux: which of us would gain control. Oh, God!" he suddenly cried out, covering his head with both hands. "If only I had understood, had had the sense to keep myself out of it, not interfere in any way; if only I had put myself completely in your hands, become *your* agent, much as you were Holy Mother's—"

"Why do you keep calling her 'holy'?"

"Because She is . . . like you. . . . But wouldn't yield control," he went on about himself. "Instead of trusting, loving you, loving unconditionally, I har—hardened, hardened the—the, uh." Andrew faltered, searching for the right word. "Art!" he declared, but promptly struggled to correct himself: "H-h-heart! . . . Art—arteries, he thought, imbecile! That was how I lost you—hardening . . . to spare myself, spare myself the chaos, chaos of feelings, fend off feeling, feeling almost anything, fearful of the pain—lost you both, not only you but Holy Mother. Lost you both," he lamented, "made you disappear."

"Well, even if you did"—Raphael, seeing Andrew in tears again, tried to cheer him up—"here I am, I'm back!" As if to corroborate the fact, the boy hopped up from the wheel-chair.

"Yes!" Andrew breathed the word into audibility. "Yes . . . so you are . . . and in the flesh. Yet if you're here, and in the flesh"—he divined step by step, his tearful eyes intense and radiant with discovery—"then disappearance can't be *all*, can't have put an end, for good, to reappearance."

"Not on your life." Raphael played along.

"But—" Andrew hesitated, perplexed. "—If there's no way out, no way back, how—how's it possible, reappearance?"

"There's always a way," Rafe remarked philosophically; "everything is possible."

"So I see. But how?"

From the wealth of his experience the boy came up with the only answer he was certain of: "Love."

Though it didn't explain the mystery of reappearance, Twister's answer suggested something else, of even more immediate importance to Andrew. "D-does it mean, your reappearance, th-that . . . you forgive?"

"Sure do."

A little high-pitched wail, which seemed to issue not from Andrew's throat but from the crown of his skull, expressed his thanksgiving. "Means that She . . . She, too, forgives?"

"Uh-huh."

"Forgives us all?"

"Uh-huh."

"She—She's ready now to take us back?"

"Why not?"

"Oh!" Overjoyed, Andrew held out his arms to the boy who, for his part, entered them readily. "Twister"—he hugged his son with all his strength—"oh, my Twister!"

Since Raphael was all but unfamiliar with the nickname (Mathew seldom mentioned his dead brother, and then only as "Chris"), he didn't know what to make of the word. "What is it, Andrew? Something hurt you?"

"No more . . ." He released the boy and straightened up. "Ready now."

254

"For what?"

Andrew gestured toward the wheelchair.

"To take a ride? Cool! man, cool."

"Bathrobe," Andrew said as soon as the boy had helped him to his feet.

"You're right—need it." Fetching the robe from the foot of the bed, Raphael held it up for Andrew, guided his arms into the sleeves. "Kind of nasty out, cold for summer. Serves them right, those astronauts, to have such lousy weather— just what they deserve." His crowing lasted but a moment, whereupon Rafe realized with an awkward giggle how inapt his reasoning was. "Dumb of me: Doesn't follow, does it, that the weather's the same? No telling what it's like up there."

"Up where?"

"The moon."

While Andrew waited for the boy, who was having his difficulties with the bathrobe belt, to tie a satisfactory bow, he said with patent curiosity, "What *is* it like?"

"Grim, I guess. You'll see for yourself tonight."

"Tonight," Andrew repeated in a murmur, anticipating the event with rapture.

When, at last, Andrew looked presentable (the boy himself didn't understand what was making him fuss so, why he was taking such pains dressing and grooming his grandfather, as though he were dressing a doll, but he went so far as to run his own rather scurfy comb through Andrew's little bit of hair), Raphael brought the wheelchair closer to the bed. "At your service, sir."

"Hold it steady."

"Don't worry—brake's on."

After a good deal of backing and filling, Andrew finally lowered himself like a nesting fowl into the wheelchair. "Can't imagine that it's grim."

"Oh, good!" exclaimed Peggy, as she came into the room with her granddaughter, "you've got him up; but why the wheelchair?" Since Andrew was relatively mobile, she preferred to resort to the wheelchair only when going outdoors. "Where's the cane?"

"Don't blame me," Raphael protested, "talk to Dad, he's the one—"

"No one's blaming," Peggy said, reminded of how touchy

her grandson could be. "All right now, let's have supper."

"Hi, Grandpa," said Wendy.

Releasing the brake, Raphael towed the wheelchair backwards into the open and turned it a quarter turn. Only then did Andrew spy the younger woman—no more than a girl, really, however tall—whose golden hair streamed like a sun shower over her head and shoulders, framing her sun-tanned face; streamed like the sun itself in shafts of golden light, spilling down from her shoulders, over her breasts, and almost into her reposeful hands—those sturdy, reliable-looking hands with which Andrew associated some kind of musical instrument. "*Viola d'amore.*"

Puzzled and self-conscious, Wendy turned to her grandmother who was quick to explain, "That early instrument, like a viola—we saw one at the Met."

Wendy didn't remember. "We did?"

"Angel," Andrew said to the young girl as if he were addressing her by name.

Wendy smiled, showing her beautiful teeth, intensely bright in contrast with her sun-tanned skin. "How you doing, Grandpa?"

"Angel," repeated Andrew.

"That she is," Peggy agreed without a trace of sentimentality.

"Watch out there, 'angel'!" Raphael cautioned his sister.

"No rough stuff, Rafe," Peggy in turn cautioned her grandson, as the boy, relishing his all-important role, dipped the back of the wheelchair and whisked his grandfather out of the bedroom.

Since there was no dining room as such in the apartment, and the round table in the kitchen could accommodate no more than four, the sizable entrance hall, in which there stood an oblong wooden table, served as the dining area for company. The table had already been pulled away from the wall and set for six by Lois and Wendy. On a big ironstone platter in the center was an abundant chicken salad garnished with hard-boiled eggs, tomatoes, gherkins, and asparagus, as well as a smaller platter of potato salad, a dish of rolls and butter, and three pitchers: one of milk, one of iced coffee, one of iced tea. When praised for the spread, Peggy refused to take any credit, commending, instead, Mrs. Lexy who, she claimed, had "done it all" the day before, prior to leaving for her day off.

Once the chair at the foot of the table had been removed to make way for the wheelchair, and Andrew was securely in place, Peggy seated the rest of the family. Knowing how much her grandson liked to be the center of attention, she had him sit at the head of the table, flanked by Lois and Mat, while she herself, concerned to help Andrew with his food if necessary, took the chair on Andrew's right and seated Wendy opposite. Though Andrew said nothing for the longest time—he simply couldn't fathom the purpose of this gathering—it was his presence that nonetheless determined the course of conversation. Since no one could tell just when he was lucid and when he was not, no one felt the least bit free either to include him in the conversation or to ignore him and speak openly of what was on their minds. Still uppermost in Mathew's mind was the question of the nursing home. After what had happened in the bedroom, he felt more convinced than ever that his father belonged in a nursing home. At the same time, Mat wavered, had his scruples. He wanted to be sure that he wasn't reacting subjectively, vindictively, to his father's rancor, punishing his father. But even so, the subject was taboo. Peggy had seen to that, had taken Lois aside before dinner to tell her to tell Mat that she didn't want to hear "another word" on the subject. Nor did she want to discuss Ben's check, which was still tucked, together with the cherry pit, in the pocket of Mathew's polo shirt. Mat took the position that his mother should keep the check, deposit it; but she could find no justification for doing so, had rather tear it up. To complicate matters, Mat and Lois and the kids were due to start their summer vacation shortly, the first day of August, and the prospect of leaving Peggy alone for a month worried Mat. Both he and Lois had begged Peggy to come and stay with them as long as she liked. Not only did they think she could use the rest, they considered it a necessity. Much as Peggy hated being put in the position of always having to say no, she nevertheless refused. She could see no way of leaving Andrew alone with Mrs. Lexy —"wonderful" as the woman was—not even for a weekend; it would give her no peace. Nor did she take to the idea of bringing Andrew along; the change, she feared, would prove too abrupt, disorienting, no sort of vacation for anyone. No, all things considered, Peggy thought it best—best not only for Andrew but also for herself—to stay in the city. In response Lois, unbeknown to Peggy, went so far as to suggest cancelling the vacation, but Mathew wouldn't hear of it. As far as he was concerned, the only solution—much as he hated "coming back to the subject"—was a nursing home; short of that, the next best thing—much as he hated "agreeing with Ben"—was to hire a registered nurse. However, since none of these thoughts could be aired in front of Andrew, the dinner conversation tended toward more neutral topics such as the accident, the night before, at Chappaquiddick and the moon landing.

When it came to Chappaquiddick, Mathew feared that the death by drowning of Mary Jo Kopechne ("If indeed it was by drowning!"—Rafe had his doubts, suspected "drugs") would remind his father of Christopher and lead to further outbursts—a repetition Mat preferred to forestall. In consequence he tried to change the subject, but Rafe was much too fascinated by the scandal to let it go at that. What it all came down to, the boy insisted, was "dope and sex," and no one could tell him otherwise. Only when Lois accused him of being a worse gossip than Letty and declared that Rafe's interest in the case revealed more about his own prurient imagination and personal drug habits than about the accident—"Want to bet!" Raphael resorted to his favorite final retort—did the conversation turn to the Apollo landing.

At mention of the moon Andrew perked up, spoke for the first time. "Why the delay?"

Peggy, attentive to the fact that Andrew hadn't touched his food, took the opportunity to start feeding him while she explained about the housekeeping that had to be performed before the astronauts could emerge from the capsule.

At first Andrew resisted. He had misgivings about being fed by the woman, knew it should be the other way around. And yet it soon occurred to him that in the transition from disappearance to reappearance—so imminent now, according to Twister, due to commence tonight—the roles were reversed: The woman fed the man. Andrew was satisfied, therefore, to co-operate, chew his food diligently like a child aiming to please, and, when done, open wide to receive the next mouthful; but he wasn't satisfied with the woman's answer. "Why the delay?"

Now, as always, Rafe assumed that he alone understood what was on Andrew's mind. Jumping up, he fetched the second television set from the living room, placed it facing his grandfather on the unused dining room chair, and plugged it in. At the same time, he launched into a familiar screed about the space program, which in his opinion was either a cover-up for the war or, worse, an expansion of it. Either way, the establishment had better watch out because if anyone thought that the student riots had been bad this semester, just wait till they saw what was in store next fall.

"They've run their course," Mathew said, and Lois, herself a schoolteacher, agreed.

"That's what *you* think!"

"Middle-class rebellion," Mat concluded, "not in any way a revolution, just a way to punish Daddy."

"Want to bet!"

"Where did you get that expression, Rafe?" Peggy turned to her grandson. "Reminds me of Twister. Whatever you said, that was the answer, 'Wanta bet!'" She protruded her lower lip belligerently in playful mimicry of her dead son. "Once, at the zoo—you were with us, Mat—I said, 'Look! there's the camel.' 'Wanta bet!' he said, sticking out that lip. For a moment I thought, well, maybe I'm wrong, maybe it's a dromedary—never did know which was which, like turtle and tortoise; maybe he's going to take after his brother"—Peggy shot a provocative glance at Mat—"correct every blessed word I say. 'What do *you* think it is?' I said. 'Reindeer,' he said." The memory made her chuckle. "Remember, Mat?"

"The boy was right," Andrew said.

"Oh! so that's what Andrew meant," said Rafe; "Christopher! forgot you called him Twister."

"Meant about what?" Mathew was curious to know.

"Before, in the bedroom."

"He called you Twister?"

"I don't know, didn't understand," said Rafe. "I thought he meant—"

"Don't stop eating." Peggy coaxed Andrew to take another mouthful, but to no avail.

"Twister," Andrew said, his needful eyes fixed now on

the boy at the head of the table.

"Wh-what is it, Andrew?" Rafe responded, not to the name but to his grandfather's pleading gaze.

"Why? . . . delay?"

"Have to eat," Wendy said, "vital."

"What was Twister like?" said Rafe.

" 'Wanta bet!' " said Peggy in answer to her grandson's question.

"Like his father," added Mat, eyeing his own father intently. By saying this, Mat was trying to tell Andrew that he both understood and accepted now what had happened in the bedroom. That his father had called Rafe Twister only meant that the dead boy was uppermost in Andrew's mind, that he saw *himself* as Twister, the victim of a cerebral hemorrhage, for which Andrew held not only Mat and Ben and Peggy to blame but the world itself. What Andrew called a "bowlinism," the embolus, was analogous in Andrew's eyes to the artery that had burst in Twister's cerebrum, killing him—hence all that talk of killing; and by forcing Mat to eat the "bowlinism," he was merely trying to get even with the world, make the world take a dose of its own medicine, the medicine responsible for the death of his son, the death of himself. "Right, Dad?"

"Reindeer," said Andrew.

"Look!" said Peggy, pointing to the television screen, even as she winked at Rafe to drop the subject. "Isn't that *2001*?"

"Sure is." Rafe picked up the signal.

"Must be showing it," Lois remarked, "in conjunction with the moon landing."

"Not overly imaginative," Wendy said.

"Sweet white fat," said Andrew, whereupon he picked up his fork and started to mash, as finely as possible, the potato salad on his plate. When satisfied with the results, he put down his fork, mentioned, "Vital food," and helped himself to the puree with his fingers.

The sight disturbed everyone. Not only was it saddening to see someone you loved reduced to such behavior, it was estranging. By eating with his fingers, Andrew automatically cut himself off from the rest of the family, became at once unapproachable, alien, outside human intercourse. Embarrassed, Wendy lowered her eyes, pretended not to see. Her brother, wanting to maintain his "cool," went right on talking about *2001*, albeit in a tone more strident than necessary. Lois kept a discreet watch on her mother-in-law, as if to learn for future reference what the appropriate response to such behavior should be. Peggy's immediate instinct was to hand Andrew his fork, but she suppressed it, concentrated instead on her own food. Though she considered what was happening a setback, a sign of further damage to the brain tissue, she also took it for a sign of health, his appetite—you had to look at things that way, from both sides, or you wouldn't get through a single day—and therefore did nothing to discourage him from eating, with or without a fork. It would be easy enough, once he had finished, to fetch a washcloth for his hands. Mathew, for his part, reached into his pocket—the gesture was only half conscious—for Ben's check. In doing so, his middle finger touched the cherry pit, and he was reminded once more of what had happened in the bedroom. Instead of strengthening his conviction that Andrew should be sent to a nursing home, the "bowlinism" seemed utterly pathetic now, heartbreaking, and it prompted Mat to be more accepting of his mother's view. But if Andrew stayed, then surely there was all the more reason to hire a nurse. Just think how much a nurse would simplify the present situation: relieve his mother of the chore of feeding Andrew, cleaning up after him; enable her to eat her own meal in peace. Besides, if she used the check to hire someone, she could come down to the shore in August. . . . Yet the moment Mathew produced the check, his mother, who took it as a challenge, was quick to respond: "I thought I asked you to tear that up."

"You did. Personally, I think you should deposit it."

"So you said." Without another word Peggy got up from the table.

Mathew tried to stop her, appease her. "Mom, where are you going? Please don't leave the table."

"To get a washcloth," Peggy said as she disappeared down the hallway.

"Flowing marrow," Andrew said, sucking his fingers, even as he eyed the pitcher of milk.

Now Lois, too, got up from the table. Before Mathew had a chance to ask why, she switched off the television. "Sorry, Rafe, but Andrew isn't watching."

"Well *I* am!" Rafe protested.

"I just can't bear that computer talking"—Lois resumed her seat—"gives me the creeps."

At this moment Peggy returned with the washcloth and commenced wiping Andrew's hands. He liked the feel of the warm damp cloth, liked being prepared for disappearance, and readily submitted. "Vital food."

"That's right, Grandpa," said Wendy.

"Yes, it is," Peggy agreed. "Had enough?" she said to Andrew.

Andrew nodded. "Ready now," he informed the boy at the head of the table.

"For dessert?" said Peggy. "There's pound cake."

"Ready," Andrew repeated with impatience.

"For what?" said Rafe.

"Go back." There was a note of urgency in Andrew's voice, and he tried in vain to push the wheelchair away from the table.

Jumping up, Rafe came to his grandfather's assistance, released the brake, but Peggy intervened. "Too early for bed—he'll be up half the night. Know what I think?" She turned to Wendy. "Time for the recital."

Everyone agreed, and Rafe, taking charge of the wheelchair once more, led the way to Andrew's workroom. The move disoriented Andrew. He didn't know why he was being brought to this out-of-the-way place, what a piano was doing there, why he was being positioned so close to the keyboard: Was he expected to play? He didn't know how. The word *clamshell* came to mind, and he said it aloud. The white-haired woman who had fed him at dinner patted his hand and sat down on the daybed adjacent to the wheelchair. The others sat down, too—Twister cross-legged on the floor beside the wheelchair. Andrew reached down and fingered Twister's ear. In response the boy reached up and took hold of his hand, held it firmly. The contact made Andrew feel more secure. Presently the girl with hair like sunlight sat down at the piano. Twister applauded her appearance, and Andrew followed suit. The girl glanced over her shoulder self-consciously to acknowledge the applause, after which she poised her hands and started playing. Very soon, however, she stopped, apologized for a mistake, and started over.

The piece was perfectly familiar, so familiar that Andrew felt he had known it his entire life, known it from the cradle. Was it a lullaby? No, not exactly; too fraught with feeling, yearning, for a lullaby—unless the infant was dead. And yet the sense of loss was not that bitter, not that final, simply poignant; there was, as well, a sense of expectation, of something equally poignant yet to come, a simultaneous looking forward to and looking back on heartache, a double view that seemed to relate at once to both events, to what had already gone before and what was yet to come. So perhaps the infant wasn't dead after all; perhaps it had yet to be born. Or perhaps (Andrew blinked, all but dazzled by the player's hair, the agility of her fingers rippling the keys), perhaps they were one and the same, the infant who had died and the infant yet to be born; perhaps there was no difference whatever between them, between any of us, the living and the dead; perhaps we were all the same, those who went before and those who would come after, the selfsame infant, dying into life, living into death . . . and listening the while to this music, played by the girl with the sunlit hair. Was that what she was doing there? Was she a kind of go-between, carrying messages in music back and forth between the living and the dead? "Angel!" Andrew declared excitedly.

Leaning forward, Peggy stroked his arm to quiet him. At the same time Rafe, turning his head abruptly, looked back at her, his expression disconcerted. Peggy gave the boy a reassuring smile. Wendy, meanwhile, ignored the interruption, went right on playing. Peggy was proud of the child, pleased with her concentration. No wonder Andrew had exclaimed over her; he recognized her real ability. Unlike Rafe, Wendy was not averse to hard work, commitment, sacrifice; clearly she had it in her to become a professional, if that was what she really wanted and kept at it. When it came to art, "keeping at it" was three-quarters of the battle. Yet how could a child of fifteen know what she really wanted? She couldn't, had to complete her education first. At present, Wendy's incentive to play had little to do with herself, her innate desire. It stemmed from Andrew, from the fact that her grandfather was a celebrated composer. She wanted to follow in his footsteps. So did Rafe. What an innocent Raphael was, captivated by the genus, the title "artist"; he imagined you became an artist automatically, merely by electing to, without a single setback, the slightest struggle. (Peggy stared at Andrew with compassion as if his present condition were the outcome of that very "struggle.") Ben was just the opposite: recognized the struggle but not the achievement. After all these years he still thought of art as something frivolous, impractical, which didn't pay its way; a form of self-indulgence, which had to be subsidized, patronized by the likes of him writing out a check. Artist's compensation! Oh, how she resented that check. Not only did it depreciate the work, the struggle, but Andrew himself, the man's entire life. Well, she and Andrew had managed very nicely to get this far without Ben's help, and Peggy had no intention of starting now.

"What's the message?" Andrew spoke out again.

This time the interruption coincided with the end of the piece, and Wendy, in doubt as to what to do next, whether to stop or play another piece, turned to face the family, which broke into applause.

"What message, Dad?" said Mathew.

Peggy flapped her hand impatiently to silence Mat and then turned back to Wendy. "Play another."

"*Consolation.*" Lois requested a second piece by Liszt, and Wendy obliged.

In the course of *Consolation* Andrew dozed off. The nap was accompanied by a bout of snoring too audible to be ignored by anyone, including Wendy, who glanced eventually over her shoulder, not in a show of temperament but merely in doubt again as to what to do. Peggy encouraged her to go on, and the girl complied.

By the time the piece was over, the snoring hadn't stopped. A whispered consultation ensued. Wendy thought it pointless to continue, but Peggy disagreed, said that she for one was wide awake and eager to hear more, whereupon she turned to Andrew and spoke his name sharply. The snoring ceased, and Wendy played yet another piece by Liszt, this one straight through without interruption.

When the recital was over, Lois proposed that she do the dishes while Peggy and Mathew readied Andrew, who was still dozing, for bed. Despite Peggy's objections, Lois prevailed and proceeded to press into service a willing Wendy and a reluctant Rafe.

Left alone, Peggy said to Mat that she didn't really need his help (she felt on guard about the nursing home), but he persuaded her to let him stay. To demonstrate his usefulness, he started to wheel Andrew out of the workroom. Peggy stopped him. She thought it better for Andrew to walk—walking would give him a chance to wake before he reached the bathroom. "Hon," she said softly, leaning over and squeezing Andrew's arm. Andrew opened his eyes, stared at her blankly. "Time to wash up." Andrew showed no sign of recognition. "Hold the chair," she instructed Mat as she herself helped Andrew out of it. Once he was on his feet, Peggy paused to give Andrew time to get his bearings. While waiting, she said of the empty wheelchair, "That can go back to the bedroom." Obligingly Mat rolled it out of the workroom and down the hallway. Peggy and Andrew soon followed, moving slowly, Andrew at a shuffle.

In the bathroom Peggy guided Andrew to the toilet, then turned him around to face her. It was like partnering Coppélia; he stood motionless, uninvolved. "Come on, now," she coaxed, opening his bathrobe and untying the pajama cord. He seemed particularly listless tonight, wrung out—too many visitors. "You know what comes next," she continued to coax. Co-operating at last, he lowered the pajama bottoms and sat down on the toilet seat. She adjusted the bathrobe, draped it behind the bowl. "Wasn't Wendy good?"

"She really is," Mat concurred from the hallway.

Impulsively Peggy pushed the door half closed with her foot, as though to protect Andrew's privacy. From his own son? No, doubtless it was hers, her privacy she wished to protect. "Call when you're ready," she said to Andrew as she withdrew from the bathroom, leaving the door ajar.

Mat followed her into the bedroom. She could tell from his restlessness that he wanted to talk about Andrew, but she was in no mood. On her way to the windows to pull down the shades—it was dark out now, and as usual Peggy greeted the night with a sense of both relief and apprehension—she took up where Mat had left off about Wendy.

"Yes, she is, but you mustn't push her—much too young. If she really wants to become a pianist, she will—with or without encouragement. Best to remain neutral."

"Lois agrees."

"She's right, knows from teaching. Let the child find out for herself, make her own choices. The worst thing we can do"—coming out from behind the settee, Peggy headed for the bed—"is make choices for each other."

Mat couldn't help but grasp his mother's meaning. Prompted now to sit down on the settee, he watched her as she stripped the blanket and top sheet off the bed. What, he wondered, must it be like for her to lie there every night next to his father? What other couple their age and in their predicament continued to share a double bed? What guts the woman had. "Can I help?"

Peggy shook her head. "Routine."

"Even so."

"Keeps me going." She retrieved the sheet from the rocking chair. "That's what you don't understand: It keeps me going," she repeated with telling emphasis.

"*I'm* not making choices."

"I didn't say you were."

"For *you*, I mean."

"I know what you mean." She gave him a pointed look.

He met her gaze. "I just wish you'd think about next month."

As the billowing blanket settled on the bed Peggy suddenly abandoned it, turned in silence to the night table, and picked up the Thermos jug. At the same time, she noticed the bowl of cherries. "They're going to rot," she said to herself. "Here"—she handed Mat the bowl—"put them in the icebox, will you? I have to fill the Thermos," she added, on her way out of the room.

Back in the bathroom Peggy said to Andrew, "How's it going, hon?" He didn't answer, stared instead into space. She could smell that he was making progress. Pleased, she filled the Thermos jug, then questioned him again. "Finished yet?" Still he didn't answer. "I'll be back," she assured him.

Emerging from the bathroom, Peggy was startled momentarily to find Mat waiting once more in the hall. "Shadowing me?" she bantered. "Your father always used to say that. His 'shadow' he called you, when you were little." The recollection, juxtaposing, as it did, images of Andrew then and Andrew now, made Peggy uneasy, impelled her to move away from the bathroom door. "You *were*—his shadow."

"Not yours?"

"Never," she answered matter-of-factly as she re-entered the bedroom. But then, conscious of Mathew trailing her, she had to chuckle, amend her statement. "Till now." Replacing the Thermos jug, Peggy resumed making the bed. "Your brother—" she started to say, but thought better of it.

"Was yours?" Mat took his former place on the settee. Since his mother had her back to him and didn't answer, he had no way of discerning her response. "Your shadow?"

"Or I his. We're all each others', it sometimes seems." Peggy sighed audibly. "Hard, those moments, like at dinner, when he goes back—your father—calling Rafe Twister."

"Hard on *you*, not him."

"You don't know that," she disputed Mat's opinion sharply. "Not hard on me at all."

"Nothing is, to hear you tell it. Hard to believe, Mom."

"What's hard," she retorted, her back still turned, "is the interference: you and Oxenburg and—and Ben."

Properly rebuked, he sat in silence, while his mother executed a perfect hospital corner. Reminded once more of Ben's check, Mat took it out of his pocket again and slipped it under the ashtray. He had had his say, now let her do what she liked with the check. The sight of all the cherry pits in the ashtray reminded him of the one still in his pocket, the "bowlinism." Fishing it out, he stared at the pit soberly and turned it in his fingers. What was hardest of all was this, the "bitter pill" the gods had in store for each of us. "I've left Ben's check here on the table."

"For what?" Peggy, having moved to the opposite side of the bed, was now facing him. "What exactly do you want me to do with it?"

"Hire a nurse."

"What for, with Mrs. Lexy?"

Mathew toyed with the cherry pit, pressing it hard. "It's not the check."

"Poor man, means well," she said of Ben, as much to give the devil his due as to forestall whatever Mat was leading up to. "Must feel so outnumbered, ganged up on—a daughter who works in an art gallery, a brother who composes, a sister-in-law who teaches modern dance—or—or did—a nephew who's into movies, a niece who plays the piano—Art, art, art, till it must be coming out of his ears. No wonder the man resorts to bribes. How else can he assert himself, hold his own against so many? I shouldn't have called it 'conscience money.' "

"He *is* on his way to Europe."

"*Tant mieux.* No, maybe not," she paused to reconsider, "his presence keeps me on my toes."

Mention of Ben's trip brought Mat back to the subject of his own vacation. "Mom." He waited until she looked at him. "I wish you'd think it over."

"What over?"

"Coming to the shore."

"That again." Peggy shook her head. "Can't." As if to illustrate her reason, she busied herself with the second hospital corner. "Keeps me going, I told you. Learned that years ago—when *you* came to adolescence, in fact. 'What happens now?' I asked myself, 'now that he's growing up.' Had me in a sweat. I know myself, how quirky I can get, if I don't keep busy. That's why I persuaded Sarah to let me open the school. Thank God! Saved my life, those kiddies. Turns you into Plato overnight, teaching does. No need to have a lot of kiddies of your own; *all* are yours . . . and *not* yours," she added perspicaciously. "And they keep coming—that's the wonder of it—new ones every year, children of the former ones, one more gifted than the next . . . keep coming."

"Till now," he suggested softly, sensitively, considerate of her feelings.

"*They* still do; it's *I* who don't." She shrugged off the distinction. "That's all right. It's like that, life, unfolds in phases. First there's one thing, then something else, more important, comes along. No particular logic; you do what needs attending to, depending on the moment. *This* does now." She indicated the bedding, which she was in the midst of turning down. "Would have had to stop pretty soon anyway, whether or not your father got sick; these bones, they're getting old."

"That's what I mean, about the country, why I want you

to come. Try it, at least. Just for a week, see how it goes."

"Don't need to see, know already. Impossible."

Mathew dropped the cherry pit into the ashtray. "You owe it to yourself, Mom." His authoritative tone did little to conceal his impatience.

"Myself! You think I'm doing it for *him?*"

"Mostly."

"Not at all." The contradiction was accompanied by a slow insistent head shake. "For *me*, I'm doing it for me."

"Doing what? Putting yourself through this grueling ordeal day after day. Is that what you call doing something for yourself? Never stopping, never sleeping—"

"I sleep."

"He scarcely recognizes you—anyone! anyone anymore. I—I *know* he didn't recognize me this afternoon." Mat hesitated. "Almost certain he didn't."

Finished with the bedding, Peggy came now to the foot of the bed and turned to face her son. She looked relaxed, composed, her expression, as she gazed at him, seemed at once ironic and merciful. "*I* still recognize him."

Averting his eyes, Mat focused again on the mass of cherry pits mounded in the ashtray, as if on the mass of his father's brain. "Only makes it harder, more painful."

"Suppose you let me be the judge of that."

After a moment he lifted his head, looked her straight in the eye. The contact left him short of breath, made it difficult for Mat to speak his mind. When he did, his tone was frail, hushed almost to a whisper. "It can only get worse, Mom."

She looked back unflinchingly. "I know that . . . accept it." Now, for the first time since leaving the workroom, Peggy sat down. She did so deliberately, choosing the corner of the bed nearest Mat, as if finally to acknowledge the fact that they were having a discussion, a discussion that took precedence over everything else. The slacks she wore enabled her to spread her legs and lean far forward, facing Mat diagonally across the coffee table, her elbows resting on her knees, hands enfolded between her thighs. "We've lived together fifty years—almost that—your father and I. After that amount of time it's more than habit, marriage, it's—it's like a broken limb that's healed; you grow together, knit, the two of you, into bone, a single piece of bone.

That's why I can't go away—restricted. Haven't the leeway anymore, the freedom to detach myself. Not a matter of dependency, mere dependency, more than that—physiological!" Bringing her hands to her blouse, she pressed them flat against her breasts. "He *is* me, my body now—strange as that may sound, coming from a dancer—I him. These hands—" Peggy paused to squint at them as if they weren't hers; "brain, eyes, all are his . . . his dying mine." She could see that Mat wanted to interrupt her, but gave him no chance. "Something for myself, you say. You think I'm being dutiful? Self-sacrificing? What? Guilt, you think? Nonsense! Everything I do, every last little thing, is being done for me, selfishly, to prolong . . . survival. *Ours*," she added tersely. "Don't know how much time is left, what you do once the limb's rebroken. Final then, the pieces"—she gazed again at her upturned palms as if they held the splintered pieces—"too old to knit. . . . Price of love: final fracture. . . . But while it's whole," she rallied herself, "while he's here—however long God grants—I'm here, too, have to be, nowhere else, not with you and Lois, not even for a day. No choice."

"I understand. But even so, sooner or later, Mom"—Mathew weighed his words with care, compassion—"you—you'll have to start—try at least—to detach yourself."

"When God rebreaks the limb, I'll start."

"Him, too—Dad—has to be given a chance to do the same, detach *himself*."

"My son, the doctor." Peggy smiled patronizingly. "Just what do you suppose has been happening all these months, *why* he didn't recognize you?" Satisfied that she had made her point, Peggy's tone changed suddenly, appreciably, turning fierce. "But not in a nursing home—enforced detachment. Never! He'll do it here"—she brought her hand down squarely on the mattress—"where he belongs."

"I agree."

Taken by surprise, she looked at her son in disbelief. "You do?"

Mathew nodded.

Clearly relieved and thankful, she closed her eyes for a moment and heaved a sigh. "Well, that's something." Having said all that she had to say, Peggy ended the discussion now by standing up, her posture characteristically erect as she headed for the door. "Better get him out of there, before he falls asleep."

As she went through the nightly ritual of readying Andrew for bed, Peggy found him peculiarly unco-opera-tive—not, as sometimes, stubborn or spiteful but simply pas-sive, disengaged. He paid no heed to Mat, who was leaning against the door and making occasional remarks; not even when she tried overtly to call his attention to their son did Andrew take any notice; but then, maybe that was under-standable, since Mat's presence was a novelty. Less under-standable was why Andrew broke his own well-established custom of tying the towel biblike around his neck; Peggy had to do it for him tonight. And though he took the soap when she handed it to him, he scarcely moved his hands; and when the soap slipped out of them, he made no effort to retrieve it, merely gazed into the sink. As for the wash-cloth, he didn't even try to take it, waited for her to wash and dry both his face and hands. On some nights, while she prepared the denture bath, he would produce his denture voluntarily, almost proudly, but not tonight. Even when she asked for it, he failed to respond, seemed not to know what she was talking about, and Peggy was saddled with the tricky job of removing it herself. "Come on, now, darling, you can do better than that," she said, offering him the toothbrush. To her surprise he took it. Yet no sooner had he stuck it into his mouth than he stopped, became motionless as a statue, his elbow crooked, arm upraised, the toothbrush handle jutting from his lips like a lollipop stick carved in stone. And thus he stayed for half a minute, ab-solutely motionless, his teeth unbrushed, till finally Peggy took hold of his arm and sawed it gently back and forth. "Don't know what's the matter tonight," she remarked with concern to Mat.

"Think it's me?" he speculated. "Because I'm watching?"

Peggy shrugged. "All right, now,"—she turned to An-drew, "beddie-bye."

By the time they got him into bed Andrew's eyes were closing. "Better have the children come and say good night," she prompted Mat, "he's half-asleep already."

While Mat was out of the room, Peggy collected in her palm Andrew's nightly dose of medicine, then poured a glass of water. "Here, my love." One by one she transferred the pills to Andrew's hand. He accepted them, much as earlier he had accepted the soap, passively. She could see that he was thinking about something else. Raising his head from the pillow with her right hand, she held the glass of water for him in her left. "Come on, now." For a moment, as his fingers closed over the pills and he began to retract his hand, she assumed that he was preparing to take the medicine. But then, halfway to his mouth, the hand stopped short and started moving laterally, from right to left across his chest. When it reached the nipple, the hand came to a halt, but only momentarily, soon the forefinger began to stir. From its wavering erratic movements Peggy couldn't tell whether the finger was in search of something or merely trying to scratch the nipple. "What is it, hon?" Andrew eyed her briefly, suspiciously, before returning his attention to the problem. By now the finger had found its way into his pajama pocket. After considerable struggle, evidenced by several painful-looking hand contortions, other fingers followed. "What are you doing?" she said, at once amused and puzzled; but even as she asked, Peggy could see for herself: He was stashing the pills in his pocket. "Sly puss." She had to laugh. "Unh-unh, none of that—cheating." Setting down the glass, she reached toward the pocket, but Andrew resisted, flattened his hand over the opening, and stared at her defiantly. Rather than struggle with him, she tried to reason. "Aren't you being silly? Have to take your medicine."

"Final medicine."

The remark sent a shiver through her body. "Don't say that—nothing 'final' about it."

"Lot you know," Andrew sassed the white-haired woman.

"Know about what?" Mat chimed in as he came back into the bedroom followed by Lois and the children.

"Won't take his medicine," Peggy explained.

Mathew shrugged and made a face as if to say, What's the difference, one night in the year?

"He'll take it from *me*, I bet," boasted Rafe.

As the boy approached the bed Andrew braced his feet against the bedstead, stiffened the hand protecting his pajama pocket. He was determined to let no one lay a finger on the bowlinisms—not the boy, not the girl, not the woman, not the man, not the white-haired woman, all of whom had by now closed in on the bed. On guard Andrew watched as both the white-haired woman and the man motioned the boy to desist, while the other woman, who was standing next to the boy, placed a restraining hand on his shoulder and then said good night to Andrew. She, at least, kept her distance, unlike the boy who leaned now clear across the bed (in self-defense Andrew shielded himself with his shoulder blade), kissed him on the cheek, and whispered in his ear, "Love you, Andrew." Still on guard, Andrew said nothing, tightened his grip on the bowlinisms until the boy backed off. Nor did he let down his guard with the girl who, holding her hair in place with both hands, also leaned across the bed, kissed him on the cheek, and said good night. After the girl, came the man, but to the near side of the bed, Andrew's side. The white-haired woman stepped back to make room for him. As the man bent down, Andrew braced himself once more, compressed his lips. "Still angry?" said the man. The question only worsened Andrew's scowl. "Don't be, Dad." Andrew's eye began to twitch as the man, bending closer, kissed him on the forehead. Immediately thereafter the white-haired woman flapped her hands energetically, and the group dispersed, moving toward the doorway. Not until everyone, including the white-haired woman, had left the room did Andrew finally relax his grip on the bowlinisms. As he did he felt his muscles slacken, his body subside, dropping almost with a thud, it seemed, into the mattress, as if something more than his resistance had collapsed. Utterly exhausted, he saw the outline of the rocking chair grow indistinct, double before his closing eyes, recede into darkness, disappear. . . .

When he next recovered consciousness, someone was talking in an undertone, talking by fits and starts about a descent of some sort; "ladder" was the only word Andrew clearly heard. A phrase, *the long way down*, came to mind. Though it seemed at once familiar and obscure, the phrase, which he repeated to himself several times, intrigued and pleased Andrew, made him feel unaccountably secure, secure enough to open his eyes.

The surface overhead was dimly lit by a dull unsteady light. Lowering his eyes, he perceived, through a row of bars—the ladder? to which the voice had been referring and continued intermittently to refer—perceived the source of illumination: an oblong screen on which there appeared an image too murky to make out. All he could see—due no doubt to his failing sight—was a pattern of shadows, pitch-black, amorphous shadows, barely visible against a meager ground of ghostly gray. That silhouette on the left, was it of a kneeling reindeer, crowned by giant antlers? . . . Andrew tried by squinting to improve his vision, bring the image into sharper focus, but to no avail. What he saw had no highlights, no perspective, no contrast to speak of, not even any movement; he saw a static inkblot.

"Ladder," repeated the voice he had heard on waking, speaking still in an undertone but now with bated breath. At the same time, Andrew's eye was attracted to the upper part of the screen where something had in fact begun to move. Again he couldn't make out what it was, could only see an indeterminate shadow moving downwards, edging toward the reindeer. Before long the downward-moving shadow reached the reindeer's silhouette, touched the animal's shoulder blade. The reindeer didn't bound up, didn't budge, remained absolutely still, head down—was it lapping water?—even as the shadow, extending steadily, merged at its base into the reindeer's back. For a moment the image became static again.

"Foot," said the voice, still in both an undertone and with bated breath; whereupon the shadow moved once more, downwards once more—*the long way down*—deep into the reindeer's body.

"Lunar soil," said the voice. Then all at once both the reindeer and the shadow disappeared in a burst of light, and Andrew saw the looming lopsided silhouette of a tree monster or troll with threefold spindly legs in front of which an eerie incandescent figure took a loping step and stopped, while a voice that wasn't the familiar one began to speak. Bothered by the harsher light, Andrew shut his eyes.

"Leap for mankind," said the unfamiliar voice. When Andrew looked again, the incandescent figure, luminous and active in contrast with the somber stationary tree monster, was moving about—sometimes at a leap, as though mindful of the unfamiliar voice, sometimes at a shuffle—while the voice itself, which had resumed talking, spoke of "powdered charcoal." By and by, as the voice fell silent, the incandescent figure left the ground and floated smoothly upward, rising upright like a bottle imp, straight up, past the base of the tree monster, past its spindly arms, past its listing upper side, till the figure, having risen higher than the tree monster's crown, merged into the background light and floated headless in midair. Its levitation prompted Andrew to lift his own head off the pillow, prop himself up on his elbows.

"Andrew?" said a voice, different from the two that had been speaking heretofore, even as the first, the muted voice, resumed speaking.

Confused, Andrew peered at the screen. The incandescent figure, back now on the ground, its head restored, was cavorting all over the place.

"Can you see?"

Shifting his eyes, Andrew perceived another figure, nearer at hand than the first, a woman's figure, standing half in shadow, her face aglow, though not with incandescence like the cavorting figure, but bathed in a cool unearthly light the color almost of her hair.

"They've made it!" said the woman in a voice more hushed, yet somehow more immediate, than the other voice, which was speaking simultaneously. "We're there! on the moon."

A thrill coursed through Andrew's body. He hadn't the strength to receive such tidings sitting up, sank back down into softness. The sight, overhead, of the lunar crust, glowing now like the woman's face, filled him with an ineffable sense of blessedness. He felt at once hot and cold—hot as the radiation coming from the incandescent figure, cold as the nimbus enveloping the woman's head and shoulders—his body being consumed, burning up and evaporating with gratitude and joy. In the presence of such providence what was there to do but close your eyes and bow your head?

"Don't you want to see?"

From the intimate sound of her voice, which sent another thrill through Andrew's body, he sensed that the woman was closer now, much closer—standing next to him or even bending over him. Not daring to open his eyes and look on Holy Mother, he turned his head away. "Not ready yet."

"Why not? . . . So amazing."

"I'm sure."

"Then look."

"Can't."

"Too bright?"

Andrew shook his head. "Unworthy."

"What is?"

"I."

" 'Unworthy?' Of what?"

His lips had gone dry, and Andrew licked them before answering. "Your love."

There was a brief silence, broken faintly by an arid susurrant sound, the sound perhaps of footsteps retreating over lunar soil. "Bounding weightless," said a voice that wasn't Holy Mother's. Shortly thereafter, Andrew heard a stifled gasp, succeeded by a snuffle. Another silence followed, broken once more by the susurrant sound, swelling somewhat this time. Then all at once he felt a gentle jolt, felt the surface under him rock, dip to one side, and rise again, as something bore down on his hand. Not until he felt Her breath did Andrew figure out that what was pressed against his hand was Holy Mother's cheek.

"You *are* My love."

"I?"

"So how could you be unworthy?"

The question, which only made him feel that much more unworthy, more inadequate to express his thanks, brought tears to Andrew's eyes, and he compressed his lips to contain the sobs he heard mounting now in his own throat.

"Don't . . . please! . . . don't cry."

"Gratitude." His head still turned, eyes still closed, still too timorous to look, Andrew reached out tentatively, reached with his free hand toward Holy Mother, touching first Her hair, then Her shoulder—level, surprisingly, with his. Was She kneeling? kneeling to *him*? The inappropriateness of the gesture made him squirm, but before he could object, She took his hand and kissed it. Her cheek felt moist. Was She crying too? "You kiss . . . *my* hand? kneel to *me*?"

"Why not? Comfortable like this."

"Ought to be the other way around."

"Don't see why."

"Your hand . . . warm."

"Why does that surprise you?"

Too discreet to say what he had expected, that Her touch would be ice-cold, Andrew said nothing.

"Wish you'd look at Me—"

He felt Her hand squeeze his, urging him to satisfy Her wish, but modesty restrained him.

"—tell Me what's making you cry."

"Being . . ." Despite his modesty, Andrew turned now toward Holy Mother but only halfway, his head in profile, tearful eyes still closed. "Being taken back like this."

"Taken back?"

"By You."

"Me? . . . You—you felt . . . cast out?"

"At first."

"By Me? . . . When? . . . When, My love?"

"In the beginning."

"Af-after twister?"

Not knowing what She meant by "twister," but sensing Her distress, Andrew tried to mollify Holy Mother. "Didn't know any better. Ignorance . . . arrogance . . ."

"Imagine thinking such a thing—that I would cast you out. Can't imagine— Mat! was—was it Mat gave you that idea? said—said something this afternoon? . . . Cast you out? No, indeed. Never. *With* you, with you . . . always."

"Know that now. . . . Imaginary, all the rest, beginning to end, the whole travail, imaginary."

"What travail?"

"Appearances . . . personal appearances. . . . *You*"—he tightened his grip on Her hand, as if to re-enforce his sense of its tangibility—"You alone . . . real."

"Where I probe," said a voice that wasn't Holy Mother's, "stark beauty."

Almost simultaneously Andrew felt Holy Mother's arms enfold him, lifting him slightly, hugging him hard. . . . Was this the way it happened, held in Holy Mother's arms? Was She about to work his disappearance, take him back into Herself? . . . Unafraid at last and even eager now to effect the union, Andrew opened his eyes. Holy Mother's head was resting on his chest. He couldn't see Her face, only the moonglow of Her hair. Yet for that very reason, because he couldn't see Her face, Andrew felt emboldened. "Adore You," he declared in a whisper. Suddenly Her body began to heave, shake with sobs, shaking his. The agitation made him wonder whether disappearance, like delivery, caused Holy Mother pain. He wanted more than anything to deliver *Her*, take on himself Her suffering, but soon realized that that was precisely what She Herself was about: delivering him from his. "How?" he besought Her, "how can I thank You?" Presently, as the sobbing subsided, he felt the weight of Her head lift, felt Her arm slip slowly out from under him.

"Sleep."

"That's all?"

"All."

As he closed his eyelids Andrew felt the surface under him dip and rock once more, heard a sound resembling the sound of cracking knuckles. "No other way—" he began, then stopped, drowned out by another sound, the sound of someone blowing his nose, and Andrew waited till the interruption was over. "No other way to show my thanks?"

"You could take your medicine."

Even before he fully grasped what Holy Mother was suggesting, Andrew's hand found its way to his pajama pocket. Through the thin material he felt the bowlinisms, hard as stone, nestled to his heart. . . . So that's what they were really for, the bowlinisms, to work your disappearance! To come to disappearance, you had first to deal with the hardenings, the remains of the gift imperative, take back into yourself whatever was indissoluble, irreducible— the pits, the waste, the hard-core clots of heart that choked the flow. . . . With difficulty Andrew fished from his pocket two of the elusive bowlinisms and brought them to his mouth. "Happily."

"That's My love."

Much as he wanted to co-operate with Holy Mother, who was now cradling his head and holding to his lips something firm, it seemed to take all the energy he had merely to open his mouth and insert the bowlinisms.

"Drink."

Taking in as much as he could of the lukewarm liquid, Andrew held it in his mouth a moment while he juggled the bowlinisms on his tongue and then, with an heroic

278

exertion of will, swallowed. Almost at once his throat tightened and he gagged a bit as the liquid carried the bowlinisms bumpily down—*the long way down. . . .*

"Now, the rest."

"Rest," he echoed with thanks.

"Of the pills. Too tired?"

Bravely Andrew shook his head.

Once the process had been repeated, he was conscious of nothing but the bowlinism deep inside his body. He could feel its solid mass, feel it unmistakably, concretely, deep down in his gullet or, deeper still, settled in his belly (to determine its exact location, Andrew touched the spot, his navel, under which he felt the bowlinism buried), no longer in motion but planted now, planted in one place and moldering, moldering already, even as it grew—he could feel that, too, its growth, the bowlinism growing gradually but unmistakably, steadily, swelling his belly with each breath. In wonderment Andrew brought his other hand to his belly to witness its labored rise and fall. Then suddenly he became aware, uncomfortably aware, of something else, lower down—a pressure in his bladder. To relieve the stress, he relaxed his muscles, releasing a stream of liquid, the selfsame liquid, he surmised, given him by Holy Mother to wash the bowlinism down—*the long way down*, borne on Holy Mother's blood, Her hallowed blood, flowing immemorially from Her to us to lunar soil and, thence, to earth—the waters of the moon falling back to earth; and all at once, considering the fall, Andrew understood that they were one: the bowlinism and the blood—through Holy Mother's providence the pits and waste that choked the flow and led to disappearance contained as well the seed, the sacred seed of reappearance—the pit and seed were one. "Thank You."

"Are they down?"

"*The long way down . . .*" Now, at last, the rest of the phrase came to Andrew's mind, and wanting to share it with Holy Mother, he tried to utter the words aloud but produced no more than a gurgling sound. With great effort he took another breath and tried again but failed. Finally, drawing as deep a breath as possible, he blurted out, "*Into reappearance*," and said no more.

Sanford Friedman was born in New York City and educated at Horace Mann School and Carnegie Institute of Technology. He has written seven full length plays, the first of which, DAWN FROM AN UNKNOWN OCEAN, *was produced when he was nineteen, at the University Playhouse on Cape Cod. Shortly after his discharge from the army in 1953, he, with several associates, leased and renovated Carnegie Hall Playhouse (presently Carnegie Hall Cinema) and co-produced works by Beckett, Ionesco and Brendan Behan. His first novel,* TOTEMPOLE, *a chapter of which received an O. Henry Award, was published in 1965, and was followed by* A HAUNTED WOMAN *in 1968, and* STILL LIFE *in 1975.*